FAITH OF THE DRAGON TAMER

BY COLE PAIN

BOOK 2 OF THE ORACLE SERIES

Map completed by Sherry Kitts. Thank you for believing.

CHARACTERS REFFERENCE

The Lands

Newlan Kingdoms
Zier*
Wyrick Razon – King
Renee Razon – Queen
Ren Razon – Crown Prince
Quinton –Ren's Captain
Neki – Swordsmand
Galvin – Swordsman
Bentzen – Swordsman
Markum – Librarian and Seer
Lazo, Jasta, and Justin – Triplet
Advisors

Oldan Kingdoms
Yor*
Ramie Augustus – King
Javi Augustus – Queen
Reese Augustus – Crown Prince
Ravi Augustus – Princess
Fraul – Ramie's Captain
Tec – Swordsman
Nigel – Ramie's Brother
Meg – Ramie's Sister
Sherri – Nigel's Love

Crape
Valor Kahn – King
Chris Kahn – Crown Prince
Manda Kahn – Princess
Ista – Collective Leader/Sorceress
Vos and Yov – Twin Advisors
Bor – Captain of Valor's Guard

Fest
Lorlier – King
Davis – Crown Prince
Marianne – Princess
Alise – Princess
Gregory – Lorlier's Captain
Korin – Swordsman
Brice – Stablehand

Ketes
Bostic – King (Renee's cousin)
Paul – Crown Prince
Sass – Princess
Raymond – Head of Castle Guard

Quar
Alezza – Princess
Bort –Alezza's Captain

Other Characters
Michael Razon – Ren's Uncle
Eli – Stardom's Priest
Grauss – Sage (Neki's Grandfather)
Presario – Recluse, Man of Most
Knowledge
The Black Knight – Nigel
The Avenger – Aaron
Zorc – The One (Wizard from
Alcazar)

Druids
Marinus – Drek (Druid Leader)
Feher – High Priest
Avalon – Marinus's son
Welch
Morrus

Controlling Kingdom

CHAPTER 1

Ramie stood on his balcony, deep in thought. The third messenger had come that day, strongly encouraging him to send people to train under Ista.

Ramie grunted. He wondered how long it would be before Ista attacked them all. Probably only long enough for her to build the Collective, and that wouldn't be long, not with most of the kingdoms embracing her with open arms.

Days after his homecoming, news had come from the border. Hundreds had been seen traveling to Zier, not only from the border regions of Fest and Quar but also the outer regions, many from his own kingdom of Yor.

After days of little sleep and many orisons he had made a speech to the city of Yor, ordering none to travel to Zier. First, he said, Newlan must prove it truly opted for peace and not war. He thought it a fair concern, seeing Newlan had a new leader who insisted on training men to become soldiers of the Quy.

The people hadn't seen it that way. They had become angry and rumors had spread that Ramie was opposed to magic.

Wouldn't the people be surprised to learn if he opposed magic he also opposed himself and his children?

Ramie's heart sank at the thought of Ravi and Reese. They both had the power and were almost out of their minds to travel to Zier themselves. He had told them what had occurred while he had been away, and although Reese understood his concern Ravi was unconvinced. She was more rambunctious than any child he had ever seen. He wouldn't be surprised if she hid in a cart to begin the pilgrimage herself.

He had sent messengers to all the lesser Oldan kingdoms ordering them to cease letting their citizens pass. Ramie had never made such a demand, but it was in his jurisdiction. Although he couldn't directly control how each ruler governed he could control the interrelationship between each kingdom, and this affected every nation. Every king had politely sent a messenger back indicating that even if they made the order their citizens would be impossible to contain.

Ramie understood. He could barely control his own kingdom. It wasn't the soldiers. They obeyed without question. It was the commoners. It seemed the less one had the more one wanted the Quy. Ista was building an army of hungry, greedy people.

He had tripled the guards at the border but the patrol was still outnumbered. There had even been some deaths, both guards and citizens. One thing Ramie didn't want was the blood of the people on his hands.

He had to do something but he didn't know what. He couldn't sit back and allow his citizens to migrate to Zier, but he couldn't go against magic with his army alone. He knew nothing about magic. Ista could very well be powerful enough to kill his entire army down to a man.

His father had taught him to think quickly on his feet and his aptitude had surprised many on more than one occasion, but he feared he hadn't reacted quickly enough this time.

If only Ketes would answer his message! If he went after Ista alone he would be one army against an army with magic. If Bostic would answer his message and join him in the attack they had a chance, but the message he had sent to Ketes remained unanswered and news had come that Bostic had closed his borders.

Ketes was the only kingdom in the Lands with a wall surrounding its boundary. It wasn't an ordinary wall. It was the king of walls, rising over twenty paces in height. It stretched from the outlying cities to the deserted rice fields of its rolling country. If anyone could have closed its borders it was Ketes. The wall was broken in places and shattered in others, but if Bostic had wanted his citizens inside the wall there was no doubt he could have rebuilt the broken sections overnight and forced everyone to remain inside.

The wall was one of the many mysteries of the lands. The first people were in Yor. As they migrated east, the wall was discovered. It was no manmade construction. The aid of magic was even discounted because of the slight imperfections in the wall's design. If magic were the cause the wall would have held few, if any, flaws.

If Yor had a wall around its borders Ramie could at least stop his own citizens from leaving, but Yor was surrounded by water, and water was a double-edged sword. On one hand it offered an excellent defense, but on the other if people wanted to leave it was next to impossible to stop them. Yor was filled with hundreds of canals that spilled into other canals and led to easy escape in the surrounding waters.

Ramie turned his thoughts back to Ketes. He had been nervous about sending the message, but now he knew it had been right to do so. It surprised him that Bostic had yet to respond. It was clear Bostic was loyal to Ren and had somehow gotten wind of Zier's takeover before word of Ista had spread, but why hadn't he answered the message?

It was perplexing. Although Bostic was known for his boisterous laugh and love of pleasantries he was also known for his loyalty and quick anger.

Could Bostic be hiding behind his walls? Or could he be planning something on his own?

Frustration coursed through Ramie's veins. If only he knew one way or the other he would be able to act or react. He would know if he stood alone against Ista or if he was backed by another force of strength.

Lorlier would have been an invaluable ally, but Ramie had received only a short message from the king of Fest. Lorlier wasn't hindering his citizen's from leaving, but he had ordered his soldiers to remain. Ramie didn't know how to interpret that missive. Was Lorlier questioning Ista, or because he was a fighting man was he just loath to release his soldiers?

Ramie heaved a weary sigh. If only Nigel were here to help him. Although Ramie was the natural leader Nigel had an eye for paths that evaded Ramie. Nigel went where no one dreamed there was a way. Ramie needed that instinct now.

Ramie began to pace. He had to think as if he were the Lands only chance. He was the only one with the truth and the only one in a position to do something about that truth.

He had waited too long. What was wrong with him? Just because Ista had magic didn't give him an excuse to hide in a corner! He was a man of action. It was far past time for his reaction.

It was time to attack.

The problem was he needed a reason to attack. He had no proof of Ista's deception. Ista rallied for peace. If he started a war it would only make her hold stronger. So what was the solution?

He looked to the southeast, toward Zier, wondering what was happening. The people seemed content. There was no news of unrest from the spies he had left in the city. Ista hadn't forced her way into command. The people had accepted her.

Or had they?

If the Zier people rebelled they would be accused of treason. Treason was punishable by death. What citizen would risk his life, his family, for a fight doomed to failure? But if there was a strong resistance they could join . . .

Ramie rubbed his tired eyes. He desperately needed rest. He needed to clear his mind before he made a decision to send the Lands into a war involving magic. His people needed something to fight for, a clear evil to fight against.

If only he had another to consult with, but he dare not trust any in his own keep for this kind of counsel. Ista was sure to have her pawns in his own kingdom. He couldn't take any chances. He needed someone neutral in all respects, someone who had nothing to do with either power or country. He could confer with the Advisor Convent, where twins, triplets and those with intense knowledge were trained, but its leaders would only refer him back to his own advisors.

Ramie heaved an exasperated sigh. It was late. He needed to call it a night. Maybe with sleep his mind would clear and he would have a solution in the morning.

He glanced inside the room where Javi slept. Sometimes he wished he could be so easily pacified. Nothing worried Javi, which was why they made such a good pair. He was always busy trying to find solutions before a problem appeared. She only moved when there was need. He was the only thing she ever fussed over. He was lucky to have her. Without Javi he would probably forget to eat.

The familiar scent of sandalwood wafted to him as Ramie stepped through the arched balcony door. Javi had left some candles lit like she always did when he stayed up late, which was almost every night. Ramie found himself wishing for the thousandth time he felt more than fondness for Javi. She deserved much more than what he gave her. Everyone thought her beauty and warmth could rival Chance herself, but the man she married only thought of her as a dear friend.

Ramie frowned with self-loathing and walked to his bureau. He shuffled through the stacked documents but made no attempt to examine them. Normally every paper was read and responded to by nightfall, but since returning from Stardom he had been unable to concentrate. Everything seemed petty compared to what had happened in Zier. He was worried about his kingdom, his children, and most especially Ren and Nigel.

The statue he kept on the corner of the desk caught his eye. It was a man, half-flawless, beautiful and pure and half-deformed, twisted, and ugly. It had been his father's memento mori, or reminder of his failures. His father had used it on more than one occasion to teach Nigel, Megglan, and him a lesson. Their father had always said that with the dawn of each day they needed to strive to be the man of beauty and not the man of deformity.

Jarek told them continuously to use their station for peace and prosperity, not for power or greed. Ramie could still remember the first time his father had shown him the statue. He had asked Jarek in childlike innocence if Presario was evil.

His gasp sounded like a defining blast in the stillness of the room. Javi stirred but didn't wake. She rolled over and tenderly drew a pillow toward her, where he should have been.

The deformed face of the statue frowned at him, seemingly annoyed at his thoughts. Presario! Why hadn't Ramie thought of him before?

Ramie recalled all he had heard about the man, disregarding most to exaggerations of ignorant minds. Presario was portrayed as a legend and a monster. He had been a child prodigy, and at the age of seven he had proven himself among his peers and obtained entrance to the Advisor Convent. He far surpassed anyone's expectations and was the most sought after advisor at the age of eighteen, when he had completed the training. Even triplets didn't finish until they were in their early twenties, twins when they were slightly older.

Before choosing which kingdom to serve, Presario had traveled back to his father's lands. While he was there a fire broke out. No one knew the details of the event, but Presario was burned beyond recognition. Instead of seeking healers Presario went into hiding.

Now Presario resided in the sections of his father's home untouched by the flames. Only one servant stayed with him. The Advisor Convent had tried to meet with him after the accident, but Presario wouldn't receive them. His teachers had sent messages imploring him not to waste his life, but Presario met them with silence. The man chose to stay closed to the world. He never ventured out of the castle walls and no one to Ramie's knowledge had ever been allowed inside. The only accounts of Presario were from his servant, who sought books to keep the man occupied.

Because Presario was trained as an advisor some people tried to gain an audience. For a time all accounts were refused, until one day the servant told a woman to write down her vexation. Presario replied in kind.

If added together, Ramie recalled multiple accounts of Presario's instructions. It seemed as long as the questions were sincere and heartfelt Presario replied.

Ramie gazed at the statue with conviction. It was imperative he speak with Presario. There was no end to what the man must know. Presario could possibly know everything happening in the Lands.

Those who obtained his replies raved about how much Presario knew about their own lives – secrets even.

And books, Presario's servant paid handsomely for rare books. If there was a book in the Lands about magic Presario was sure to have it.

Ramie turned to Javi's balled form. She wouldn't approve if he left without telling her, but he didn't want to hear her objections. Time was of the essence. If he waited until sunup, those who saw him leave would insist on an escort, and an escort was out of the question. Presario didn't like people. If Ramie went with an escort even a note would be turned away.

He shuffled through the parchments on his desk until he found one of little worth. After tearing off a small section he reached for his stylus, scrawled a short note to Javi, and propped it against her jewelry chest. She would find it when she woke.

He donned his deep navy cloak and slipped out of the bedroom. Ramie nodded to the puzzled guard and walked down the marbled hall before he was questioned.

The Crest castle was grandiose. He had always wished it was less so but it was built for beauty as well as defense. Ramie admitted it was beautiful, but he also thought it bordered on the verge of being obscene.

The hall was alive with colors: pinkish gray marbled floors, burgundy walls decorated with golden accents, vessels of gold on gray marble tables, and painted ceilings exploding with hues of every tone imaginable. As boys he and Nigel used to peruse each scene and create monumental fabrications of the figures residing within the brushstrokes.

His lone footfalls breached the sanctity of the hall, disturbing the slumber of the painted faces. When he reached the smaller corridor leading to the stables, he turned. Although the smaller hall still held extravagant decorations they were less frantic, with softer pastels, and longer, more soothing brush strokes. With the way he felt now the pastels clashed with his impassioned resolve.

Underlying his focus he felt something he had little use for – desperation. Ramie Augustus felt desperate. He had never been desperate in his life. He suddenly realized he had felt desperate ever since leaving Zier. He didn't like the feeling. As a matter of fact he was on a mission to be rid of it.

When he arrived at the stables he released a breath and reached for the cold iron handle that separated him from the freedom of the ride. He knew he should take a minimum of ten men with him, but he didn't know the extent of Presario's knowledge or sight. He would take no one, humble himself before the man, and if he had to he would insist on an audience with Presario.

Ramie took a quick surveillance of his clothing and scowled. He was a king and he looked the part. He would be a sure target for vandals if he went out as he was. It would be hard enough to conceal his face since his portrait was imprinted on every coin in Oldan. He had argued avidly against his facial imprint but his advisors had won the fight. After all, he was the youngest controlling ruler in history. His advisors insisted he follow tradition and have his portrait imprinted on all currency to assure loyalty to his visage.

Ramie opened the door and went straight for the storage bins where the stable hands kept spare garments. After a short search he chose a well-worn brown buckskin shirt and baggy trousers. Shoving his father's memento mori into one of his pockets, he pulled the disguise over his clothes. Although the fit was tight he didn't want to leave his clothes behind. He wanted to appear the stable hand while traveling but he may very well need his royal attire when he demanded to see Presario.

When the façade was in place he took one of the ropes hanging on the peg near the door and tied it around his waist, spitting invectives when he saw how much of the trousers remained bunched at his ankles. He found a blade in the storage area and cut the trousers to size.

As he made his way to Mortar, his steed nickered a greeting and pawed the earth. Just as Ramie was about to open the stall, he paused. "My friend, you're much too regal for a stable hand."

Ramie walked the length of the straw-filled stable, finally selecting one of the horses used to pull heavy cargo. The wooden sign on the stall christened the inhabitant as Foster, a rust-colored mare that looked fast if not well bred. Foster looked at him with disinterest but allowed him to stroke her muzzle. After a quick rubdown Ramie guided his chosen mount out of the stall and saddled her, feeling like a little boy trying to sneak out of the castle for an adventure.

But it wasn't so much an adventure as it was a crusade.

CHAPTER 2

Foster proved faster than Ramie expected. The horse could rival Mortar in the races. Although she wouldn't win, she'd put up an incredibly good fight. He would reach Presario's hometown of Mintree by dawn. Ramie praised the Maker Presario resided where he did. The man could have lived in some far off region, making him impossible to reach quickly.

Foster hungered to move faster but Ramie held her back, fearing the rocky terrain would cause her harm if she went at full gait. As they cantered in the dark, sparse trees jutted out into the gloom like hands waiting to grab him. It was flat in Yor, extremely flat, contrasting with the hills and mountains he had been to of late. Although Yor was surrounded by water the internal sections appeared as if water never reached them. The soil was rocky and dry and if you didn't know better you would have sworn water was the farthest thing away.

The Crest castle had been built on the water's edge, where canals, lily vines, and moss-covered trees dominated the landscape. It was as if you were in a paradise, but only paces away lurked the Abyss. Ramie loved the variety, and he especially loved nighttime excursions. The peaceful sounds of the echo bugs brought back memories of nighttime jaunts with Nigel. But as he rode toward Presario's castle he had an ominous feeling. He felt watchful eyes on him. Every so often he would reach under his tunic and finger the hilt of his sword.

When the sun started to peek through the clouds Ramie reined in Foster and reached for the map he had tucked into the saddlebag. Ramie swiveled in the saddle, cursing as the right bottom leg of his frayed breeches hung on one of the saddle's brass ornaments. Mumbling invectives about his height, Ramie dismounted, tearing his breeches in the process.

Ramie detached the satchel and pulled the map from its contents. He knew the roads leading to Mintree, but he wanted to be sure he took the one leading directly to the center of town. As he remembered, Presario's castle sat at the end of the main road and he couldn't afford to waste time coming at it from odd angles.

He was about to unroll the scrolled parchment when Foster screeched. Ramie bounded back just as Foster toppled to the ground.

Ramie stared, dumbfounded and incredulous, as a weasel-like creature attached itself to the fallen mare. Blood spurted from the

11

sides of the creature's gaping jaws before it settled into a comfortable position and relaxed to feed.

The creature's beady eyes swiveled to him. Ramie felt their power just as he remembered the childhood stories.

It was a nesbit, and nesbits attacked things standing still.

Ramie started running. He didn't know if there were any more nesbits in the area but he didn't care to find out. As a child he had never thought to ask if nesbits hunted in packs or alone, but he hadn't known he would ever need the knowledge. All he knew was that Foster was dead as soon as the nesbit had bitten. He had to run and he had to run fast.

He kept fit by continuous swordplay and occasional forays in the summer games, but he knew he would soon tire. Slowing to a jog, Ramie set a steady rhythm. He kept a leery eye on the barren landscape, but all he saw was scattered trees, rocky terrain, and occasional patches of night flowers, reminding those passing that life could grow in a barren land. He kept jogging anyway.

With the full light of dawn Ramie slowed to a quick walk, but his eyes darted to each side, continuously watching for more magical creatures.

The sun rose in the distance, outlining of buildings of Mintree. At one time Mintree had been one of the most populated inner cities of Yor. Although water was scarce, Presario's father had produced a large livestock trade. Mintree thrived and many craftsmen moved in, increasing the population even further. When Presario's estate had burned the city ceased to have the inflow of capital it once had, and most townsfolk were forced to leave.

As Ramie strode down the center street he felt ridiculous in his tattered clothes but refrained from taking them off. No one would believe a king would walk into Mintree on foot, especially without an escort. If he voiced his true identity most would only think him a fair look alike.

It appeared Mintree hadn't seen a visitor in some time. The structures on either side of the wide street were in their last stages of life. Rotten boards hung over doors and windows, roofs were sunken and decayed, and soiled rags fluttered in the breeze, waving farewell to the city they once knew. The structures squeaked every so often in response to either a slight breeze or their own aging.

Presario's castle stood at the end of the street, a herald of the city's ruin. It loomed over the rest of the city in blackened shards, its hollow windows smiling at the disparaged scene below. Only the top left-hand corner of the castle remained untouched, and though it was beautiful, with cream turrets and gold trim, it looked appalling attached to the rest of the mansion, as if the black, festering wound would seep into its purity and mar any chance of salvation.

Ramie shook off his foreboding thoughts and started for the keep, but stopped short as a few noises drifted to him. The city looked deserted but the sounds were unmistakable. Perusing the street Ramie noted a few of the buildings looked less rickety than the others. One of the sounds came from a building a few paces up and to his right. The sign had long since faded but the horseshoe nailed to its surface betrayed its purpose.

On careful examination, Ramie could see the blacksmith through the open window, long gray beard wavering as he pounded on something he would soon fire into shape. Thinking the man may have a horse for sale, Ramie approached. His soft leather shoes made no sound on the dusty street.

"Excuse me, do you happen to have a horse for sale?" Ramie asked in the most respectable tone he had. He wasn't used to asking for things so he hardly knew how to go about doing it.

The blacksmith jumped, dropping what would soon become an ornate sword, and looked at Ramie with a mixture of startlement and ire. The clanging of the dropped weapon rang through the morning's air like thunder. Ramie couldn't help but chuckle as he apologized for his sudden appearance.

The blacksmith shook a blackened finger at him. "Don't ever do that to another being again! I could have dropped that iron on my foot! Then where would that leave me, hum?" The blacksmith leaned out the open window and peered at Ramie with wide eyes. "I would be blind and crippled now, wouldn't I?"

It was only then Ramie noticed the man's blank stare. The way his eyes wavered in the sunlight should have given him away, but Ramie hadn't been looking for anything out of the ordinary.

"I'm sorry," Ramie said. "I meant no harm. I just thought you might have a horse I could purchase. Mine gave out on the ride over."

The man grinned. "Here to see Presario?" His teeth were rotten, a few gone. The man's fetid breath caused Ramie to take a step back.

"Yes, I am," he said, glancing at the castle. It towered above him, grinning in mockery.

The blacksmith picked up the unfinished sword. "Only Presario can tell you if I have a horse for sale," he said, dismissing Ramie as if he were a fly on a horse's ass.

Ramie raised his eyebrows. "Presario isn't a king or a god. He has no power to tell you what you can and cannot do."

The blacksmith's blank stare and crooked grin reminded Ramie of something from a child's nightmare.

"Oh yes he does, my friend." The sightless eyes sparkled. "Oh yes he does!"

- - -

Ramie was furious. He had been trying to purchase a horse from the blacksmith for a degree of the sun, but all the man could do was point to the castle.

"What if I told you I was Ramie Augustus?"

"I would tell you to talk to Presario. Ramie is nothing in this town; Presario is all."

Ramie's blood boiled. He spun from the man and marched toward the castle. His sense of foreboding evaporated with his anger like steam from a kettle.

The blacksmith's raspy voice called after him. "I wouldn't try if I were you. Presario doesn't take kindly to visitors."

Ramie spun to ask how he was supposed to request a horse from Presario without visiting, but the blacksmith's window slammed in his face. Ramie resisted the urge to take a broken board from the street and shatter the hazy glass.

Ramie stalked off, muttering oaths of every degree imaginable. He would not allow Presario to have domination over the few people who remained in the city. How dare he! The man was a recluse. He had shut everything down. What gave him the right to order these people to obey him?

Ramie would ensure Presario's game ended, or he wasn't the king of Yor.

A second sound echoed down the street. It was a soft grinding noise and it emerged from a shop to his left. Having no intention of stopping, Ramie marched on, but turned his head to catch a glimpse of what other imbecile would remain in a forsaken city at the hands of a recluse.

What he saw made him stop. A man peered from the shop's doorway, sightless eyes staring at Ramie as if they could sense his specter.

The implications made Ramie's head spin. Had Presario allowed only blind men to stay in the town? Or had Presario been mad enough to blind the remaining people so they would be unable to look upon his features if he came out of his sanctuary? Ramie drew a deep breath to calm his rising fury and strode toward the man. The man backed up, terror scrawled in his round face.

Ramie stopped and held up his hands to insinuate he meant no harm. Scowling, he dropped his arms. The man was blind. He couldn't see the action.

"I mean you no harm," Ramie said. The man stopped his retreat but stayed in the shadows. "How were you blinded?"

The man cocked his head to one side and glanced back to the safety of his shop. "Birth."

A grinding wheel stood behind the man, wood chips scattered around it. A chair, still needing a back and one leg, sat beside it. From what Ramie could see the shop was well kept and the finished furniture in the back was some of the finest he had ever seen.

Ramie remembered the famous blind furniture maker, Matadon. His pieces were known throughout the Lands, and they brought a large sum. Ramie even had a few of Matadon's pieces in the Crest castle. Sensing this man would be more reasonable than the last, Ramie took a step forward. The man took a step back.

"Matadon?" he asked. The man's face broke out into a grin and he nodded, suddenly unafraid.

"You live here under Presario's control?"

Matadon cocked his head to one side, making him appear more disheveled than before. Although Matadon kept a good shop, he cared little about his appearance. His matted hair and tattered clothes could use a good washing. "In a way, yes."

"What do you mean, 'in a way?'"

"Presario makes rules and we follow them."

"Then you are under his control."

"If you say."

Ramie's anger rose to new heights. "Only the king makes the laws. Those who preside over cities only follow them and oversee the community in which they're in."

"Not in Mintree. It's different in Mintree. Presario is all in Mintree."

Disgusted, Ramie resumed his march down the street.

Matadon's voice followed him. "I wouldn't go there if I were you."

Ramie turned in a streak of fury. "And why not?"

"Presario doesn't like visitors."

"And what is he going to do, kill me?"

"He might."

Matadon turned and walked back into the shadows of his shop. Ramie couldn't make himself move. Matadon's words left him more than a little shaken. No guard was with him. If Matadon was right and Presario killed him, who would know?

But the more Ramie thought the more furious he became. No man in his kingdom would be allowed to treat people as slaves. There were no slaves in Oldan. Slavery had been vanquished long ago.

It seemed his business here was twofold. Not only did he need information, he also needed to have a light chat with Presario.

He gazed at the castle. The colossal blackened shell towered over him, the smell of burnt wood still strong. Ramie was surprised it was still standing, and slightly appalled someone would continue to reside within.

Now that he stood directly beneath the castles precipitous height Ramie noticed the hastily constructed stairs. They had been added to the outside and led up to the unmarred section. Despite his anger the foreboding stole over him again. Something was out of place: the two men, the broken buildings. It was almost too perfect.

As he reached the last standing building before the castle a woman dashed out and blocked his path. The sign on the building read: *House of Harlots*.

She was the most beautiful woman Ramie had ever seen. Her thin, white smock, covering a precious small amount of skin, was ripped to the thigh, revealing one long, tan leg, and the scoop at her neck hung so low her ample breasts were overflowing.

She placed a hand on his chest, halting his approach. "Please don't," she whispered.

Her voice was so fragile, so afraid, Ramie immediately took her hand, wanting to reassure her. She leaned into him, trembling, and wrapped her arms around his neck. Her long, dark hair tickled his chin.

He stood, stunned, unsure if he should console her or push her away. She moved closer. Her breath was warm, tantalizing. The smell of her was enough to drive any man mad.

He thought of Javi and had to fight to regain control of his desires. He could feel every contour of the girl's form: the shape of her chest, the flatness of her stomach, the curve of her hips, and the strength in her thighs. He felt all the doubt and uncertainty surrounding his marriage filter through him. He felt himself weaken. With sudden yearning he reached up to feel the girl's hair.

His hand halted in midair. He looked at the castle before him – a tingle of warning, a shimmer of deceit.

16

Ramie focused on Javi and his duty to her, to the people of Yor, and to the people of all the Lands. He felt his mind become sharp.

This wasn't natural. The entire town wasn't *right*.

He pushed the girl away and looked into her eyes. They were two black pits, devouring all light. "Why shouldn't I go?"

"He won't be happy if I let you pass, he'll . . . " Her voice trailed off as she placed a slender hand on her breast. She whispered, "Tell me your troubles. I can provide you with much more than Presario."

Ramie fought back his feelings and pushed her away.

He looked at the castle again. He thought he saw a curtain drop in the upper window.

He shoved past the woman even as she yelled for him to stop. He closed his eyes, fighting his desire to turn back. He wasn't that strong. He may be a king, but he was also a man. He wasn't strong enough to resist a second time.

He tensed, prepared to deal with more diversions, but none appeared. When he reached the castle he scaled the outlying fence and dropped to the ground.

The enclave was well landscaped. Although it was a simple design, with few flowers, it was attractive and comfortable. Even the grassy section below the charred ruins remained carefully tended.

But he didn't take long to survey the area. He started for the stairs as soon as his feet touched the ground. He pulled off the stableman's tunic and untied the rope at his waist, bemoaning the fact he had left his cloak on Foster. It had the emblem of Yor embedded in its threads and would have proven his identity at first glance.

Ramie's mind turned to what he would say, knowing he would have to contend with Presario's servant before he reached Presario. He would not let Presario deny him entrance. He was the king for the love of the Maker!

A rudely constructed, heavy wooden door stood at the top of the stairs. It tilted slightly, creating an immediate impression of lunacy. Ramie was truly beginning to think Presario mad. Although it went against all he had heard, what he had seen so far did nothing to discount the theory.

Ramie banged on the door and waited. Just as he lifted his hand to knock again, it opened. An old man peered out. Wrinkles covered the man's gaunt face and no smile touched his lips, but neither caused Ramie to forget his words. It was his eyes. They were solid white, no pupil or color in them.

The man had been blinded by fire. The mere thought of fire touching his eyes turned Ramie's skin. It must have been horrible.

The man's brows furrowed as he cleared his throat, indicating for Ramie to speak his mind.

"I've come to see Presario." Ramie's natural authoritative tone flowed from him like melted butter.

The old man raised his eyebrows in surprise. "No one sees Presario. If you have a question write it down. He'll decide if it's worthy of a reply."

When the old man began to shut the door Ramie's temper flared. He caught it with his hand, but the old man's strength surprised him. Although Ramie was able to stop the door he was unable to force it further open. It held steady, only a finger's width from the frame.

One white eye peered through the crack with unusual perception. "Release your hold, my lord. Presario is now off limits to you."

"You had better change your tone, old man. I'm Ramie Augustus, King of Yor and Ruler of Oldan. If you don't grant me entrance I'll declare you a traitor of Oldan and have you hung."

One white eye regarded him, almost as if it could see. A chill went down Ramie's spine. There was nothing right about the town, the man, or Presario. Ramie wanted answers now more than ever.

"If you are who you say, where's your guard? And why are you here? Kings have advisors and courts. Why would a king need to see Presario?"

Ramie cooled his anger in order to answer without exploding. He didn't like games, and that was what he was in. He also didn't like wasting time, and that was precisely what Presario was forcing him to do.

"Kings have advisors and courts, but when war is close you never know whom to trust. I need an objective opinion and guidance on issues that must remain concealed. That's why I'm here. I don't think I have to worry about Presario flapping his tongue, seeing that not even a king is welcome in his home. I have no time to write my questions. I need immediate answers." Ramie paused and cocked one eyebrow. "That is, if Presario has them."

"Presario has them," the old man stated as if Presario was the Oracle itself. "You speak with the hauteur of a king, or close to one. I'll tell Presario you're here."

Ramie nodded and released his hold on the door. It slammed in his face. Sighing, Ramie did the only thing he knew to do, and that was to sit and wait.

- - -

Ramie paced on the small landing, glancing at the door in silent fury. Arri, the old man, had come back and told him Presario would see him, but only at dusk. Ramie had started to object when the door had slammed in his face for the second time.

If Presario was a respectable host he would have invited him in to wait, perhaps offer some tea or wine. But no, not Presario, not the man who had retreated from the world of the living to abide in a sepulchered keep of mourning.

Presario ruled like some kind of omnipotent being, commanding people to do what he wanted, when he wanted. After careful deliberation Ramie decided to ask his questions first, calmly if he could, and then deal with what Presario had done to the town. The more Ramie thought about Presario's actions the more enraged he became. Presario had closed his lands for the sole purpose of driving people from Mintree, forced blind men to stay behind and monitor all who passed, and turned away those who entreated him for knowledge. What right did one man have to decide the fate of a city, the fate of other souls, and the fate of the future? Mintree was once the highest producing province in Yor. It could be so again.

Presario was beyond Ramie's comprehension. Although the fire was a tragedy, Ramie would have never done what Presario had done: shut out the world, denying himself life, love and friendship, and most important, denying others a wealth of knowledge. Although some entreaties were rewarded with Presario's reply, it took an act of the Maker to make it through the town to see the man.

Ramie thought back to the accounts of Presario's replies and stopped pacing. Ramie turned to the town, eyes falling on the building closest to the keep: *House of Harlots*. His mind spun.

Presario only answered women!

Ramie glanced at the crooked wooden door as if it alone could reveal Presario's secrets. Why did Presario only answer women? Why did he turn men away? Ramie glanced back toward the town, thinking about the two men and the girl. Did they only show themselves when men walked through the town? He wondered. The girl would be a useless deterrent for women, unless she focused those midnight eyes on them and screamed.

The door opened, shattering his thoughts. Arri stood back, allowing him entrance. It was the first full view Ramie had seen of the castle's interior, and all he could do was stare.

Books lined the walls from floor to ceiling. He had come to the right place. He would be surprised if there was a book in the Lands Presario hadn't read at least ten times.

Arri shifted. "Are you coming, or are you going to stand there gaping all day?"

Ramie stepped inside, a shiver running down his spine at the old man's words. It was said the blind had better senses than most, but Arri's white eyes were uncanny.

Arri closed the door behind him, bolting it quickly as if an army had lined up outside. A portrait of a boy with brilliant blue eyes, cherry-brown hair, and a kind smile hung behind the door. The boy was just reaching manhood. He sat up straight and proud, daring the artist to capture all his nuances. It was Presario, as he was before. The painting had been slashed in anger, slicing the boy's face and causing the painting to appear ominous and not enchanting.

Maybe Ramie was being too harsh on Presario. No, he thought, Presario should have picked up the pieces and gone on.

But Nigel hadn't.

The thought knocked Ramie off balance. Although Nigel's situation was different, it had the same result. Both Nigel and Presario had denied everyone a chance to know and love them.

Ramie followed Arri without question, suddenly feeling like a knave in a shrine. Torches were placed every few cubits in standing wrought-iron holsters. Light danced with chameleon subtlety over the profusion of books, which seemed to have no end.

Arri turned down a dark, narrow corridor halfway down the hall. Ramie was about to follow but he stopped short. The skeletal shell of the blackened castle loomed only cubits away. Ramie took a step forward, morbidly enchanted by the sight. The boards below him became a jagged, precarious precipice. The bony bowels of what once been one of the most glorious mansions in Yor reached upward with twisted features. Only a small section of hall remained visible in the distance. Paintings hung unrecognizable, tattered curtains fluttered in enigmatic drafts, and ashes and dust were pilled high in every corner. Though furniture was sparse, there was enough evidence of former inhabitance to cause the torchlight to bring shadowy specters to life.

All evidence of Ramie's anger evaporated. Why didn't Presario board up the sight? It must be painful to look upon one's former life and be reminded of its tragic end. Ramie made a mental note to offer his own men for the job, maybe even help rebuild the entire keep.

Fearful Arri would grow weary of his hesitation, Ramie turned and hurried down the smaller passage. A lone light flickered from under a doorway at the end of the hall. It danced just enough to help Ramie maneuver through the books surrounding him.

He heard soft, eerie music as he approached. It climbed higher and higher until Ramie's hackles began to rise. The old man turned toward him with iridescent white eyes. It was an experience Ramie would never forget: the darkness, the music, and the eyes.

Arri stepped aside, indicating for Ramie to enter alone. Ramie nodded his thanks, trying his best to keep his regal demeanor, but his hands shook with the same unnatural twinge he had sensed in the streets of Mintree.

Presario may be a recluse, but he was far from an ordinary man.

Arri left without a word, his soft footfalls echoing impending doom. Ramie leaned into the wooden door until he had regained some of the Augustus confidence. He concentrated on why he was there: Ista's lies, his kingdom, the Lands, and most importantly Ren and Nigel. If he was there for one reason it was for Ren and Nigel. He couldn't let them down. He wouldn't let them down.

He opened the door and stepped into a large library. Books were arranged from floor to ceiling in exquisitely polished shelves. A huge redwood desk, covered with papers, styluses and scrolls, sat in the center of the room. All items were arranged with careful precision.

The knowledge residing in the room was fathomless, and Ramie knew the books held in the library and the halls only scratched the surface. How many other chambers had he been led past? How many floors were still useable? How many thousands upon thousands of volumes were hidden in Presario's castle? Presario was called the man of most knowledge. Now Ramie knew why.

Despite the overwhelming number of volumes, what drew Ramie's eyes were the paintings. They surrounded the room, but instead of being hung – for every wall from floor to ceiling supported a shelf – they were propped against the shelves. Not an inch of floor space was untouched by their frames. Some were even stacked one on top of another.

They were all images of water: waterfalls, lakes, streams, rain, floods, oceans, and glaciers. Every depiction of water was represented: water, the opposite of fire. Ramie's chest tightened. He had no right to judge this man. He had no idea what kind of pain Presario had lived with since the fire.

Ramie swallowed his pride and turned to the corner fireplace from which the only light in the room emanated. A huge chair sat before the fire, the back far taller than the man who sat within its depths. All Ramie could see of Presario was one wrinkled hand clutching the arm of the chair.

With quick calculation Ramie determined Presario was only thirty-five. Ramie turned away. The wrinkles weren't from age. Ramie had only seen one other hand as melted as the one before him, and that man hadn't lived through the night. The memory was painful to recall. Ramie couldn't imagine living the memory. If the rest of Presario's skin was as festered as the hand Ramie couldn't begin to conceive the torment Presario had endured.

When Ramie turned back, the hand was gone. A winding sound shattered the silence and the music started again. Ramie hadn't even noticed the music had stopped, but as it rekindled the spectral drone seemed to enwrap his soul in a pod of loneliness.

Ramie took a step back, unsure if he wanted to feel what the man before him felt every day.

"It seems the Augustus family will not let me be."

Ramie jumped at the sound of Presario's voice. It was pleasant, soothing, even compassionate, but it was contrary to what he had expected. The voice didn't parallel the foreboding feelings, the ominous castle, and the shriveled hand. Ramie thought back to the picture he had seen of the young Presario: the cherry-brown hair, the brilliant blue eyes, and the kind smile. The voice fit that face.

Ramie cleared his throat. "I don't understand. This is my first visit."

"And you believe you are the entire Augustus family?" Presario's tone was sarcastic, condemning. Ramie balked, but his confusion overpowered his anger.

A hollow laugh came from the chair. "Yes, that would be what the mighty Ramie Augustus thinks. He and he alone constitutes the name."

Ramie drew a furious breath, but before he could speak Presario's voice marred the silence.

"Years ago the Black Knight came to me. He was near death. I had to make a decision. Would I help him live and be seen? Or would I maintain my heterodox haven and perhaps be responsible for his death? I chose the former. He was the only one, until you, I have allowed into my halls.

"So I say again, it seems the Augustus family will not let me be." His voice stayed in an advisor monotone but Ramie sensed the inflection of Presario's voice at the irony of his words.

Ramie finally found his voice. "Then I owe you my gratitude for saving my brother's life."

Presario's chuckle sounded like paradoxical music: happy but sad, enticing yet distant.

"Ironic, don't you think? You threaten me with your title and then discover the Augustus family owes me a blood debt. An old adage theorizes that since you have threatened me, the very person who helped your family parry death, your very soul is given to me to command in death. The nullity commanding the sovereign, very ironic indeed."

Ramie's anger ignited. "You forced me into a threat I had no intention of carrying out. You shun the world, molting your genius when it appeals to you, denying others even parcels from your hand. You were the most talked about advisor of all time, Presario, not a twin, not a triplet, but you. I don't use my title for its own sake but for the sake of the people of the Lands. My need is great, Presario, and you would have turned me away without thought or care. Are you that deformed in heart as well as in body?"

Ramie winced as soon as his words were out, but there was no taking them back. The music had stopped and the only sound was the crackling fire. Ramie wondered how Presario could endure to sit before the flames. Ramie supposed it might be Presario's way of defying the memories.

"You put me in an awkward position, my *king*," Presario hissed. "Do I listen to you because of the sincerity of your need? Or do I banish you because of your haughty words and arrogant judgments? I believe you could take lessons from the Black Knight, my *king*. Ironic don't you think? The brother who kills has a pure heart and mind, yet the brother who rules has less worth because of his foul mouth and swift dictums. Anger leads to destruction, Ramie Augustus. I am proof of that. You need to peruse the mural for its theme before you judge the artisan's purpose."

Ramie didn't want to admit the truth of Presario's words but was unable to avoid them. He was passing judgment on someone he knew nothing about. He had secretly condemned his own brother without thinking through the implications: the perils Nigel would face if he had stayed, the danger to their family, Nigel's feelings. No, he had only thought of himself and how Nigel had deserted him.

"When your brother was here he mumbled a lot in his sleep. He was concerned more about you than his own life. He wept over and over, praying you would forgive him if you gleaned the truth. I wonder if you have?" Presario's words cut. Ramie remained silent.

"Now whose heart is deformed?" Presario asked. "I wouldn't leap to judge me if I were you. You need to purify your own soul much more deeply than I. All I do is try to live in peace. Would you castigate a blacksmith who didn't want to fire another piece of iron?

Would you condemn a furniture builder who didn't want to carve another piece of wood? How am I different from someone who doesn't care for his profession any longer?"

Presario paused to wind the music box once again. "You debase me for the town's demise? Be wary of that imperious thought. I don't control the town as you think. Those who remain do so on their own accord, although I do reward them for their efforts. All they want is a solitary place to practice their craft. All I need are a few to turn away those who seek my advice.

"The only thing I'm guilty of is ceasing production on my father's fields. Yes, it has caused the town to die, but it's my land and Yor isn't destitute of soil to raise cattle and grain. But I know your mind. You still believe I'm vile. You think I've forced people to leave, but you still don't ask the reason behind it. What you don't see, what you don't care to know, is that it pains me to see Mintree a ghost town. I'm alone. I'll always be alone. It's by choice, yes; but that doesn't make me apathetic. I liked looking out the window and seeing children at play. I enjoyed chance sightings of trysts between lovers. I delighted in the bustle of the market and witnessing the latest garish fashions. No, I didn't close my father's fields to bring the town to ruin. I chose to do so because I loathed everything about my father at the time. It may seem trite to you, but it was everything to me."

Presario paused, heaving a sigh. "I don't explain my actions for your consent. To be brazenly honest, I don't explain myself to anyone, king or no king. You may deplore me or you may extol me. I don't care which. I allow you to ask your question because of your soul. Although it's quick tempered, it's true. You're the only man, besides your brother, who has made it past the girl. All others give in to her, married or unmarried, devout or heathen. All." Presario slapped his hand down in harsh judgment. "But know neither your title nor your heart gave you leave to come into this house. I allowed you entrance because of a man I know and respect. That is your brother, my king, not you. Nigel has given you entrance. Remember that. Ask what you will."

Ramie knew Presario was right, about everything. His own admittance was belittling. Closing his eyes Ramie tried to regain his former confidence. It evaded him. He thought of Ren and why he was there. It gave him what he needed to speak to the man he had degraded without righteous cause.

"The crown prince of Zier has been pronounced a traitor and his kingdom has fallen to a sorceress who has survived since the Wizard War. She claims the crown prince is the one to fear and rallies the

Lands behind her. She has encouraged all kingdoms to send those with the power to train under her, and people go, hungry for the rewards the Quy can give them. She is forming a force she calls the Collective, claiming it will be under no rule but will work for all the Lands. I know she lies. This woman's tentacles reach through the Lands as it is. With a collective force under her she'll be able to infiltrate the Lands and crush all resistance."

Ramie waited for Presario to speak. When he did not, Ramie continued. "I'm in a perilous position because I know the truth yet I have no proof to show. Currently no other kingdom will join me in the fight against her. Without regard to magic my army is insignificant compared to hers. With regard to magic my army is dead before the first taut of the bow.

"I would wait longer but I fear with each breath I take her hold strengthens and mine weakens. I'm here to obtain advice on attempting an offensive against the Collective. The crown prince of Zier has fled, but I want to assure when Ren returns it won't be too late. He's honorable, Presario, much like Nigel. If you like my brother you would like Ren."

Presario remained silent. The crackling of the fire continued but the embers were burning low and there was an acute chill in the room. Ramie rubbed his arms, wondering if Presario would risk being seen to rekindle the flames.

"I didn't realize the synergy would be a prince," Presario said.

Ramie looked at the back of the chair in confusion. "I'm sorry?"

A variegated hand lifted from the confines of the chair and slashed the air for silence. The fabric of Presario's robe crawled up his arm, exposing seething flesh far more dreadful than the hand.

"It's of no importance." Presario laid his hand back on the ball of the arm, long fingers careening over it with slow precision. "You've come for nothing. You know what you must do. You're looking for reassurance, something I cannot give. All I can do is help you understand your thoughts.

"You've just said Ren is honorable and has been pronounced a traitor by a knowledgeable sorceress. If that's true you don't want this sorceress training people with magic. She'll mold them into shadows of herself. Your decision isn't whether you should oppose her. Your decision is when and if you should go against her with force. On one hand emancipation will bring freedom for the people and an ultimate good, but it will also shed an unfavorable light on you. You'll have conquered Newlan. There will be suspicion and outrage. You'll have also killed the people's channel to learn the Quy. On the other hand, if you choose to remain idle any more time without an offensive is time this sorceress has to train those with her. The more time passes, the greater the threat. You are a king. You know what is right. Although the road is perilous, you already know the answer."

"But how do I mount an offensive against something I know nothing about? What defense do I have?" Ramie asked, his voice betraying what little hope he held.

"Go to the table," Presario said. "I've left you a book. Although most accounts of the Quy were plundered some were hidden and many have found their way here. I pay a handsome price for rare books, and people from across the lands come here to sell them. Over the years I've collected many on the Quy. The one I now bestow to you is my most prized piece. It should be of use. It's called a Patois Paragon or patoi for short. Do you know this term?"

"No," Ramie admitted, walking to the book and laying a dubious hand on its leather cover.

"Patoi means 'the model of words.' Books holding the patoi cognomen are literally teachers of what is contained inside. This book is a patoi for the Quy. The emotional weaves inside start from the most simplistic and finish with the most convoluted and precarious. It's old, as old as the Alcazar I should think. The first Calvet, Omar, created it. From that day forth every new thought and emotional weave he found significant was recorded in the book. With each generation the book has been added to, up until the destruction of the Alcazar.

"The book's words, shall I say, come alive to the reader, so you'll be able to learn with swiftness."

Ramie stared down at the monstrous book as Presario droned on. He could feel the power residing within, enticing him to open the cover and learn what was held in its depths.

The book would be a guide to him and to his army. He would be able to fight Ista with magic.

The fire blazed hotter, banishing the chill in the room. Ramie turned to find Presario had put another log on the flames. Ramie frowned. He thought he would have noticed Presario's movement. He turned his attention back to the book.

"How did you know what I needed before I asked?"

"What would compel a king to come alone, in the dark, dressed as a beggar, other than something as mystical as magic?" Ramie heard the smile on Presario's lips. He smiled himself. What else indeed?

Ramie opened the book. A shade of a figure only a finger's length in height leapt from the pages. Ramie bounded back a step.

"You've opened the patoi of the Quy," the figure said with balmy smoothness. The accent was so eccentric Ramie had to concentrate to make out the words. "I'm Omar, First Calvet and founder of the Alcazar. I'll be your guide. Before you turn to the beginning I need to cover the rules.

"First, you must not turn a page until mastery of the emotional weave held therein. Proceeding onward is dangerous and insensate. If you disobey this rule the patoi will know and it will lock itself from you forever. Second, don't let this be a teacher to those of lesser knowledge. Warnings aren't given, only what needs to be done to culminate the emotional weave. It's for one of long learning and study."

The small figure smiled and cocked his head to one side. Ramie could feel the humility and love emanating from the mien, but he also felt power. His mind tingled. He took another step back.

A troubled expression crossed Omar's features. The small specter rubbed his chin and hovered to Ramie. Ramie remained frozen in place as Omar tapped his nose.

"Not of Calvet quality."

Ramie blinked at Omar's statement. Presario's wry laughter rose from the chair. Ramie was too flustered to be irritated, but his anger took residence just below his startlement.

Omar tapped Ramie's nose again. His brows drew down over sharp hazel eyes. "State your lineage."

Presario spoke before Ramie could reply. "Omar, he's the one I spoke to you about. He's the king."

The specter turned to the chair. If it was possible, its frown deepened. "No, Presario. This can't be allowed. There is too much anger in him. He'll try to learn too quickly." Omar's eyes wavered back to Ramie. "He'll close the book for his generation."

Ramie drew in a breath. When Omar said the book would be locked from him forever he hadn't realized it would be locked away for as long as he lived. Once again he felt humiliation. It had crossed his mind to read a page and keep passing it to another, then another, until the entire book was read, in order to expedite the learning process.

Omar read the verity of Ramie's thoughts and snorted. "I don't choose to go with him."

"You have no choice, Omar. You're the words in the book. The Alcazar no longer exists. There's no Calvet to pass you to. I own you. I bequeath you to the king."

Omar's sharp hazel eyes regarded Ramie once again before releasing another snort. The minuscule figure twisted in the air, hovered back to the book, and dissipated over the pages. The leather cover closed with an acute slap.

Ramie stood stunned. Had Omar rejected him? No, Omar hadn't rejected him. Omar just wasn't happy Presario had given him the patoi.

He stepped back to the book. It was cold now, not tingling with the warmth he had felt before. He thought of what Omar had said. He would have to keep his anger at bay. There was no one else he could trust with the book. He would just have to master one page before he went on to the next.

The thought was almost jocular. Patience wasn't something he possessed. He knew he would soon close the book to his generation. Although his impatience was a weakness, that weakness made him a good king. He would stand for neither idling nor delay.

Ramie felt his one ray of hope wink out. Whom could he trust to use the book with swiftness as well as patience? The etching on the cover seemed to mock him. A familiar snort came from inside. He refrained from opening the book and strangling the little mite within. If the book was aware why couldn't it just keep him from turning to the second page if he hadn't mastered the first? Why did it have to close itself to him, to his generation?

When he turned to ask Presario, he froze in place. A piece of wood drifted through the air to replenish the fire.

As the implications manifested, Ramie stepped toward the chair. "Presario, you have the Quy. You heard what Omar said. You already know the book. You've read it from cover to cover before magic was alive to awaken its specter. You could come with me and teach my men far more quickly than I. Presario, I can't stall any longer. Many people are crossing the border against my command. The longer I delay the more powerful she'll become.

"You already know the Quy. You're the only one in the Lands who has studied it for years, who's read the words from generations of Calvets. Please, Presario, help me train my men. Help me liberate Newlan from the threat that could soon consume us all."

His supplication sounded strange to him. He had never pleaded with anyone in his life, but it took all he had to remain standing and not get down on his knees to beg. The music droned on, the fire crackled and popped, but no reply came.

When Presario's cynical laughter finally wafted through the air, it sounded as if he had repressed it for some time. "My king, surely you jest. You knew my answer before you asked the question. I intend no disrespect, but I am where I am and this is where I'll stay."

Ramie knew he was about fight a losing battle, but he had to try. "Presario, please. The book will give us some knowledge but learning won't come fast enough to defeat Ista. We'll be dead men, fighting a battle we can't win. You're the only one I can trust. You're the only one who can give me the edge I need."

"No, only the Chosen can do that. I'm a grain of sand compared to him. He's the mountain, not I."

"But one grain of sand can tip the scales," Ramie said. "One grain of sand can cause a blister to form on the foot of a monster. One grain of sand in the right position can make or break a battle because one grain of sand can help the one man who can make a difference."

"I'm not that grain of sand."

Ramie's temper flared. Didn't Presario understand the Lands were at stake, that his own precious stronghold would be subject to Ista's rule? Was Presario so egocentric that he would turn his back on humanity?

Ramie exploded. "You've wallowed in self-pity and denial for years! Can't you see the world is now in need of your knowledge? Will you allow innocents to die in this war when you have the unique opportunity to save them?

"You're well-known throughout the Lands, not for your shard castle or your deformity, but for your knowledge." Ramie trembled so violently his vision blurred. He put his fingers to the bridge of his nose and took a breath, trying to calm. "You need to put the past behind you and go on as my brother has. Nigel may die in the process, but that won't stop him from helping the Lands.

"What about you, Presario? Will you sit in your haven and never see daylight again, never see the smile of a child, never feel the love of another human being, never feel the joy of witnessing how your intellect has saved thousands around you? If that's what you choose then you truly disgust me. Is your appearance so important you'll put it in front of countless lives? Are you vain enough to think it matters?"

Ramie was about to say more when Presario rose from the chair. The firelight cast his body in shadow, shielding his features from view. Presario was a large man, much larger than Ramie had first imagined, and if the fire had burned him, it hadn't weakened him. As Presario approached his appearance began to manifest.

The skin outside his long brown robe was fraught with ridges and crevasses, like a pot of boiling water that had never cooled. One eye

29

was seared completely shut, the skin dripping down to cover the fissure for eternity. The other eye was the piercing blue Ramie had seen in the picture, but there was none of the winsomeness left, only profound sorrow, anguish, and currently, rage.

Although Presario was broad, he was bone thin, and the scant hair growing on the motley skull was just a reminder of his former self. Ramie wasn't prepared for the sight, but he didn't recoil. If he balked Presario would never again allow another near him.

"Would you ask me to do as you say now, my king?" The smooth voice sounded strange coming from the molten face, but Ramie didn't turn. Instead, he stepped closer.

"Yes, I would. I place no emphasis on beauty. You're the only one who can help me defeat a woman I know to be sinister. You've said my heart is true. If it is, you know I'm right. How can you deny me your intellect when you know good and well I'll fail without it!"

"Control your anger, my king," Presario hissed. "It will be the end of you. I have foreseen it."

"So you claim to be a seer, Presario? A seer? And still you choose to wallow in the dark and shun the world?" Ramie threw up his hands and stalked to the door. Enough of Presario and his demented mind!

He stopped with his hand on the knob. When he spoke his voice was a harsh whisper. "A seer is no seer if he isn't seen. A prophecy is no prophecy if it isn't read. You're a sorry excuse of a seer if that's what you claim to be. You're just a deformed man who will never be whole."

Ramie withdrew the statue from his pocket and placed it on the bookshelf beside him. It was the reason he had come. It was only a small relic of his father, but it meant more to him than all the gold in the Lands. All the lessons his father had given had always ended with him holding up the statue, challenging him to be the face on the right, beautiful and pure.

Ramie knew part of him had become the face on the left. He had failed his brother, and he had failed in other areas he was unwilling to admit. Presario saw through some of those, and perhaps Presario's understanding was the reason Ramie felt so disturbed. The one who lectured on actions and judgments hid behind a mask, using it as an excuse to disregard what the Maker had bestowed on him.

All anger drained away. Ramie didn't understand Presario's actions, but he couldn't condemn Presario for them. Presario was a man who had been burned both emotionally and physically. Although

Ramie didn't know the reason, he did know Presario only injured himself by denying himself life.

Ramie traced the statue with his finger. "My father left me this statue when he died. I've cherished it because of what my father used to say. He said we needed to strive to be the man of beauty and not the man of deformity. He said with every action we need to reach for excellence. When I was young, I heard about the fire in Mintree and how a young man destined for greatness was burned beyond recognition. The same day my father gave us a lecture about being the man on the right. I asked in childlike stupidity if you were the man on the left. My father looked at me and said, 'No, son, that man is more beautiful than even the one on the right. You'll see. He'll be one to admire for years to come.'"

Ramie opened the door and walked down the corridor, shoving past Arri who was standing watch. When he reached the main passage, he felt a hand on his shoulder. Turning, he looked into Arri's uncanny white eyes. Arri waved him onward as he glanced back down the hall as if he could see. A familiar chill passed down Ramie's spine as he followed Arri to the main door.

White eyes regarded him. "Thank you for telling him what you did. I'm in your debt. He's truly a beautiful man, my king. He just won't allow himself to be. There's much pain in him, even now."

"Why so long?" Ramie asked, concerned he had left Presario with ill words. Although he felt Presario was wrong he didn't like to burn bridges.

The old man looked toward the charred cavity of the castle. "The night of the fire he had returned home from the Advisor Covenant to choose where he would serve. He found his mother in tears, entreating his father to stop seeing his mistresses."

Ramie already feared where the story would lead. At one time it was perfectly acceptable for men of influence to have concubines. Now only kings were allowed to give in to their dalliances, and sometimes even kings were shunned if an illegitimate child was born. Affairs still happened but all were kept well hidden for Oldan law frowned on such promiscuity. If a man was caught in the act his wife could take half his possessions. If a woman was caught the husband could discard her and strip her of everything she owned. Most women were forced to prostitution afterwards, which was how many of the harlot houses had begun in the first place.

Arri continued. "Presario's mother was one of the most beautiful people I've ever had the pleasure of seeing, and her love for his father

31

was unbounded. All thought he matched her love. That wasn't the case.

"A year before Presario's return she was thrown by a horse. Her ankle caught the stirrup and the horse inadvertently crushed her jaw and shattered one of her legs. Her beauty was marred and Presario's father rejected her, fulfilling his desires with other women."

Ramie closed his eyes. It was the one excuse for a man to seek pleasure elsewhere. If a woman's beauty was damaged it would be lawful for him to have others. Ramie vowed to change that law.

"When Presario came home he overheard his parents arguing: his mother imploring his father to love her, his father refusing to listen. Presario's father quoted the law, saying it gave him the right to deny her, to choose others to satisfy his needs. It was only right, he argued. She was now a cripple and not as she had once been, not the same person he had married."

Arri sighed, white eyes filling with memories. "You should have seen Presario, my king. He was blinded by rage. He burst through the door and yelled at his father. Words turned into shoves and soon a torch was overturned. A tapestry covering an entire wall ignited like dry grass and began to fall. Presario's mother was directly underneath and her leg didn't allow her to move without assistance. Presario dove, covering his mother's body and taking the flames. Only after he had broken a window and hurled her to safely did he douse those flames.

"Presario could have followed his mother out the window. Although he was burnt he wasn't as he is now, but a beam fell on me." Arri shook his head as if he wanted to die. "The boy jumped through a wall of fire to save me. While his own clothes were burning he pushed me out the nearest window, saving me from greater harm. That was when the house seemed to ignite on its own accord. The fire swept the bowels, collapsing the inner shell and trapping Presario.

"When we found him it was almost too late."

The old man's voice broke. Ramie put a hand on his shoulder, trying to give what little comfort he could. Now he understood why Presario tested every man who came through the city.

"What of his mother?"

Arri blinked as if confused as to who stood before him. When a flash of remembrance crossed his features he herded Ramie out the door.

"When she heard her husband was dead and her son trapped in the flames she took her own life."

Ramie's breath caught. Presario had said his anger had led to destruction. Presario and Nigel were very similar creatures indeed. Nigel blamed himself for the deaths of Sherri and Megglan. Presario lived with the weight of his parents' deaths.

The door began to close but Ramie stopped it with his hand. Somehow, he had to convey his sympathy.

"I'm sorry," Ramie said. "That's why you're blind?"

Arri straightened, eyes wide. "Oh no. I'm blind because Presario wanted no one to see him. I burnt my own eyes long after the fire so Presario would let me serve him."

Ramie was stunned enough to release his hold on the door. It closed, iron hinges fastening from the inside. Ramie banged on the door, pleading with Arri to let him speak to Presario one last time.

He was desperate. He didn't want to leave Presario without some token of understanding, without telling him he would change the law. But Arri didn't answer, and soon Ramie knew it was futile.

Ramie started down the stairs. When he reached the fence he turned and glanced up at the window. The curtains were parted. A small flicker of firelight glimmered in the pane. Heartbeats later the curtains dropped, betraying a shadow that quickly turned away.

CHAPTER 3

Ren stumbled down the steps as the Oracle collapsed behind him. White dust and pieces of stone came at him from every direction. He shielded his eyes and dove for the nearby trees just as the Oracle's edifice began to sway and the columns beneath it crumbled. With a paralyzed soul, Ren watched the complete destruction of the building before he collapsed on the ground.

He wanted to rest but the commands of the Oracle kept twirling through his mind, condemning any hope of sleep.

He grabbed a rock and threw it. It hit a nearby tree, nicking its bark. The light wound stood in stark contrast to the gray knots of the tree: light and dark, love and pain.

As he thought about the charges before him, he shivered: kill his mother, deny his love, and destroy his soul.

How could virtuous beings, lecturing of love and pain, ask him to do things bordering on the very emotion they had warned him against? He felt his anger begin to rekindle. He clung to it.

The third element rose inside him like a deprived monster. It wasn't a pure hate, a complete hate, but it was enough to shield him from the anguish, enough to shelter him from the torrent of agony that threatened to swallow him alive.

He caressed his anger, forming it into a steep culmination inside his soul.

Then he thought of the words written in the Oracle, the Quy's enchanting song, and the two men he would have to become. He released the darkening corruption, recoiling as the pain rekindled.

Light or dark, they said, one or the other. He wanted the light. He desperately wanted to help the Quy live in the light. He couldn't allow hate to swallow him or the Lands would become darkness. What was it the Quy had said? Love was strong but the pain of love was stronger. She had also said the two together, love and love's pain, could crush the darkness.

But would the pain ever go away?

He forced his body to move. Every muscle cried out for him to rest but he refused to heed the cries. He surveyed the rubble of the temple. It rose before him, mirroring his shattered heart. Ren ascended the pile of glimmering white stone, catching glimpses of words and occasional bits of paintings. Under one hollow he saw his face, or Barracus' face, staring up at him. White dust coated his features, further blurring them into Barracus' own. He looked at the painting without emotion. Why did it matter? The Oracle said he would become both men. There was no escaping that end.

The eyes of the dead mage mocked him. Ren wondered if he was already forming into Barracus because of the hate lurking just below the surface. Was that how the former mage had turned vile?

A breeze stirred. Ren almost thought he heard it whisk away a man's laughter.

Kill, deny, and destroy. The verity of the Oracles charges crashed inside him once again.

"Why are you asking me to do this?" he shouted at the crumbled stone.

There was no response, only harsh silence.

A table protruded from the rubble, paces from him. A small box rested on top. He didn't recall seeing a table with a box. The only tables he had seen were by Choice and Chance, with arrows and dice.

Ren stepped over the remains of his partitioned face and approached the table, cautiously testing each stone before he went. The box was a small, metal pyx, the type used to carry healing herbs to kings and men of fortune centuries before. It was rumored all pxyes had been blessed by the fates in order to magnify the properties of the herbs and expedite the healing process. Ren had always wondered how a pyx could be blessed by the fates if the fates were intangible. Now he knew. They were blessed by the Oracle's Fate.

Ren picked it up. It couldn't be here to heal him. He was sick at heart, not in body. Could it be another message? A sweeping aversion resonated in every limb. He couldn't take another message. The last three were more than he could endure.

Small chiseled runes lining the edges of the pyx caught his attention. They consisted of a multiple backward-slanted Z's, the symbol for victory, the same symbol etched on the hilt of his sword.

What was victory without his mother, Aidan, or his own soul?

The sun sunk lower in the sky. He needed to hurry back to the others. He was tired, but he desperately needed to see his friends.

He placed the pyx on the table.

"No more," he said.

The pyx's sides collapsed. An explosion of colors shot skyward with the force of the ten winds. Ren fell. A stone's jagged edge sliced through his shoulder.

The colors pulsated faster and faster. The turbulence whipped around him, flailing his hair and threatening to tear his clothes from his body. The skin on his face burnt from the vitality of the color's

35

movement. The air surrounding him, the air providing life and nourishment, was whisked away, leaving him parched and drained. His lips dried, his eyes stung, the nausea in his chest caused him to swivel and relieve himself of his last meal.

When he turned back to the colors they were forming a picture. Ren shielded his eyes from their brilliance but was unable to turn away from the images before him.

As the wind beat and the colors pulsed, he saw an image of himself killing his mother with his sword, running her through with lethal intent. Then the scene changed. The colors turned dark as screams of horror filled his mind. He clutched his mother to him, watching as others fell around him in death. With each death he pulled Renee closer. The look on their faces was defiant and heinous. His mother, one of the most beautiful women in the Lands, was laughing at death.

The colors surged again, forming an image of the silver dragon. He stood over it, as the painting showed, plunging his sword into its heart. Ren tried to turn away as the silver dragon's violet eyes began to weep, but before he could the image changed into one of darkness.

He walked toward the manacled dragon. Barracus' face smiled in anticipation. The silver wailed a warning through its clamped jaws as he sliced a gouge deep into the silver's flanks. The dragon howled in pain as fire spewed through its muzzle, creating a red ball that grew larger and larger, dominating the scene and blackening out the horizon.

The colors pulsated again until they created an image of him kneeling before a man of darkness. The shadow moved toward him, swallowing his essence. Suddenly a ray of light shot through the dark man, shattering the shadow's form into thousands of minuscule black pieces. He rose from the soot, drained and torn but whole.

Then the scene changed. He saw himself walking toward the sheet of darkness and standing proud before it. As he drew his sword the darkness swallowed him. His body shuddered and twisted until he became a torrent of madness.

When the scenes ended, the colors swirled faster. They became a stark white hand with long, sharp fingernails. The hand opened and moved toward him, wrapping around his neck and choking all air from his lungs.

Just before he lost consciousness he heard them and he knew if he didn't heed their voice the second image of each scene would become reality.

"Heed us, Chosen. Heed us or you will fail. Truth above all. Truth above . . . "

\- - -

Manda stood on a rock, heedful of the poisoned black water sloshing at her feet.

People she loved were dying on the shore, but there was nothing she could do. She couldn't reach them even if she could tear free from the chains that encompassed her entire length. She would die as soon as she hit the water.

Evann floated by, eyes wide and lifeless. Blood seeped from his chest, but the black poison washed it away. Manda turned her head, unable to bear the sight any longer.

She heard familiar laughter and turned to find Alezza gliding toward her on top of the water, the hem of her golden gown bobbing in the poisoned darkness. Manda was sure Alezza would begin to scream as the liquid ate her flesh, but then she realized Alezza was poison. The black liquid couldn't harm her. A chain dangled from Alezza's hand and disappeared into the water. Alezza lifted the chain.

Chris emerged from the dark depths, twisting in torment as the poison ate his flesh. His green eyes, filled with holes from the poison's touch, entreated her for help. Manda jerked, tearing at her chains. One of her feet slipped into the water. A hollow moan rose in her chest as the water bit into her skin. She watched as her foot became a bloody, bony stub.

Alezza dropped Chris back into the water, smiling in amusement as Manda begged for his life.

"Like this?" Alezza lifted Chris' degenerating body out of the water once more. His flesh was gone. All that remained was a bloody mass of tissue, but he still writhed on the chain. Surrounded by crimson, the whites of his eyes looked horrific. There was no life in those eyes, only madness.

Alezza released the chain and let the last of Chris disappear under the poisoned depths. Alezza reached for Manda. "You're next, my dear."

Alezza began to pull her into the water.

Manda resisted, gripping the stone as hard as she could, screaming out the atrocious acts she would do to Alezza when she was able. Alezza only laughed, tugging harder.

A calm stole over Manda. It was a peace she couldn't describe. Why was she resisting? Everyone she loved was gone. There was nothing left to fight for.

She forced her muscles to relax and let Alezza pull her toward the icy darkness. Manda felt the poison begin to creep up her ankles, prickling her flesh with its tongue of death.

A voice came from the distance, whispering of hope and telling her how much she was loved.

She listened, ignoring the pain as the poison rose higher. She felt something on her face and tasted tears, but they weren't her own. In the distance she saw Lazo coming toward her in a boat.

Alezza snarled, pulling harder. Manda fell, expecting the bite of the poison to envelope her. It did not. When she opened her eyes she found herself in the boat. She could hear the poisoned liquid eating the wood, but the small boat still had buoyancy. Lazo began rowing to shore. His one blue and one green eye were filled with harrowing loneliness, but when he met her gaze determination and love overcame the desolation. It didn't matter. Nothing mattered anymore.

"Lazo, I don't want to live."

"If you give up, Alezza will win."

Alezza will win.

The phrase hit her like lightning.

She would never let Alezza win. Manda rolled to her knees, watching the tiniest sprays of dark water enter the cracks in the wood and willed the boat to move faster. She had to reach the shore. She had to find a sword and prepare for Alezza's return. Alezza would pay for harming her brother. She would pay dearly.

Manda opened her eyes and brushed away the moisture on her face. Blinking, she tried to focus. The world was different. The sound of lapping water was gone. Someone drew her into an embrace as the cool touch of the breeze tickled her face. She pushed away, needing to understand. She looked into the contrasting eyes she had seen in her dream.

"Lazo?"

Lazo smiled. Relief tumbled through her. It was only a dream.

She looked around. The naked Sierra Mountains jutted into the dusky light. Horses grazed in the distance. A fire crackled from somewhere beyond her vision.

"Where?" She forced Lazo's arms away and stood as the memories washed over her. Lazo caught her as her knees buckled. She struggled, trying to break free. She had to find Chris.

When she finally broke from Lazo's hold she ran toward her horse. From her peripheral vision she saw the Avenger. The pain she had sensed in him before was now etched in the smallest contours of his face. She changed direction and dropped to the ground before him.

"Did you?"

Aaron nodded his assent as his eyes filled with pain. It took her a few breaths to realize the pain she saw in them was her own.

"Did he feel it? Did he feel everything he did to us?"

"More," Aaron said.

Manda sat back on her heels. She didn't feel the satisfaction she had hoped for, only a hollow emptiness. She studied the Avenger, sensing he already knew her thoughts.

"I need to find him," she said, referring to Chris.

Aaron took her hand. She could still feel the power pulsating within him.

"We will help."

"You're avenging both of us?"

"No."

"I don't understand. I thought you only feel power when you're avenging a betrayed."

"When I avenged you I avenged your brother. The power within me isn't the same as the avenging power. It's less intense but more painful. My purpose is to save your brother, Manda. That's why I still live."

The gray haired man beside the Avenger began to hum a tune she hadn't heard since she was a small girl.

If he can't find the purpose there
If he can't give his love away
The Avenger will walk the land no more
And the world will be betrayed.

She looked at the Avenger, unsure what the song meant.

Aaron's eyes glowed golden in the firelight. In them, Manda saw years of pain, centuries of living with the agony that could only come from love's betrayal. It was too much for her to fathom. The depths of his gaze told her he was never free of the anguish. With every breath he felt the pain of love.

His love was the only thing saving him from the pain. How would he survive if he gave his love away?

She wanted to help him. She took his hand and kissed it, holding it to her face in silent thanks.

He smiled. When he did, his entire face lit with caring beyond comprehension.

"Thank you, Manda. You've given me a purpose. Your heart is pure. You remind me of someone I knew long ago. I'll do my best not to fail this time. I'll do my best to save your brother."

Manda wrapped her arms around the Avenger's neck, too overcome for words.

- - -

"I want you both to remember not to judge people by their appearance," Ramie said, looking between his children, "and to strive to be beautiful on the inside."

Ravi stared up at him with wide wet eyes. Reese sat in silence as he always did after one of his father's lessons, contemplating what he had just been told. Javi watched from across the room with a smile on her face.

"Is he all alone, Daddy?" Ravi asked.

Ramie pulled his daughter into an embrace. She had been calling him Father for years. Her reversion to the more childish name betrayed how much the story had touched her. "Yes, he's more or less all alone."

"Make him come here. He wouldn't be alone here. Reese and I would spend time with him," Ravi said quietly. Ramie smiled into her long, black hair. Ravi was going to be even more beautiful than Javi, if that was possible, and just as tender hearted.

"I tried, Ravi. He wouldn't have it. That's another lesson to you both." Ramie glanced at Reese to see if he was listening. "You have to want to help yourself before help will come. Even a king has to rely on others. You must let others help you in order to become the great person you strive to be. Do you understand?"

They both nodded. A lone tear slid down Ravi's check. She brushed it away before Reese noticed.

Ramie sighed and looked out the window. He had been back for two days but he still couldn't banish Presario from his mind. He had replayed the experience over and over, regretting his harsh words but still angered by Presario's obstinacy.

He only wished there was a way to mend the bridge he had burned, but he knew Presario would never allow him into his home again. He had failed.

And he had left the book, foolishly left the book. Presario said Ramie's anger would be his destruction. Anger made him forget the book. It may be that very slip to which Presario alluded, but now his pride wouldn't let him return to claim the patoi. His men would face Ista without magic.

His troops were almost ready to march. They would leave the following morning. He was terrified to face Ista, but it was the only way.

Wrong was wrong. If magic was on the wrong side, so be it. He had waited long enough.

The only light was the messenger from Ketes. Tec had been waiting when Ramie had returned to the keep, apologizing for the delay. Bostic had responded to the message as soon as it had arrived, but Tec had a little trouble with Ista's troops, not to mention a few bouts with creatures of magic. Tec had only brushed the surface of his journey, but it was enough for Ramie to knight him on the spot. The things the boy had gone through were harrowing. Ramie was surprised Tec made it to Yor alive, much less in the short time he had.

Bostic was ready to launch a full attack, but like Ramie knew more fighting power was needed. Ramie had just sent word back to Bostic. In a fortnight their armies would meet on the road to Zier. He hadn't told anyone what the messenger carried. If spies were among his men it was one surprise he would have on his side.

A gentle brush on his shoulder broke Ramie out of his somber thoughts. Ramie looked over into Ravi's brown eyes. "What is it, pudding?"

Ravi rolled her eyes and twisted her hair over one already elegant finger. "Don't call me that, father. I'm almost sixteen years old."

Ramie bowed his head in submission. "Yes, forgive me. I forget how fast you've grown."

Ravi repressed a smile. "Can magic mend Presario's wounds?"

Ramie blinked. He hadn't thought of the possibility. Could it? "I don't know, Ravi. I don't know how the Quy works."

"It could, Father," Reese said, looking much older than his fourteen years. "I'm sure of it. Ravi has already healed a few scrapes. She's going to be a powerful shaman. When she's older she could alter a burning easily."

Ramie's face colored. He spun to Javi. She lost her smile and held up her hands in defense. "I can't stop them, Ramie. You know how incorrigible they are. I can't be with them every sun's click."

Reese paled. Ravi quickly retreated.

"I told you two not to use the Quy!"

"But – "

41

"No buts, Reese! You could harm yourself by doing too much too fast!"

"But you won't let us learn!"

"Silence!" Ramie stepped toward them. Ravi and Reese shrunk into themselves. "I told you there are people wanting to control those who have the power. You both could be taken and used to hurt me, this kingdom!"

He spun to Javi. "This isn't something we can afford go unchecked. Do you want your children captured?"

Javi's dark eyes welled with tears.

Ramie softened. He didn't want his last conversation with his family to be in anger. He was leaving tomorrow. He didn't expect to return.

"I'm sorry. I just can't bear the thought of any of you coming to harm. I'm leaving tomorrow. I'll be gone for a long time. I want to know you're safe."

Reese's face drained of color. "Are you marching to war?"

"Yes."

Reese stiffened. "I want to go with you."

"You're my heir, Reese. You'll have to maintain Oldan until I return."

Reese blushed with pride but frowned when he realized he had been turned away. Ramie wished his request was in jest, but it wasn't. He couldn't trust anyone else with his kingdom. Because responsibility had been forced upon him at a young age Ramie had wished many times Reese would take an interest in something other than his studies, but Reese hungered for knowledge the way the desert hungered for rain. He had matured far more than other children his age, Ravi included. Now Ramie thanked the Maker Reese was the way he was for he felt confident Reese could handle the responsibility that would now be forced upon him.

A sharp knock at the door startled him out of his thoughts. His brow furrowed. His men knew better than to disturb him when he was with his children.

"Come," he said, quickly changing into the king of Yor and not the father of two.

One of his guards hesitantly stuck his head inside the door. "Two men wish to speak to you, my lord. We've tried to turn them away but they won't hear of it. They claim they're from Mintree."

Ramie couldn't believe it. He stood to walk from the room but hesitated. If it was Presario he needed to be greeted in an informal setting, not as a king would greet a subject. Ramie turned to the guard and nodded. "Show them in here."

The guard's face registered surprise, but he bowed and retreated. Ramie could almost feel Reese's excitement at being allowed to witness the exchange.

"I want you both to be on your best behavior. Make these two feel welcome."

Before he could say more the door opened and two men were ushered inside. The first was tall and thin, with a long cream cloak hanging loosely about him. A dark brown cowl covered the man's head and shoulders, completely concealing his face. He carried a book in his gloved hands. It was the patoi of magic.

Arri stepped forward, white eyes regarding Ramie with a shadow of a smile. Before the silence became awkward Presario's advisor tone sliced through the air. "It seems you've put me in an awkward position once again, my king. You left the book and I had to stare at it until my conscience couldn't forgive me unless I delivered it to you myself."

Ramie smiled, unable to contain his delight. "You will train my men?"

The cowled form gave a slight nod. "Yes, but understand I'll leave as soon as I feel you can manage on your own."

"We march tomorrow at dawn. I can wait no longer. You'll come?"

Ramie held his breath. After a few heartbeats the brown cowl bowed. "I can teach in the saddle."

"That's all I can ask of you, Presario, and that's far more than I expected."

Ravi's breath caught as soon as Presario's name left Ramie's lips. Before Ramie could stop her, Ravi walked to Presario and took one of his gloved hands. Ramie tensed. If he chastised his daughter, it would embarrass Presario more than if he did nothing. So he did nothing.

Ravi reached out and touched Presario's hood. Presario grew taut. Ramie closed his eyes, praying to the Maker Ravi wouldn't do what he knew she would.

When he looked again Presario's hood was off. His face looked even more horrible in the light of day, but Ravi remained unflinching. The air thickened with silence. Ravi stood on her tiptoes and kissed Presario's cheek. After a few breaths, Presario pulled Ravi into an embrace.

Ramie turned away, too overcome for words.

CHAPTER 4

Davis peered into the Yor Lake and wiped his brow. If it hadn't been for the circumstances he would have laughed at his reflection. His shaggy brown hair was now cut close to his scalp and dyed a midnight black. His royal clothes had been discarded for a tattered green tunic and well-worn doeskin trousers. He carried a sword but it was cheaply done and had no ornamentation.

Ramie would never believe he was Davis Tresvent, prince of Fest. Actually, he wouldn't be surprised if Ramie laughed in his face. Sighing, Davis straightened and walked toward the Crest Castle. It rose before him in both beauty and splendor. It turrets were a rich cream, decorated with gold ribbons and glittering stone. All windows were filled with stained glass images, some of scenes, others just awash in an array of colors. But despite its ornate trimmings the castle was built for beauty as well as protection. Every few cubits richly polished wooden machicolations blended in with the decorations of the castle and would be open if attack was imminent, housing guards with quivers of arrows or boiling kettles. The gates surrounding the keep were high and housed armed gatehouses every twenty paces.

As Davis approached the inner wall, a procession came out with Ramie leading. Davis picked up the pace, running through the crowd. He had been so preoccupied he hadn't noticed the large ship docked in the lake. From the way Ramie was dressed he wasn't leaving for an afternoon ride. He was riding to war.

Davis pushed his way to the front of the crowd. The things his father had revealed to him came back in a maddening rush: the needles, Korin. Holy Maker.

Ramie had almost reached him when a guard shoved him back.

"Out of the way, friend."

"Please," Davis said, "I need to speak to the king."

The guard looked at his clothes before shaking his head. "Not today, son."

Davis held up the message with the wax seal of his father. "I have a message from Lorlier." Although it was Lorlier's seal, Davis knew the guard wouldn't believe him, not with the way he was dressed. The people jammed closer, shoving Davis back. The guard turned away, ignoring him.

Ramie walked by him.

Davis cursed and shoved past the guard, shouting Ramie's name. His heart raced. He had to reach Ramie. He had to tell him Lorlier would meet him at the split in the Divi.

The guard caught his shoulder and threw him to the ground. Davis grabbed the man's leg and twisted, toppling him, knocking over other onlookers. When the guard regained his footing, he forced Davis to his knees and manacled his hands. Davis looked up at the king, now halted before him.

A brief flicker of recognition passed over Ramie's face, but before Davis could speak the guard brought him to his feet and shoved him back through the throng.

"My king, a message from Lorlier!" Davis shouted over his shoulder. "I have a message from Lorlier!"

Davis was unsure if the king heard. The guard dragged him forward. The crowd parted.

Then the king was before of him, peering up at him with questioning eyes.

"My lord," Davis breathed frantically, "a message." Davis diverted his eyes to his pocket where he had placed the message. "And a request to join you on board the ship."

The guard guffawed, but Ramie's eyes stayed on Davis.

"I was sorry to hear about Davis," Ramie finally said. "Lorlier must be heartbroken. I can't imagine losing a son, but these are dark times. Were you close to the prince?"

Davis nodded, catching Ramie's hidden question. "Yes, my lord."

Ramie walked past him without even reading the message. "This one comes with me. I'm in need of a new attendant."

- - -

Bentzen fell, but he did not feel. He hadn't eaten in days. He hadn't slept in days. Part of him knew he was slowly going mad. At times he didn't remember. Other times he did. When he remembered he gave himself more pain. He deserved it. He had failed, miserably failed.

His breath came in shallow gasps as he lay there. He suddenly wondered why he was on the ground. He couldn't recall. But the grass felt good. He decided to remain there for a time, until he remembered why he wanted to leave.

His eyes opened and he watched the treetops sway in the breeze. He heard their rustle and exquisite dance. As a child, when the buds were new and the chores done, he used to escape to their highest branches. He loved to sit and listen to the breeze talk to the leaves, stirring them into song. Trees made him feel like he was above the world.

He decided he wanted to climb one.

Slowly, he moved. His feet dug into the grass. His hand pushed his weight.

Then he saw the blood.

What had happened to him? Blood coated his arms. A moan escaped his lips.

Tol had been taken from him. Tol had died in his arms.

He began to weep. He had never cried before. He never knew he could cry. The tears felt odd against his cheeks. One fell into his mouth. It tasted salty. The taste startled him. He licked his cheek. Yes, he tasted salt, but it was mingled with another flavor. He thought about it for a short time: salt and moisture and . . . pain. That was it. Tears even tasted like pain.

Why did the Maker have to take Tol away? Why couldn't the Maker have taken him: a man who would never be missed, a man who had never looked at someone with such love or need, a man who wasn't innocent?

He had grown up with unloving parents. His father stayed drunk and beat him every night. His mother watched but never intervened, never shed a tear. He held no love for either of them.

When he was thirteen his mother had given him a large sum of coins to purchase supplies for the winter. He had never returned.

He went to the next town and found employment with a farmer. He had always been tall and broad and was able to pass for being older. He worked there three years. The owner treated him admirably. He was well paid and well feed. The farmer's daughter tried to talk to him on more than one occasion but he just smiled and walked away. Why would he want to let anyone close if his own parents could be so cruel?

That was why he was the way he was. When he left the farm he had gone directly to Stardom to try out for the guard. It had been a mere dream in his mind. He couldn't even hold a sword. But he had a driving need to try. When Ren had allowed him in, despite his clumsiness, Bentzen had been humbled. His prince believed in him when all others took him for a mere beggared. He would do anything for Ren.

As Bentzen watched the trees bend in the breeze he suddenly hoped Ren knew how much he respected him. Even when Ren asked

Bentzen to be in the guard little if any emotion had touched his face. He had decided long ago to feel no more. His parents had taught him that.

Now he knew love. Bentzen felt the knife wounds on his arms from where he had sliced his flesh in punishment. Would he have rather never felt love? He thought about it for a time. He honestly didn't know. He was used to being unfeeling yet determined, liked but unknown. No, he didn't want to be the old Bentzen, but he didn't know if he wanted to be this one either. The pain was too great.

He heard horses. Bentzen lifted his head. Galvin and Neki cantered across the field. Neki had a cocked arrow aimed at a scurrying doe. Bentzen cried out, but his voice was only a whisper. He cursed himself for his stupidity. He owed Ren a report yet he had wounded himself almost to the point of death. He could always end his life after he had done his duty. Now he may have ended two more lives he cared about, that Ren cared about.

"No." Bentzen forced his legs to stand. He concentrated on putting one foot in front of the other.

A horse stopped beside him. Bentzen looked up into Galvin's dark eyes.

"Fates, Bentzen, what's happened to you?" Galvin bent down, encircled Bentzen's waist, and heaved him up on the palomino. "Hang on. I'll take you to camp."

Bentzen leaned into Galvin, feeling the other man's heat. He felt so cold.

Bentzen forced his eyes open when Galvin's mount came to a stop. Quinton and Markum tended a fire, but Ren was nowhere to be seen. Bentzen furrowed his brow. Where was Ren? From the looks of it the camp had been set up for quite some time. Neki dropped from his horse and flung the doe before the fire, lips broadening into a wide grin.

"We eat well tonight, my friends,"

Quinton looked up from the fire and smiled. His eyes flickered to Bentzen. Then a hollow curse escaped his lips.

All eyes turned to him. Bentzen smiled, managed a wave, and fell. Galvin caught him before he hit the ground. The world swayed. The faces surrounding him were fuzzy. Galvin's deep voice yelled for water. Almost immediately cool water entered Bentzen's mouth. He drank greedily. He hadn't had water in days.

He mumbled for more. He heard someone say not to give him too much. Someone else started washing the wounds on his arms. He tried to shake them off but he only managed to flop his arms like a fish out of water. More water entered his mouth. He drank again, this time not as quickly, hoping they would let him have more if he slowed his pace. They did not.

He heaved a sigh as cool salve was applied to his arms. They were healing him. He didn't want to be healed. He deserved death.

"One of the Collective captured Renee and Marva. He's taking them to Ista. Tol is dead, he died in my arms from the pain. I don't deserve to live. Let me die. Please let me die."

- - -

Ren woke, disoriented and confused. Every limb ached; every muscle throbbed. He twisted to get a better view of his surroundings. He was in the middle of a forest path, encased by tall spindly trees. Vines clung to their trunks, threatening to choke them. Some of the branches were already shriveled, the vines cutting off their vein of water.

Nothing looked familiar.

Ren rubbed his neck. A sharp pain shot through him. Then he felt the welts.

Visions of the stark white hand flashed through his mind. It had choked him, burnt him. Ren felt around his neck. The claw marks were real. The welts were real.

The images were real.

Truth above all. He had to trust the Oracle's commands. He had to betray his mother, deny his love, and destroy his soul. He had no choice. If he disobeyed worse would happen.

He needed to see his friends. He desperately needed to feel the touch of another human being. He stood and looked around him. There was no clearing, no remaining rubble, no large trees, and no air of life.

The Oracle was no more. Not one stone remained.

It was turning dark. Ren started down the path, knowing his friends would be worried. His mind turned to the paintings, the words, the stone faces, the hand, and soon he was running to escape the things he had seen, what he had to do, and who he was.

The wind picked up. Tree branches thrashed down, blocking his path and slashing his skin. They cut him time and again, but he welcomed the pain. With each cut the physical pain demanded his concentration and steered him away from the emotional pain. But after each assault the internal pain seemed to escalate, giving his soul to bleed. He ran faster, pushing on until he saw the light of a fire in a distant clearing.

He heard the familiar sounds and smells of camp: Neki's sarcastic laughter, Markum's soft voice, Galvin's worried speech, the smell of boiling tea, burnt wood, and roasted game.

A debate was taking place. Neki said they should search for him. Galvin agreed, saying he had been gone too long. Markum refuted. Sometimes the Oracle kept people for weeks, he insisted. They shouldn't worry yet. Besides, Markum said, if he hadn't emerged the Oracle still had him and there was nothing they could do. Despite Markum's words his voice was fraught with concern.

Weeks?

How long had he been gone?

Ren stumbled into the clearing, startling them all. Galvin caught him before he fell.

Ren barely heard Galvin's demand to bring food and water, that he had lost weight. Ren thought about the air of life. It had kept him alive. At the mention of water, real water, his stomach rumbled.

"How long?" he whispered.

"Ten days. You've been gone ten days."

Ten days? How could he have lost that much time?

Markum put a bowl of stew before him. Ren picked it up and slowly began to eat. It tasted bland. The air of life had been so sweet nothing could compare, but as his stomach began to fill the memory of the air dissipated and the stew began to form a flavor.

The water felt cool sliding down his throat. He had never tasted anything so good. It almost felt purifying – almost. Nothing would be able to purify his soul, not after the Oracle.

Ren forced his mind from the images of the Oracle and surveyed the camp. Something was wrong. His eyes fell on Bentzen.

Bentzen was supposed to be with Renee. Blessed Fates, was it already starting? Ren rose to his feet and stumbled to the swordsman. He fell before Bentzen and gripped his hands. The desolation in Bentzen's eyes terrified him. Ren turned to the mounts tied a short distance away. Michel and Quinton's horses weren't in the group.

He turned back to Bentzen. "What happened?"

One of the Collective took Marva and Renee." A silent tear fell down Bentzen's cheek. "Tol died in my arms, Ren, from the pain."

Ren placed a hand on Bentzen's shoulder, heart melting as the swordsman bowed his head and wept. When Ren spoke, his voice was barely above a whisper. "The band didn't work?"

Bentzen shook his head. "It worked, my prince. The man took it from him. I didn't notice until it was too late."

Ren turned to Galvin, the silent question in his eyes.

"Quinton and Michel are after them. They left as soon as they heard, just after sundown."

Choice's words echoed in his mind.

It had begun.

The Oracle's meaning was clear.

Galvin stepped forward, broadsword propped on one shoulder. "If you want to go after them I suggest we leave now. They were riding fast, but if we hurry we can catch them."

"No." He said it too quickly. He saw the look of surprise on Galvin's face and closed his eyes, trying to banish the image of his mother's torture. This was his choice. This was what he had to choose. The Oracle had ordered him to allow fate to play her course. He couldn't help his mother. He had to continue his search for the One.

He understood. If he went back Ista may claim him and he would be unable to battle the darkness that would lead to the Lands ultimate destruction.

He remembered the scene from the pyx where his mother laughed as people died around her. If he went back that was her fate. He felt the white hand encircling his neck. He couldn't search for Renee.

Choking back his anguish, he looked up at his friends' stunned expressions.

"It's probably better," Galvin said. "Michel and Quinton would be the Abyss to catch."

"Burning cinders, Ren," Neki said, trying to lighten the mood. "Those two lit out of here as if the children of the Mynher were after them. Fates, they didn't even take their packs. I had to chase after them until they slowed enough to let me hand them over."

Ren managed a smile before he buried his face in his palms, unwilling to meet his friends' eyes. All thought he had just betrayed his mother. And they were right.

But he couldn't tell them why. He couldn't reveal what the Oracle had told him.

Feeling a hand on his shoulder, he looked up into Markum's worried gaze.

"Are you all right, Ren?"

Ren blinked up at him, specters of the Oracle dancing in his eyes. "I've never been worse, Markum. I've never been worse."

- - -

As Korin approached the inner ward of the castle, he felt the noose tightening. The presence was a heavy constant in his mind, a force he couldn't deny. One of the Collective swung the gate open without even asking his name or interest, and Korin didn't volunteer the information. He passed by without a smile, a nod, or a word.

Ista already knew he was there. He didn't have to say or do anything to gain entrance to Stardom. His life was Ista's to command. After she used the Red Eye on the Chosen, she would use it on him. As of today, his life didn't matter.

All that mattered was saving Marianne.

He hadn't eaten or slept since leaving Fest. He had stopped caring after leaving Lorlier's family. Salvation would never be his to grasp.

The New Alcazar loomed to his right, signifying the massive strength and power Ista had already acquired. Its black stone shimmered deceptively. Its turrets were almost complete. Soon the Lands would be under the New Alcazar's power. Before, the structure would have put the fear of the Abyss in his soul. It did nothing to him now. Nothing else mattered.

People with shaved heads littered the grounds of the castle. They took little notice of him as he rode by. Everyone talked in excited whispers about magic, about what they could already do. Fools. The greed lighting their eyes was so replete Korin knew nobody had questioned Ista's methods. All were just hungry to learn. The whispers of the Collective were already so strong no one would need the pain lessons Ista had used at camp. All would just follow blindly, the force in their minds making them puppets on a string.

He already knew where to go. He didn't have to ask. The force inside him pulled him closer with each click of Salve's heels. Only Mari invaded his thoughts. She would die if Ista didn't send a cure.

Korin remembered her brittle toenails, the terror in her eyes – and the betrayal.

His heart constricted. Soon he wouldn't have her eyes haunting every waking breath. Soon he wouldn't even remember Marianne's name. When the Red Eye was used on him the Korin he had fought so hard to become would die.

Korin dismounted at the entrance to the castle. He didn't bother to tie Salve. He would never see his horse again. He leaned his head against Salve's neck and whispered a tender goodbye. Salve nickered. It was an entreaty not to leave, an urging not to enter the castle. Korin thought about jumping on Salve's back and fleeing. He would feel the elation of the ride before the pain came. He would have a few fleeting heartbeats of freedom.

But the thought was whisked away as soon as Mari's eyes entered his heart, as soon as her kiss lit the dark corners of his mind.

Korin walked up the steps. Salve nickered and pawed the ground. Korin forced himself not to look back. Nothing mattered anymore.

Inside, the people were as thick as the grass in the field. Many lingered on the black floors with memories of home stored around them. Where before the Razon castle had been a maze of splendor, now the black floors were dirty and the golden accents were tarnished with the fingerprints of many. But Korin barely registered the stark difference before focusing on the marble staircase leading to the second floor.

He took the steps with quick strides, unconcerned about hastening what was to come. He knew there would be pain. He knew there would be punishment. But what was to come was to come. There could be no denying it, no salvation.

The guard posted at Ista's study stepped aside and let Korin enter. Ista stood at the window, gazing over her creation. She was in her beautiful body, and Korin briefly wondered why, but as soon as the door clicked shut the pain came. All thoughts were whisked away as he fell to the floor, clutching his head as the incessant pulse of anguish exploded inside his mind.

It lasted far longer than it ever had before. But then he knew it would. While it continued to wrack his body he tried to focus on Mari, on Lorlier, and on his duty to them. When his mind finally cleared Ista's melted face peered down at him with such animosity he wondered how she had hid it all these years.

How she hated him!

"How do you deny me, Korin?"

Korin bowed his head. "I focus on other things, Ista. I pretend I'm someone who obeys you without hesitation. My true self is safe from you, hidden away deep inside. He comes out when I don't feel you, when I'm not doing those things I abhor."

"Ista, Marianne is dying – "

The pain was worse than the first, but it didn't last long.

"I don't care, Korin," Ista said. "I care little for what happens to Marianne."

"But if you want me to marry her she needs to live. If you don't send the cure now there will be nothing left for me to claim."

Ista's eyes bore into him. Korin heaved a heavy sigh. Ista knew he was right. Although she knew she could take any nation by force it went against the web she was trying to weave. She had portrayed herself as the savior to the people. She needed to reinforce that theory.

When Ista turned away he knew he had won. It gave him no satisfaction, only profound relief he may have saved Lorlier's daughter.

Ista walked to a large desk that sat beneath a portrait of a former Razon leader and dipped her hand in the ever-present basin of water. After dousing her brow she opened a top drawer and pulled out a shed section of silver dragon's skin – a blanket of the power.

Just as a boiling cloth could absorb the poison from dragon's flames, silver dragon's skin must absorb magic. It would draw the disease from Marianne.

Korin heaved a sigh. He had done all he could. He had helped Mari and he had denied Ista. Little did she know he had told Lorlier everything, and when he returned to Fest he would die at Lorlier's hand.

He barely heard Ista call the guards and send for a scroll. He barely remembered signing his name to the parchment and seeing the carrier leave. He barely remembered being thrown into the dungeon to await the day Ista could control the Red Eye. He barely remembered anything. For the entire time he was living in a body of pain.

CHAPTER 5

Manda watched Lazo tremble by the fire. The past few days her friend had put all his energy into helping her rise from the pain and have hope for the future. She had remained silent and unresponsive. She was in her own dark world, not really wanting to venture out. In the dark there was no hope, and no hope didn't leave any room for pain or hurt.

Now, as she watched Lazo's brow bead up in sweat, his hands fumble for water and his eyes move in and out of focus she realized how selfish she had been. She hadn't even asked why he had left the twins. Now she knew. On occasion Fraul and Aaron mentioned the word Lazo had always spoken with fear in his eyes – the Mar.

Fraul stuck a bowl full of venison stew in front of Lazo, encouraging him to eat. Lazo shook his head, eyes moving with unusual speed. A mournful cry rose from Manda's chest. Fraul turned toward her, acute gray eyes surveying her with concern. He pursed his lips and turned away. His look didn't escape her. Fraul didn't think Lazo would survive the night.

Manda remembered what Lazo had told her about the Mar: no twin had ever survived it; no triplet had ever tried.

Lazo enwrapped his legs with his arms and rested his head on his knees. Even in his compact position she could see his spasms. He pulled tighter, but the shaking continued. Her eyes flickered to Aaron. Aaron's hawk-like gaze was already on her. The Avenger was a mystery to her. He rarely spoke, but she could sense his thoughts as if he spoke them aloud. The pain in his eyes was unfathomable. The love radiating from him was unbounded. Yet he was extremely distant, not in the physical sense but in an emotional one.

She knew the Avenger lived with the pain and love of all the betrayeds, but she would have thought the exchange of emotions would bring him closer to the avenged. Yet he barely spoke to her. Despite his distance, she felt an unshakable bond with him. When she tried to form it to words she drew a blank. It was neither a bond of carnality nor one of righteousness, neither a bond of love nor a bond of pain. It seemed to be a bond of delicate devotion, but why she had no idea. He knew her every feeling. He was the Avenger. But she had no idea what made him who he was, how he felt, or why he would hold her in such an honorable regard.

She met his gaze without flinching, unembarrassed by his scrutiny, and he in kind did not turn. Aaron was tall and handsome, with a mane of ebony hair and eyes that drank the light. His body was perfection: broad shoulders, narrow waist, muscular build, angular jaw, and large hands. Although she found him handsome, his emotions dominated his features and drowned his affable looks in their intensity. His emotions scared her. She didn't understand how he could do anything other than drown in them.

Before, she would have been attracted to him. Now the thought of any man frightened her.

Lazo rose and staggered toward the distant tree line, mumbling about making his bed away from them that night. He said he needed the comfort of the surrounding trees. Manda knew the truth. He was leaving them to die.

Aaron and Fraul watched him go. Each wore a concerned look.

"The closeness of twins and triplets is without bounds," Aaron said. "Without that closeness Lazo's heart will just stop beating, the pain of separation too great to bear."

Fraul fingered his goatee and gazed in the direction Lazo had disappeared. "There's nothing we can do?"

Aaron's eyes flickered in the firelight. "Nothing."

Manda listened to their words but tried to deny their truth. She didn't want Lazo to die. For days Lazo had loved her enough to shove his own anguish aside. For days Lazo had overcome the Mar to help her live.

There was too much pain in this world. Chris may be lost to her forever. She could see the truth of that in the Avenger's eyes. She could feel it in her own soul. Ren was in dire trouble, fighting something no one understood. Her father had betrayed her. And now one of her closest friends was about to die a horrible death.

Warm arms encircled her. She leaned back into Aaron's chest. He stroked her hair and kissed her forehead. She didn't recoil. Something about his magic abated the visions of the rapes. She clung to him, and he held her until she calmed.

Lazo needed this kind of warmth and tenderness. A moan escaped her lips as she thought of the one thing that may be able to save him.

Just the thought drove her back into her blackness. But it was the only way. She might not have to allow it all.

Manda twisted in Aaron's arms and looked up into his gentle eyes, fully aware he knew her thoughts. Aaron nodded, admitting she was Lazo's only chance. Manda swallowed back her fear and rose, focusing on Lazo and his friendship. With every movement she felt the bruises, the lacerations, and the deep ache where Bort had entered her time and again. Hands still moved over her body: groping, grabbing, and hurting. She had bathed in every frigid stream they passed but not one had washed the hands away. They clung to her like leeches.

She walked toward the distant trees. Their branches still swayed from Lazo's entrance. She focused on their movement, murmuring to herself that this time was unlike the others. This time she was saving another's life. No matter how much it hurt, no matter how many memories it brought, it couldn't hurt her any more than she had been hurt. It couldn't even begin to come close.

Manda moved the branches away and ducked under the sheltering trees. The mournful sounds of the night greeted her. A cricket chirped a lowly tune, an owl cooed to a distant love, the leaves fluttered in the plaintive breeze, but her own footfalls tolled of doom. A gust of wind spurred past her, cooling the soreness of her limbs but causing her skin to crawl as if the wind had hands of its own.

She found Lazo in a mossy bed surrounded by trees. As soon as she had ducked under the low hanging branches she realized why Lazo had chosen that particular haven. The branches dipped and waved over the ground, sheltering the inhabitant in a loving embrace.

Lazo was facing her with eyes closed, shivering violently. Before her heart felt only pain. Now it lay broken before her. She closed her eyes, concentrating on the warmth of the surrounding trees and the freedom of her choice. She was free to choose this. Above all else she had to remember that. Freedom made the difference.

She began to undress. Her hands shook but she ignored them. She fumbled at each button until every one popped free. Lazo needed to be as close to someone as he possibly could. If she wasted time trying to ease into it he might die and she would have failed in her task. It was all or nothing, and as she undressed her conviction deepened.

She would do anything to save Lazo. He was her mentor and her friend. At one time she even held a silly girlish notion of being the first to have a triplet fall in love with her. Although she didn't harbor those foolish thoughts any longer, Lazo would always hold a special place in her heart.

Hearing Lazo's intake of breath, she turned to face him. The slightest breeze licked through the surrounding shelter, chilling her and bringing the crawling hands back to life.

Her flesh was a patchwork of purple and black bruises. Some of the bruises had turned a jaundiced shade, reminding her of mucus in sick horses.

"Manda." Lazo turned from the monstrosity she had become.

She knelt beside him. His contrasting eyes looked at her with profound love for her gesture but held horror at the implication. She forced her mouth into a grin, feeling nothing of the blithesome humor she filtered into her voice. "You don't find me attractive, my friend?"

His mouth fluttered open. He forced his eyes to lock on the branches. "No, Manda, I mean yes. But this can't be after . . . "

She loved him even more for understanding her pain, but before he could resist, she began to take off his robe. He stopped her with surprising strength and peered into her face with his old vigor.

"No."

Manda cocked an eyebrow and started to rise. "Lazo, you need to be close to someone. Fraul offered his services. I'll call him if you like."

Lazo pulled her back down, reddening in embarrassment as his hand brushed her bare thigh. He turned away once again but a small smile threatened his lips.

"Fraul isn't my type. I've always been partial to redheads."

"Good. It's settled then." She reached out again. This time she managed to yank his robe out from under him. When he started to force it back down, she stopped. She had to make him understand. Closing her eyes, she released her façade.

"Lazo, I can't go on if you die. Yes, this will hurt me. Yes, I'm terrified at the thought. But if you die . . . " Her voice broke. She bit her lip and looked into the contrasting eyes that had first attracted her. They were filled with tears, not for himself, but for her. Her conviction grew. "Please, Lazo. Let me help you. Help me help you."

"I'll be fine, Manda," he said as a surge of tremors shook his body. A choking fear rose inside her. With energy she hadn't felt in days, she tore his robe from him and pried his arms open, forcing them around her. He gave in. He pulled her closer, almost suffocating her.

Rivers of revulsion ran through her at his touch. She gritted her teeth, concentrating on who he was and why he held her until her feelings of repulsion subsided into one of mere queasiness. She allowed her head to sink to his shoulder.

Soon the warmth of his body became soothing. The force of his hold hurt but she didn't stir, fearing any movement would cause him to retract. She dozed. When she woke Lazo's clutch was desperate, and he shook with such force his teeth chattered. She was doing little good. She forced him on his side and pulled him closer.

His body was a sheen of sweat. She soothed the hair from his brow and whispered encouragement. She didn't know if he heard. His spasms became even more violent. His eyes flickered open. The madness residing within was bone chilling.

He managed to say her name. It sounded like a tender goodbye.

She crushed him to her and kissed his head, telling him to hold on. His body was hot, trying to accommodate for the twins' missing minds with its own warmth. It was futile. Lazo needed what only she could give. Fates, give her the courage!

As her own tears coursed down her cheeks, she found his lips. He was unresponsive, awkward.

She knew Lazo had never kissed anyone, never been with anyone. It was rare when a twin had any desire or opportunity for such things. His lips fumbled over hers. She knew he tasted her tears but when he tried to pull away she wouldn't let him. He groaned in frustration, but she only kissed him harder. After a time he gave in, crushing her with his weight, drinking in her breath.

Lazo pulled away. She buried her face in his chest, not wanting him to see her pain and repulsion. The memories flooded through her: the ripping, the tearing, the beatings, and the hands. Dear fates, the hands, over and over again.

"No, Lazo, you must stay close." She tried to pull him back, but he resisted. He lay on his side, kissing her cheek and whispering his apologies. He ran a slow hand down her arm.

Manda shivered as the hands of many rubbed her. She groped for Lazo, found his lips and forced him to kiss her again. He tried to retreat but soon leaned into her. His lips began to learn. He kissed her with tender warmth, unlike the others.

She tried to move him closer, determined to hold back her tears this time, but he stopped her.

"No, no, Manda. Just talk to me. I need to know you. Talk Manda. Please."

He brought her hand to his lips. He kissed each fingertip before entwining her hand in his own.

His breath was warm, sweet. His beard tickled her neck as his lips explored her.

"Talk to me, Manda."

She didn't understand why, but she closed her eyes and began to talk. At first she just rambled, telling him of her likes and dislikes. She told him of her love for horses and the forest, how she always looked forward to trips across country, and how her favorite color was pink but she could never wear it because of her hair. Soon she spoke of different things: what she and Chris had done when they were younger, her days at her cousin's house and how much she looked forward to coming to Stardom, not only to see Chris and Ren but to see him.

Lazo listened, acknowledging her accomplishments, chuckling at her stories, but all the while he was massaging her bruises, feeling every curve and kissing each cut.

She felt the tenseness leave her muscles, the ache in her chest subside and the torment of her memories fade into the distant horizon.

Whenever she stopped talking he always whispered he needed more. She always thought she could think of nothing else but then she began again.

When the night had finally dissipated they lay in each other's arms, watching the distant sun begin to fill the world with light. Lazo stroked her arm in silence, still needing to feel her close.

Suddenly, he chuckled.

She twisted in his arms and looked into two distinct, smiling eyes. She raised her eyebrows, indicating for him to let her in on the joke.

His eyes danced with mischief. "I was just thinking the Mar wasn't so bad. It forced one of my whimsical dreams into a reality."

Manda buried her face in his shoulder, hiding her widening smile. "Mine too, Lazo, mine too."

CHAPTER 6

Sim flew low in the sky, searching. He still hurt from where he had fallen, and Aidan's emotions were still a resonating rain inside him: beautiful, yet sorrowful. He was unsure if he ever wanted to feel those emotions again, and what he had felt only brushed the surface of Aidan's soul. He still didn't want her to leave, but now he knew why she yearned to do so, and for once he understood.

"Sim," Aidan thought. "Thank you."

Sim was shocked. The Bane never thanked him, just demanded without explanation. Sim did the only thing he knew to do and that was to change the subject.

"I've found his trail. We'll find him soon."

Sim felt Aidan moving through him, breathing the night air as he did. He knew it took a lot of energy for Aidan to bring herself his senses. It was far easier for her to stay in the darkness, but her determination was too great. She had to know. Sim liked that. It was as he was. He had to know. And now that he knew her feelings he knew why she had such resolve to do as she did.

But before he could warn her to be cautions, before he could tell her the Bane was right, and the more she used his senses the harder it would be to stay herself, the Bane spoke.

"Careful, my child. The more you are the same, the less you are different, and the less identity you'll have."

"I have my faith. Nothing can take that," Aidan replied.

"The dragon can. Without meaning to, the dragon will."

- - -

"I don't think the Old Sea could compare to this damnedable place," Neki said as his horse trudged out of an ankle-high, stagnant pool of water. Neki's scowl caused Galvin and Markum to chuckle.

"Don't complain," Galvin said with a grin, "at least we're moving."

"That's debatable." Neki scowled again.

As much as Ren hated to acknowledge it, Neki was right. He doubted they had traveled over fifty dragon tails from where the Sphinx had appeared. And they had been traveling for almost a full day.

If exasperated was the word for their moods it didn't come close to matching Ren's inner turmoil.

The same night he had emerged from the Oracle the rain had started. It wasn't an ordinary rain, it was a deluge, the kind of rain nothing could move in, at least nothing that had any wits. Visibility was infinitesimal, the constant dousing of icy pellets was maddening, and if that wasn't enough the Oracle had decided to appear at the edge of the worst region of Crape, the Rancor, where a heavy rain would take days to permeate the red clay soil, leaving a slippery, treacherous, unclear path. If they had tried to ride in such weather they could have lost each other, the way, or a horse to a lame foot glutted by the uncompromising soil.

After two days of waiting under a make-do shelter they were finally moving, at least in theory. The scenery seemed to take forever to change. If it was the type of scenery that warranted ogling the trek would have been tolerable, but it wasn't. The brushy undergrowth, littered with thorny plants and spindly, vine-filled trees stirred up a medley of confusion. It was said when the Maker created the Rancor he couldn't make up his mind and tossed everything on his shelves into his creation pot, simmering it for days to produce a scattered and inharmonious terrain.

Frequent curses from Neki, colorful invectives from Galvin, and cautious whispers from Markum drifted in the sultry air like beacons of warning. Ren didn't know why he had insisted on leaving the shelter when the rains had stopped. He knew how dangerous it would be to traverse the Rancor when the soil had yet to imbibe the water.

No, that wasn't true. He knew why. Although the horses' hooves were sinking like quicksand, his own soul felt like it was already covered.

He had to find the One.

The urgency of that truth had first come to him the night he had left the Oracle. His urgency was suffocating, his need immense. One thing kept repeating in his mind: he had to find the One before the dragon found him.

But then the rains started. Everywhere he turned he heard the whispers of the Oracle. Sleep had managed to come, but fitfully. Every time he would sleep dreams of the Oracle plagued him and his urgency grew: he had to find the One before the dragon found him.

His men tried to talk to him, but all he could do was look into their faces and voice a meager reply.

On the second night the rains continued to fall. He cursed the rain and condemned his own stupidity for failing to leave as soon as he had emerged from the Oracle.

A fire grew inside him during that time. He wanted answers and he wanted them yesterday. The One was the key. If he could reach him before the silver dragon landed he held hopes he could rout the Oracle's demands. If the One knew how to sever the dragon's hold on Aidan there was a chance his words wouldn't have the effect he feared.

Only the kota's loud purr brought him comfort. He stroked her neck as he rode. Keena had grown, so he didn't have to bend far. Her horn now reached a hand's span in length and she stood at eye level with a few of the other horses in the group. Brown eyes swiveled to him. A small smile threatened his lips as he gave in to her silent entreaty and pulled a piece of dried apple from his pocket.

Neki's sudden exclamation caused him to turn. They had just reached the outer rim of the Rancor and were now trudging out of the bog and up a sharp rise that led to the middle plateau of Crape. The horses trotted forward without command, gleeful to shake off the red clay coating their underbellies and flanks.

The mood of the men quickly rose. Laughter floated to Ren, raising his own spirits as they topped the rise where lush, verdant grass stirred in the breeze. The undergrowth and thorny plants of the Rancor were banished, and instead broad cedar trees coated with falling moss careened over the plains. The sun began to creep from behind the clouds, exiling the rains and sending a blanket of solace ahead of them.

Ren urged his mount into a fast canter. His men followed, eager to put distance between themselves and the Rancor. The thundering drone of their horses' hooves soothed Ren's mind, but it was only a few heartbeats before a shadow eclipsed their flight. Ren looked up.

Instead of looking at the sky, he looked at dragon's wings.

Ren urged his mount faster, pleading to the Fates the dragon would fly by, praying to the Maker it wouldn't land.

"Not yet Chance," he whispered.

He felt more than saw Galvin and Bentzen flank him protectively. Markum voiced a warning behind him.

The world was suddenly bathed in shadow. Silver scales carpeted the sky before the dragon glided to the ground, blocking their path.

The horses reared, eyes wide with fear. Keena pranced at his side, thinking it was a game. Harsh curses indicated Neki had been thrown. His muttered exclamations faded as he ran after his fleeing steed.

It took all Ren's strength to keep his mare from running, and still she bucked. Galvin dismounted and grabbed Ren's reins, cooing his mount into submission. Ren dropped to the ground and turned from the dragon.

"Ren?"

A hand touched his shoulder, another found his back, still another his arm. The dragon thundered a greeting, closer this time, almost directly behind him.

Ren looked between Galvin and Bentzen's concerned faces. Markum paled as he muttered something about the Oracle. All eyes turned to Ren. A sudden understanding rose in each.

Bentzen stepped forward. "Do you want me to kill it for you, Ren?"

Ren shook his head. "No, Bentzen, that isn't what I have to do. It will live, physically that is."

Bentzen studied him. "Will you, my prince?"

"I will, physically."

"Can we do anything?" Galvin's voice brought Ren a small comfort.

Ren drew a deep breath. He looked at his companions, feeling the warmth of their friendship. He had been selfishly distant since the Oracle. His friends surrounded him, offering him comfort, yet all eyes were filled with disquiet. He had put it there.

He put a hand on Galvin's shoulder. "No, Galvin, there's nothing you can do. Only I can carry through the Oracle's demands, but I'll regret this for the remainder of my days. If I understood why I could accept it more readily. But I don't."

A slight breeze stirred. Galvin's jaw tightened as he glanced at the silver dragon. "I don't know what the Oracle commanded, but know the Maker isn't cruel. Trust him to the why. You just follow the how."

Ren bowed his head, knowing Galvin was right. The Maker didn't direct him to do this without a purpose. He remembered the saying at the Oracle's entrance: *Everything happens for a reason and in that reason there is divine good.*

He may not understand why he had to do this, he may never understand, but he needed to trust the Maker. As long as he followed the Oracle's commands all would turn out well.

Ren drew a deep breath. It was time. He could wait no longer.

When he turned to face the dragon, his limbs moved on their own accord. Ren felt his entire life flash before him. No emotion he had ever experienced felt as wrong and as terrible as the one he was currently feeling. With each step he took the more his hopes slipped through his fingers.

The dragon rumbled a greeting. Ren clenched his jaw, trying to find strength to voice the words he feared.

The dragon's eyes turned a deep violet as it lowered its head and brushed his hand. Ren tried to force his voice to come but as he stared into the dragon's eyes it took all of his energy to breathe. Aidan was whole, and once he spoke she wouldn't be. He would never be able to explain the reason behind his words. He would never be able to tell her how much she meant to him. When he felt his resolve begin to shatter he turned away, knowing his face would betray him.

Warm breath gusted over his neck as the dragon smelled him. Aidan had seen his face and couldn't believe the coolness it held.

He started to talk, telling her he denounced their union. There was no reason, he lied, to have the link now that she was in the dragon. It would just keep him from loving another and having a normal life. He was better off without her.

He fell to the ground as the dragon bellowed in pain. Markum screamed a warning. Ren felt the intake of breath and tensed for the inevitable fire to storm around him. He didn't care. He loathed his words, his fate, and what the Oracle had forced him to do. He deserved to die. Maybe this was what Fate had meant when she said he had to destroy his soul. He would welcome it.

The fire came. The heat seemed to be all around him, but he felt no pain. Nothing could match the pain inside his heart. A gust of wind encompassed him as the dragon took to the air, screaming into the fading sunlight. He would never forget that voice for it wasn't a dragon's roar – it was Aidan's scream.

Now he could destroy his soul. His soul's destruction would seem easy compared to what he had just done. Maybe it was better this way. If Aidan felt as much for him as he felt for her she could never bear his destruction. He prayed she would find comfort in the dragon, the most beautiful creature in the Lands. At least the dragon matched her beauty.

"I love you, Aidan," he whispered into the grass. Familiar hands touched his back and rolled him over. He heard Markum tell Galvin to heat some water and douse a blanket in order to draw the fire's poison from his system.

Aidan had burned him. Ren smiled. He remembered the riddle of the sphinx: Through fields of fire I am made. Yet for some reason he couldn't recall the answer to the riddle, even though he knew it was important.

Blackness descended, but before it encompassed him he heard a voice echoing in the darkness.

"*Blind faith,*" it whispered.

- - -

Sim didn't know what to do. The emotions he had felt before tore through him once again. But he didn't want them. He didn't want them at all. It meant only one thing: Aidan was beginning to merge. Sim could barely hear the Bane's voice trying to reach her, but Aidan wouldn't listen.

The emotions were frightening: love and pain, pain and love. But the pain was more than Sim could bear.

Foreign liquid oozed down his silver cheeks as Aidan's emotions riveted through him. His love became more than he had ever dreamed. It was beautiful, hopeful, sensual, and wonderful. It felt like Mezuzah's warm tongue, a dragon cub's first step, a waterfall's spray, and the sun on his back. But the pain was more than he had ever feared. It was without hope, fathomless, eternal, and black. He would much rather have every bone in his body broken, every dragon in the Lands slain, every sun in the universe dark than to feel Aidan's pain.

He thought of Ren's eyes. They were eyes that felt the same tearing pain Sim was now experiencing. They were eyes that revealed a tormented soul.

Before Sim lost his senses he tumbled to the ground, desperate to tell Aidan what he knew.

For he knew the truth. He knew.

Ren lied.

If only Aidan would realize that in time.

CHAPTER 7

They had ridden hard, stopping only briefly in the night to rest their horses and catch a few moons' clicks of sleep. They barely talked. They barely ate. They were on a mission.

When Bentzen had first relayed the story Quinton had jumped into action, thinking what men of war were trained to think - kill.

Now, after riding for days he had been through every emotion he could possibly feel: anger, hatred, pain, desperation, anxiety, worry, and fear. The fear came whenever he thought about the one possibility he didn't want to consider. He may never see Marva again. The thought always left him off balance. He didn't know what he would do without his wife: her smile, her bravery, her stubbornness, and her ice-blue fiery eyes. Those same passionate eyes now haunted his dreams.

Quinton felt like he was on the spiral of fate, descending to the point of no return. He knew this could be his last ride. He just wished he had been able to tell Ren goodbye.

But if this was his last ride he would take as many as he could down with him, especially the man who had taken Marva and Renee. He would suffer a thousand times over for what he had done. Quinton had no doubt he would recognize him. He had memorized Bentzen's description of the man called Ickba. Marva's captor also plagued his dreams, but in every dream Ickba died screaming.

They had just crossed the Sierras where they had ridden through a storm of dust and Quinton silently welcomed the dense forests of Zier. He steered his horse to a small cave he used to frequent as a child. It would be a perfect place to rest. Stardom was only a day's ride away. They needed to gather their strength before they attacked.

As he broke through the small clearing containing the hidden hollow, he reined his horse to a skidding halt and waited for Michel.

Michel's horse bolted through the clearing heartbeats later. Since leaving the others Quinton hadn't seen Michel in the bright of day. Although they had stopped briefly every night to catch a little sleep, Michel appeared to have slept little, if at all. He looked years older. Quinton had fallen asleep immediately every night. He was trained to do so. Sleep was necessary for strength, and if he had no strength, Marva had no chance.

"In the midst of battle," his father used to say, *"you must rest."* And it was true. The first night had been difficult but he had managed

to do what his father had trained him to do: clear his mind and delve into a dream state.

As Quinton watched, Michel's eyes fluctuated between sanity and insanity, and every few heartbeats he trembled with the force of the ten winds. Quinton stepped forward, concerned, but when Michel drew a breath the trembling stopped. Quinton relaxed, realizing Michel's movements could have been from tears. Michel hit his horse's flank and stepped aside as the horse trotted off to graze. Quinton marveled at how Michel could communicate with animals. The horses he rode were never fettered but were always there the next morning, nickering for his hand.

Over the past weeks Quinton had surprised himself by feeling the same loyalty toward Michel as he did his prince. Although he had many he called friends he had precious few he felt close to. He was, after all, the captain of Ren's guard. He needed men to admire him, call him friend, but he also needed to remain objective and slightly distant from each. He didn't mind. He had always been friend to many but close to few. There was something different about Michel, however, something special. Ren took after Michel more than he did his own father. Quinton supposed that could be the reason he felt an unexplainable bond toward Ren's uncle. Michel and Ren were of the same mold, both in looks and in beliefs.

Michel stood in the clearing, back to him, gazing in the direction of Stardom. Quinton's heart went out to him. He and Marva had years together, one in courting and two in marriage. Michel had only a fleeting heartbeat with Renee, and now, just as a door had opened and allowed him entrance, someone was threatening to take her away.

"Michel?"

When Michel turned Quinton had to force himself not to start. His copper eyes were almost inhuman. Their discoloration was far worse than Quinton had first realized. It appeared Michel hadn't slept in weeks. Quinton was unsure if Michel even recognized him. Quinton took a step back, leery under Michel's gaze.

"Michel, we rest here. We don't move until high moons tonight. We need to be strong and have our wits about us."

Michel's eyes focused. A small amount of recognition crossed his features. Quinton was about to say more when Michel grabbed his bedroll and walked off. Quinton watched him go, the hackles on his neck rising. Michel had been slightly distant since Ista's camp. Had something happened to him there? The thought was chilling. Just in case, Quinton walked in the opposite direction, casting a furtive glance over his shoulder.

- - -

Marva was seething. She was a blasted fool, accepting Ickba as just a lowly stable hand. How could she have been so blind!

Ickba was taking his time riding back. He was having too much fun during his frequent breaks. Marva was now ready to rip out his eyes and carve the rest of him up with slow precision. At first she had been worried about the queen, but Renee had surprised her. Renee hadn't cried, called out or screamed as most women would. She did exactly what she should have done. She lay under the vile man like a sack of grain, not allowing his blows or his torture to break her. Marva was proud of her and had proceeded to put Renee on a higher level in her internal ranking of people.

Marva inched a little closer to the large boulder on her right, all the while keeping her eyes on Ickba, who was torturing Renee for the last time. His back was to her, and soon she left caution to the ten winds and began to roll, over and over, moving faster and faster. She was sure Ickba wouldn't notice. The man was laughing in glee as he prodded Renee with a knife.

The boulder hit her back. It had a hooked protrusion that looked to be just the right size to pry the silver band off her head. Marva moved into position and forced the rock's hooked edge under the band, allowing it to dig into her skin. She drew a deep breath, closed her eyes and flung her head forward. The edge tore into her skull, ripping her skin to the bone. She bit her tongue to keep from crying out. Blood seeped into her left eye, but the silver band was loose.

She leaned forward. The band slipped from her head and fell into her lap.

She didn't know how to use the Quy, but she figured she was mad enough to learn. She peered at the ropes binding her ankles and concentrated on her rage. Ickba would be done with his torture soon, knowing that Renee would be valuable to Ista. Marva would be next. Marva's torture always lasted far longer than the queen's. Instead of panic claiming Marva, her resolve deepened. Marva leaned closer to her feet, eyes wide with conviction.

"Loosen, curse you."

As if on their own accord, the ropes slackened and one of her feet dislodged. Marva jumped to her feet and ran toward Ickba. He never knew what hit him. Her foot impacted his backside so hard he rolled over Renee's head. As soon as he hit the ground he looked up at her with malice so intense her temper flared even further. How dare the man look at her like she was the detestable one!

The force of her next kick flung him into a small tree. The impact slowed him, but only briefly. The trunk of the tree severed and he fell with it. His eyes registered surprise, and that spurred her even further. She reached for the sword Ickba had discarded before his games with the queen.

Before the rogue could stand the sword impaled him in the throat. He choked, face still in shock, and went limp. Marva went to Renee and cut the ropes on her hands and feet. No words were spoken. No words were needed. Each knew what she had to do.

Renee ripped a large piece of cloth from her gown. Marva turned to Ickba, but before she could raise the sword above her head Renee held out her hand. Marva handed her the blade and watched as the queen brought the weapon down on Ickba's throat, severing his head.

Renee held out the cloth. Marva picked up Ickba's head and placed it in the thin, white threads. Renee tied it closed. Blood seeped through the cloth, marring the white brilliance.

Marva looked up at the queen. Ickba's blood was splattered on her face, but her blue eyes blazed with fire. She glanced toward Zier before turning back to Marva.

"Proof."

Marva smiled. "Let's go."

- - -

Quinton woke during the night and stared into the eyes of a madman.

Michel stooped over him, face straining with tension, a dagger raised above his head. "Stop . . . me," he said. Michel's arm shook to control the dagger's downward movement.

Quinton rolled to the side just as the dagger plummeted to the earth. Without a second thought, Quinton toppled Michel and knocked the dagger from his hand.

"Michel, what's happening to you?" Quinton asked through gritted teeth.

Michel flailed back and forth, his strength uncanny. His eyes alternated between the man Quinton knew and a rabid animal.

"Something . . . Ista . . . kill the Chosen's companions. I'm infected. Help me. Kill me, Quinton."

The plea in Michel's voice tore Quinton's heart, but before he had time to respond Michel flipped him over and grabbed the dagger. Quinton cried out, dodging another blow, and darted away.

Michel crouched in an animalistic stance. His eyes became huge, the whites glowing in the night with mad intent. Holding the dagger in front of him, he grunted. His eyes suddenly cleared. He turned the dagger on himself, straining to plunge it into his heart.

"No, Michel!"

"Ren . . . Quinton. Don't let him see me like this! Kill me!"

"Maker of Fates, Michel. I can't. We'll find help. Just put the dagger down."

The fear in Michel's eyes slowly turned to rage. Quinton backed up. If Michel lost control Quinton would be unable to stop him. The man was stronger than a dragon, and then some.

But as Quinton looked into Michel's eyes they transformed into Ren's own.

"Please, Quinton," Michel said softly. "Before I can't control it."

"I can't, Michel. I could never."

And then Michel's eyes began to glow a sickening green. He growled.

Quinton turned and ran. The last thing he knew was a sharp stabbing pain. He fell. Wolven howled in the distance. Quinton wondered if he would even be alive to feel them tearing his flesh.

CHAPTER 8

Alezza blinked in surprise as the heir of Crape fell to his knees before her. She had ordered her men to clean him up. She could barely touch him, he stunk so. His soiled pants were rank and he had lost so much weight his clothes seemed to be hanging on a skeleton. The man placed before her now was nowhere near the horrendous figure she had been with a short time ago. The release from the pain and the wash had done wonders.

Chris' blond hair shone like spun gold and his skin gleamed a golden bronze. Bowing his head, he heaved a heavy sigh as if he cared little about what happened to him. Ever since Manda's escape he hadn't fought her at all, and she hadn't been kind. She had punished him day in and day out. Where before Chris had tried to control his screams, now he did not. Where before Chris had tried to control his convulsions, now he did not. Where before Chris had managed to hold his bowels, now he did not. If it was because of the excruciating pain she was sending she would have been pleased, but it was not. Chris had finally broken because of Manda's departure. He hadn't wanted his sister to bear the misery of his suffering.

Alezza had been careful not to take Chris too far with the pain. She couldn't allow his death. He was the key to her future. If she rode into Crape with Chris she would be revered. A prince, now the crown prince, thought dead, would be found, and he would declare his love for the princess who had saved him. It was too perfect.

Only after the wedding could she allow him to give up on life.

Alezza glanced briefly at the tent flap as if she could see beyond to where two of her men still searched for Manda. She silently wished them a swift kill. She grew weary of the girl's games. Apparently Manda knew how to cover her trail. Manda had traveled through every stream, followed every rocky path and had somehow managed to evade her. Alezza was surprised Manda had the heart to leave. Manda knew Chris would suffer for her deception.

Alezza was still furious. If Manda managed to convince someone of her story, Alezza would be hung, unless Chris negated Manda's claim.

A slow smile stole across Alezza's face. Chris was hers to command. When those green eyes looked her way they weren't only filled with hate they were also filled with insanity. Now all she had to do was send him opposing feelings and he would do anything she wanted. During Manda's rape Alezza had tested her theory. If she could stimulate the needles to send anguish, why not ecstasy?

She had been right. It had worked. Now came the true test. The pain she had sent him over the past few days was so intense sometimes his skin seeped blood. Now, if the pleasure could match that intensity, Chris of Crape would be hers.

Her thoughts circled back to the man who had been found with Chris the morning of Manda's escape. Who was he? His clothes were gone, his sword generic, and he was dead before she could ask any questions. Was it one of Chris' guards? She doubted it. A guard would have come with more support. No one would send one lone scout to look for two heirs believed dead. No, it could only be a farmer or some traveler who had heard the screams and taken pity on the bonded. But he could fight. The man had killed nine of her men before he was brought down.

That left her with only eighteen guards. No, seventeen. Manda had killed Bort.

Alezza's resolve deepened as she refocused on Chris. His head was down. From the rhythmic rise and fall of his chest she knew he was sleeping. She hadn't granted him any sleep of late.

Tonight would be no exception.

She slowly lifted his head until his face came into view. Alezza licked her lips. Tonight would be perfect. Chris stared up at her, unblinking and without fear, but with the most intense animosity she had ever seen.

"Not appreciative of the bath?" He was handsome in a boyish kind of way. His huge green eyes, shaggy blond hair and thin build shouted of innocence, but his sunken jawline, broad shoulders and sheer height argued for a man worth the title of prince.

It would be a pleasure to break him.

She ran a finger down the side of his face. "My sweet." He flinched, but she ignored him. He wouldn't flinch long. Instead, he would be begging. "I won't bring you any more pain, only pleasure, but you must do one thing for me."

Alezza saw the hatred intensify in his eyes. It sent a tantalizing chill down her spine. She liked challenges, and this wasn't only a challenge, it was fun.

"Now, now," she whispered as she found the needles in his mind. She sent a powerful surge of the Quy. His face quickly registered surprise. He hadn't known the assault was coming. But she had to be careful. She didn't want him to break completely, at least not before he had given her the throne.

Instead of sending fire into him she sent a tantalizing breeze. At first she made it barely discernable, then she gusted it in short blasts. Chris set his jaw, brows furrowing. She chortled deep in her throat. Her own vitals felt what she was sending. No man could resist for long.

Kneeling, she stroked his cheek, forcing the breeze inside him to build in severity. She saw the effects of her frolic on his face. After the pain, the small erotic sensations caused his eyes to roll back into his head. She kept her sensations slow and easy, running her hand over his chest and shoulders.

"Don't try to resist, my love. You can't resist," she teased, sending a small amount of pain down the needle's shaft, reminding him she could revert to the pain if he didn't give in to her demands.

His body began to convulse as if she had sent a quick, intense surge inside him. Alezza released the pain, surprised. She hadn't sent enough for him to react so. She knew his limits. Curious, she tried again. He reacted the same way.

After the eroticism the pain was a shock. Alezza tittered. This would simplify things. He would be much easier to control.

She started the process again, then again. When the carnal sensations came Chris jerked and trembled with euphoria. During the pain he screamed as though she were sending a fiery wrath inside him.

Alezza knelt beside the prince and started to build the pleasure. She watched as his chest rose and fell as the feelings grew. Alezza whispered her love and promised no more pain. Her hand stroked his face. She wanted him to grow accustomed to her touch.

The emotions she was sending caused her to feel flush. She began to take off her outer garments, letting the heat-filled breeze wash over her thin frame. She wished she were willing to lay with a man before she wed. As soon as the thought was out, she looked at Chris. If Manda evaded the guards and told her story, Alezza would be hung unless there was an heir. Alezza released a throaty laugh and brushed Chris' face. Chris was, after all, going to be her husband, and if he gave her a child before he died no one could condemn her to death. She would be allowed to live and raise the child.

And if she matched physical contact with inner sensation how much faster could she break him?

- - -

The fire had long since died. Ren shivered, but he welcomed the cold. It made him think about something other than Aidan and his mother. He touched his left shoulder, the only part of his body the silver dragon had burned. He felt the ridges of flesh underneath the pledget. It would scar, forever reminding him of his deception.

He was only supposed to stand watch for a moons' click, but he hadn't woken Galvin to take his place. He knew he would be unable to sleep. He honestly didn't know if he would ever sleep again, at least without nightmares.

Ren sighed softly to the night, trying not to wake Galvin. Galvin had been so concerned over the past few days he woke at any movement. Galvin stirred, but only to bring his arm under his head. The previous night Galvin refused to sleep unless Ren did first. Needless to say, neither of them had slept.

Ren walked to the nearest tree. He rested against its trunk and stared into the dark forest. They had wasted precious time. Bentzen and Galvin insisted he rest his burnt shoulder for a day before moving. Now they were only a day's ride closer to the Alcazar. Ren's frustration was starting to overcome his reason. That night he had forced his men forward until most had fallen asleep on their horses.

He would have thought the urgency to find the One would abate after his encounter with the dragon. On the contrary, it had escalated. It was a constant buzzing in his mind, an imperative force that wouldn't leave him alone.

The air turned colder. Ren tensed. A shiver of warning rippled down his spine. Overhead the nightbirds stilled their eerie song. Ren looked out into the night, sensing something moving his way.

It took every ounce of energy to remain still and search with his eyes. A rustle stirred but he couldn't lock the sound's position. It seemed to be coming from everywhere.

He didn't know what to do. Some creatures of magic reacted negatively to movement; others reacted just as violently to stagnation. Ren tried to clear his mind of all else, concentrating on the danger but distancing himself so as not to lose his reason.

He sensed movement below him. Tiny black snakes slithered over his boots. His mind quickly connected the rustling sound to the snakes' movement. Adders!

Ren drew in a breath and turned his head. The rest of the camp was already crawling with tiny snakes. He heard a shout and saw Markum standing as a black snake fell out of his tunic.

"Markum, freeze!" Ren yelled. But it was too late. Markum's body tumbled to the ground in death.

The snakes bit at first movement. Their venom was immediate death. The Adderiss always sent her snakes ahead of her, making sure they stopped everything in her path. Once the target was covered in the vile creatures the Adderiss demanded things. If she didn't get her wish she let her snakes feed on the victim. It was that simple.

Pain swept through him as he heard Galvin scream Markum's name. Markum was dead. Curse the Fates! Markum was dead.

"Ren!"

Ren swiveled his upper body. He locked eyes with Bentzen. The swordsman, careful not to move the bottom portion of his body, now crawling with snakes, tried to reach for the Quy's sword, but it was just out of reach. Bentzen's muscles strained in effort, only to drop back in exhaustion. Looking into Bentzen's eyes Ren felt his own fear reach a zenith.

Ren had never seen Bentzen afraid, but the look in Bentzen's eyes betrayed his terror. The implication shook Ren more than his own apprehension.

Bentzen's eyes widened as he looked past Ren. Ren tensed, feeling the warm venomous breath of the Adderiss on his neck. He reached toward his sword. He felt its metal, its weight. In the next heartbeat the sword was in his hand.

Turning, he posed ready. He was unprepared for what he saw. Twin pools of moss-green sordidness marred by thin viperous slits of black pupil peered at him. The Adderiss threw her head back and hissed in laughter. Her eyes rolled back to reveal their red undercoat.

"You think you can kill me with a sword?" she hissed, narrow tongue flickering dangerously close to his face.

He grew taut as her moss eyes roved over his men with slow, hungry precision. Their red edges made her look like her insides were on fire.

As a human, she would have been beautiful. Her form was human, though if you looked closely her skin was an ivory reptilian. A raised ridge of scales crowned her head and trailed down the sides of her face and neck. Thick, coarse black hair fell in waves to her shoulders. Ren's eyes dared to flicker down her body. What he saw sent waves of nausea through him. The only thing covering the rest of her tall, thin form were adders, slithering over her in waves. Two large ones, apparently the two that produced the countless others, slithered sensuously around her hips and shoulders.

The Adderiss smiled at his repulsion. Sharp incisors clasped over her bottom lip. She placed a hand on his shoulder and hissed. Her fetid tongue hit his cheek. Some of her adders glided over her hand and down his shirt.

"Stay put, Chosen." She walked past him.

Sweat beaded on his forehead as he turned himself to stone. The thin snakes twirled over his chest, making sure he remained motionless.

The Adderiss' laughter echoed through the night. He gritted his teeth, forcing the memory of Markum's lifeless body from his mind. The Adderiss hissed as if she had found a prize.

Ren couldn't see what was happening. She had already killed Markum. He refused let her kill anyone else.

"Adderiss!" In response to his shout the snakes moved over him with more speed. Although the Adderiss laughed at his demand, he sensed her moving closer.

"The Chosen speaks. Let me not deny him his words."

She stepped into view. More snakes had left her, revealing more skin than Ren cared to see. She gurgled deep in her throat as she circled him, touching him in places he didn't care to be touched. When she faced him she bowed. The snakes stirred around her in a frenzy.

The Adderiss stepped closer. Her moss-green eyes burned a hole through him. His anger slipped away. She would get what she wanted or she would kill them all.

"Don't ever speak to me in that tone again." Her hot breath steamed off his skin. Perspiration rained down his face. He willed himself to ignore the itch.

"Then be on your way."

A sinister grin slit her face as she hissed in laughter. The intensity of the sound sent her covering writhing with glee. The adders in his tunic nipped his chest as if tasting what was to come.

"I see the Chosen is well read in magic. But does the Chosen know the Adderiss must get something for his safe passage?"

"Let my men go. Then I will grant your demands"

She scowled. "You don't make the rules. I make the rules."

Ren remained silent.

She fastened her hand on his arm and pulled him closer. Her hot breath seared into his nostrils. Her eyes radiated contempt and evil. His skin crawled with lewd disquiet.

"I want your fire."

Ren blinked in confusion, thinking he had heard her wrong. "I don't know what you mean."

"Your fire," she demanded, "for your men."

Ren hesitated.

"I warn you, Dragon Mate choose and choose now. I grow weary of your hesitation."

The term caught Ren off guard. Chance had used the term "Dragon Mate" when referring to him, and her decree had been about the silver dragon and Aidan.

"Agree!" Her eyes darted behind him.

He screamed for her to stop.

A thud reverberated in the night. Galvin's intake of breath told Ren another man had fallen.

The Adderiss' moss eyes turned to him, wide with rage. He searched his mind, frantic to think of what his fire could be. Her eyes darted back to his men. He grabbed her arm.

"Agreed," he said. His movement caused the adders to nip furiously at his flesh, sending him into a torrent of darkness.

- - -

Ren slowly opened his eyes and looked into the faces of his friends.

Galvin collapsed on the ground beside him. "We thought you were dead. Fates!"

"Help me up."

Galvin looked at him with concern but didn't argue as he lifted him into a sitting position. A tingly sensation flowed through Ren's chest and arms but he had only been stunned, nothing more. He looked at Galvin with a slight hope.

"The others?"

Galvin's face turned ashen. He shook his head. "Bentzen and Markum are gone."

Ren bowed his head. Bentzen his loyal follower, the one who was just beginning to allow himself to feel friendship and love . . . and Markum.

How dare she do this! Ren stood, still feeling numb in places on his upper body where the snakes had nipped his flesh. But he had agreed to her demands before they bit and was therefore protected from their venom.

He faced the camp. Many travelers had used the clearing. No grass grew in the large circular area, and a fire pit lay at its center. Rocks were stacked around it to thwart any unwelcome breeze. The fire had been rekindled once again. It blazed high into the night, trying to ward off anything else looming in the darkness. Markum and Bentzen lay where they had fallen, eyes wide and lifeless.

Ren searched the forest until he found a sharp rock. Finding a large area beneath a sheltering cedar he began to dig the graves.

Soon Galvin and Neki joined him. They worked in consoling silence, each concentrating on the task at hand. It was slow, and at times Ren thought about taking Markum and Bentzen farther inland where the red soil wouldn't be as prevalent, but each time he thought of moving them he quickly dismissed it. Moving them didn't seem right.

The red soil was difficult to dig. The others took breaks in silence. Ren did not. He needed a purpose, and his purpose at that point in time was to dig.

He felt a hand on his shoulder and looked up into Galvin's concerned face. Ren hadn't noticed the rain. Galvin's blond hair was drenched and water ran down his face like perpetual tears.

"Tomorrow the ground will be easier to work because of the rain. We're all exhausted. Let's get some sleep. We can finish this after we rest."

Sleep was the last thing Ren wanted. He needed to occupy himself with something physical, something that would help block his thoughts. Just as he was about to argue he saw the weariness in Galvin's eyes. He glanced behind him. Neki faired no better. Ren nodded reluctantly. Galvin gave his shoulder a sympathetic squeeze before he turned to erect the thatched shelter they had constructed during the previous rain.

Ren let the cool rain wash the dirt and sweat from him, not really caring if he ever sought the shelter. The rain wasn't the pelting rain of the prior storm. It was a cleansing rain, soft and cool. The intermingled clay soil didn't absorb the water quickly but it didn't repel it like the lower Rancor. Ren stood in silence, watching the two shallow graves fill with water. The rain continued to ping down, making the pools dance and sway with ripples of pain.

Neki stepped beside him. All humor had drained from his face. Dark hair clung to his neck, accentuating his thin frame. Ren could see a resemblance to Grauss as rivulets of water careened down Neki's face. They had the same slender nose, the same high cheekbones, the same curve of the mouth and the same deep-set eyes. Although Neki was taller, his build was the same as the sage, broad shouldered and lean.

Neki's lips twisted into a worried frown as he searched Ren's face. When he didn't find the answers he sought he turned back to the graves. Where before the rain was soothing, now the droplets sounded ominous as they splashed into the shallow pools.

"What did you give her?"

The question took Ren off guard. He had already forgotten he had agreed to anything. Bentzen and Markum's death had shadowed all other consequences.

"I gave her my fire."

Neki's face twisted in confusion. The look caused him to appear comical despite his urgent tone. "Your fire? What do you mean your fire?"

"I don't know. I wish I did. That's what she asked for. When I hesitated she killed Bentzen. I didn't hesitate again."

Neki nodded as he turned back to the graves, but a heartbeat later he turned back and grabbed Ren's arm. "If you don't know what it is it could be important. She may have taken something you need to defeat Ista. Do you feel any different?"

"No, no different, but I did use fire on the wolven. The Quy said I was the first to conjure fire. The Adderiss could want that ability for some reason."

"So you can't burn anything?"

"I don't know, Neki. I can't use the Quy as you do. I can't find the power on a whim. Even if I wanted to try to ignite something I wouldn't know how. I call the Quy by instinct and only in dire need."

Neki didn't appear satisfied. Water dripped in a steady rhythm from his nose. "Is that the only fire you have? Think about it symbolically. What about dragons? Could she have meant dragons?"

"Dragons are free creatures. They aren't mine to give. Even if Aidan," Ren paused to draw a breath, "even if Aidan is whole I couldn't give the Adderiss the silver dragon."

Neki shifted and put his hand on his hip. Lowering his eyebrows, he grunted. "Burning cinders, I don't like it. She would only want something with profound significance. I don't like it at all."

CHAPTER 9

Chris looked at the beautiful woman, tired and confused. She had been giving him pleasure and pain all day, but he couldn't comprehend why he was given pleasure for doing the things he did and why he received pain for asking questions. He supposed he shouldn't ask questions, but he had just drawn her a glass of water. Now she was asking him to draw her another glass of water and she had yet to take a sip from the first glass. Why shouldn't he question that?

"Chris, I want you to draw me a glass of water," the lady asked again, this time with a slight edge to her voice

He was so tired. All he wanted to do was rest. Surely, if he told her she already had a glass of water she would see the foolishness of her request. "But you already have water."

The pain wasn't pain – it was martyrdom. He doubled over, waiting for his life to end. The wait was maddening. After the pleasure she had just given him, the pain shot higher than it ever had before.

With the same abruptness the pain started, it ceased. He found himself face down in the dirt, inhaling dust. She kicked him. He clutched his ribs, trying to rationalize why a beautiful woman who could give such pleasure would relish such anguish. But she loved it. The more violently he reacted, the more intense his screams, the more intense the pleasure, the more intense the pain.

And then came the instructions: draw some water, take a bath, and comb her hair. Do this and that, not strenuous things, but things. During those times he tried hard to obey her, but his mind wandered. The red uniforms of the soldiers called to him, spoke to him in ways he didn't understand. He decided red must be his favorite color, but as the days passed he began to envision a more subtle red. In his mind he saw a lock of red hair, bleached blonde from the sun.

He focused on that image when the pleasure was rising too fast and he felt himself about to drown in its depths. When he focused on the red image it always pulled him out, helped him survive. He really didn't know why he fought to survive. Maybe it was the pleasure. Yes, the pleasure, surely that was it.

Sometimes he fought hard to remember why he clung to the red image. That was when he reached for the second image.

It was a stone, a black stone, pure and without blemish. It wasn't as comforting as the red but he clung to it when he wanted to deny the beautiful woman. A powerful force radiated from its midnight depths. Chris clung to it, welcoming the strength of the stone. He had put his memories inside it, he knew, tucked them away from the beautiful woman. He had formed the stone to keep himself alive. For some reason if he had the memories he would deny the woman each time, and if he denied her his mind would rupture. And he wanted to live. He desperately wanted to live. He needed to do something. He didn't know what, but when he was able to claim his memories he would know – hence the stone.

He hungered to remember. There were times when he held the stone, ready to take the memories that would end the mystery. Each time something stopped him: the snickers from the soldiers, the woman's laughter, the erotic longings, or the stabbing pain. It wasn't time to remember. He hoped one day he would be able to draw from the stone. Now was the time to hold onto sanity.

"Don't question me, my sweet. How many times must I make you understand that all I do is in your best interest?" The woman bent forward. Her long locks tickled the side of his face. She smiled but the smile seemed as breakable as glass. "I won't make it a point to explain, but this time I'll make an exception. You need to learn that I can be trusted. I want you to draw another glass of water for you, my dearest. As you said, I already have a glass. You see," she said, lifting an eyebrow. "I only think of you."

He blinked, unsure. But he knew not to question a second time. If she sent the pain now neither the red nor the stone would be enough. His mind would be gone. At times he wondered if it was already. Was it insanity that formed those images? Were his memories something he had created in his imagination? Was this who he truly was?

Clutching his ribcage he rose and went to the water. He continued to hold an anguished look, feigning that the kick had injured him more than it really had. If she didn't think it hurt he might very well get another clout.

Careful not to spill any of the liquid he trotted back. She didn't like dawdling. He had learned to be swift. As he handed the cup to her he felt an expected wave of pleasure pass though him. The woman smiled and ran a finger down his cheek.

She guided the cup to his lips. "It's yours, didn't I tell you?" The water tasted wonderful. Normally he was only allowed one glass a day, at mealtime. It seemed she was telling the truth. His brow furrowed. She said she did everything for him. If that were true then why did she hurt him?

81

She smiled again. All he could do was stare. She was beautiful. He wanted to reach out and touch her long, dark hair, but something held him back. His mind couldn't understand why he felt repulsion when he touched her, but the feeling wouldn't leave him. It wasn't because she hurt him. He had gotten used to that. It had to do with the red image he carried.

Just as he was about to reach for the red image the pleasure swept him away. He rode the waves as they swept him under. Soon they were too much for him to withstand. He released himself and plummeted into their depths, swallowing the galvanizing pulse, letting the shock flow through his entire essence.

He twined through the sea, releasing every muscle, not even bothering to breathe. The pleasure was so enveloping he couldn't move. His mind was black, like the stone.

The top of the water was too far out of reach. Soon he would drown. He struggled, but his arms moved only a fraction.

Too much. Too much. Too much. The pleasure started to hurt. Desperate, he flailed in the water, but he only managed to shiver as he continued to plummet to the painful bottom of pleasure.

With anguished force he reached for the red image. It came immediately. He clung to it, fighting the pleasurable pain. The red formed a rope, a saving rope that floated to the surface of the pool of pleasure. His lungs burned from lack of air but he began to climb, higher and higher, until he reached the surface. When he broke free he screamed, releasing water from his lungs, but he didn't stop there. He continued to climb until he reached the place the rope had started. It was a landing, a pure black landing. He collapsed on its smooth, ebony surface to regain his breath. The strength of the stone seeped inside him, caressing him with emotions he couldn't place.

He crawled to the edge of the landing and looked down at the pleasurable water below. He knew he couldn't do without the pleasure for long, but he didn't want to go back. He wanted to remain on the smooth stone.

Something touched his cheek. Something else lifted his hand. He wanted to brush it away but he was too weak. It wouldn't go away.

He opened his eyes and looked into her face. For a fleeting heartbeat he saw her brows wither in concern, but as soon as the worried expression came it evaporated, leaving nothing but a stoic smile. The woman dropped to her knees and cradled his head in her lap. His entire body ached, but he was accustomed to the feeling. He was so tired. He just wanted to rest.

He closed his eyes. A shade of a huge, burly man flashed before him. He heard a woman's laughter, another's scream. His heart raced. An intense loathing filled him. When he looked at the woman again he wanted to recoil, but he was too tired. All he could do was deny her on the inside.

"Do you know who you are, Chris?"

Chris. The name sounded familiar. He thought about trying to reach for the stone but decided against it. He was too tired to care, far too tired to care.

He managed to shake his head.

"Chris is your name, my sweet – Christopher Eric Kahn to be exact. You're a prince, my love. Your people believe you dead. Thankfully, I've found you and will restore you to your people. They'll be exuberant. When we arrive at your home I want you to marry me. Would you do that for me?"

A soft lap of the pleasurable water found its way over his black stone, sending an oscillating pulse inside him. As he forced the stone higher the waves followed. It was a losing battle. His feelings were out of his control.

He looked into her eyes. He didn't want to marry her. He hated the feelings of pleasure, and he abhorred the intensity of the pain.

"Never," he managed to whisper.

As soon as the word was spoken he was racked with a stabbing anguish. It was so intense he felt himself falling from the stone, mind exploding from the change in emotion. He began to pray he would forget his loathing, the red, the stone, and just agree to the woman's demands. If he agreed he was sure to be left alone. That was all he wanted, wasn't it?

Yes, that was what he wanted. He would agree. He had to agree.

He began to mumble pleas of forgiveness to names he didn't remember, surprised his ignorance was what hurt him most of all.

- - -

It was well past midnight but Marva wasn't tired. She walked beside the queen down the well-lit streets of Ziera to the most populated bar in the city, *The Dragon's Bane*. Even from their distance she could hear the night's activities commencing, but although loud chatter and the clinking of glasses seemed normal, Marva could sense the undercurrent of tension.

The few people they had passed jumped at their own shadows. Marva had a good mind to clout every one of them. People who shrunk inside themselves instead of fighting for their beliefs infuriated her. She knew good and well the people in the city still believed in Ren, despite the evidence against him. Marva shook her head and mumbled under her breath. Beside her, Renee remained silent.

Renee hadn't spoken since their escape. At first Marva thought Renee had gone slightly mad due to the desecration of her body, but she soon realized Renee was healing in her own way, rationalizing the injustice of the Lands in her own mind.

Marva knew there was no rationalizing their torture, but she was also trying to come to grips with what had happened. She had lost her unborn because of Ickba's dalliances. Why? What did the Maker want her to learn from the experience? How could the death of her unborn serve to benefit the Lands?

Placing her hand on her stomach Marva was surprised to find she had to stifle tears, but beneath those tears her fury took on a new dimension. She was almost blinded by the intensity of it. Maybe the Maker wanted her to be furious. Maybe fury would help her fight. Currently, she felt furious enough to demolish Ista's entire army with a mere thought.

Marva shifted her gaze to the tall shadow dwarfing Stardom. The left side of the structure had yet to be completed, but with the speed it had been built the New Alcazar would be finished in days. The feat was almost unfathomable until she thought about what Ren had done with magic.

The laden bag still swung at Renee's side. Blood had long since saturated the white cloth, so at the outskirts of the city Marva had rewrapped the prize in one of their traveling blankets. Renee hadn't refuted her actions, but before Marva had finished Renee had taken it from her once again.

The burden hadn't left the queen's side since their escape. The fire in her eyes told Marva that if anyone doubted Renee, the queen wouldn't hesitate to use the sword again.

They knew where they needed to go. *The Dragon's Bane* was well known for it patrons. They were both rich and poor, merchants and ruffians, but all of them had one thing in common: they had connections.

If you wanted to find a man, seek swift action, begin a revolt, or have word spread quickly you went to *The Dragon's Bane.* However, the pub was well tended, and if Elderec, the pub's owner, didn't know you or want your kind inside you didn't get inside. It was that simple.

Even Ren, during his occasional escapes to the city, had been observed in the pub. Marva had questioned him about it once. He had just smiled and said, "Well, Marva, if you only had a short time, and wanted to learn as much as you could during that time, where would you go?"

And Ren was right.

The clinking became louder the closer they went, and soon the pub could be seen in the distance. *The Dragon's Bane* was an imposing structure. With two floors taking up a good city block, the building looked more like a large stable than a pub. Marva had heard it could house hundreds of people without anyone brushing shoulders.

Marva stopped and let Renee walk up the steps that separated them from admittance. Renee knocked, softly at first, but when clinking glasses inundated her entreaty she rapped louder. A few patrons close to the door stopped their loud chatter and yelled for Elderec. Heartbeats later a large, wide shadow opened the door and peered down at them.

For the first time Marva really observed what she and the queen were wearing. She blinked in surprise. Her gown was filthy, and Renee's gown was splattered with blood. It was a wonder the people they had passed hadn't run away screaming. They looked worse than two beggareds.

The shadow moved its head. "Don't take your kind here." Without another word the door slammed in their faces.

Renee didn't make a move to leave. She knocked again.

Muffled curses came from inside before the door swung open for the second time. Renee stepped forward before the shadow could speak.

"Elderec, if you don't grant us entrance I'll have you hung for treason."

There could be no mistaking the queen's voice. This time Marva saw the whites of the shadow's eyes widen in shock. Elderec backed up, mumbling apologies under his breath.

When they stepped into the pub a hush fell over the crowd. The minstrel, oblivious to the sudden quiet, kept playing a lively tune on his flute. He was soon silenced as one of the patrons reached over and ripped the instrument from his grip. Blinking in shock, the minstrel opened his mouth to speak, but when his eyes fell on Renee no words followed.

Marva wished she had a talent for painting. The shock reverberating through the crowd was worth a thousand strokes of the brush. The crowd was just as Marva expected. A few wore coats of the finest make. Gold trimmings and silver brocades decorated their shoulders and armbands. Others wore less extravagant styles, the type

85

wealthy merchants would don, with leather trimmings and brass buttons. Still others wore outlandish attire, the kind those of the lower ranks would wear to flaunt the little wealth they did acquire. The remainder wore shabby garments but their hair and teeth marked them as the upper of the lower class. Servants bustled about in all directions, filling orders with deft speed. Although there were a few women in the crowd they weren't harlots, on the contrary, they were from the city's underground, a few possibly from the black market.

A small boy with blond hair and eyes the color of almonds pushed his way to the front of the throng. He was young, no older than five, but the sparkle in his eyes betrayed his intelligence, and the dirt coating his clothes suggested he could find trouble as well as a hound could hunt rabbits. One of the women grabbed him by the arm, silently ordering him to mind his manners.

Once Renee's face was bathed in the soft light of the pub no one could mistake who she was. Her blue eyes swept the crowd with both regal authority and harsh judgment. A few faces held a touch of fear, but most held adoration. After the initial shock had passed a few reverent utterances of, "My queen" could be heard filtering through the throng.

For the first time in Marva's life she held her tongue. Everything would be better coming from the queen.

Renee stepped forward and put the bundle on the bar. It hit the wood with a loud "thunk." A few of the rougher crowd blinked in shock as they placed the package's weight with its shape.

"I don't know whose side you're on, and I'm not here to sway you in either direction, but if any of you know Ren there should be no doubt who or what to believe." A few whispers started but quickly silenced.

"I'm here for one purpose and one purpose only: to tell you Ista is controlling the Collective. She inserts needles inside their minds and controls them with magic. Once you're one of the Collective you're a pawn, nothing more."

There were more whispers, now a few angry.

Renee motioned to Marva. "Marva and I were captured by one of her pawns. We killed him."

Renee turned and opened the blanket. A few muffled gasps wafted through the air as one of Ickba's eyes, now dark and murky, stared at the crowd. Elderec took a step back, his obesity shaking the floor. After running one hand through his greasy hair he grabbed a bottle of whiskey and took a long haul.

"I'm leaving this with you. You can examine it at your leisure. If you split open his skull you'll find the needles. If any more proof is needed I'm sure one of you can arrange for a few of the Collective to have tragic accidents."

After an awkward silence a tall, thin man stepped forward. He looked to be a lower class merchant. He wore a thick red coat with brass buttons, but adorned no other decoration. His boots were tall but they were well worn and a small hole was visible near the heel.

"My lady, I don't think any of us doubt your words, but what do you propose we do? Ista has magic. We don't. Mere swords will do nothing to her or her kind."

Renee's gaze swept the room once more. Even in tatters she commanded attention. When she spoke her voice was like an executioners. "I'm not asking you to fight magic; I'm asking you to spread the word. I'm not asking you to oppose Ista; I'm asking you to watch and wait, for when I return I'll return with an army. And when I do, I don't want you to fight openly but covertly. Take as many of the Collective down as you can before we enter the gates."

The queen turned and walked to the door, expecting Marva to follow. Marva did so, thinking of the queen's words. Now they would ride to Ketes, as Ren had first charged them to do, and entreat Bostic to attack.

Before the queen reached the door she spun and surveyed the room with an icy glare.

"And I warn you, if any of you side with Ista, be far, far away from here when I return."

- - -

Aaron studied Manda as he sat before the dwindling fire. She was incredible to him. When he had first touched her he had felt the unbelievable pain and torment she had endured, but he had also felt the unbounded love she held for her brother. Although he had avenged more horrible stories, Manda had felt the most pain.

The amazing thing was the pain she had first felt was none of her own. It was the agony of seeing her brother suffer. Only after she had left to seek help did she give in to her own pain. And that, on top of her worry for Chris, was what sent her into what Aaron called, "The first death." He hadn't seen any survive the first death until Manda.

Aaron turned his gaze to Lazo. The familiarity of the triplet's voice, his soothing words, and his pleadings were the only reason Manda lived. Aaron had witnessed it, but he hadn't thought Manda would wake. The first death was strong. He had held many during their stupor, and each one had died in his arms. Manda's pain was no less, and perhaps more. Yet she lived.

Manda amazed him. After her own anguish she had faced her memories days later. Lazo lived as well, without any sign of the Mar or its effects. In fact Lazo had emerged from the trees with his head held high, clutching Manda's hand in tender affection and daring the Mar to claim him. And Manda had been reborn.

Now Aaron was witnessing the Manda Lazo had whispered of: the fiery eyed, witty, vivacious, winsome girl whose sole purpose in life was making people smile.

Manda and Lazo whirled past him as Fraul bellowed an out-of-tune jig on his hastily carved flute. Manda's laughter sent rivers of happiness down Aaron's spine, but a smile didn't find his lips. He had almost forgotten how to smile. It had been so long since he had felt anything but pain.

Aaron watched Lazo and Manda dance around him, still enthralled by the pair. They had found strength and hope in each other, had cleansed each other's wounds and shared a profound intimacy, yet it was clear they would never join to one. What had happened between them was sacred, Aaron could see it in their eyes, but their friendship was only enhanced, not in any way altered.

Lazo was now as protective of Manda as a mother was of a child. He insisted on helping her with everything, frowned when either Aaron or Fraul unintentionally caused her discomfort, and bit his lip in consternation when she put herself in harm's way. Manda took his doting with stride but laughed at his mannerisms and never missed a chance to tease him about his care.

Despite all her banter, Manda was no less affectionate concerning Lazo, although her caring surfaced in different ways. She hugged Lazo repeatedly, touching his hand every so often in tender affection and fussed over his bedroll when he went to wash, pacing until he was back within her sights. When he did return, although she always teased him for taking too long her eyes sparkled up at him in a way Aaron yearned for someone to look at him. But Manda's look wasn't a romantic look, and Lazo's grin wasn't a romantic grin. The looks they gave each other were deeply affectionate but in no sense carnal. It was almost as if Lazo had superimposed Manda as his twin, and Manda had found someone else to worry about besides her brother.

Aaron still couldn't believe it. He had seen the terror in Manda's eyes before she had followed Lazo into the forest, and he remembered Lazo's tremors beforehand. When Aaron had insinuated Manda's sacrifice was Lazo's only chance he hadn't believed it would be enough.

Yes, Manda was truly the most beautiful creature he had met since Kyra.

Aaron looked into the fire, trying hard to banish Kyra from his thoughts and then feeling remorse for doing so. Kyra was his soul, but she would try to take it, as she had done so many times before. And it would be soon. She had waited longer than she had in years. He wouldn't be surprised if she came in the next breath.

Manda's laughter echoed around him. His lips formed a grin, a real grin, not one of irony or conquest but one of unfettered happiness. Aaron closed his eyes and relished the feeling. Manda's laughter tickled his spine. It was contagious. He found himself chuckling for no other reason beyond the joy of being with her and hearing her obnoxious giggle.

His feelings shocked him. The last time he had felt joy was heartbeats before he had become the Avenger. With Kyra in his arms nothing but joy could be felt, and nothing could ever compare, not even the joy he was feeling now.

For him to be feeling anything but pain was a phenomenon. He was pain. By definition, the Avenger felt so much pain if his pain was given to another, even slowly, that person would die within heartbeats. It was too much for anyone else to bear.

The Avenger had been born through so much love and pain nothing could surpass the intensity of those feelings. So with each avenging, the love and pain of the betrayed just soaked into him, making his love and pain all the more strong; but because his last thoughts were saturated with pain, because those he avenged were experiencing love's pain at its culmination, pain was his dominate element. He had to concentrate on the love to feel it. But when he did . . .

Aaron closed his eyes and blocked out the surrounding sounds. He dove inward and immersed himself in the pool of pain. It was much more than the surface pain he felt. It was complete, seeping into his every pore. He swam down to its icy depths, gritting his teeth, every fiber telling him he wasn't going to make it this time. When he crashed through the bottom of the pool, love engulfed him.

He collapsed in its warmth and tried to calm his rapid heartbeat. The love oscillated over him, pulsed through him, cleansing every pore. As he lay there he felt Kyra, smelled her natural perfume and heard her whispers. He relished his thoughts, clung to them like a lover, knowing they would soon be gone. Kyra was always the first one he felt. Then the others came: the love of all the betrayeds in the order of his avenging. He awaited them, welcomed them, felt the love they held for the betrayer. Finally, Manda's love tore threw him. It was unadulterated, unblemished, and shone like the morning star.

But the love quickly faded, which was why he rarely came to this place. Although he could find love he had to go through pain to reach it and to leave it. He looked above him at the pool of pain. When he reemerged he would remember little of the love. He was the Avenger. Love was second to the pain. The pain was his magic: love's pain, the strongest emotion of all.

The distant flutter of laughter resonated through the pool, giving him the strength he needed to dive through once again. As the cold black sorrow ripped through him he repressed a scream. When he opened his eyes only a trace of the love still held firm. Despair rose inside him. He yearned to feel love again, love without the pain, but that was a tenuous dream. If he ever did feel love again it would fall far short of his love for Kyra, and that alone would cause him to turn away.

Manda and Lazo were still dancing. Manda's giggle rolled through the air like a refreshing breeze. Aaron watched her. Or could he love again? When he heard Manda's laugh his entire body tingled with pleasure. It excited him and frightened him at the same time. He was the Avenger. The Avenger came and went. But then he was supposed to live again, as Aaron, not as the Avenger. That was the very reason Kyra came to him after each avenging.

Aaron fingered the hilt of his sword and frowned. This was his last chance. Magic had been reborn. If he didn't agree to Kyra's demands he would never live again as the Avenger or as Aaron.

He had refused Kyra's request for centuries. Why would this time be different? It wouldn't. He could never do what she asked. How could he?

"Kyra," he whispered, "My beautiful Kyra, how can you ask such a thing of me?"

Aaron heaved a weary sigh as his eyelids sunk. The first thing he saw was Kyra's heart-shaped face. Although Fate had blessed her with beauty, her beauty had taken her away. Kyra's beauty was blinding. Her outer vision was perfection and her inner was a mirror of that perfection, but no one else had been able to see her inner beauty because of the carnality of man.

A loud chortle from Fraul caused Aaron to start. Manda was pulling Fraul to his feet, handing Lazo the flute. Fraul wore a crooked grin. He bowed and kissed Manda's hand. Aaron watched in envy as

Fraul began to dance in a sultry style, causing Manda's laughter to ring through the night once again.

Manda didn't have an external beauty that blinded men like Kyra, but she had a subtleness that snuck up and took your heart just as quickly. It was her spirit, her smile, her laughter and her openness that made her love and give herself freely. Kyra had always been reserved because of her external beauty, but her very presence had lit up the room. Manda had the same effect on people, except it filtered first from her inner self and shone through her external self, brightening her attractive features into something spectacular. When she was present there was just an aura of light, an electric current of elation. Yes, Manda's beauty equaled Kyra's own.

Aaron rested his head in his hands. If there was ever a time he could do as Kyra asked he wished it could be now. He found himself liking Fraul's wit and skepticism, Lazo's intelligence and conversation, and Manda . . .

No. Even if he agreed to give Kyra what she requested he could never love another as much as he loved Kyra. It would be unfair to ask another to love him if he couldn't match that love.

Someone put a hand on the back of his neck. He knew it was Manda because the scent of lilac tickled his nose. She always put lilac in the water before she washed her hair.

He looked up at her. She smiled and held out her hand.

"Come on, goof, don't you hear the music? I'm asking you to dance with me."

Aaron took Manda's hand and slowly rose to his feet, feeling awkward. He hadn't danced in ages, centuries even. He forced his legs to move, and soon he was dancing as he had with Kyra. It was an age-old dance, sure to be out of style. At first Manda was unsure, but soon she treaded around the fire as if she had known it since birth. Her long hair whirled around her, sending out the scent of lilacs. Aaron began to feel lightheaded, not knowing if it was the lilac, the dance, or the exhilaration. But he felt wonderful.

Fraul picked up the pace of the song and Lazo began to clap. Aaron found himself laughing and spinning and twirling and dipping.

When the dissonant song had came to a screeching halt, he turned to see Fraul doubled over in laughter and Lazo snickering at their show. Surprisingly, Aaron could still hear his own deep laugh echoing though the night's air. If felt good to laugh. He hadn't laughed in earnest for a long time.

Manda's slender hand slipped into his own. He looked down into her beautiful green eyes, full of life and energy. Standing on tiptoe, Manda drew his head down and kissed his cheek.

"You're beautiful when you're happy, Aaron. Please open your heart to feel happiness. I assure you, we'll help you find it."

The sincerity in her eyes tugged at his soul. His heart ached to hold her. Despite his fear, he pulled her to him.

Fresh lilac tickled his nose. "You make me beautiful, Manda. You make everything beautiful."

CHAPTER 10

Aaron woke as the air stirred around him. A breathy sigh enveloped him. He closed his eyes, remaining still to drink in the sensation for all he could.

She was forming.

A lump caught in his throat. The love he held burgeoned within him like flint to flame, cleansing his age-old anguish, purifying his soul and once again stealing his heart.

The air filled with tingling effervescence – with her – his Kyra. Aaron smiled, unable to be saddened by his ultimate end or her final goodbye, because for a few heartbeats he would once again be with the most glorious thing in all the Lands.

The air around him formed hands and wrapped him in a celestial embrace, touching his face, his hair, his hands, and finally pulling him to his feet.

Aaron relished the anticipation before he turned to face the glowing figure silhouetted beneath the light of the twin moons. Even in shadow his Kyra was glorious. Long, wavy hair careened down her sides and sparks of power twirled around her frame.

As he approached, her face became clear. He drew in a breath, surprised he had once again been unable to remember her beauty. It was as if he couldn't comprehend her radiance and disregarded his memories as surreal. He knew part of his reflection was how Kyra had been in life, and now she was far more glorious. At first it had saddened him, but after a time he had decided it was only appropriate: he avenging their love by avenging others, forcing people to fear him and their actions; her sustaining their love by gracing all with wonder, filling people with reverence and splendor.

Kyra was far too magnificent to love only him. He had always known that. Although their love had been unprecedented, he knew the day would come when she would be taken in some form or fashion. That wasn't to say he ever thought she would love another over him. It was to say he knew the Maker had some greater purpose for her. He just hadn't realized the extent of those plans.

He trembled with love when he reached her. For a time all he could do was look into her eyes, but when his tremors escalated he bowed to one knee, hung his head, and whispered the words he had uttered for centuries.

"Kyra, my heart and my soul, my love and my pain, my future and my past, I give to you all that I have and all that I am. But I beg you, don't ask me to release you. If I do I'm no more, we're no more, and you'll be nothing to me but a name in the stars."

"I must ask it, Aaron." The air quivered with a song that hadn't yet been sung. "Give me your emotions. Give me your pain and your love. I beseech you. The time is at hand."

After all the times she had asked, a dagger still tore his chest at her words.

He looked up into her solid silver eyes, full of power and love, and choked on his next words. "Kyra, if I grant your request I'll never see you again. I would live a life without remembering our love, without remembering you. How could you ask me to do such a thing? Have you forgotten our love?"

When her face twisted in anguish he quickly regretted his words, but they were the truth. This time he didn't want her to leave him without knowing why he chose to refuse.

"If I die so be it. At least I'll die with you as part of me. What you ask of me is living an eternity without you, an eternity, Kyra."

A lone, silver tear trickled down her cheek. Aaron reached up and gently wiped it away. When his fingers touched her, her power coursed through him with frightening speed.

"I have never, nor will I ever forget our love," she said, turning her heart-shaped face from him, staring at memories he could almost feel, memories she wanted him to betray.

"But that's what you ask of me."

"I know," she said quietly. "And I know how hard it must be for you, but you must, my love, or all will be betrayed."

Aaron blinked. It was the first time she had ever referred to the song sung about him. "How can the Avenger betray all? I fight betrayal. I take on its pain. I am its pain."

"Oh, Aaron, my love." She knelt, taking his face in her hands. "I can't . . . " Her silver eyes filled with tears. "You just must."

The way she held his face brought back sacred memories. She had always taken his face when he came home, tantalizing him before she allowed him a kiss. Before she died she had done the same thing, but with her touch she had charged him to avenge their love.

With the touch of her hands her power seeped through him, but it couldn't distill his past horror: Kyra being skinned before his eyes, Kyra being raped and beaten, and he unable to reach her.

She was the Quy now, not his Kyra Goodenspy. Their love had made the power possible. Their love had made him the Avenger.

94

"Oh Kyra, my Kyra, stop being the Quy."

Her eyes saddened. "I can't, Aaron. The world needs me. I am what that Maker wants me to be. I am no more or no less, but I am more powerful because of your love."

"And if I give it away?"

"Then I'll still be as I am. I'll still know."

"But I won't."

Her brow furrowed. "No."

Aaron sighed and leaned into her, wrapping his arms around her, shuddering as her current surged through him. "I'm not that strong, my love."

"You can love another," the Quy said softly.

"No."

Kyra turned and looked toward camp. Aaron's chest constricted. She would use his friends to make her point, so this time he wouldn't fail.

"She's beautiful, Aaron. Let her help you."

"Please, Kyra, don't."

She ran her delicate hands through his hair. He felt his tears falling, sizzling off her body like steam. He didn't want to give up his pain, his love. That was all he knew, that was all he was. Who would he be without them? Who would he be without Kyra?

"I would be empty, Kyra. Your love is all that helps the pain. All I know is pain. Where would I be without either?"

"You would be a man. You would live again. That's your reward for bearing the pain all these years. You would be free."

"Free without you."

"You'll always have me, my love."

"But I won't remember."

"No." Her voice was sad, mournful. "There's a girl over there who needs you. Although she's strong, without you she won't be. If you don't give me what I ask you'll die, and it will shatter both her heart and her spirit. Unlike you, she can't take any more pain."

Aaron slowly raised his head and turned toward camp. Manda and Fraul were watching. Manda blushed and turned away. Aaron's heart split in two. Kyra was right. If he didn't do as she asked he would die and he would be unable to help Manda save her brother. Could he do that to Manda?

But could he release his love for Kyra?

- - -

Fraul woke with a start, sensing something. The air wasn't right. It was too . . . shimmery.

Leaping from his bedroll, he landed on his feet, but before his hand he could reach his sword his eyes locked on the two figures in the distance. He froze, mouth agape, and immediately knew Aaron Goodenspy and Ari Goodspeed were one in the same man.

The fact Fraul had been right in his query didn't send him any pleasure.

"Holy Maker of fates," he whispered. He felt like an intruder, but he couldn't look away. His legs moved on their own accord. He stepped toward the woman who seemed to be wearing a gown of stars. She bent toward Aaron and took his face in her hands.

The pain etched on Aaron's features was far greater than any Fraul had ever seen. He had already seen anguish enough to move mountains in Aaron's eyes. What Aaron was now feeling would have killed another in a heartbeat.

Then he remembered Aaron's words.

"I can't betray the one I love."

Whatever Aaron had to do to live again was happening. Fraul's breath caught as he closed his eyes. He had grown fond of Aaron and held hopes he could help the Avenger overcome what he had to overcome, but this was something far out of Fraul's reach.

Aaron and Kyra, pain and love, bound together by past love and created out of pain. There was nothing anyone could do to help Aaron. No one aware of his story would ask Aaron to betray her. Why she was asking was beyond Fraul's grasp.

Manda stepped beside him, eyes wide with wonder. Fraul put his arm around her shoulders. They watched in silence as Aaron shook his head. The Quy lost her smile and saddened. The air shivered. She turned their way.

Fraul's heart hammered, but not because they had been discovered. It was Kyra's eyes. They seemed to enwrap him with love, draw out his fears and leave a purified soul. Manda drew a sharp breath beside him. She felt it too: the love of the Quy for the Maker's children.

Aaron turned their direction. His pain amplified even further and his face twisted with worry. His eyes locked on Manda. She released a whimper and turned away.

Fraul stood, dumbfounded. The Quy was using Manda to convince Aaron to yield his love and pain. Manda knew it too. Fraul opened his mouth to try to say something comforting but nothing would come. Then, in stark amazement, he watched Aaron nod in acceptance.

The air around them stirred, moving with frenetic ardor. Aaron collapsed on the ground as Kyra released him and stepped away.

"No," Manda whispered.

Fraul didn't know what to do. Aaron was giving up his love for them. Blessed Fates! He had helped the Avenger betray his love. It tore Fraul's heart.

The Quy raised her arms. Her lips parted and she began to chant. At first her voice was so high Fraul mistook it for the wind whistling through the treetops, bending and swaying until it whirled to the heavens. But as he listened, he heard her words:

> Black as night the hate it thrives
> Cold as hollow bones
> Take my love's hate from him
> And form the fated stone
>
> White as light the love it grows
> Fervid as molten flame
> Take my child's love from him
> And mold the choosing stone
>
> Clear as glass the pain it lives
> Cutting as the blade
> Take my guard's pain from him
> And cast the chancing stone.

As her voice ebbed and flowed her silver light began to intensify, lighting the woodlands like noonday. When the verse was through she bent her head to Aaron's still form.

"Aaron, draw you sword and take my hand."

Aaron did as the Quy asked. The Quy's silver glow surged into Aaron. His jaw tightened; his chest heaved; he began to shake and tremble. He threw his head back and screamed.

Fraul stumbled backwards. The air oscillated over him, crashing with madness and sorrow and passion. The emotions tore through him, sending him sprawling over the crackling remains of the fire. Ash and debris whirled around him. Aaron's sword began to glow, but not with a white light. It glowed with a darkness so profound it seemed to swallow the night.

Still Aaron's scream continued. It was harrowing. Fraul thought his own heart would rip from him. He covered his ears but he couldn't force the pain to dissipate. He wanted to reach Aaron, help him, but he couldn't move.

Only one thought dominated his mind: Aaron was pain, he had lived with pain for centuries, but whatever he was feeling must be pulling the skin from his bones for no one could survive what was driving that scream.

- - -

Aaron was reliving every betrayal he had ever known, but not one at a time. All of the emotions came together and mingled into one. Hate thrived, pulsed and howled: anger at the countless betrayals, anger he could only do so much. The love grew, soared and shouted: the betrayed's first comfort from the betrayer, the betrayed's love held for the deceiver. But the pain, fates on fates, the pain! It wasn't only the betrayeds' pain, it was also the first, intense, shocking realization of the betrayer's identity. The pain not only lived, it thrived. It not only breathed, it grew. It not only cried, it screamed.

The pain, love, and anger were always with him, but tears always washed the anger away, love always concealed the dark clouds of anguish, the pain was never the pain of the first realization, and it never, never grew.

He collapsed on the ground. He thought his heart was going to rip open. He thought surely he would die. Then his brother's betrayal rose above the others with tortuous speed. His brother crashing down the door, beating him to the point of death, chaining him to the ground; his brother raping Kyra, passing her to his men, laughing at his inability to reach her; his brother skinning Kyra before his eyes, lips sneering in victory; his brother coming at him with a knife as Kyra's broken body fell to the floor; Kyra, blue eyes still shining with life, slowly turning silver; the silver light blinding him, breaking his chains, killing his brother, resonating through the world with thunder; Aaron crawling to her, holding her as she cupped his face and whispered what she would have him do:

"Aaron, you must be our Avenger. You must be . . . "

A silver light engulfed him, and for the second time Kyra died in his arms.

Then there was nothing. Thoughts he had held only heartbeats before were gone. He knew they existed. He remembered feeling . . .

something. He searched for them, knowing he had lost something precious.

There was nothing but emptiness. Who was he? The answer didn't come. He groped for any memory. He scraped his chest, trying to uncover what he had lost.

The emptiness overpowered him. He tried to regain his last memory. Why was he on his hands and knees? Why did he feel so alone? But he couldn't.

He felt a movement and raised his head. Silver eyes stared down at him, flickering with emotions he couldn't feel. But the woman was beautiful, far more beautiful than any memory could be.

She reached out and touched his cheek. Memories crashed into him, filling his marrow with feeling. Aaron steadied himself with his hands and gazed into her silver eyes, desperate to hold on to consciousness.

"Kyra?"

A silent silver tear slid down her cheek. He brushed it away.

"Did you think our love could ever be crushed, Aaron, even by magic? You needed to give everything you had. That's why I've told you for centuries you wouldn't remember. But nothing could break our bond, my love, not even draining you of all feeling." Kyra ran her hands through his hair. He felt her power tickling over his new soul free of the pain of others, free of the anger of betrayal, and free of love's anguished cry.

A flicker of images still lingered, but they were a story, not actuality. The reflections were lore, not truth. Yes, he remembered, but no, the memories weren't his own. He drew in a breath, buried his head in the flat of Kyra's stomach, and wept. She stroked his hair, letting him feel the relief he could have had years ago.

"Why did I need to do this?"

"The world needs your feelings, Aaron." Kyra opened her palm, revealing two flawless, polished stones, one white as snow and the other clear as light.

"All our love and all your betrayeds' love is in the white stone. All our pain and all your betrayeds' pain is in the clear stone. All your righteous hate is in your blade."

Aaron looked at his sword. The silver blade had turned deathly black. It was so black at first he thought the blade was gone.

"You have little hate, my love. Our tragedy happened too fast and then we died. You had no time for hate. You were too busy feeling pain. The betrayeds you avenge are the same. They haven't gone past the pain to feel anger. The anger you do feel is your own anger at the betrayer, your own righteous hate. It isn't strong enough to form the stone. You must find the man who can help you form the stone.

"When you saw me you remembered our love, as I knew you would. Nothing can break true love away from your soul. It's in you," Kyra said, putting her hand over his heart. "Nothing can ever shatter it. But your pain is gone, as it should be, so you can live again."

"I don't want to live without you," Aaron said. Although his role as the Avenger was now complete, his love for her was growing again, faster than he would have liked it to.

"Yes, you do. You're a man, and now you can live freely, without bounds. I'm the Quy. I love you but can never love you. I'm not human. I'm the power. That's how I was able to hold on. That's how the Maker granted us life.

"I remember our love, but only with idyllic charm. I don't want it back. I don't know how to want it. I love you, but I love everyone. I'm the Quy. You're a man. I want you to live again, breathe again. I want you to find someone who can love you without bringing you pain."

Aaron touched her hair, feeling its silky weightlessness, knowing she spoke the truth. She was the power, not his Kyra. The happiness he had felt only breaths ago dissipated. She didn't love him as a man. She loved him as a child. "You didn't bring me pain, Kyra. Others brought me pain."

"I did bring you pain," she said. "I unintentionally hurt everyone I touched. Women met me and it pained them. Men met me and it pained them. Only you weren't harmed, for I loved you. But my love brought you pain. I want no more pain to come to you. I want to be inside your mind and feel your joy of living. For in that I'm with you, as I'm with everyone with the power.

"I love even the dark ones, Aaron, because they love me. I just am. But if I can be in your mind like this . . . "

She cradled his face in her hands, shut her silver eyes and tilted her head back, exposing her long, slender neck. Aaron's heart twisted, remembering his Kyra in life, but as quickly as the feeling came it was taken by a sudden jolt in his mind. He felt the power of the Avenger being born in a new way. He shivered, not from uneasiness but from feeling her within him.

A small smile reached his lips. He touched the thread and felt her, his Kyra, existing inside him.

Although he felt her he knew it would never be the same. His smile withered. She remembered their love with blissfulness. He remembered it with longing and need. It hurt, but as he looked at her his spirits rose. The Quy, pure beauty, had once been his bride, not out of necessity but out of love. That love had been the catalyst to birth the power."

"Take these," she said, placing the stones in his hand. "You can strengthen them even further. They're replete with love and pain, but they aren't saturated. You can make them stronger when you form the fated stone. Your sword is the catalyst that can accomplish that end. It has turned black. Your purpose is to go and use it. Find the other defender who can form the stone. Once the stone is formed, its magic will draw you to the one with need. Then you can save me from the darkness."

Aaron's mind reeled. Strengthen the stones? Find the other? Save her from the darkness?

As he opened his mouth to speak, Kyra began to fade from vision. "But how will I know?"

"You will know, my love," she said, brushing her lips against his. "You will know."

Aaron watched her fade, desperate to stop her, but paralyzed by her kiss. It shivered through him like the morning mist, brushing each nerve with tantalizing sensuality.

Only when the last silver fleck had disappeared from the air did he open his palm to study the stones. They were perfectly formed, blinding in their brilliance. As he held his former feelings in his palm he sensed their power and wondered how he had been able to survive with those emotions inside, and how they could become any more saturated. He felt the power in his sword as well. Where would he find a man with righteous hate, a man who could form the stone?

He placed the stones in his belt pouch, thanking the Maker he wouldn't be the one to bear the burden of wielding them when they were complete. Whoever it was had to be far stronger than anything the Lands had ever seen.

CHAPTER 11

Ren woke with a start, the dream slowly fading from vision. His heart banged hard against his chest. The darkness had been reaching out to claim him. He had fought it, slashing the air as the black cloud came closer, but his resistance only made the cloud stronger, and when the black mist touched him the fingers of hate and greed wrapped around his spirit. He tried to pull back, but the darkness was too strong. Slowly, he had started to change.

He reached up and touched his face, ensuring himself the dream wasn't reality. It had felt like a thousand maggots were sluicing underneath his skin, but it had been his own face bubbling, forming into something else. Ren tried to calm his rapid breath as he recalled the painting of Barracus in the Oracle. He shivered on the cold ground. He would do anything to repudiate that horror.

A twig snapped. The kota came awake and sniffed the air with rabid intensity. Ren tensed, fearful the Adderiss had returned, but he heard no further movement, only a deepening silence.

Ren tried to see through the darkness, but the twin moons had vanished behind the clouds. He could only see past the first shadows of the surrounding trees. He tried to hear something to give him an indication as to where the threat would come, but all he sensed were hard eyes peering through the trees.

Blood pounded in his temples. He was tired of surprises and tired of death. At the thought of Bentzen and Markum something ignited within him. Enough was enough.

Ren jumped to his feet and drew his sword. The dragon's eyes glowed with his rage: one pair white, the other dark: two sides of the spectrum; two beings he could become. *Which will it be, Chosen?*

He ignored the voice and culminated the anger inside him. The black eyes pulsated with power. Ren made two arcs in the air and settled into an attack stance.

"Show yourself!" he demanded to the night.

The camp immediately came alive. He heard the soft release of swords. The tip of Neki's curved blade entered his peripheral vision, glimmering in the light of the twin moons. The ruby glowed with brilliant intent: luck in battle. But the emerald, the stone to ward off evil doings, was torpid.

Although the torpid stone should have brought Ren comfort, it did not. The hairs on his head stood on end. For precious heartbeats only the sound of crickets greeted them. Ren studied the trees directly in front of him, sensing something. Ren gripped his sword tighter.

Three men appeared out of the depths of the forest. They were robed in gray cowls, long hoods shielding their faces from vision. They held their hands below their chins. Only the tips of their fingers touched, leaving a chasm exposed to the air, symbolizing an unanswered prayer.

Ren stood in silence as the three Druids released their unanswered prayer and lowered their hoods. Three pairs of eyes focused on Ren: one set dark, one set light, the other a murky brown. In the Druid fashion their heads were shaved except for one long strand of ebony hair starting at the top of their skulls and descending to the base of their necks. Their skin was dark, almost almond in color, and blended into the night. Once unveiled, their hands returned to their unanswered prayer position.

The dark-eyed leader stepped forward. He wore a thin mustache, signifying his importance. Only those high in the Druid ranks were allowed to sprout any hair beside their jet-black tufts.

He was tall, almost three hand spans taller than the others, and well built, with kind, intelligent eyes. Ren had only seen a few Druids in his life, but he had seen enough to know the dark-eyed Druid was an exception of his kind. Druids were slight men with fragile bones and less masculine features.

The other two Druids fit Ren's remembrance: small men with hard eyes. The one with the murky brown gaze reminded Ren of a petty thief he had once caught in the castle. There was no love in those eyes, only greed and envy. The third had no distinct features. If Ren hadn't been looking at him he might have gone unnoticed.

Ren's eyes flickered back to the leader.

The leader gave a small nod of greeting. "You're the Chosen." His voice was so deep it almost shook Ren's bones. "You must come with us. The One is waiting for you at the Obelisk."

Ren blinked in shock. The Obelisk, the temple of the Druids, resided on the Druid island of Dresden. Ren stared into the leader's eyes. They held no malice, no deception, only a profound desire to help. But why would the One be with Druids? Animosity between wizards and Druids had been waging for centuries. The Druids would shut the One from the power faster than dragons could spew fire.

Galvin stepped past Ren, casually resting his broadsword on one shoulder. "Ren isn't going anywhere." Although Galvin looked nonchalant he gripped the sword so hard his knuckles were white.

"You don't have the One any more than I have the One. Be on your way."

Ren put a hand on Galvin's shoulder, indicating for him to hold his position. The Druids remained impassive. Their eyes never veered from Ren.

"Why would a wizard be with Druids?" Ren asked.

"Safety for him and safety for you. I believe you're hunted, yes?" the leader asked, raising one eyebrow. "The Obelisk is the only place no one will search. It's the only place your enemy won't go."

The leader's voice resonated in a droning timbre. Ren had to concentrate to understand where one word ended and the other began. Druids were known to be sedate, their meditations running together even in waking movement, but the leader seemed more tranquil than most.

"Why should I believe you? What proof do you have?"

The small, greedy-looking one scowled. "Aren't we proof enough, Chosen? A Druid hasn't been out of the Obelisk in years."

The leader released his "prayer" and held one hand in the air, demanding silence. His dark eyes turned to Ren. "Forgive Avalon. He is too defensive of our line." He paused. "We have no proof to give. The proof is inside you."

Galvin shifted with impatient energy. His silver teardrop danced with fury. The three Druids didn't even bat an eye in his direction.

Neki raised an eyebrow. "If you have the One why didn't he come with you?"

Avalon was about to say something but decided against it. The leader's eyes flickered to Neki and studied him in silence. He glanced at Neki's sword, eyes betraying slight emotion, but when he looked back at Ren the Druid once again wore a calm mask.

"The One is the One, meaning he's the only one. If he were killed where would that leave the Chosen? The One is safe in the Obelisk. He needs you to come to him. That's the only way."

Although what the leader said made sense, Ren's gut told him something was amiss. He had learned to trust his instincts long ago. But it would be next to impossible for the Druids to know about the One unless he was actually there.

"What will the One do?"

The animosity in Galvin's voice surprised Ren. He turned to look at his friend. Galvin stood as if the forces of the Abyss were trying to claim him.

The leader's gaze lingered on Galvin. "Insist the Chosen go behind the door."

"Morrus!" Avalon exclaimed.

Morrus held up his hand for silence. "I won't lie to him, Avalon. What he has to do is for the Lands. I have faith the Chosen knows this and will come in spite of what this could mean to him as an individual."

Ren looked between Avalon and Morrus. Go behind the door? He was the Chosen. If he went behind the door it would solve nothing. He would be unable to recall friends, relatives or entire years of his life. He may be unable to remember his own name. He had to destroy the darkness. How could he destroy the darkness without the Quy's power?

Then he heard Fate's voice echoing in his mind.

"You must destroy your soul."

And with a surety he couldn't describe, he knew.

Fate had ordered him to go behind the door.

The haunted eyes of the portrait in the Oracle seemed to loom in the air, staring into his heart. Those were the eyes he would have, eyes of a man without memories.

Neki stepped forward, brandishing his sword with frightful enthusiasm. "The Maker curse it, do you think we've lost our minds! If Ren goes behind the door he'll be unable to defeat what he needs to defeat. All three of you are mad! Burning cinders, Ren, tell them no!"

The leader's eyes remained on Ren throughout Neki's remonstration. "It's either go behind the door or become Barracus."

Ren thought of the other portrait, the one with half of Barracus' body as his own. He hesitated, confused as to how the portrait could become reality. His breath caught – the Red Eye.

Morrus stepped forward. "The Red Eye can pass spirits through to this realm. Spirits who had the Quy in life need a vessel with the Quy in order to use their power. The vessel in which they pass determines the strength of their power. If the vessel is weaker than the spirit the spirit will be hindered, unable to use its power to the fullest. If the vessel is stronger the spirit can thrive. The darkness the Chosen has to defeat is a force only he can bring. The only way to stop the darkness, the threat of Barracus entering his body, is to go behind the door. If Barracus enters through another he'll be defeated. If he enters the Chosen the threat will be too great to be crushed."

Ren remembered his dream: the darkness forcing him out, the fingers squeezing his soul and the terror as his skin bubbled into a horrible monstrosity.

When Galvin read the truth in Ren's eyes he gripped Ren's arm so tightly Ren thought his bone might shatter. "Ren, you must not. I don't care what the Oracle told you. This isn't the way."

"It is, Galvin. I've been having dreams of becoming Barracus."

Galvin's eyes filled with desperation, but before he could speak the Druid leader stepped closer.

"You don't want to become the darkness."

The dream flashed through Ren's mind again: the terror, the bubbling flesh, and the grip of fingers on his soul. No, he didn't want to become the darkness.

"I won't remember my life, will I?"

"I'm sorry, you may not. You may remain somewhat whole, but you will lose some of your memories. There's no way to be sure until the door is shut."

Ren saw the Druid's lie. Morrus was trying to spare him. Most remembered very little of their past. The implications suddenly crashed down on him. He may not even remember Aidan.

"Ren," Neki said, an edge to his voice. "Let them go. We can discuss this in private."

Morrus shook his head. "There's no time."

Galvin's hand tightened on the broadsword. "We demand the time!"

Before any of them could blink the broadsword was in the Druid leader's outstretched hand. The force of its impact caused Morrus' tuft of black hair to sway in the moonlight.

Morrus' dark eyes pierced Ren's own. The forest was bathed in a sheet of silence.

Although the leader displayed no aggression there was a violent conviction in his eyes. He would take Ren by force if necessary.

"Violence is unnecessary. I choose to go freely."

Neki shook his head. "Ren!"

"Trust me," Ren said, "this is the only way."

Galvin turned from him. Ren wanted to say something but there was nothing to say, no words of comfort to be given. In a way he was agreeing to his own death. He couldn't blame Galvin for being angry.

Ren turned back to Morrus. "But I go on one condition."

The leader tilted his head, causing his thin length of ebony hair to shift to one side. "What's that?"

"I speak to the One before you attempt my closing. I have something I must request of him."

The power of Ren's tone caused the leader to blink in surprise. "I can't assure you the One will grant your request, but you'll see the One before the closing."

For some reason Ren found himself inherently trusting Morrus. "Thank you."

"We leave now," Morrus said, beginning to turn.

"We go where he goes," Galvin said, jaw clenching in determination.

Avalon turned. "No, you cannot."

When Galvin faced Avalon, his look was death. "Try to stop me."

Morrus stepped between them. He handed the broadsword to Galvin and put his hands back into the unanswered prayer pose. Ren noticed he put them closer this time. He wondered if closing his door was Morrus' current prayer.

"I regret you cannot," Morrus said, his tone kind, even apologetic. "Our horses have been blessed by the One and can ride much faster than your own. Your horses will never be able to keep the pace. They can try, but they will fail."

The three Druids turned and walked back the way they had come, expecting Ren to follow. The kota whined beside him. Ren reached over and scratched the tender place under her horn. She leaned her head against him and began to purr. He felt a stab of sorrow. She would try to follow. It would pain her a great deal when she was unable to keep up. He wondered if he would ever see her again, or remember her.

"Stay with Galvin, Keena," he whispered. The kota breathed a sigh as if she understood but pressed against him with more force. Ren turned and looked into the faces of his friends. Galvin's eyes were sunken and there was a look of lunacy about him. Ren almost asked why he was so anxious but then decided against it. If he knew Galvin's reason it might shatter his own resolve.

"It's the only way, Galvin. Believe me. It's the only choice I have."

Neki shifted, looking uncomfortable. "Burning cinders, Ren. Did the Oracle tell you to do this?"

Ren glanced to where the Druids had gone. "In a way."

"In a way!" Neki said. "Ren, please reconsider. This is foolhardy at best."

The third Druid came through the trees, leading Ren's mount. "It's time."

Ren nodded and bent to grab his pack. When he had tied it to his new mount's saddle he absently patted the mare's neck, whispering greetings, and mounted with a heavy heart.

"We'll follow when we can and wait for you at Port Vy," Neki said, indicating the port city close to the island of Dresden.

Ren nodded, unable to look at his friends. He may not remember them after the closing. He knew he should say something but couldn't find the words.

Then Galvin was beside him, clasping his hand. Ren felt something cold slip into his palm. Before Ren could see what it was, Galvin shook his head. It was a slight movement, but it was enough. Ren nodded, keeping his fist closed. For some reason Galvin didn't want the Druids to discover his gift. The Druid stopped his horse and turned to watch.

Galvin's dark brown eyes peered into Ren's with unmistakable desperation. "Believe in yourself. Remember this," Galvin said, eyes flickering to Ren's closed fist.

"May the Fates be with you, Galvin," Ren said. "If I'm able to retain some of my memories I pray to the Maker you're among them."

CHAPTER 12

"Please, don't stop." Chris hugged the dark haired woman tighter. They had been riding all day and she had been giving him feelings he both longed for and abhorred, but it hurt to be without them. She shifted in the saddle and leaned back. Her dark eyes drew him closer.

"Kiss me."

He hesitated, wanting to resist, but when her eyes heated he remembered the pain and leaned into her. Her lips were soft, sensual. Confusion seeped inside him. Why hadn't he wanted to kiss her? The question quickly dissipated as she sent him a tingling pleasure. His body shook with need, but she only allowed the pleasure to pulse within him, keeping it high enough for him to tremble but low enough for him to be coherent. It was maddening.

"Do you remember what you must do?"

He let her question hang in the air. He had already said yes multiple times but tried to rationalize answering anyway. He felt a doubt form within him and was about to dispute her question when a sharp stabbing pain ripped through him. Why shouldn't he answer? He didn't want to die. There was still something he must do.

"I remember," he slurred as a wave of pleasure engulfed him. When the feelings subsided into a small pulse he opened his eyes and squinted into the sun.

"Who are you, my love?"

"Whoever you want me to be."

She laughed and reached back to stroke his cheek. He shivered, unsure if her touch was something he enjoyed.

"I'll give you more intense emotions for the rest of your days if you say your name is Chris Kahn."

He couldn't imagine emotions more intense than those she had already given him. He didn't know if he wanted anything more intense. But if he didn't agree the pain would come. He knew if the pain came it would be too much. He could be Chris Kahn, the name did sound familiar.

"I'm Chris Kahn."

She chuckled and turned away. Chris looked to the horizon. They were approaching a castle. A pang of familiarity surfaced, but as soon as it did the pleasure intensified.

"Do you love me?"

His brows creased. Love? No, he didn't love her.

A sharp pain pierced him, and he smiled, thinking it was the pleasure, but then the convulsions began. No, he didn't love her. He hated her, but not for the pain. He hated her for something he couldn't recall. The pain just always reminded him the something else existed.

"You hesitate, my love. If you want me to bring you pleasure you need to tell me you love me."

He gathered his courage to tell her to go to the Abyss with her pleasure when she sent it inside him again, intense this time. It was too strong. He heard himself murmur his love, praying she would release her hold.

The surges subsided. He opened his eyes. The castle rose before them. The lady was holding his hand and talking to a man in a green uniform. When his eyes met the man's a look of shock stole over the man's features. Then there was shouting. It was loud. He wanted to cover his ears but he didn't want the people to think him rude.

People swarmed around them with tears streaming down their faces. Trumpets blared. He smiled, unsure of what to do. Some screamed and fell to their knees, thanking the Maker for keeping their prince out of harm's way. The lady raised his hand above her. The crowd went wild. He smiled until his jaws ached.

When they stopped at the gates of the castle a man in a green uniform, trimmed in a brilliant gold, clasped his hand. Tears glistened in his eyes. "It's good to see you, my prince. I'm sorry about . . . " He paused and turned away. "We all loved her. I have some other news, I'm afraid. I fear to tell you with your health deteriorating but I pray I must. Your father has been murdered. You're the king of Newlan, my lord. We must send word to Zier as soon as possible."

The lady stiffened beside him, but he barely noticed. The slow pulse inside him wasn't enough. He began to shake. The man in the green uniform's brow creased in worry.

"Help him down, captain. He just needs rest."

The lady turned to him. The pleasure increased but her eyes could shatter stone.

He understood.

As he leaned against her he spewed the words she wanted him to speak. He would have died without her. She had nurtured him for days. Although he knew he wouldn't recover, he wanted to marry her. The people needed to have hope. He wanted to give them an heir. The man started crying as he helped him up the steps.

The man yelled for a priest. People scurried around him, bowing as they went. He wondered why they were bowing. Something tickled his mind, but then it left.

A uniformed man led them up the stairs. He was so tired. Soon the man in the green uniform with the gold trimming picked him up and carried him through a bedroom and out to a balcony.

The man sat him down but remained beside him, supporting him. The warm breeze felt nice. He turned to look over the balcony. Hordes of people were crying, smiling, cheering up at him. Many waved, calling the name the woman had told him to don. He waved back, perplexed at their fervor. The people cheered.

He knew his mind was failing. He reached for the ebony stone. It soothed him. A man cowled in a black cloak hurried to him and bowed. The man raised a black book and began to read. The woman smiled and clasped his hands. He shuddered, but the pleasure surged higher, overcoming his revulsion.

She mouthed a vow of love. He remembered to agree with her and did so. The man with the gold-trimmed uniform chuckled and told him to repeat what the priest had said. When he did the pleasure rose higher, but he didn't want it. He tried to tell her with his eyes it was too much, but she merely reached up to take his face. He watched with mild interest as their lips met.

The man with the gold braids lifted him and took him to the bed as the pleasure dissipated. The bed felt wonderful. He sank into it and sighed. He was so tired. All he wanted to do was rest. He waited, expecting the lifesaving pulse to come. It did not.

There were no feelings at all.

There was nothing, only darkness with a thread of light dangling at its center. He tried to reach the thread but he was too tired to move. He lay directly under it, watching as it swayed in the darkness.

The man in the gold-trimmed uniform ran out the door, yelling for a healer.

The woman smiled at him and patted her stomach. "Thank you, my sweet. You've done your duty. Now that you have an heir on the way I can rule in your stead."

Her words evaded him. He reached for the stone when he felt himself shake with need.

A wave of men ran into the room. Some had green uniforms. Others were dressed in gray robes, their only adornment being a silver chain with a silver leaf pendant. The lady began to cry. She held his hand. He didn't want her to hold his hand. Her touch was repugnant. All he wanted was an emotion, any emotion.

The gray men swarmed around him. She backed away. He didn't like the look on her face.

A painting caught his eye. It was a portrait of a young girl with red hair. She smiled in amusement at the artist.

He stopped moving. His breath seemed to come from a vacuum.

The black stone burned in his palm. He closed his fingers around it. With the force of the ten winds the images pelted him: Manda being raped and beaten, Evann falling to the ground in death, Alezza laughing, Manda screaming, Bort grunting, soldiers snickering, his father sneering, his father betraying, his pain, Manda's pain, the rage of humiliation, the rage of his helplessness, the rage at being unable to reach Manda, and his loathing of those causing the pain.

When he released the scream inside no one heard. As spasms shook his body he focused all his remaining energy and jumped, barely grasping the thread that swung in the darkness. He felt his mind begin to tear and quickly forced his memories back inside the stone. He held his mind together by clutching the thread. It sent power inside him, purifying his soul.

When all his memories had left him he just swayed in the darkness, holding on to life.

"I don't know if there's anything we can do," a soft voice said. "I can't find anything physically wrong with him."

"He's heartsick, captain. He and Manda were close," another said.

"I'm surprised he's lasted this long," the first voice said. "It appears he wanted to come home."

As he swayed in the darkness he wondered why he held on. Why would he cling to something when he was nothing, saw nothing, was in nothing? He was about to let go when rage coursed through him. It was something. It was an emotion. He felt rage.

He better hold on.

Sooner or later someone would come. Someone would find him.

The stone burned in his palm.

- - -

Renee watched Bostic's approaching army with open admiration. It appeared as if Bostic had recruited every male citizen in Ketes. His army was the sea hurling toward them.

Last night, when she had spotted the approaching hoard, she and Marva had stopped and made camp. There was no sense riding toward

Bostic just to ride back again. Bostic was marching toward Zier. Somehow he had discovered Valor's treachery.

Bostic's massive form dominated the front lines. He lifted his hand, motioning his soldiers to halt. The animosity in his gaze saddened Renee. Her cousin had always been quick to smile. Ista had taken that smile from him. Renee didn't know if he would ever find it again.

Bostic perused Renee's tattered clothing and bruised face. Dust and grime lingered around his eyes, but instead of making him appear disheveled, it only emphasized his rage. His lips curled into a frown.

"I'm fine, Bostic," Renee said before the king could speak. "I know about Sass."

Bostic closed his eyes and nodded. When he looked back at Renee, the rage had intensified. "I'm incapable of losing."

Renee smiled. "So am I."

"Ramie's meeting me at the base of the Sierra's. I'm sorry I can't offer you a proper greeting, but I can't be late."

Instead of replying Renee mounted her horse. Marva did the same. Bostic clicked the reins and started forward. Renee flanked him and took his hand, trying to offer what little comfort she could.

- - -

They had ridden into Crape that morning, passing small villages and keeps along the way.

It had taken some time to find Alezza's trail. Although Manda had found Alezza's camp easily, when they arrived it was deserted and a recent rain had erased all tracks. After days of searching Fraul had spotted fresh hoof prints. They led directly to Crape.

Aaron insisted they stop at an inn to wash before they rode into town. Manda had agreed, but reluctantly. She knew she needed to ride to the Crest Castle looking like an heir and not a battered, worn girl, but it still flustered her. She wanted to take her brother from Alezza's grip yesterday.

But Manda had to admit the warm bath was a much needed and a much welcomed luxury. It did wonders to her remaining bruises and boosted her energy. She tried to think of the last time she had taken a real bath but finally gave up. The rocky streams and chill pools of the countryside were forever ingrained in her memory.

When she finally conceded to leave the bath and pad naked to the dressing room she was surprised to find a new outfit laid out for her. It was a deep, forest green, so deep it was almost black. The pants fit tightly had a slight flair to the hips, creating a look of femininity despite the mannish style. The cream smock was well fitted but still movable and, praise the Fates, didn't have any billowing lace around the collar or wrists. A cape completed the outfit. It had slits for her arms and was adorned with glittery cream beads that tapered into a stitched vine pattern across the chest. The outfit was simple enough to be tasteful but the cape was ornate enough to give her an aura of regality when she entered the gates of the castle.

Manda glanced in the mirror, giving the outfit her final approval. The tight cloth with the hip flair gave her more shape than she had in actuality. Unfortunately her new shape was concealed underneath the cape. She scowled, releasing the capes heavy folds, but quickly brightened when she saw the effect the cape had as it swayed around her. The cape clung to her shape more so than other coverings.

Manda suddenly realized she had a figure. She stepped closer to the mirror and blinked in surprise. She had dropped at least ten stones of weight, and what weight she did carry was taut muscle. When her eyes flickered to her face, she jumped.

She was never one to dawdle over appearances. She always thought it a fabrication to put on the pompous frills most women would never be seen without. Luckily she had big eyes, pouty lips and dark eyebrows that didn't require much of the abominable paint. As she stared at her new image she was taken aback. Her face had thinned, her cheekbones were evident, her chin now came to a point, and her brow was wide and strong. Although her broken jaw had mended a little off center, it gave her an alluring charm. But that wasn't what made her breath catch in her throat.

It was her eyes.

They had deepened in color to a green so rich they matched her cloak, and the brown flecks that had always dotted her irises were no longer brown, they were golden, like the Avenger's eyes.

Manda smiled as she stared into the eyes of a stranger. Nothing of her father remained besides the color of her hair, and the sun had even bleached it to a lighter shade. If she hadn't been peering at her own reflection she would have considered the image pretty.

Without further ado she made her way down the stairs to meet the others. When she entered the foyer the men stood and bowed. Fraul bent to kiss her hand, reciting poetry far surpassing anything she would ever become; Lazo gave a low whistle, murmuring his approval; and Aaron swept her length, golden hazel eyes shining with open admiration. Manda blushed and managed to escape through the door, insisting they hurry.

114

She couldn't let herself feel anything more than friendship for Aaron. She had seen Kyra. Kyra was exquisite and regal. She would never be.

Ever since she was a child she had laughed when pedagogues tried to teach her the ways of court and she purposely ignored every foolish tradition. She didn't know why she was the way she was. Her mother had been a model example in solemnity, her father the paragon of refinement, and Chris the image of a prince, but Manda wanted nothing of the masquerades.

That had been what first attracted her to Ren.

Ren laughed when he thought a joke was funny, he frowned when he was unhappy, and he didn't play games. But it wasn't Ren she was infatuated with. It was his principles, his ideals, and his visions.

Now, after her feelings for him were but a fond memory, she still loved him, but it wasn't in a romantic way. He would always hold a special place in her heart, as she would in his, but that was as far as it went.

She turned to Aaron. What did she feel for him? Was it just infatuation? Or something more? She wasn't sure and she really didn't care to find out. No one could come close to equaling Kyra's beauty. She felt sorry for any woman who tried.

As they rode toward the castle Aaron kept teasing her that he had never seen a more handsome pair of woman's legs, clothed that is, as her own. His booming laugh rolled off his tongue with ease, but Manda wasn't embarrassed in the slightest. She laughed with him, teasing back that he better get a long look at them clothed because that was the only way he would ever see them. Fraul leaned back in his saddle and enjoyed their banter, chortling casually and chewing on a few wisps of hay he had plucked from a large bale. Lazo wore a continuous grin, either because of their repartees or because he remembered her legs in other ways. That and that alone caused her embarrassment.

When they reached the inner city she knew something was wrong. She was easily recognizable, and although some people shouted in joy when they saw her, many averted their eyes as quickly as they could. Aaron, riding beside her, drew his black sword. After that the people gave them a wide girth.

Just before they were about to pass through the outer portcullis a woman stole up to her and handed her a rose. Manda looked down at it in mild confusion. It was a white rose, symbolizing hope life would continue. Valor was dead. The woman should have given her a red rose for sorrow and pain.

"I'm sorry, my lady. We all pray he won't die, but they tell us it's bleak."

Terror gripped her. She looked at her three companions. Aaron's eyes glowed with incomprehensible power. Manda spurred her horse into a gallop, only hesitating long enough to allow the iron gate of the inner ward to rise.

Her vision blurred. She let her horse have free rein, trusting it to steer her around impediments. When she reached the castle, a guard greeted her with tear-rimmed eyes.

"My lady, we feared the worst."

"Where's Chris?"

"Her majesty said she presumed you dead. "

Her majesty? Manda felt sick. "Where's my brother?"

"In the wedding suite, my lady."

Manda drew a sharp breath. It had happened. She was once again under Alezza's command.

The guard shifted his weight. "I'm sorry, my lady. You mustn't know. Everything has happened so fast. Your brother married Alezza of Quar. She's very stricken by his illness."

Manda strained to keep her emotions under control. Aaron grabbed her arm and warned her with his eyes to stay calm. They couldn't give away their entrance.

She nodded, allowing Aaron to guide her up the steps. The few men who passed her stopped to tearfully welcome her home. She didn't hear them. All she heard was the blood in her temples, her own heavy breathing, and her rage churning underneath her fear.

When she reached the wedding suite she drew in a breath and rested her head on the doorframe. The last time she had seen Chris there had been madness in his eyes. What would he look like now? She braced herself and swung the door inward.

The room was dim. Aaron parted the curtains. When the fading sunlight fell on the figure in the bed she choked back a cry.

Chris was as pale as death. She dropped to her knees and rested her face on his chest. At first she sensed nothing, then a weak heartbeat. Her eyes swept his white tunic and pants. Color rose to her cheeks. All royalty was buried in white. It appeared Alezza expected him to die at any time.

"Chris, what has she done to you?" Manda squeezed his hand, silently ordering him to come back to her.

Chris' eyes flew open. He grabbed her wrist and pulled her down to meet his face. She tried to move away, frightened by the madness in his pale green eyes.

116

"Chris, it's me."

His fingernails dug into her arm. Lazo tried to pry them loose, but Chris wouldn't release her. His chest heaved. His eyes widened. He pulled her closer.

"I have the stone."

"The stone? Chris, please," she said. "You're hurting me."

"He'll never come back to you."

Alezza!

Chris released her wrist at the sound of Alezza's voice. Alezza's gaze could have smote iron. Manda cringed as the memories stole over her like a phantom.

Aaron put his ebony blade against Alezza's neck. "Don't move and you won't die."

Recognition passed over Alezza's face as she risked a quick glance at the Avenger.

Manda grinned. "I don't know if you have the upper hand anymore, Alezza. I have some powerful friends on my side."

The door behind them pushed open. Harman, the head of the castle guard, stumbled in. The gold-braided uniform marking his rank seemed out of place in the dim light. Harman drew his sword and pointed it at Aaron.

"Drop it," he demanded.

Manda's eyes remained locked on Alezza. "Harman, I've known you since I was five. Lower your sword."

Confusion passed over Harman's face when he saw her. His eyes flickered with joy, but his jaw clenched. He was doing his duty. He was defending the queen. Manda was about to speak when Harmon nodded. "I'm listening."

Manda turned to Alezza. "Do you want to tell him how you forced needles into Chris' mind, had me raped, and beat us both consistently, day after day, or should I?"

Harman's mouth dropped open. "But, my lady, Chris loved her very much!"

"Love?" Manda said. "Do you think he was in his right mind when he came here, Harman? No. Alezza forced those words from him and fooled you all. She's almost succeeded in killing her new husband, and now she's queen of half the Lands."

The silence in the room could have shattered glass.

"Kill her, Aaron."

Before Aaron had a chance to reply, Alezza's eyes flickered to Chris. Chris started thrashing on the bed like the ten winds were inside him.

Aaron pushed Manda aside. When their eyes met, she knew.

"Forgive me," he whispered, bending to kiss her cheek. "It can't wait." Aaron turned and plunged his black blade into Chris' heart. Chris' back arched. A blinding light erupted around them.

Then they disappeared.

- - -

Manda collapsed next to the bed. She didn't understand. What had Aaron done? Where had they gone?

Manda slowly raised her head. She could still see Chris' indention, the only indication he had been there at all.

"Not as confident now, are we my sweet?"

Manda turned to Alezza. Images of what Alezza had done to Chris came flooding back: the beatings, the needles, the pain, and the terror.

In one fluid motion Manda knocked Alezza down. Her ring – the ring of rule, the ring of Crape, the same ring Alezza now wore – tore Alezza's jaw.

Manda wasted no time. She drew her sword and brought it over her head, surprised she felt none of her own rage, none of her own hate for the woman beneath her. As she began to bring the blade down upon the woman who had destroyed her brother she felt her inner power. Aaron had passed some of his magic into her, and now that magic screamed for justice.

She was an instrument of death, wielding the blade of verity. She may not be the Avenger, but her path was clear. She would wield her blade for righteous destruction. She would become death for those following the darkness.

Just as her blade was about to drink Alezza's blood Harman's weapon stopped its fall. She spun to him, righteous rage searing her core.

Harmon stepped back. "My lady, she's carrying your brother's child."

Her blade, before hungry for Alezza's blood, tumbled to the ground.

A searing pain smarted through her heart. She had almost killed her brother's child. In a daze she heard Alezza screaming for the guards, shouting that Chris had been murdered.

Alezza rose to her feet, dark eyes flaring with animosity. A deep cut from Manda's ring dripped blood. Alezza screamed again.

Harman looked perplexed. His loyalty was with Manda, but his duty was with the new queen.

Lazo stepped beside Manda. Distant sounds of boots echoed in the stillness. Manda's eyes flickered to Harman. It was her word against Alezza's. She could even see the doubt in Harman's eyes. He had seen Aaron use his sword on Chris. He had seen her try to kill her brother's wife and child. How could she explain that?

She couldn't.

With a sick feeling in her gut, Manda realized that even if the people believed her, Alezza would walk free. There was only one circumstance in which a woman could rule a kingdom: if the heir to the throne was a child of less than sixteen. If Alezza bore Chris' child, Alezza could escape justice and rule Newlan for sixteen years. No matter the accusations against Alezza, her sins would be wiped free until her son was of age to rule or her daughter of age to marry.

Manda saw the truth of her thoughts in Alezza's eyes. Alezza's lips twisted into a victorious smile. She stepped closer, the Quy's light shimmering around her.

Then Harman was beside Alezza, grabbing her from behind, holding the sword under her chin. He motioned to Manda. "Get out, my lady. Now."

Lazo didn't hesitate. He took Manda's hand and forced her to run. Manda tried to take one last look at Harman, but they were through the door before she could meet his eyes.

As they ran down the hall guards came at them from both directions, but when she pointed to the wedding suite they passed her without question. She took the stairs two at a time, Lazo right beside her. She spotted Fraul at the entrance. He turned, gray ponytail whirling behind him, and ran to their horses. They were all mounted and galloping toward the inner ward within heartbeats. The toll of the death bell rang through the air with gruesome finality. Manda leaned into her horse and urged it faster. Horns blared, ordering the gates to be secured. Manda's resolve deepened.

She had to live to take Chris' child from the spider's womb.

Manda glanced at the sun and calculated when the child would be due – late spring. She would find Alezza late spring. Then her blade wouldn't fail.

They pounded through the inner ward without incident, but as they approached the main portcullis the gates were shut. Reining her horse to a stop, Manda grabbed the tunic of the closest guard and put a dagger under his chin.

"Are you loyal to Christopher Eric Kahn?"

The guard blinked in confusion as his eyes flickered to the men coming after them. "Of course, my lady."

"Then listen carefully. If you're loyal to the Kahn name you'll open the gate and let me pass for I'm the only Kahn left. When I return none loyal to Alezza will remain. Am I clear?"

Hazel eyes stared into her soul. "My lady, I anxiously await your return." His hand dropped the iron lever. The portcullis began to rise.

The horses were getting closer. "Your name?"

"Gren, my lady."

"You won't be forgotten, Gren." Manda clicked the reins and her horse sprang into the busy city streets of Crest. When she dared to glance back, her breath caught. At least twenty soldiers followed them. Most were in Quar's crimson but a few were in Crape's forest green. There were too many to fight.

The people in the city were falling back, trying to move out of her path. She shouted her name, imploring the crowd for help, realizing her pleas were probably futile, but the villagers started moving their carts into the street, slowing the men pursuing them. She prayed a silent thanks to the Maker and continued down the cobblestone road. When they reached the edge of the city the streets gave way to rolling hills.

As they topped the first hill Manda slowed and turned. Only six men followed. Fraul motioned for her to continue as he dismounted to fight the onslaught of soldiers. He brandished his mace in one hand and his sword in the other. If Manda hadn't known him she would have thought he looked the fool, standing with two weapons, facing six men on horseback, a slow grin spreading across his face. But Manda knew Fraul. The man was a trebuchet about to hurl destruction at the six soldiers riding toward them.

Manda gritted her teeth. Her sword would see blood this day. Spinning her black stallion, she rode back to Fraul and dismounted, drawing her own short sword.

Fraul looked over at her and raised his eyebrows. "Don't try to be gallant, Manda. Get to safety. Aaron would burn me alive if anything happened to you."

At the mention of Aaron's name her determination built. "There'll be worse than this, won't there? I have to learn to fight sometime."

Fraul studied her carefully before nodding.

Lazo stepped beside them. "Unless you want me to fight them with my charm you're going to have to give me a sword." Fraul mumbled something incoherent before tossing Lazo his blade.

Fraul drew a hidden dagger from his belt as he surveyed the coming men with stealth-gray eyes.

"I'll take the three in the lead. They look to be taking this entire affair a little too personally. Manda, you take the one on the far left. Watch his eyes. He'll give away his next move. Lazo, that leaves you the two on the right. The one on the inside favors his left side, meaning he leaves his right unguarded. He'll be an easy kill. The other will be a little more difficult."

"I don't suppose you have time to give a quick lesson in swordsmanship?" Though Lazo spoke in jest there was a nervous edge to his voice. Manda winced, keenly aware Lazo had never held a sword.

"Lazo, maybe you should leave."

"There'll be worse than this, won't there, Manda? I have to learn to fight sometime," Lazo said, using her own words against her.

Manda turned to face the men. The lead soldier glared at them with deep fury. He was one of her father's personal guards. Apparently he had fallen pray to Alezza's charm. Four of the six were Alezza's guards. Manda knew them all very well. All had taken their turn with her. The guard Fraul had assigned her was one of those. She would be incapable of missing.

Fraul twirled his mace in the air, drawing the leader's gaze, and let his dagger fly. It impaled the man in the forehead, toppling him easily. He was dead before he hit the ground.

Fraul strode toward his next target as Lazo danced around the horses of his opponents with comic grace.

Manda stood as immovable as stone as Alezza's guard rode toward her. When his eyes flickered down her length, he sneered. It was exactly what Manda needed to ignite her fury. As he leaned down to run her through she careened out of the way and impaled him in his back. She heard his spine break and watched the look of shock spread across his face as he spun for another pass. His legs dangled uselessly at his sides, and this time when he came at her she sliced his throat before he could counter.

She surveyed the others. Lazo darted between his two opponents, the sword looking out of place in his hands. Blood dripped down his right cheek from a near-death miss.

Fraul was laughing, apparently having a grand time with his two rivals. As she watched he swung his mace and bashed one guard's head like a melon. Looking at her, he winked.

She grinned and ran for Lazo.

Before she could take one of the men by surprise, the other spun and shouted a warning. It was a shame it wasn't one of Alezza's guards. She didn't have the fury this time, but impaled him just the same. When he fell off his horse she stood over him and looked down into his dying eyes. She felt nothing as she pierced his chest and watched the last of life leave him.

Lazo still fought, or evaded, the remaining soldier, though he had managed to unhorse the man. Fraul casually sauntered over and swung his mace into the soldier's back. The man staggered briefly before falling to the ground.

Fraul leaned on his mace and looked at Manda. "Where in the name of the Maker did you learn to use a sword, my lady? By the fates, those men didn't stand a chance."

Manda grinned. "When I was young, instead of training for court, I trained for war."

"Lances? Battle-ax?"

"No. I was always too short to wield them."

Fraul grinned. "Not anymore. At the next town we'll stop and purchase more supplies. I take it upon myself to teach my men, and it seems you two are my men. But let's not tarry," he said, glancing back down the hill. "She'll send more after us."

Manda suddenly realized she hadn't thought about where they would go after she had found Chris.

Fraul saw her confused expression and smiled as he began searching the fallen men for anything of value. "We'll travel to Oldan. Ramie needs to know what's happening, and it appears he needs to rid Crape of some pests."

Oldan. It sounded reasonable to her. Fraul had spoken well of Ramie Augustus, and although the king sounded a bit arrogant he was on Ren's side. Maybe they could talk Ramie into much more than just attacking Crape. By the way Fraul's eyes sparkled, that was his angle precisely.

CHAPTER 13

Galvin stared into the distance and touched his chest. He felt naked without the star sapphire, but Ren needed it. He didn't know if the stone's power was dead or alive, but if it was alive it may be able to save Ren.

A clear blue stone with a brilliant white star at its core, the star sapphire symbolized light in the darkness. If used by one powerful enough the stone could augment the wearer's memories. His father believed in its strength and told him it would be his guide in times of trouble.

It had been created for one of his distant ancestors: Agamonium, king of Ketes, who had the power of the Quy. Agamonium was a benevolent king, devoted to his people and beloved by all, but the law of the land forced those with the Quy from power. Agamonium had no desire to become a wizard and hid his power for many years. When Druids came to Ketes he shunned them, feigning ill heath, and managed to evade suspicion.

When his deception was discovered, the Druids stripped him of the Quy. Agamonium lost all his memories, including any recognition of friends and relatives. He went mad and butchered nearly his entire family.

Agamonium's distant cousin, Jeiken, traveled to an old wizard and begged the man to create something to help Agamonium regain his memories. The wizard had obliged by creating the star sapphire, but when Jeiken had returned home it was too late. After killing his family, Agamonium had killed himself.

The star sapphire had never been tested for its true purpose, but it had been handed down to each descendent of Jeiken. It served as a reminder of the family lineage.

The stone meant the world to Galvin because he wasn't his parents' child. They had found him abandoned when he was newly born and raised him as their own. His mother had called him her miracle because she had been unable to bear children. His father had given him the sapphire as a small child. It was the first time Galvin truly knew how much his parents loved him.

Neki turned to him with a troubled expression. "You know something about Druids, don't you Galvin? Do you think Ren will be all right?"

Galvin was about to relay Agamonium's story when he decided a long explanation was unnecessary. Galvin stared into the night where Ren had gone. It was almost dawn. He had been standing there for some time.

"No, I don't think Ren will be all right."

"Then we need to hurry," Neki said, starting toward the graves. "Let's bury the men and be after those damnedable Druids. I just don't know what possessed Ren. He reacted with the sense of a toad."

Galvin remained silent. Who was he to question the orders of the Oracle?

They worked in silence, eager to finish so they could follow the Druids. Galvin thought his haste disrespectful of Bentzen and Markum but he knew both his friends would tell them to forget the burial and follow Ren. He worked faster.

With each click of the sun his worry grew.

Without Ren the camp seemed desolate and hope seemed lost. After what seemed like days, they placed Bentzen and Markum in the earth.

When they stood before the graves the finality hit again. Bentzen was gone. Markum was gone. The kota whined beside Galvin, looking between him, the graves and the direction Ren had gone. She seemed to understand the Druid horses unearthly swiftness and hadn't tried to follow, but if they didn't saddle up soon the kota would leave without them. Galvin put an arm around her neck in silent reassurance. Neki began to push the mounds of sod over the bodies.

"I wouldn't do that if I were you."

Galvin drew his broadsword and whirled to the new voice. A man with long, dark hair peered past them into the graves. His silver-gray cloak was unlike any Galvin had ever seen. Pockets and silver clasps littered its length, concealing multiple inner compartments. Beneath it, a midnight-blue robe swayed with a life of its own. Silver swirls careened through its uncanny texture.

Coal black eyes holding far more knowledge than could be possible given the man's age, looked at Galvin and winked. Reaching into one of the compartments the man brought out a handful of silver dust.

Galvin's eyes veered to the man's widow's peak and pointy eyebrows.

The man flung the dust over the graves.

Markum's eyes flew open.

"Not dead!" the One said, laughing gleefully. "Only sleeping!"

- - -

Markum opened his eyes. He felt strange. Sensing cold stone beneath him he sat up and tried to focus. It was useless. Complete darkness surrounded him. His ears rang the way they did when it was far too quiet, as if they were trying to compensate for the stillness.

The stone underneath him felt unfamiliar. He wished for a torch and almost bolted up in alarm when one appeared in his hand. It took all his energy to remain calm. Had he slipped into the unknown? He blinked at the torch, trying to rationalize its appearance.

Images of the Adderiss stole through his subconscious. He jumped to his feet and swung the torch around him, feeling the snakes on his body. And then he saw the doors, thousands upon thousands of doors.

The prophecy came back to him with crashing speed.

The dreamweaver will remain in death
When magic will choke his mind.
And he must choose only one
Door to open wide.
For if the wrong one he chooses,
The darkness will settle in
And the Chosen's heart and soul
Will be forever cold.

Remain in death. Remain in death. His breath caught. The Adderiss had come, the snakes had encircled his body, and right before they bit he jumped.

It was the only way he knew to describe it.

He had leapt from the scene. He had never felt the snakes' bite. He rubbed his eyes, trying to force himself to wake. He did not. Panic threatened to claim him. His chest constricted into a scream.

And then with a flash of realization he calmed.

He wasn't dead. He was dreaming.

A nervous laugh escaped his lips. Somehow he had jumped into a dream, and somehow the dream had saved his life. He breathed a sigh of relief and looked at the torch in his hand. Was the torch something he dreamed into existence, or could he use magic in his dreams?

He remembered back to the times he had tried use the Quy. He had never been able to feel it, not even a flicker. But he had made the torch appear.

No, that was a fluke. He was dreaming. In a dream you could command anything into existence. He had just dreamed the torch. If he wanted to see in the darkness without the torch he could. It was his dream.

The torch disappeared.

Markum waited. After a dragon's breath of grueling darkness, the torch reappeared. He shrugged. So his dream didn't want him to see without a torch. He would accept it and go on.

He looked around again. Below him, above him, beside him, in front of him and behind him was door after door after door. The stone landing was only a small circle in a vast expanse of blackness. Markum stepped to its edge, expecting to see a walkway that would take him from the landing to one of the doors.

But only darkness greeted him. The doors just floated in the air with no path to them or from them. How was he supposed to choose the right door when he couldn't even reach them? He searched for anything that would help, but there was nothing.

Sighing in frustration, Markum sat down. He had to reach the doors! He had to discover the meaning behind the prophecy. What did the doors hold? Lands? People?

His eyes flickered to the torch. He could feel the heat of the flames as if the flames were real. Where they? He had wished for a torch and a torch had appeared, but when he had wished to see in the darkness without the torch he couldn't. Was the darkness reality? Markum shivered as he studied the torch.

"I wish there were walkways leading to every door."

Within a blink of an eye walkways began forming in the darkness, falling and rising, entangling each other until nothing shy of a stone spider's web swirled around him, each tortuous thread leading to one of the floating doors.

Markum grinned. At least he could do what he wanted here. He took a walkway leading to a large cluster of doors. Each door had a symbol or phrase etched on its surface. Now he had to discern why he had to open a door, why it would help Ren, and what, if anything, lay behind it.

He thought about the prophecy.

Remaining in death meant leaping into his dream. Somehow before the adders' poison took hold he had jumped here.

The dreamweaver part was understandable. He was a seer. He could read prophecy from his dreams.

Markum straightened and turned to the tangle of stone webbing he had constructed. It was a dream weave of webs.

Each door was an entrance to someone's dream!

He wasn't in his own dream. He was in the catacomb of dreams!

And he had to open Ren's dream at the right time.

Markum collapsed on the pathway. How would he recognize Ren's dream? He looked around again. There were thousands upon thousands of doors!

"May the Maker have mercy."

Markum drew a wavering breath and walked to the first door. He held up the torch and inspected the symbol on the knotted wood: three wavy lines below the spiral of fate.

"The symbol of prophecy," Markum whispered. His voice resonated off the wooden frame as he fingered the deep grooves of the lines, hoping he could sense something from the inscription. He felt nothing besides the intricacies of the wood: no foreboding, and no allure.

How could he choose one way or the other on "prophecy?" He could see where it could be the right door or the wrong door. He had to think. Why would prophecy be right or wrong? He thought back to all he had read. One truth kept entering his mind: prophecy was right in its context but could be wrongfully interpreted. Prophecy sometimes clouded the truth and clouded judgment. No, prophecy wasn't the right door. It was far from the right door.

He studied the next door. It displayed a saying in the old tongue. Markum searched his mind, trying to recall all he had read about the language of the first people and how it had transformed over the years. Then he remembered his very first dream.

It had haunted him for years and it was the very reason he had become an erudite. Beasts had surrounded him, but he hadn't fought the beasts with ax or sword or any other weapon. He had fought them with books. And every beast he touched with a book disintegrated before his eyes.

He wondered if the beasts were doors. He wondered what would happen if he didn't open Ren's door in time.

Would the beasts win?

His determination deepened. There was no time to waste. Ren needed him.

Markum sat down. A full glass of burgundy wine appeared in his hand. He drew a long swallow. This was going to take a long time. He might as well get comfortable.

- - -

"Dreamers can live if they reach the catacomb of dreams before death takes hold," Zorc said, unable to disguise the pride in his voice. It had been a long time since he had used magic to help someone. Stopping these men from burying the poor boy alive made him feel as light as air. This was what wizards were born to do. He felt the love of the Lands building inside him again. He rocked forward to his toes and then backward to his heels, praising the Maker he was at last out of that damnedable cave.

"Now get him out of there and tell me what happened."

"Ah," the blond one stuttered, looking as if he had seen the gossamers of the Fates themselves.

"The Adderiss," the tall one said. "Her snakes bit him."

Zorc knitted his eyebrows together. "Oh dear. I held hopes she wouldn't be reborn. Very well," he said, waving his arms in a flourish and turning to the woods. "I need one of you . . ." Zorc pointed to the blond.

"Galvin, and this is Neki."

Zorc nodded to each in turn. "Yes, pleased to meet you both. I need one of you to boil water while I go in search of some thistleberry. Thistleberry will kill the poison in his system. It will take some time, probably weeks, but the lad should be able to heal, physically that is. The rest is up to him. He'll have to find his way out the dream world and back into this world. Nothing can do that for him. Some have been able to do so, others haven't."

The men had gone pale.

Zorc looked between them, fearful he had revealed too much too fast. Perhaps these men knew little about what had occurred in the Lands. He made a note to watch what he said in the future. Zorc studied the duo. They were an odd pair. The blond appeared acutely serious while the tall one appeared not far from a jester in a passing parade.

Zorc decided to look at them through wizard eyes.

When he did he drew in a sharp breath.

Galvin was strong internally, not unlike a wizard or a twin. Although Zorc sensed a trace of the Quy in him, it had died long ago. Neki was young, far too young to have the Quy emit from him with the force it did. An uncontrolled, chaotic pattern spewed out of the boy like an inclement tempest without direction. Neki was trouble, not as a person but because of his lack of training. The coy grin he wore caused Zorc to scowl. No one with that much power needed to be glib. But the easy manner in which Neki leaned on his sword calmed

Zorc's reaction. Neki was someone who was intelligent, if not wise. He was a victim of the times, nothing more.

There would be many more like Neki, some perhaps even stronger. Zorc needed to warm to that and set his mind to train them, after he found the Chosen.

He nodded to each in turn, hoping his wits were still true and he didn't like them only because they were the first people he had come across since leaving the hideaway.

"My name is Zorc Val Vincent. I'm grateful to meet you." He bent forward and put a hand behind his back, as a proper Calvet would do. It felt strange. He was used to bowing completely, with back parallel to the floor, but he was the last of the wizards, hence the Calvet, the leader of the Alcazar, or what was, or was not, left of it.

"I don't suppose any of you have seen a man," Zorc paused, brow furrowing with self-reproach, "or I think he's a man. He could be a woman for all I know, although I have never considered the possibility." He mumbled under his breath, scratched his chin and chastised himself for not thinking of it sooner. The Chosen could be anybody: boy or man, woman or girl. It didn't matter. All that mattered was that he find him or her.

Zorc whirled to Neki. The boy took a step back, eyes widening under Zorc's glare.

"You," Zorc said, stepping closer to the power he had sensed heartbeats ago, fearful he might have missed the obvious. The Chosen would be strong. Neki was that, much more, but Zorc would have thought . . .

Thought what? He chastised himself. Older? More rounded in feelings? More intense in desire? More handsome? More ugly? More muscular? More serious? What?

Zorc stepped in front of Neki and had to look up slightly. What he saw in Neki's dark eyes scared him but didn't convince him.

"Something isn't right," he murmured more to himself than to anyone else.

"You're the One." Galvin said, eyes vacillating between fear and hope.

Zorc lost his smile. How would they know him? He looked at each in turn and then down at the dreamweaver in the grave. The boy bore an uncanny resemblance to Galor, a very uncanny resemblance.

He spun to Galvin, almost screaming. "Where's the Chosen?"

Galvin glanced at Neki before he replied. "Druids."

"What? What's he doing with Druids?"

"They said they had the One. They convinced him you were with them."

Zorc listened as the two pieced together the story. The Druids were going to put the Chosen behind the door. They were going to destroy the world. Ista had gotten to them. The thorn had pricked – the same thorn that had taken his Christa.

He would destroy her.

"What does this mean?" Galvin asked as if the weight of the world was on his shoulders.

"It means we have to find him before the door is closed," Zorc said through gritted teeth. "The Chosen is too strong to remain behind the door. If they shut it and Ren doesn't die, he'll be a shell of a human.

"Barracus will be able to enter a shell without problem. That's Ista's plan. Ren, the most powerful person in existence, will be unable to fight, and Barracus will be able to tap into the Chosen's power without any difficulty. Ren, as he was, had a chance to defeat Barracus. Ren behind the door will be easy prey. Barracus will claim him, and all hope is lost."

CHAPTER 14

They were moving fast. Ren could see in the distance but if he looked to each side the view was, at best, the ten winds come to life. They had covered hundreds of dragon's tails since leaving the others and their horses still didn't show any signs of slowing.

Ren had become used to his eyes shedding tears from the force of their speed. He had also become used to Fate's words echoing in his mind.

Your belief will damn you or raise you. Believe in choice and chance. Believe in love and pain. But believe in you.

Galvin had said something similar: *Believe in yourself. Remember this.*

Ren opened his palm and studied the star sapphire, perplexed as to why Galvin had given it to him. It was a beautiful, costly stone. If the gift were a token of friendship Galvin would have given it to him openly, but he had given it to him covertly, entreating him with his eyes.

What was Galvin trying to tell him?

The stone lay dormant in his hand, but the white star at its core glowed with an inner light. It wasn't an ordinary stone. Ren felt a warmth coming from it, almost an entreaty.

Even though he had its leather thong wrapped around his wrist, Ren feared the stone would be hurled away by the wind and closed his hand.

His stomach growled. He almost laughed. He was riding toward his death yet he yearned for food.

No. He couldn't think that way. All hope was lost if he did. Somehow, some way, he would fight. And he would fight with everything he had. Something tickled his wrist. A narrow stream of blood careened up his forearm. He had gripped the stone so tightly his fingernails were cutting his palm.

His mount slowed and the world around him began to form a concrete image. His horse threw back its head and snorted, annoyed at the pause in flight. Morrus dismounted and motioned for him to do the same. The third druid, Welch, built a fire. Ren's stomach growled as an aroma of spices and savory sauces filled the air.

"I'm sorry this is our first stop," Morrus said, "but our horses have only two days left of their swift pace. It gives us just enough time to reach Port Vy."

Ren studied Morrus. In the light the Druid's differences were even more apparent, but despite his sizable mass and prominent presence Morrus had a demeanor that made him curious to Ren. Druids were a solemn race, taking temperance to the extreme in every aspect of their lives. Ren had never seen a Druid look upon anyone without hauteur.

Ren wondered if the other Druids would be like Morrus. He hoped so. It surprised him but he found himself liking the Druid. He smiled at the thought: the condemned venerating the executioner.

But Morrus was a Druid who wanted him behind the door. He remembered Morrus' expression when the Druid thought he would refuse to come with them. Morrus wouldn't have hesitated to take him prisoner. The Druid may not be a man of war but he would do what he felt he should.

"Would you walk with me while they prepare the meal?"

The question took Ren off guard. Although Morrus had shown him all signs of courtesy, Ren hadn't expected the Druid to befriend him.

"I would be honored."

Morrus nodded, still expressionless, and walked from the fire where Avalon and Welch worked with quick, quiet movements. Ren fell in beside Morrus, but not before he saw Avalon turn to watch their departure with silent contempt. Ren was glad Morrus was in command. Avalon would have had him bound and gagged by now.

They walked in silence. Ren tried to concentrate on the grassy fields of the Fyl region. He always liked riding in the flatlands. It was vastly different from the mountainous region of his home, but after a few days of the plains he always missed Zier's lush woodlands and naked rock mountains. He suddenly wondered what the island of Dresden would be like.

As if on cue, the Druid spoke.

"What would you have done if you had remained in control of your kingdom? Would you have considered the old laws and chosen either wizardry or reign, or would you have disregarded the old laws and ruled Newlan with the Quy?"

Ren hesitated, unsure of how to reply. The Druid's eyes were on him, but he didn't rush his thoughts. He sensed the question was an important one for Morrus.

"I would have considered the old laws first, but I wouldn't have let them dominate my decision. If I had known without a doubt others in the position of power would honor the old laws, I would have relinquished the throne.

"But if other rulers with the Quy remained in power I would have remained. How could I step down and allow others to take advantage of Newlan? I would have retained the throne in order to help fight against them."

They walked on. When Morrus didn't speak, Ren grew nervous. He knew the Druid would dislike his response, but the last thing he wanted to do was lie.

Finally, Morrus cleared his throat. "I understand."

Ren glanced at the Druid. Morrus was smiling, drawing prominent lines around his eyes and lips.

"I didn't know what to expect when we were ordered to find you," Morrus said. "They told me you would be unreasonable and wouldn't accept your fate. They ordered me to take you by force. I agreed, but along the way I decided everyone deserved a chance to prove themselves, and I vowed to give you the benefit of the doubt before I resorted to force. You did as you should. I admire you for that."

"The One ordered you?"

"Yes, the One."

A chill colder than the peaks of the Jaguars flitted down Ren's spine. He thought the One would be someone who would be his teacher, his mentor. Now it sounded as if the One would be his keeper, his holder. He suddenly felt odd, like there was something he was missing, something he had overlooked. He recalled Markum's description of the One from his dream.

"What's his name?" Ren asked, trying to keep his voice casual.

"Zorc."

That sounded like a wizard's name. "Describe him to me."

"I can't. I've never seen him."

Ren stopped. The tall Druid looked down at him with an expressionless face. "What do you mean you haven't seen him? Magic was destroyed almost four centuries ago."

One corner of Morrus' mouth lifted into a grin. "He hasn't been with us since magic's destruction. He only came to us a short time ago to wait for you. Since his arrival he's been guarded with whom he takes company. He remains in the upper temple and only lets the High Priest of Dresden in to see him. Although he stays with us and trusts us to a degree, he's also vigilant. He told us some of what is to come, but not all, and certainly not how the prophecies will come to pass. The One had to trust us enough to tell us of you, but he's kept us at arm's length. If I were he, I would do the same.

"Wizards are stronger than Druids and can crush us if they desire, but one wizard against the entire city of Dresden? He wouldn't stand a chance. He's on guard, as you'll be. But you have nothing to fear. We only do what is right for the Lands."

The chill still hadn't left Ren. Morrus' words sounded rehearsed. Was the One really with them?

Ren glanced at the horses and forced his muscles to relax. The One had to be at the Obelisk. Only a powerful wizard could have produced such an effect in their mounts. Druids certainly couldn't.

If something was wrong it wasn't that he had made the wrong decision. He had made the right one, but something underlying the right decision was corrupt. Even so, it didn't change his fate.

Ren turned back to Morrus. The Druid was watching him closely.

"If you haven't seen him, did the High Priest tell you to find me?"

Morrus nodded. "When the One first arrived the elders on the High Committee were allowed to speak with him. They were convinced by his words. If Barracus comes through the Eye and enters someone with your power there will be no defense."

An image of the Oracle's painting flashed through Ren's mind. He didn't want to become that horror.

"The One says Barracus needs someone of incredible strength to enter. You're the Chosen. If Barracus enters you after being in the lower Plains he'll have gained in strength and severity. Pain in this world will be nothing to him. He'll wreak such destruction that few, if any, will survive." Morrus' words seemed to dim the bright of day.

"I'm sorry you must endure this. You were born with a great ability and now you must destroy it because of something that happened centuries ago. I don't like it any more than you."

Ren nodded. They continued to walk in silence. Only one thing dominated Ren's thoughts, and for once it wasn't Aidan. It was a premonition the One wouldn't be his friend or mentor, but his keeper.

- - -

Galvin rode behind Zorc, the wind forcing tears from his eyes. The wizard had put the same charm on their horses as the Druids had on theirs, but the Druids were almost a day's ride ahead of them. Ren would probably set sail for Dresden before they were able to overtake him.

The outlook was grim. Hiring a ship to Dresden was comparable to pulling teeth from a live dragon. It didn't happen. No ship's coxswain wanted any part of the Druid island. Although the Black Knight's phantom still kept the Druids from the mainland, all feared close proximity to Dresden. Ships passing Dresden had been known to be "freed" of their vices, and those who went to the island without permission were fine targets for the zealous Druids. Sailors liked to drink and whoremonger. The thought of vanquishing their secular cravings sobered any ship's coxswain and put the fear of the Maker in the crew.

When Galvin had reiterated that fact to Zorc, he had witnessed the backlash of Zorc's terror.

Zorc had spurred into action faster than if his robe had caught fire. He found the thistleberry within heartbeats and with a flick of his wrist had boiled water to steep the berries that would draw the poison out of Markum's body. He had ordered Neki to give Markum the thistleberry tea as he was flinging silver dust over their mounts.

Through all of the wizard's irate sputtering Galvin saw the terror in Zorc's eyes. That frightened him more than anything. Ren was in far more trouble than he had first realized.

They had ridden from the clearing within a sun's click of Zorc's appearance, Markum tied securely to his mount, padded by blankets and extra clothing. Galvin was sure the ride would be hard on Markum, but there was no other way. They needed to be after Ren. Zorc said they had done all they could do for Markum. It was now up to the dreamweaver to awaken.

Zorc's long black hair flew behind him like a banner of doom. Galvin almost felt sorry for the Druids. He didn't think Zorc would let any of them live after this.

Zorc slowed at full moons to give their mounts a moons' click of rest. Neki dismounted with his short dark hair in disarray. He wore a silly grin as he staggered the first few steps to regain his equilibrium.

"That was incredible!" Neki said, eyes shinning with fervor. "Zorc," he yelled up to the wizard, "why don't you travel like this all the time?"

Zorc looked at Neki as if he were a burr on his blanket. "The horses will die if you ride them like this longer than five days. It's already shortened these horses lives by one third."

Neki sobered and gave his horse a reassuring pat on the neck. Zorc sat down on a large flat rock and stared west, where the island of Dresden resided.

"I'm worried," Neki said.

Galvin glanced at Neki, surprised to find dark circles under Neki's eyes. Galvin quickly changed his opinion of the swordsman.

Neki wasn't flippant. His humor was his defense in times of peril to stifle his own fears. His defense didn't look to be currently working. The pulse at his throat beat like the Abyss was reaching out to claim him.

Neki heaved a guttural sigh. "I need to do something or I'll go mad. Tell the wizard I go in search of some berries or roots to gnaw on. I'm famished, and in our haste we forgot food. Tie him down if he tries to leave without me."

Neki walk off in the direction of some distant brush. When Neki's shoulders slumped, Galvin wondered if Neki kept up the banter for himself or for others.

Galvin ambled toward the wizard. He had so many questions he didn't know where to begin, but when he reached Zorc he didn't have the heart to ask even one. He could almost see the frantic thoughts spinning around Zorc's head.

Galvin settled down in the grass, content to just be near the wizard, feel the aura of Zorc's power and know that it was all being directed to help Ren. He studied the rolling hills before him. He could see the beginning of the Fyl flatlands in the distance, where creeks were abundant as the water from the Divi shed its tears. Galvin could almost smell the difference in the air. Here the air was replete with grass and late-blooming flowers. In Crape, as well as Zier, it was saturated with woods and moss.

Galvin turned to find Zorc regarding him with penetrating eyes. The wizard's eyes were just as Markum described – twin pools of ageless wisdom. The profusion of emotions coursing over Zorc's face only intensified their depth.

Zorc broke the silence. "I need you to do me a favor."

Galvin blinked in surprise, unsure of how to respond. He didn't have to.

"There are a lot of Druids on Dresden and I don't know if I'll be strong enough to keep them from trapping me behind my door. If I become trapped I will be unable to help Ren, and I'll be another shell Ista can use at whim.

"The Druids will be unconcerned with you until after both Ren and I are behind the door. Kill me if it looks like I'm going to become trapped, before I'm forced behind the door. Kill me without thinking, Galvin. Do you understand?"

Galvin lifted his eyebrows in shock. "No, I don't understand. Why should I kill you before I'm sure you're behind the door? I understand the reasoning for after, but not before."

"Because that's the only way you'll be able to take my knowledge and teach Ren," Zorc said. "Take out your sword."

Galvin hesitated, but the look in Zorc's eyes quenched any doubt. Zorc was doing this for Ren. Galvin couldn't refuse. Galvin drew his sword and nodded. Zorc reached into his robe and drew out a small bag of silver dust. Zorc slowly sprinkled the dust down the blade. He made the symbol for magic at the sword's tip: an inverted triangle inside a larger triangle inside a circle. Then Zorc drew a parallel line back up the sword and sketched an arrow at the top, pointing toward the hilt. The wizard waved his hands over the blade. The dust hissed and smoked. Then the sands vaporized before Galvin's eyes.

The sword shivered and a tingling rushed through Galvin's hands, up his arms, to his shoulders, only to plummet down to his toes. It was the Quy learning his form. As soon as the tingling had dissipated it came again, this time from the toes, retracing the same pattern until it emerged from his fingers and flowed back into the blade.

Galvin staggered backward, yearning for the sensation again. It had been blanket of warmth titillating his senses, filling him with something he had always known but had always been lacking.

A hand encased his shoulder. Zorc's resonating voice poured over him. "You had the Quy, Galvin. As a child you had the thread. It should have been born in you as it was in Ren and Neki. I see it in your eyes. You have an inner strength that only comes from the gift. I don't know what's happened in your life, but something has taken it from you, stole it, if you will.

"You've just felt what you might have known. I regret you had to feel it. It would be better if you never had to endure it, given your loss. I would have charged Neki with this task but he can't accompany us to Dresden. The risk is great for him. Although powerful, he's untrained. The Druids could force him behind the door faster than an arrow flies.

"I'm sorry, Galvin. I feel your spirit. I know killing me will be hard if it comes to that, but what must be done must be done. If there's a chance I'll be trapped take my life without pause. You'll gain my words, if not my power, and be able to teach Ren what he needs to know to defeat Ista."

Galvin didn't know what to say. If he had the Quy, where had it gone? He had always feared magic because of his lineage. Now the remnant of the Quy within him made him long for it. As he looked into Zorc's gentle eyes he knew once the Quy was gone it couldn't be recovered. He wanted to weep with the finality but forced himself to think about Dresden, and Ren.

"How will I be able to save Ren if you're gone and I'm surrounded by Druids?"

Zorc smiled, eyes twinkling as if he were a teenager out for a prank. "Even if I'm unable to keep them at bay, I'll give them the Abyss to fight." Still grinning, Zorc leaned back on the rock. "If a Druid wants to close someone from a vice, or close something unrelated to the Quy, he can do so easily by himself. It takes at least three Druids to shut the door on someone weak in the power, even if the person allows it. For a Druid to close a four hundred year old wizard, who doesn't want to be closed, well, according to my calculations it would take almost one hundred Druids."

That didn't sound too bad to Galvin. "How many Druids are there?"

Zorc lost his smile. "In my day, almost five hundred."

Galvin's hopes sunk.

"My point is this," Zorc said. "It will take a plethora of them to trap me. If they've already put Ren behind the door they won't have the strength to put me behind the door. Ren's closing, I'm sure, will take at least as many, if not more than mine. It will drain their strength. They'll be unable to fight back when you and I enter their temple. But if they haven't closed Ren, may the Maker bless this end, I'll be able to hinder them enough to allow you and Ren to escape."

Zorc leaned forward, eyes glowing with wicked intent. "I'm a soldier in this war, Galvin. If I become trapped don't hesitate to kill me. For all I know that's why I live, so another can take my knowledge. If it looks like there's a chance I'm losing the battle, kill me. If you don't, all hope is lost."

CHAPTER 15

Ren could tell his horse was tiring. Every once in a while the mare gave a gruff, wheezing sneeze, but she didn't slow.

Ren patted her neck and glanced up at the sky, immediately finding his constellation. The previous night he had quite a scare. The hazy white cloud signifying the One had retracted, buoying farther and farther away from his star. It had terrified him.

Try as he might his horse wouldn't slow, and it would have been suicide to jump. But when he looked again, the haze had begun to move closer. He had never been so relieved. Of course the heavens didn't synchronize to the middle plane with perfect precision. Of course there would be lags between the physical world and the outer realms.

Now the hazy white cloud drew closer than ever, almost covering the constellation's center star. He was riding to the One. There was no doubt. Soon he would find answers. No, he would demand answers.

His horse sneezed and stumbled. This time when he drew back the reins, the horse obeyed. A blur passed him on the left. When Ren's horse blundered to a stop, Ren quickly dismounted. He patted the mare's neck and whispered words of encouragement. Her eyes were dull, mucus dribbled from her nose, and she had thinned as if she hadn't eaten in weeks. As he stroked her she heaved a sigh and toppled, dead before she hit the ground.

Morrus stopped beside him and silently extended his arm. Ren took it and mounted. Within a dragon's breath they were running with the Divi River. The Druid ship rose in the distance. It was a large merchant ship with a wide hull and a large black lateen. It looked ominous. A sharp, stabbing doubt pierced Ren's mind. He looked back at the synergy constellation, letting his doubts dissipate with the wind.

Druids were easily identifiable scurrying around the deck. The ropes holding the massive ship at dock had already been untied. The Druid crew still had on the traditional gray but they weren't robed. Instead they wore baggy breeches and knee-length tunics, belted at the waist with a black sash.

Morrus slowed his mare and let her trot up the plank at her own pace. When they reached the smooth, polished deck, all eyes turned to

Ren for silent inspection. Ren felt like a sheep in a dragon's lair but managed to keep his eyes focused on Morrus' black strand of hair.

Morrus dismounted and strode to the bow of the ship, shouting orders that were immediately whisked away by the wind. Without the Druid beside him Ren reached for the star sapphire, now concealed under his tunic, and walked to the ship's railing. The boat swayed in the water and broke free of the bank. Its sails caught the wind and it lurched forward, sailing down the Divi with surprising speed.

Ren watched the mainland move farther and farther away. Even though the air was muggy with the sweat of the water, a chill passed though him. The boulders of the coast loomed over the ship in judgment. The twin moons' light haunted the banks and painted faces in the rocks. They were faces Ren feared he would never see again.

He longed for a glimpse of Zier: the bald Sierra Mountains, the massive redwoods, and the lush green forests. He thought back to the time when his only worry was leaving the castle without detection. It was amazing really, how insignificant his life had been before the Collective. Now he was the Chosen, ordered to close his door, without friends and without promise of return.

Morrus leaned next to him, dark eyes and emotionless expression making him appear sinister in the dusky light, but when he spoke a quiet compassion was discernible in his voice. "How do you fare?"

"Not so well." Ren looked down at the black water. A light mist hit his face, as if the Old Sea were trying to cleanse him for burial. "But thank you for asking."

Morrus didn't reply. Ren tried to concentrate on the sound of the water. The torches around the boat gave an eerie cast to the waves.

"What will you ask the One?"

Ren had wondered when Morrus would ask that question. "When I go behind the door I may be unable to remember certain things. I want the One to help a friend. I had to lie to her to fulfill this quest. I want him to find her and tell her I meant nothing of what I said."

Morrus chuckled. Ren held his tongue. The Druid clearly didn't understand the importance of his request.

Morrus shook his head. "I don't laugh at your request. I laugh because you continue to amaze me."

"I don't understand."

Morrus' eyes sparked with humor. "You come willingly, you speak to me as if I'm your friend and not someone who is trying to, in a way, change you, and then you think of another when you're about to do something that may destroy your mind."

"What did you expect me to ask the One?"

"I honesty don't know, but nothing like that."

"I do this because I have to, Morrus. I don't understand why I have to, and I don't like it, but it's the fate the Maker has placed before me. I can't change it. There's no sense fighting what can't be changed."

Morrus fell silent, but Ren felt the Druids eyes boring into him. "I've always been intrigued with the idea of a Maker."

Ren turned in surprise. "What do you mean?"

Druids were pious, devout and even ardent in their religious beliefs, which was why they wanted to rid the Lands of vices. Ren always assumed Druid theology was the same, only more fervent than others. Morrus' words claimed otherwise.

A small quirk to the Druid's lips lit his emotionless face. Morrus' eyes flickered behind him and lowered his voice. Ren leaned closer to make out his words.

"Druids are a religious race, but they don't believe an ultimate power created the Lands. Although they do believe in another realm, it's only in the sense of where the spirit will go once it leaves the body. They believe once we die in one realm we go to another and continue on. How good we are in this life determines what we will be in the next. This can go on indefinitely, depending on how good or bad one is. If one is incessantly good, eventually he will become a god."

The water lapped up the side of the ship and echoed around them. Morrus remained silent as he waited for a few of the ship's crew to pass.

"Druids believe a man stays in a realm until he's achieved the highest order in that realm. He's then born in the next realm where his goodness allows. And so the process continues. This realm is believed to be the highest of all realms, and the highest being in this realm – "

"Is a Druid," Ren finished.

Morrus nodded. Ren thought he saw a hint of distaste pass over Morrus' features.

"And when the Quy was first born long ago, the Druids felt as if they had been superseded."

Morrus nodded again, face returning to the emotionless mask. Ren thought about the history of wizard and Druid animosity and finally understood why it went so deep. If the Druids didn't consider themselves to be the highest order in this realm it meant they were another step removed from becoming a supreme being.

"So," Morrus continued, "Druids found a way to rationalize their supremacy. They discovered a way to close wizards from the Quy. Because they could conquer them, they were still supreme.

"Although this realm is the last, the epic of the soul may continue. When a Druid dies in this realm, if he passes the test he will become an all-knowing, all-seeing being, capable of anything and everything. If he fails he will sink to the lowest realm and begin the process again, no matter that he has achieved the highest realm or the highest status."

"What's the test?"

When Morrus turned toward him his dark eyes flickered with dangerous shadows. "The god the Druids believe they will become is one god. By that I mean a combination of countless Druids will make the god complete. Until it reaches consummation the god won't function. When this god made of Druids is in fruition the realms will be no more. Hence there are only so many Druids that will become the god you refer to as 'The Maker.' Upon completion this god will make new worlds, new realms, and will dominate them with power beyond imagining. The Druids reference the Quy as petty compared to the powers they will possess."

Ren's mind spun. The Druids thought only a select few would achieve divine status, which was why they were so zealous among each other and the Lands. They were competing to become a god. Ren was shocked out of his thoughts by Morrus' continued speech.

"But you ask about the test," Morrus said, eyes glowing with either fervor or fury, Ren was unsure which. "The Druids of this realm pray to those Druids, or the High Order, who have gone on before us to achieve divine status. The High Order urges us forward in our quest for divinity, and they inform the Drek, through the High Priest, what those tests will be."

Ren thought through the implications. If the Drek revealed what to do and what right or wrong was, the Druid cultus would believe him. During the ride of the Black Knight the Drek had ordered the Druid race to rid the Land of vices.

Morrus interpreted his thoughts and nodded. "Yes, the former Drek ordered the Druid race to cleanse this world of all evil. He said those cleansings would buy all Druids the promise of a higher being."

Ren noted that Morrus invariably used the word "Druid" when referring to his kind, not "we." Ren studied his friend. "Do you believe as the Druids believe?"

Morrus ignored the question. "I say all of that to say this. I hope you're right and there is a Maker, one Maker, and he will help you through this. Although it may be too late to save my soul, let me just say this, and don't take offense, but if the Druid ways are right, and when you die, because you aren't the highest order in this realm, you'll once again sink to the lowest, I condemn my gods and abhor my own spirit for helping them bring you to this end."

Ren didn't know what to say. Morrus had given him a high honor, and nothing Ren could say could express how much Morrus' words meant to him.

The crescent moons cut the water in two golden strips. Ren suddenly wondered what Grauss knew about the moons and if there was a story about them as well.

They had drifted into the sea. Ren looked down into its icy depths. Something large stirred just below the surface. Shouts echoed from the other side of the boat. Ren turned to see one of the fallen horses mounted in a sling. The Druids lowered it into the icy water.

The ship drug for a few heartbeats, as if the horse was an anchor trying to stop their progress, before breaking free. The Druids went back to their tasks in silence.

"What was that for?" Ren asked as he caught a glimpse of something large descending deeper into the water's depths.

"The Protector."

"You mean the creature that once lived in the sea to guard the Druids?" Ren asked. He had read about it a few times, but it wasn't written about frequently. Not many had seen it.

"Yes." Morrus spoke in a monotone. Ren could tell Morrus wanted the conversation to end there. Ren obliged, not wanting to anger the man he considered the last friend he would ever see.

"It's time to retire," Morrus said. "A bed is set up for you. Shall I show you where?"

"No, I want to stay awake." Ren wanted to say he wouldn't think of sleeping the night before his death, but he knew that would be cruel. He wasn't going to be put to death. He was just meeting his fate.

"Good night," Morrus said softly. "May the Maker smile upon you."

"Morrus?"

The Druid paused. "Yes."

"How many will close it?"

"For you? You're very strong. If you're willing, I would say no less than a few hundred."

"Does someone lead it?"

"Yes."

Ren nodded. Morrus turned away.

"Morrus?"

The Druid paused and looked back. Ren didn't want to anger his friend, but he felt the need to say what he would. "It's never too late for anyone's soul."

Morrus hesitated but finally retreated. Ren listened to the Druid's fading footsteps. He felt empty, drained, but he wasn't tired. Actually he was more awake than he had ever been. He thought he would feel bitter, but he only felt acceptance: kill his mother, destroy Aidan's belief, and sacrifice his soul. He had already done the first two, now there was only the sacrifice of himself. He almost welcomed it. He had hurt the two people he loved most in the world.

He leaned against the railing, welcoming the cool breeze of the Old Sea and the spray of the chill water. Something rubbed against his rib cage. Ren pulled out the prophecy book. He had forgotten all about it.

Ren fingered the silver dragon on the cover. Its blue eyes bore into him, telling him he was missing the message, overlooking a crucial piece of the plan. He opened the cover to the first prophecy. He studied it briefly before turning the pages in search of a new prophecy. With each blank page his mood deepened. He realized he searched for words to assure him he would remain whole.

Then, without warning, the book disappeared from his hands.

- - -

Markum stared at the door in front of him and tried to remember the two prophecies in the prophecy book word for word. It was impossible. He knew he didn't have the wording right, and one word could make a colossal difference in interpretation.

He wished for the book. When it appeared in his hands Markum gave a short, colorful exclamation and then cursed his stupidity. Of course he could dream the book! Why hadn't he thought of it before!

But before he turned to the next page his hand stopped in midair. The book hadn't come to him closed. It had come to him open. Markum stared at the blank pages, confused.

As the implications filled him, Markum drew a sharp breath. This was the real book. He was using the Quy. He couldn't use magic in the real world but he could in the dream world. That was his power.

Holy Maker! The implications!

And Ren had the book open. Ren had been reading it when Markum had called it to him.

When the quill appeared in the air beside him, Markum took it and scrawled a hasty note in the margin, chuckling as he recalled his dream about the notes. It had been the second dream with the wolven. Words had appeared in the margins. Now he was the one writing them.

Placing the quill in the center pages he sent the book away with a mere thought and began to pace. If Ren could read it they could communicate, help each other, but if he could create magic only in his dreams his words may be unreadable in the real world.

There were too many possibilities. When a sufficient amount of time had passed Markum willed the book back. His writing was still there, and a new note was scribbled beside his own.

Ren had replied.

Yes, I can see this. Who am I writing to?

He replied: *It's me, Markum. I'm in the dream world. Somehow I made it here before the adder's poison took hold. There are thousands of doors in here: doors to dreams. I believe these doors are what the dreamweaver prophecy foreshadowed. I have to open your door, your dream. Any ideas?*

He watched the book disappear and waited, excitement building. He had contact! He looked around him. Even though he had eliminated many doors there were still thousands left. He studied the door in front of him. No, it wasn't the one. It disappeared with a wave of his hand.

When he thought he had given Ren enough time to reply, he brought the book back. What it said drained all color from his face.

Markum, praise the Maker you're safe. I'm with the Druids. They're closing my door. Maybe somehow . . .

The words "maybe somehow" had been scratched out.

Find it, Markum. Find it fast.

CHAPTER 16

The island of Dresden crept closer, both beautiful and terrifying. White spiny birch trees lined a lone walkway leading to the stark white structure of the Obelisk. The scene would have been serene had there been any sound coming from shore, but all was still.

Ren sucked in a breath and focused on the new hope he carried inside him like a shield. Markum was alive, and Markum could help him.

He remembered Fate's words: *Believe in you.*

It was the last thing Fate had told him. He had been over and over those words, dissecting them, weighing them for their true meaning, and as the ship hit the shore Ren thought he understood.

Fate had told him everything had a divine purpose. Closing his door was a means to his divine purpose. If this was a means, it was not the end. He traced the lines on the hilt of the Quy's sword – the symbol for victory. Ren's resolve deepened in the pit of his stomach. He wouldn't let the Druids take his memories. They could have his power, but not his memories.

If he believed, anything was possible.

And it was then Ren realized a profound truth.

He wasn't a prisoner of fate but a prisoner of doubt.

As a flaw could mar a stone so a doubt could mar a soul. If he didn't believe in the Maker's ultimate purpose and in himself to rise victorious and see that purpose through he would hold something back, not give his all, and he would fail. Holding back was an excuse, a scapegoat for failures. Failures could be avoided by belief and giving all of one's self to the task at hand.

The Maker had deemed him the Chosen. The Maker hadn't put him here to die. The Maker had put him here to follow his path and rise victorious.

The ship lurched to sudden a halt. His constellation was no longer visible in the morning's light, and the latter half of the night had been overcast. It would have been reassuring to see the white haze representing the One encompassing the center star, but so were the whims of chance.

The Obelisk sat beneath a blanket of clouds. Its top was barely visible, but Ren could faintly make out the lines of the temple. It was pyramid-shaped but slender. Then he saw the large flat base hidden among the mist, forming a second pyramid that anchored the prominent yet slender culmination.

"This is where I say farewell."

Ren turned to his friend. There was a strange hopelessness in Morrus' eyes, but something in Morrus' voice told Ren the closing was the furthest thing from the Druid's mind.

"May your Maker deliver you. The Lands wouldn't be as fair without you in them. Courage to you, my prince."

The Druid turned without giving Ren an opportunity to reply.

"Morrus?"

Morrus stopped, but didn't turn to face him. Ren felt a ripple of warning. Something was wrong, and it had nothing to do with him. It had to do with Morrus. Ren glanced at Avalon. The younger Druid was watching them. Avalon's emotionless mask confirmed Ren's suspicions.

When Ren turned back Morrus was gone, and hundreds of Druids were waiting on the shore. Their gray robes swayed around them, and each one held his hands in the unanswered prayer pose with palms almost touching. All eyes were on him. He hadn't even heard them coming.

He searched the shore. There was no sign of Morrus. There wasn't one friendly face among a nest of vipers. Even the air seemed to radiate evil.

For one terrifying breath Ren doubted his interpretation of Fate's words.

But then they echoed in his mind once more, quenching his doubt. This was his fate, his spiral. He was walking the path the Maker wanted him to walk. And the Maker wasn't cruel. Although he didn't understand the why, he would accept the how. Ren drew a deep breath, the fire deepening in his soul.

Strong hands grabbed him from behind and a sharp pain shot through his shoulder. Before he could react, Avalon and Welch were beside him, fettering his wrists. Another Druid stepped from his side, holding a dagger with a bloodied tip. A stream of blood ran down his arm from the deep scratch the Druid and inflicted. Ren stumbled for balance as his vision blurred. The dagger's tip had been tainted with a drug.

He had come willingly. Why were they drugging him?

Before the thought was out, multiple feathers brushed his mind. The Druids were trying to close him before he had seen the One.

Rage surged through him. How dare they! He had made only one request. One!

The fire inside him heated in intensity. The Druids on the shore closed their eyes and raised their arms to the heavens.

The feathers became a whip screaming toward him, its spiked end seeking blood.

The wind from the whip brushed his cheek, but Ren felt no fear. He focused on his belief in the Maker, in goodness, and in his ultimate fate. He heated those beliefs higher.

As the whip touched his cheek his head came up with a hollow clap of thunder. The whip hit a barrier and bounced back. Ren was encased in a cylinder of internal power, heated by his belief and forming a shield nothing could penetrate.

The whip dissipated into distinct threads, surrounding him, pushing hard. Ren leaned into the thick wall and pushed back. He didn't try to analyze his wall, he just kept his belief hot and pushed harder. He searched the shore for Morrus, feeling betrayed, but Morrus was gone.

Avalon leered beside him. "Your friend has been taken, Chosen. I'm the LoDrek now."

Ren felt his barrier waver at Avalon's words. With an anguished cry he reached inside and threw everything he had into the block, slamming into the wall he had created with full force.

The barrier strengthened. The threads dissipated. The corner of Avalon's eye twitched violently. Ren smiled. He had won, and Avalon knew it.

"I told you to take me to the One." Ren's voice was calm, but it was laced with cold steel. "I intend for you to keep your end of the bargain."

A small chortle escaped Avalon's lips. The Druid leaned closer, foul breath full of fury. "This isn't every Druid, Chosen. On the contrary, this is only some." His eyes flickered to the Druids on the shore. Their drawn faces indicated their exertion. "If I really wanted to close you, you would be unable to resist."

"The lowest realm is too good for you, Avalon," Ren said. "Tell me, where does a soul go if it isn't taken to the lowest realm?"

With a breathy curse Avalon jerked him forward, leading him down the plank. Ren felt the drug begin to claim him. His vision wavered. The horde of gray-robbed figures undulated from his path as if he were a disease that would soil their sanctity. Images formed doubles and the Druids' pallid, emotionless faces twisted and jerked into shapes and horrors far worse than any nightmare.

The earth changed color and contour as he stumbled between Avalon and Welch, but Ren made sure to never lose contact with his interior wall.

The fog was lifting. The gleaming white moonstone finish of the Obelisk shivered with a blinding luminescence. The billowing mist swirled around his thighs and hips, sending a wet mizzle over his feverish forehead.

Ren's head felt heavy but he managed to keep his eyes locked on the tower rising in front of him.

Where was the One? Where was Morrus?

He felt his mind slowing. His feet dragged behind him. His body went limp as shouts drifted past him like the wind. The drug was claiming him, calming him into complacency, but if he lost consciousness his wall would be there when he woke. It was a wall of belief, and his beliefs did not waver.

- - -

Fraul stopped his mount and chuckled.

Manda turned to Fraul in confusion. They had been riding hard since Crape, and during the day Fraul rarely paused to eat.

Manda took the opportunity to rub her weary shoulders. Even though Fraul pushed them hard in the day, he pushed them even harder at night, training both her and Lazo to be deft soldiers. Manda's entire body ached from swinging the battle-ax, but Fraul was a good teacher. She felt more comfortable with it each night.

Fraul pointed ahead of them.

Men in Lorlier's colors of maroon and silver were riding toward the Divi where two large ships were docked. The ships were the biggest Manda had ever seen. Five huge catapults donned each end and eight mounted ballistas lined each side. On the shore, two men on horseback were waiting to greet Lorlier's brigade. One wore Yor's colors of navy and white. The second was robed and cowled. Although the two were an odd pair, Manda recognized Fraul's description of the first man: Ramie Augustus.

"It seems my king has planned a revolt without me. I'm crushed." Although Fraul tried to put some hurt in his voice, his widening smile made it sounded more like elation.

"Come. The formalities of war will escape Ramie. He'll usher Lorlier's brigade onto the ship faster than a dragon spews fire."

Without another word, Fraul clicked his reins and shot forward. Ever since their close encounter with Alezza Fraul had been hungry

149

for a fight, and his passion had put a fire in Manda as well. Manda gave Lazo a wink before following Fraul to the bridge.

Manda's blood felt like it was on the verge of boiling. The power of the Avenger was growing inside her, forming something unexplainable but strong. Although she didn't know what the power was or what it would help her do, she felt every nerve in her body screaming for her to fight for justice. At times it was so incessant it was almost painful.

When they reached the bridge that expanded the breadth of the Divi, Ramie turned to see who approached. When his eyes landed on Fraul his entire face lit with joy. Manda was surprised. Although she knew Ramie and Fraul were close, Fraul's description of the sovereign Ramie Augustus didn't match the smiling man before her. But almost immediately, Ramie's smile withered and he stood straighter in the saddle, creating a perfect picture of regal solemnity.

"Don't tell me you're planning to attack without me, my king."

The light in Ramie's eyes returned, but as quickly as it came, it blinked out. He shook his head. "I've waited far too long, Fraul."

Fraul nodded. "Have you a plan of attack?"

The king's eyes flickered between Manda and Lazo. He nodded slightly to Lazo but paused on Manda. Ramie perused the weapons attached to her saddle.

"She can be trusted, my king."

Ramie's frown deepened. Manda straightened, warning him with her eyes to hold his tongue. Ramie decided against commenting and turned to Fraul. Manda relaxed her stance. She would not let the king of Yor tell her she was unwelcome in his army. She could fight with the best of them. Better than most, she would imagine.

Ramie's voice was laden with worry. "Ista knows I plan to attack, Fraul. Lorlier discovered Ista communicates through crystal balls. I had every man in the army stripped by five others, searching for the crystals. I found three. Needless to say, I didn't think before I acted."

"Dead?"

Ramie nodded. "I'm sure those men told her the army was preparing to march. I had circulated the rumor that we were riding to strengthen the border patrol, but now that her men are dead she'll discern the truth.

"Bostic is with us. So is Lorlier, for reasons you will be unable to believe." Ramie paused, gripping the reins until his knuckles turned white. "With them we may have a slim chance." Ramie's eyes flickered to the cowled man behind him. "Meet Presario. He knows the power, has studied it for years. Magic will give us a greater chance of victory."

When Presario's name was mentioned Fraul raised his eyebrows in surprise and Manda had to consciously keep from gawking. Presario's tragedy was known far and wide.

"Ista won't be prepared for us to have magic. I searched the rest of the men three times. There are no more crystals. Even if more of her followers are here they'll be unable to communicate with her. She knows I march, but she doesn't know my strategy, and she doesn't know we'll use magic against her when we arrive.

"Although the Sierras will be almost impossible to move an army over, if we attack by sea one of her followers could see us and warn her well in advance. Because two other kingdoms are with us, I plan to – "

"There's no need to plan. She won't prepare."

All eyes turned to Lazo. The advisor gazed southeast, toward Zier. When he turned back to Ramie he bowed his head in homage. "My king, I was with her for some time, and she takes little notice of those she deems harmless. If it's truly as you say, and she doesn't know you'll be fighting with the Quy, she'll ignore you until you can literally reach out and touch her.

"Your army, three armies, even ten armies will be a mere pebble to her. You haven't seen the Collective, my king. They are like grains of sand on the shore, but they aren't warriors. They are commoners, farmers, even children. She isn't training them to march like an army, she's training them in magic. They will only know how to fight standing in one place.

"So, don't worry about strategy. Don't worry about hiding your advance. Don't worry about direction and surprise. Just march. Save your men's strength and come at her from the easiest way possible.

"For as a giant ignores a pebble, Ista will ignore you and your armies, my king," Lazo said. "But even a pebble can down a giant. And if that pebble has magic . . . "

Presario moved his mount closer. "He's right, my king. She'll take little if any notice of us."

Fraul chuckled as he rubbed his scant goatee. "Even a pebble."

Manda knew Lazo was right, but she could see Ramie didn't like the idea. He was a man of strategy, a man who wanted all his options laid out before him. He was a king.

Without replying, Ramie turned to face Lorlier's approaching brigade. In the silence that followed everyone else did as well.

Manda had observed Lorlier at the ball. He had a domineering presence, one that made you sit up and take notice, but there was a kindness in his eyes, a tender look that reminded her of a protective father. As Lorlier approached, Manda found herself looking forward to seeing Lorlier again, but as the king of Fest marched closer Manda had to blink in surprise. Lorlier's eyes were sunken and bruised, and his previous passion had been replaced by seething rancor.

He didn't acknowledge anyone's presence except Ramie's. "Is he safe?"

Ramie nodded. "Your messenger is safe."

Lorlier closed his eyes, savoring Ramie's words.

"Lorlier, based on his report I take it you've searched your army for more with crystals?"

When Lorlier looked at them again, his eyes were cold steel. "Oh yes. That's well under control."

"And Marianne?"

As soon as his daughter was mentioned, tears sprung to Lorlier's eyes. Manda grew concerned. What had happened to Marianne? She had been fine at the ball.

"She's alive, but she'll never walk again."

Ramie heaved a sigh. Manda wanted to say something but held back. What could she say? Lorlier didn't know her, and she knew nothing about him or his family. It was a few heartbeats before Ramie spoke.

"Well then, let's get moving."

"And our strategy?"

Ramie turned to Lazo. "March. That's all of a strategy we need."

- - -

Zorc stood where they had left him, hair quivering with each violent breath, robe stirring in the wind, back stiff as a blade was straight. Galvin doubted the island of Dresden would even exist when Zorc returned, or didn't return. Galvin fingered the hilt of his sword and sent a silent prayer to the Maker he wouldn't have to kill the wizard.

As they approached, Zorc turned his head from his watchful gaze of the distant Druid island. "Which ship?"

Galvin didn't want to tell him the news. Thankfully, Neki stepped forward and placed a hand on the wizard's bony shoulder. Zorc was a skeleton. Galvin didn't remember Zorc being as gaunt when he had first appeared. The wizard's cheeks had hollowed, and the only other visible part of Zorc's body, his collarbone, was just that – bone. They had to be quick about finding something to eat. The only thing the wizard ate now was his anger, and although Zorc had enough of it to fill the coffers of kings, sooner or later he would need real food.

Zorc's fiery eyes shifted to Neki.

Neki shook his head. "Every coxswain we found refused to take us. It seems the Druid crew made it clear as crystal none were to follow. I even offered them more than what you gave us for payment," Neki said, jingling the bag of gold despite Zorc's growing frown, "a small fortune. None took the bait."

Zorc spun with such violence Neki held up his arms in defense. The wizard looked toward town. All former rage drained from Zorc's face, leaving a slack, pallid, apathetic mask of indifference. Galvin wondered if this was what a wizard looked like before he hung someone by his entrails.

"Where?" Zorc asked.

"The pub."

Without waiting for further explanation, Zorc stalked off, his midnight-blue robe shimmering with a magic of its own. Its silver streaks oscillated on the surface like a raging sea.

Neki trotted after Zorc with only a hint of disquiet. Galvin followed but kept his distance. He had no desire to get in the way of an angry wizard.

Zorc appeared to be walking on air. His body barely moved underneath the silver swirls of his robe. Galvin would have thought Zorc was floating had the dust of the streets not twirled around him.

Vy was the last port on the Divi River. It was the only place for leagues having banks deep enough to hold a large ship. Most buildings in the town were three stories, which was an extravagance rarely seen except in large manors. Vy was a handsome town, well tended from the ample wealth pouring into its coffers from merchants and ship's crews. The wooden buildings were polished to a high sheen, bricks were richly painted, and when they reached the town center, dusty roads gave way to well-laid cobblestone. Music and laughter wafted through the streets in the dawn's light as the pub patrons continued the night's festivities.

With the wizards' impending confrontation, Galvin suddenly thirsted for a pint of brew. Almost on instinct, Galvin reached up and touched the silver teardrop dangling from the loop encircling his ear. The teardrop symbolized the life he had left behind by swearing the ancient oath. He had never regretted his decision. It was what he had been born to do. Although his parents had loved him completely, there had always been a vast emptiness in his life. For a time he thought marriage would fill the void, but then he came to realize he needed more than marriage. He needed a bond. The soldier's fidelity gave him that. In a way he and Ren were one. They were as close to brothers as you could get without blood. Galvin would lay down his life for his prince. He should have done just that when the Druids had come. Galvin vowed he would never let Ren put himself in harm's way again.

Zorc walked through the large wooden door of the "Knightman's Ale'ment" as if he owned the place. Although it went against his better judgment, Galvin followed Neki through the door. Neki pointed out two of the men they had spoken with earlier, the two least intoxicated. Zorc glided toward them. A knife blade could have cut the silence.

Large, brazen men stared wide-eyed and unbelieving at the sight of the robed wizard. Galvin almost wished Zorc wore his less-conspicuous cape with the multifarious pockets, but he had to admit the stunned shock of the bar's patrons was slightly amusing. In his current mood Zorc's dark eyes were twin pits to the Abyss and his skeletal frame gave him the look of walking death. His robe reeked of magical powers, and the silver specks attached to the fabric swirled violently.

The coxswain who had introduced himself as Kilmin shook his head as Zorc walked toward him. Galvin noticed Kilmin's former vigor was a little subdued as he eyed the wizard.

"I said no and I meant it. Aye, Scoti?" Kilmin said, taking a sip from his mug of dark porter before slamming it down for emphasis.

"Aye, Cox," the scant man across from him muttered. His inebriated, dirty eyes flickered between the wizard and Kilmin. The boy mirrored his superior by taking a long haul of brew. Most of the dark liquid ran down his chin before he slammed it down and burped.

Kilmin rubbed the foam from his whiskers and grunted his assent. Kilmin was a big man. His burly arms and barrel chest would be able to cut down mountains with little problem. Sticking a piece of wood into his mouth, Kilmin began to gnaw it emphatically. His sienna eyes glowed with impudence.

Zorc raised his pointy eyebrows and flicked his wrist. The Coxswain began sliding on the bench as if it were greased with butter. Kilmin's eyes widened as he tried to hang onto the table. It was no use. The huge sailor kept sliding until he bumped the far wall.

"Cox Kilmin!" Scoti leaned over the table and extended his thin arms. "Take me hand if ye need!"

Kilmin looked at Scoti's outstretched hand as if it were a snake. When Zorc sat beside Kilmin on the bench, the coxswain paled and Scoti tensed to bolt. Neki leaned into the bench beside Scoti, blocking any means of escape. Zorc's face remained emotionless.

Zorc reached for Kilmin's beer and took a long swallow. "I don't know how much you men know about Druids but they're a nasty lot."

"Aye, they are," Scoti whispered, swaying from side to side as he glanced at Neki. "That's why we ain't taken ye to their bloody island."

Zorc drained the rest of the beer and placed the empty mug on the table. Reaching above the mug, he quivered his hand. The mug began to spin. Zorc removed his hand and tilted his head, watching the quivering mug with growing interest. The mug began to rise from the table, still spinning. The eyes of the sailors became huge.

"I don't know how much you know about wizards, but they can be a much nastier lot." The mug spun in a more frenzied fashion.

"Yes, wizards can do much more than Druids, especially to the common man."

The mug rose higher. The scraping of chairs and the creaking of the bar door betrayed the flight of the pub's patrons.

"I wouldn't refuse a wizard just because some Druids ordered you to do so. On the contrary," Zorc said, pausing as he watched the mug rise to the ceiling, "I would do everything the wizard wanted." The mug fell, shattering in every direction. Zorc turned to Kilmin, eyes lighting with internal fire. "Especially if the wizard was mad."

If it was possible, the silence in the room deepened. The look on Kilmin's face would have been humorous if they didn't need him to save Ren. Kilmin moved his lips but no words followed. He cleared his throat and nodded. "Aye. When do we leave?"

"Now."

Kilmin didn't argue. "We have to get the gear and wake the men. Soon as possible, we be at the dock. Ship's name is Seawitch."

"Thank you for your assistance, gentleman. You'll be well rewarded." Zorc stood and made his way to the door. The few remaining patrons pushed their chairs well out of the wizard's way.

Neki grinned at Galvin and patted his curved blade. "Druids be warned."

Zorc turned, causing Neki to bump into him. The wizard's face was stern, but it softened as he spoke. "I'm sorry, Neki. You can't come. You must stay here with Markum and the horses."

"Oh, no," Neki said, lifting his hands in defiance. "Just because I'm young doesn't mean I can't hold my own in a fight!"

Zorc's eyes clouded with gravity. "That's not it at all. You have the power but are untrained. A handful of Druids could lock you behind the door before you could unsheathe your sword. If I could protect you I would, but I can't. I too have to fight to stay whole. If we get Ren out alive I would hate to tell him that in trying to save him one of his men became trapped behind the door and is now only a shell of a human. If I know anything about the Chosen, he cares for his men, and I can see you care for him. Don't put another notch of pain in his belt if you can help it, Neki."

Neki drew in a breath for a repartee but quickly thought better of it. He gave a brief nod. Zorc turned and floated toward the docks. This time Neki let Galvin walk behind the wizard.

The Seawitch was anchored at the far end of the dock, near the mouth of the river leading to the Old Sea. Their horses were where they had left them, tied to a post. Markum lay on a litter beside them, still deep in sleep. Galvin started to glance away when he broke into a boisterous laugh. Keena was beside the horses, munching on the sparse grass growing next to the docks as if she belonged there. At the sound of his voice her huge eyes flickered up and she began to prance.

She trotted to him. Galvin chuckled and rubbed the skin around her cream horn. He couldn't believe she had found them. They had been riding at impossible speeds.

Zorc stepped beside him. "The kota?"

Galvin smiled. "It seems she wants to help Ren just as much as we do."

A huge grin spread across Zorc's face. Galvin frowned in bemusement.

"Just a saying! Something an old friend occasionally mumbled in dumbfounded consternation. But now it makes sense! 'When the kota rides the wind, the Chosen will rise again.'"

Spinning around, Zorc lifted his robe and began to dance. Despite his prior disappointment, even Neki chucked.

The wizard's twinkling eyes had lost all of their prior anger. "All hope is not lost, my friends!" he exclaimed, surprising Neki by taking his hands and forcing him into a spin. "All hope is not lost yet!"

CHAPTER 17

Ren woke with his head pounding. Just as he was about to relax his mind a jolt of warning riveted him to attention: the Druid's betrayal, the drug, and the attempt to close him.

They were pushing against his barricade. He slammed against his internal wall, causing the few Druids on the other side to fall away.

When he opened his eyes, light ripped through him and heavy chains clanged in the silence. He fumbled to sit up. The drug still made him queasy. Although the effects weren't as mind numbing as they had been before, his head pounded horribly. It felt as if he had been hit with a mace.

As his vision cleared he found himself on a straw bed in a small moonstone chamber. Three Druids peered down at him. Avalon wore a scowl that could shatter mountains.

The man standing beside Avalon had to be the Drek, the Druid leader. Along with the black lock of hair falling from his otherwise bald scalp he donned a long black beard. Ren's eyes flickered back to Avalon. The LoDrek wore the beginnings of a mustache, as had Morrus. The third man was bald, with waxen white skin and murky yellow eyes.

The Drek gave an imperceptible nod. His jet-black beard caused him to appear young until he inched into the flickering torchlight. The Druid was old, very old, but he stood tall, and his eyes sparkled with profound curiosity.

"I'm Marinus, Drek of the Mohemiun line of the thirty third schism of the two hundred forty scions of Dreks before. I take it you're the Chosen?"

Ren didn't bother to reply.

The Drek's brows drew together at Ren's silence. After a brief pause he motioned to the others. "This is the High Priest of Dresden, Feher. You have already had the honor of meeting my son, Avalon. Thanks to you he now holds the status of LoDrek."

Ren raised an eyebrow. Honor indeed. "Where's Morrus?"

"It's none of your affair, Chosen," Feher stated, his oily voice sending a dagger of warning.

Ren forced himself to look into Feher's repellent yellow eyes. "My name is Ren. I expect you to use it."

Feher's eyes narrowed. Ren felt a smart flog against his interior wall. He hurled himself against the block, sure Feher alone would be able to tear it down, but after a few heartbeats his hold steadied.

Feher's jolt had been more powerful than the whip-like combination of hundreds of Druids, but instead of frightening Ren into submission his rage took on a new dimension. How dare the Druids threaten him when he had come willingly! How dare they treat him as little more than dirt under their fingernails!

Ren stepped forward. The chains fettering his ankles sounded shrill in the moonstone chamber. Marinus held up his hand in an effort to avoid conflict, but his frown deepened.

"Yes, Feher, please address him by name," Marinus said. He nodded to Ren. "But you are to address us with respect, not with brashness."

Ren lowered his voice. "I'd be more than happy to do so, but I've come on my own accord and you chain me without respect or humanitarianism. I consent to my own closing, requesting only to speak to the One before you begin, and you have yet to honor that request. I ask you a simple question and you strike down my importance. Yes, Marinus, if you begin to show me I'm not a prisoner of my own choosing I'll treat you with the utmost respect. I thought we were determined to achieve the same objective. Now I'm not so sure."

The room was immersed in silence, but Ren stood his ground. Finally, Marinus began to chuckle.

"Morrus said you were a good man, and you have just proven his words. I apologize for the, shall I say, 'capture' of you." Marinus' mouth lifted into a semblance of a grin. Although it was still demeaning, it wasn't unkind. "I didn't know how you would react. I ordered you to be chained before you stepped foot on the island. I'm sorry you misunderstood."

Ren's eyes flashed to Avalon. The LoDrek stood with rigid solemnity, face expressionless. The Drek hadn't ordered Avalon to close him or administer the drug. Avalon had done those things on his own. For some reason Avalon didn't want him to see the One. Ren decided to feign ignorance.

"Then why did you order your son to administer a drug and try to close my mind even before I stepped from the ship?"

Marinus' eyes narrowed. Despite Avalon's obvious efforts, his face turned crimson.

"Let's talk of what shall be done," Marinus said, ignoring the question. Ren didn't mind. His point had been made. "You said you agreed to come willingly, yet you block your mind. That's a contradiction."

"Marinus, I said I would come willingly if I could speak to the One and make a request of him. I haven't spoken to the One, so I don't yet come willingly. Morrus assured me I would meet the One before there were any attempts to close my mind. Your son has already broken that agreement. Because of that breech I don't trust you or your kind. I'll continue to resist until the promise has been fulfilled."

Ren knew Marinus wasn't at fault, but his harsh words seemed to affect the Drek. Marinus harrumphed and turned toward the others. "Feher, go see what's keeping the One. Avalon, unchain this man. He's no prisoner, only a soldier in a war."

"But, Marinus," Feher began with mock piety. "The High Order has informed me –"

"That he isn't to see the One?" Marinus asked, peering at Feher. "I think you've misunderstood them, Feher. I've warned you not to put your own ambitions to me. I know the High Order's voice from your own. Be wary you pass the test, Feher. It would be a shame if you didn't."

Feher hesitated before he made his way to the wooden door, painted white to match the moonstone walls. Avalon knelt to unlock Ren's chains without meeting his eyes.

Marinus forced a smile. It looked more like a grimace. "I'm sorry you've been treated poorly. It wasn't my intention."

Ren inclined his head. "And I intended no disrespect."

Marinus nodded, accepting his words. Ren was about to inquire about Morrus when the door swung open.

The One stood in the doorway. The wizard was just as Markum described: tall, slender, long dark hair, and knowledgeable eyes. But Ren had been correct as well. Zorc eyed him like a viper, not a human. Ren felt the faint hope he carried die within him. This was the One. This was his fate. May the Maker be with him.

As Zorc surveyed him Ren had to battle the urge to step away. There was something uncanny about Zorc's eyes, something almost perverse. The One inclined his head in the same manor as Marinus, but without the smile.

"They tell me you come willingly. You're strong to recognize the need, but that's why you're the Chosen." His voice was deep, almost as deep as Morrus' voice. Ren once again wondered about his friend.

"Please, ask what you would of me, but make haste. Time is limited. I have felt a strong disturbance in the Quy. It can only come from the Red Eye. Barracus will escape soon. If you don't go behind the door, Barracus will enter you and mold your mind to his purposes."

"Why not wait to close me? I'm among Druids. They can close me if that should happen."

Zorc shook his head as his eyes filled with anger. Anger at his question or the implication, Ren was unsure. "Think. Magic had to be destroyed the last time Barracus was in the world."

"He was immune to Druids?"

"Yes. Barracus alone knew how to evade the Druids, until the Black Knight," Zorc said, eyes careening over Ren, "and until you." Zorc waited until the point sunk in. "Do you see why we must hurry? With each heartbeat the threat deepens. If Barracus enters you we're all lost."

Ren remained silent, studying the wizard. He felt no liking toward him, but he felt no dislike either. He only felt numb.

"Feher said you had a request?"

Ren nodded, about to speak of Aidan when he realized it was futile. The man before him wouldn't care about Aidan. He would promise to search for her, but he wouldn't. Aidan would never know his true feelings. Then he remembered Morrus. Ren made a quick decision to change his request.

"I want Morrus to lead the closing."

The Druids in the room suddenly lost their calm. Feher drew a breath that would rival any dragon, Marinus' eyebrows catapulted to his forehead, and Avalon sprang toward him with death in his eyes.

Two whip-like threads crashed into Ren's barrier. Feher and Avalon were strong, but Ren was prepared. He thwarted their attack, and in the next heartbeat both men felt the backlash of his fury as they were flung away from him even in body. Avalon stumbled to regain his footing, the vehemence in his eyes unmistakable.

The Drek, sensing what had just occurred, glared at Feher and Avalon, face darkening to match Ren's own. For the first time since arriving on Dresden Ren felt as if another was truly on his side.

Now Ren was sure Morrus was in trouble. He didn't know why, but it didn't matter. Morrus was a friend.

Marinus anger melted as curiosity spread across his face. "Why do you ask this?"

"Morrus and I have talked," Ren said. "I like him, and I believe he likes me. I have no friends here. You wouldn't allow them to come. I consider Morrus a friend, so I want him to lead the closing. Surely you understand."

No one moved. The High Priest's yellow eyes glowed with deep-seated animosity. Ren didn't know why his request was so startling. They had sent Morrus after him, and at the time Morrus was considered LoDrek. Surely Morrus must be someone important in the Druid cultus. Besides, what did it matter who led his closing as long as he was closed?

Marinus' pale blue eyes sparked with humor. "A wizard and a Druid, friends?" The Drek's voice quivered between astonishment and ludicrousness. An odd grin broke one side of Marinus' downward turned lips before he released an amused chuckle.

Ren wondered if the Drek had laughed in years. The wrinkles on his face displayed tension and worry, not humor.

"I'm sorry, that honor is for the LoDrek," Marinus said. "Morrus is no longer the LoDrek. Avalon has taken that position."

Ren turned his gaze to Avalon's smug expression. So that was why Avalon reacted the way he had. The realization made Ren's concern increase. What had happened to Morrus?

Ren met the Drek's gaze with grim determination. "Let me ask you something, Marinus. Someone betrayed you, lied to you, and tried to kill you. Would you want him to lead your funeral? Or would you prefer a friend say words over your corpse?"

His words bit, but he could see the understanding in the Drek's eyes.

"I'll only yield if someone I trust leads the closing. Morrus was LoDrek on the journey. He can be LoDrek again. I'm sorry, Marinus, but your son hasn't given me much to trust."

"We have no time to waste," Zorc said, a slight edge to his voice. "If you're unwilling I'm afraid we'll have to force you."

"So be it," Ren replied. Although he didn't know how to use the Quy or how he was blocking the Druids from entering his mind, if he resisted every Druid on the island may be unable to close him. Based on the wizard's foul expression, Ren was right.

"It goes against the Druid law," Marinus said. "It cannot be done."

Ren shrugged with casual indifference. "You're the Drek. You can change the law."

After a few heartbeats of silent examination, Marinus sighed. "I'll think on it,"

"We don't have much time, Marinus," Zorc said. "Time is of the utmost importance."

Marinus turned and walked to the door. "I said I'd think on it, Zorc."

Avalon glanced at Ren before he followed Marinus out the door, Feher close behind. Zorc remained, cold eyes perusing Ren's face. "You play a dangerous game."

"I don't play games. What I do is right."

Zorc didn't reply. Instead, he turned to leave.

"Why me?"

Zorc turned to face him once again. "Why? You have great strength. Only one of your strength could have released the Quy again."

It was the answer Ren had expected, but it bothered him. Why couldn't the One give him a deeper explanation? Even Grauss had explained that he was born under the three internal and external elements. The wizard just brushed the surface.

"And so it ends like this?"

"Yes, this is how it ends."

A cold chill passed between them. Ren took back his former assessment. He didn't like the wizard at all.

When Ren didn't voice another question, Zorc turned and followed the Druids, closing the door behind him. The lock clicked shut. Ren sighed. He may not be in chains, but he was still a prisoner.

- - -

Zorc paced, glancing at the sun every few heartbeats and muttering oaths under his breath. The wizard's oaths were viler than a group of sailors at midnight, but Galvin understood the wizard's frustration. A rival crew had slashed the sails of the Seawitch the prior night, and new sails had to be hoisted, which took time they didn't have. Although Kilmin and his crew scurried around the deck like ants, glancing at Zorc with sweat-filled, fearful faces, they couldn't hurry the process fast enough.

Galvin had boarded the ship to see if he could help, but he had only managed to interfere. The crew was efficient. As a boy he had worked for a brief time under a ship maker. The Seawitch was one of the finest merchant ships he had ever seen. She was made of rosewood: lightweight, durable, and very expensive.

Kilmin's crew consisted of eight men, where it usually took at least twelve to take care of a ship so vast, but with the Seawitch's expert design extra men were unnecessary. Great care had been taken to place its gears and levers close together so one man could do two or more jobs with little effort.

Galvin wondered what kind of cargo sat under the ship's hull. On the fore and aft of the ship two large catapults were packed with rocks, ready to soar. Most ships had one catapult, maybe two, but not four. Whatever Kilmin did, it wasn't legal. That suited Galvin fine. It meant Kilmin could dodge trouble blindfolded.

The Seawitch's rosewood gleamed in the afternoon sun and Galvin itched to board. He loved to sail, and it had been years since he had boarded a vessel as grand as the Seawitch. A wooden maiden, carved with intricate detail, jutted from the fore of the ship, leading it onward to adventures unknown. Her arms swept the air beside her, her long hair lifted from her slender neck, and her parted lips tasted the sea breeze that had given her birth. Galvin wondered whose daughter she was. Most carvings depicted actual women, and this one appeared recently carved. The lines were too defined and the coloring too rich to be an old piece. He was suddenly glad he didn't know. If he had seen the woman in true form he would have lost his heart.

Someone stepped beside him. Thinking it was Neki, Galvin didn't turn.

"If you don't mind me asking, what's your purpose in sailing to the Druid island?"

Galvin started at the sound of the strange voice and found himself staring into the bluest eyes he had ever seen. The man was about his height, with nape-length wavy brown hair. A long black-hooded cloak enveloped him, concealing all other clothing from view.

When the man brought a black-gloved hand out of his cloak, Galvin noted the rest of him was clothed in black as well. Galvin's eyes widened. It had been years since he had heard of the man, but when the Knight had ridden through the Lands Galvin had been awestricken. He had even held childish whims of riding to help the man avenge the Lands.

"You're the Black Knight."

The man smiled. "I suppose I could be, but it wouldn't be such a good thing to admit so close to Dresden. Someone could sell such information and become a very rich man."

Galvin glanced at Zorc, now watching them with growing interest. "But such a man would be a great asset to what we do, although he wouldn't want to go where we go."

"Yes, Dresden would be a dangerous place for the Black Knight to ride."

The man's gaze shifted out to sea. His jaw clenched as his arms folded. Galvin knew without a shadow of a doubt the Black Knight stood beside him. The anger the man still carried wasn't only evident, it was catching.

"Although the Black Knight would consider riding on Dresden if he discovered a man by the name of Ren Razon happened to be on the island." The man's eyes narrowed. "It's about time the Druids know who I am."

Galvin's hopes soared. Without even considering how the Knight knew of Ren, Galvin nodded. "Ren's there. He's the reason we go. If you would accompany us we would be in your debt. Not only would it tip the scales in our favor, I for one would relish the show."

The Knight smiled, eyes dancing as he leaned toward him. "Between you and me, I've always wanted an excuse to make my appearance on Dresden. Once Ren is safe I'll have to thank the prince for giving me the opportunity." His smile withered. "If he's safe. May the Maker's fates be with him. If he's safe."

Zorc inclined his head. "Zorc Val Vincent humbly at your service, fair knight. As the Calvet, the leader of the Alcazar, which is no more I should say," Zorc said, waving his hand in irritation, "I've heard of your deeds and would like to express my deepest gratitude."

The Black Knight's eyes narrowed in warning. Galvin stiffened, unsure why the Knight looked at the wizard with rising animosity. Zorc didn't seem to notice. He rolled to the balls of his feet, smiling with bright enthusiasm.

"As a defender of those born with the power, I should say, fair wizard, the likes of you should have obliterated the Druid race years ago."

Zorc sighed and nodded, not a hint of irritation finding his face. "Believe me, I've considered it many a time, as have most wizards of old, but to wipe out a race is for the Maker to decide, not man. And the Druids are needed in case a wizard turns corrupt. If it weren't for the Druids more wizards would act on their hunger for power. No, I like the Druids no more than you, perhaps even less, but they're a necessity I'm afraid. Though a little less of them would be quite to my satisfaction."

"If they're such a necessity," the Black Knight said, "where were they when Barracus took the Lands?"

Zorc raised his pointy eyebrows and rocked to his toes. "The Druids were there, Knight, but Barracus had split his mind, built his own door, and took all of himself behind it, not just pieces. He remained whole and intact behind a door the Druids couldn't open, a door of his own creation. Correct me if I'm wrong, but that's exactly what you've done, I should say, put all of yourself behind a door."

After a few breaths, the Black Knight nodded his assent.

"Very admirable, Knight, very admirable indeed." Zorc tapped his lips with a finger and looked at the Black Knight with a quizzical expression.

Galvin was lost on the entire concept. He would never understand the ways of magic. A hollow ache rose within him as he remembered the glorious sensation he had felt when Zorc had charmed his sword. No, he would never understand, and now he would always yearn to know.

Zorc continued. "I've tried to create this door over the years, so my mind is empty and my soul is safe, but I've been unsuccessful. I suspect only those who have broken from tradition at a young age can do so. Has this happened?"

The Black Knight considered the wizard's words. He finally nodded.

Zorc smiled and hooked his hands behind his bony frame in humble satisfaction.

"Galvin, Zorc!" Neki was suddenly beside them, face flushed from his hurried approach. As his eyes grazed over the Black Knight a grin lit his face, but it faded within a heartbeat. "Druids are in the brush by the dock. I don't know how many, but it looks like they're watching the Divi, making sure Ren isn't followed."

"Where?" Zorc asked.

Neki's eyes shifted to the end of the dock where dense trees created a secure haven. "There's a fallen tree about fifty paces inside the cluster. They ducked behind it when they heard my approach."

"You didn't let on you noticed?" Nigel said.

A wide grin spread across Neki's face. "No. I like my memories and my vices. I've no desire to fight their kind without the likes of you."

The Black Knight released a boisterous laugh. The sound was surprisingly charming until he brought up his gloved hands and flicked his wrists. Twin daggers sliced through the air, transforming his laughter into something fierce. As fast as the daggers appeared, they disappeared. The Black Knight turned without a word and walked toward the distant tree line, cloak billowing behind him.

"He came just in time," Neki whispered as they watched the black form move toward the trees.

"Yes," Zorc said, tucking his arms behind his back and rocking forward to his toes. "He just may be the edge we need to make it out alive."

- - -

Nigel came back from the woods tucking five black locks of hair inside his cape. He had gained no pleasure from the destruction of life, only mild satisfaction that he may have obtained the ship safe passage to Dresden.

Looking down at the five flail-like instruments in his fist, Nigel shook his head and combed a hand through his hair. Druids were an abominable lot. The flail-like instruments proved it.

Each flail was a different size, the largest as big as his forearm, the smallest only the size of his palm. Each was polished to a silver sheen and had handles carved with enigmatic runes. He had read about the Druids' sacred instruments, or xectics, before, but had no idea they still existed.

Nigel shivered, unwilling to think about what would have become of them had Neki not seen the Druids in the brush. The Druids would have used the xectics without any hesitation, awakening the monster of the Old Sea – the Druidonian.

Nigel could hardly believe the Druids would call to it after all these years, even with a prize like the Chosen. The Druidonian was unpredictable and indestructible. Once, the Druidonian had almost destroyed Dresden and had come close to wiping out every Druid in existence.

Nigel wished it had. Then Megglan and Sherri would still be alive.

A small breeze stirred, carrying with it the scent of death. A soft, hollow whistle came from one of the xectics. Nigel had always wondered how the flail-like instruments could make such a sound. Now he knew. The spiked tips of the metal ball had been cut, allowing air to circulate freely, amplifying the wind's effects and causing a shrill croon to call to the monster.

Nigel glanced over the dark, gold-tipped waves of the Old Sea. He wondered where the Druidonian rested and if it had to be called to rise to the surface. The island of Dresden wasn't visible, but he could feel the Druids miens and his own violent reaction to those miens. Yes, it was about time the Druids knew his identity.

Damn them to below the Abyss! They needed to be annihilated. The wizard may very well change his mind about the Druids' necessity when he saw the xectics.

As Nigel approached the ship, the sails had been raised and the wizard and Galvin had already boarded. When Nigel stopped beside Neki, the younger man gave him a disgruntled look.

"I wish I could split my mind like you. If I could, the Druids would have a real bad day."

Nigel chuckled and handed Neki the black tufts of hair. "Souvenirs."

A smug grin stole over Neki's features. "Looks like they're already having a real bad day."

Nigel laughed, and without another word trotted toward the ship, carefully shielding the xectics with his cape.

As soon as he had climbed on board, the crew shouted oaths and barked commands as the ship veered toward the center of the Divi River. The tension of the crew was visible in their every move, and Nigel could hear the worry underlying their speech. Everyone feared the Druids.

Nigel strode to the wizard, who leaned over the fore railing as the ship broke into the open sea.

Nigel knew what he was looking for.

"It is."

The wizard's tired midnight eyes turned his way, the question evident.

Nigel held up the xectics. "There were five of them in the woods, each with one of these. I'm sure they were to call it if a ship sailed for Dresden."

Zorc's face turned sour. "Damnedable Druids. I have a good mind to eradicate every one of them."

Nigel smiled.

Zorc sighed and scratched his chin. "At the beginning of time only one race existed. The Maker granted some individuals special gifts to be more, shall I say, 'in tune' to the people and elements around them. They could call objects, communicate with animals, and enter a mind, thereby influencing how a person developed."

Nigel stiffened. Galvin leaned against the railing next to Zorc. "Do you mean the Druids were once one of us?"

"Yes," Zorc said, brows furrowing into a deep V. The Druids and we are one, yet they spun off from us and created their own cultus until they became a completely different breed. You see, those with these powers thought themselves superior and only interbred with each other. After years, every child born of a Druid pair had the same powers. And so it continued until the memories of their lineage was washed away from every heart and mind.

"After a time the Druids became zealots, stilted in their mannerisms and actions. They broke from the Maker and preached their supremacy. Although they didn't rule directly, the Druids forced their way into many political circles. Not even kings would deny them. Everyone believed in their superiority. Then the Quy was born."

Zorc paused to smile. "Druid supremacy was suddenly disputed. Their power and influence waned. Because the Druids taught spiritual unrighteousness they couldn't make war without demeaning their name. But soon the Druids found a way to rationalize their superiority even in lieu of the Quy. They learned how to close the door.

"For a time the Lands were in chaos as Druids rationalized wizard closings, claiming it was their religious right. The people were confused, not knowing who or what to believe.

"When the Druids first learned how to close the door they also knew how to keep a person whole, even if part of the person's essence went behind the door." Nigel drew in a sharp breath. Zorc turned to him with rage in his eyes. "Soon after the closings started a new Druid leader, Donnu, came into power. He was more zealous than most and saw a chance to debase those with the Quy. He began what wizards call 'The Silent War.'

"Donnu was a very charismatic person and the Druids followed him blindly. One by one, Donnu put each Druid's knowledge of how to shut the door behind their own door. He then taught them a new way of closing, one that would tear the memory or power from a man and not only shut it behind the door, but destroy him.

"Wizards began going mad and the people of the Lands turned to the Druids for help, once again believing in Druid supremacy. The remaining wizards soon learned what had happened, but by that time it was too late. All the Druids' former knowledge of how to shut the door without destroying the person was gone. But that was what Donnu wanted. He planned on driving the wizards mad and regaining power for the Druids."

"But can't someone find the knowledge again?" Galvin asked.

"It's unlikely. The Druids who knew how to shut the door and not lock it have long since died. With each new generation the shadow of the knowledge slips further and further away. I doubt even the most powerful Druid would be able to deduce how they had once been able to accomplish the task."

"Did the wizards do anything when they discovered the Druid deception?" Nigel asked.

"Oh yes," Zorc said with vengeful eyes. "They created the Druidonian."

Nigel whistled. "That's doing something."

A small smile touched Zorc's lips, but it quickly faded. "As soon as the Druid deception was discovered the remaining wizards plotted their revenge. When the Druid Caucus took place that year and all the Druids went to Dresden, the wizards put their plan into play. The wizards decided on the silver dragon, the fiercest beast known to man, to base the creature. And then they changed it, added to it, and subtracted from it, to form what is now called the Druidonian."

"So it's really just a silver dragon, only altered?" Nigel asked, not surprised. Some books called the beast the dragon of the Old Sea.

"It isn't just a silver dragon," Zorc said quietly. "It's a magical creature through and through. Although it began as a silver dragon, each part of it was molded and shaped by the wizards: each scale made perfect, each bone made stronger than iron, each talon made lethal, each ounce of blood made deadly. It's a creature that can't be destroyed by magic. It's a creature that can't be destroyed by weapons. It's a creature that can't be destroyed."

The wind whipped and lashed in haunting tones, causing the xectics to sing their shrill cry. Nigel spun, shedding his cloak and covering the flails. He held his breath. When the noise abated with no incident, only then did he begin to breathe. When he turned back to the others, Zorc had paled. Nigel wondered if the wizard had ever seen the creature.

Zorc eyed the xectics with a dangerous frown. "The wizards created the creature to keep the Druids on Dresden. The Druidonian circled the island, and if the Druids tried to leave it would attack. But something went wrong; and let this be a lesson to us all. If you transform life, it's out of your control. It has a mind of its own. That's what happened to the Druidonian. It formed a pact with the Druids and now it's their protector, not their captor."

"What's the pact?" Galvin asked.

"They feed it."

Nigel's heart began to race. He didn't want to know what they fed it. He surely did not. His eyes met Galvin's. The same sentiments were mirrored in Galvin's gaze, but Galvin finally turned to Zorc.

"Feed it what?"

"Their women."

The wind howled around them, sending a chill down Nigel's back. He looked toward Dresden, unable to see the island in the fading light. No one knew why there weren't any Druid women. It was a topic always dismissed as unsolvable. No Druid women had ever been seen and none were mentioned. When the topic was brought up the Druids ignored it, and no one wanted a Druid to be angry with them so the topic was left to die.

Nigel's grip tightened on the hilt of his sword. "I don't understand why this is unknown, or why it's allowed."

"It's unknown because the Druids don't want it known and the wizards are ashamed. It's allowed because the Druids do so, no matter how brutal, to survive. The wizards of old allow it because if the Druids were destroyed the Druidonian would search elsewhere for food. It would come to the mainland. The magic that created the creature is strong enough to keep it close to the island, but what would happen if the Druids weren't there to feed it?"

Nigel swallowed, closing his eyes. Years ago he had almost wiped out the entire Druid race. Thank the Maker he hadn't.

"Some Druids tried to escape the island when the Druidonian was first put into the sea," Zorc continued. "They, of course, died. The creature became hungry for human flesh, so much so it attacked Dresden, almost destroying the entire city. After that the Druids began feeding it their women. In those days women Druids were considered expendable, even though, in some respects, they were even more powerful than the men. I believe once a woman reaches a certain age she's forced to birth a child, then she's fed to the Druidonian."

"But magic has been dead for almost four hundred years," Galvin said. "The Druidonian has been dormant. Why aren't there any women now?"

"I don't know and I don't know if I really care to know. The Druids have always been a zealous, secretive breed. I'm sure they've rationalized their ritual sacrifices in some way; and because the Druids have sacrificed their women for so long, with the lull in magic, they may have continued to sacrifice them for other reasons."

Nigel remained silent. Now he understood why the Druids hadn't hesitated to kill Megglan and Sherri. They considered women expendable, only good for sacrifices. Yes, it was about time the Druids knew his identity. He may not come back from Dresden alive but he would take ten times a tenfold down with him. Nigel felt eyes upon him and turned to meet Zorc's coal-black glare.

"Don't do anything foolish on Dresden. If they've already put Ren's power behind the door, only you have a chance to save him. You know how to split your mind and protect yourself from them. You may know something that can break him free. If you die, Ren dies, and all hope is lost for the people you love in this world."

Nigel tensed but remained silent. Zorc turned and walked away. Nigel knew the wizard was right, but he wanted to go to Dresden without duty or moral obligation. He wanted to go to Dresden and obliterate every Druid he could. The Druidonian would have plenty more to feed on.

Before he could consider Zorc's words, Galvin locked his gaze. The man seemed to glow with an interior light of pure, unblemished confidence. The wind whipped his white-blond hair around his face like sheets of lightning.

"I abhor the Druid race. They destroyed my family long ago, leaving only one of us alive. There have been many times I wished I were riding beside you, mutilating every Druid in the Lands." Galvin paused. Nigel leaned closer, not wanting to miss what the wind was trying to tear away.

"The man you're about to save is only a man, but he's one of the best men I've ever known. I don't say that because he's the Chosen, the title doesn't do him justice, but you won't believe me until you see for yourself. I don't know why you hate the Druids, and it isn't my place to ask, but I'll ask one thing of you, and keep in mind this request comes from someone who hates Druids as well." Galvin's deep brown eyes were penetrating. Nigel had never seen so much inner strength in someone, not even his brother. He nodded for Galvin to continue.

"Focus on Ren, get him out, and save his mind. I assure you, you won't regret it."

Galvin kept his gaze locked on Nigel for a few heartbeats before he walked off into the night. Nigel leaned against the railing and closed his eyes, battling the voices in his mind.

He thought of his little brother. Ramie had grown into a man since Nigel had left. He thought about his father and mother, to whom he had never been able to say goodbye. He thought about his sister and Sherri and made himself stop there. He was fighting ghosts he would never be able to defeat. The pain would always be there. Sherri and Meg would never be with him again. He would never see his parents again. He had missed years of his brother's life. Nothing could get that back. If he killed every Druid on Dresden it wouldn't be enough.

Nigel took off of his left glove and looked at the brand. He had lived with his hate for so long he didn't know what he would do without it. Could he release it long enough to save the man on the island? He remembered the respect Ramie held for the prince and knew if his brother felt that strongly about Ren, he had to try.

CHAPTER 18

The latch lifted. Ren stood as Morrus entered the room, his customary gray robe replaced with a white one. Their eyes locked in friendship, but before Ren could speak Feher interjected, "It's time, Chosen."

Ren tensed, eyes flickering to Marinus. Avalon was nowhere to be seen.

"Will Morrus lead it?" Ren asked.

"Yes," Feher said, his distaste obvious.

Ren tried to catch Morrus' eye once more, but the former LoDrek had bowed his head. Ren heaved a sigh and followed Morrus and Feher down the hall, Marinus following.

Ren kept his eyes locked on the back of Morrus' head. Morrus had shaved off his black tuft of hair. Ren wondered if the gesture had anything to do with the closing or if it had something to do with Avalon replacing him as LoDrek.

The moonstone chambers seemed to have no end. The Druids' ceremonial robes blended so well with the moonstone Ren had to concentrate to distinguish between the white-robed Druids and the walls. The scent of vanilla hung heavy in the air and as they moved deeper in the temple Ren descried almost imperceptible hollows in the stone where small candles were lit to wash the moonstone corridor in a haunting glow.

The hallway twisted and curved, and Ren could sense their descent into the earth, but as soon as he thought they were about to reach the bottom of the temple they led him up a narrow circular stairway. They were taking him to the base of the slender culmination he had seen from the ship.

He had relived his memories the prior night, bringing them to the surface and studying each detail. Now he brought them to mind again. They flashed through his subconscious with vivid clarity. He concentrated harder. His thoughts were so strong his chest began to heat with emotion. The Druids hadn't tried to break his wall recently so he relaxed his hold, sending more of his strength into his memories and beliefs. They burned through him like a meadow fire. They were almost blinding.

The heat at his chest became painful. When he reached for the spot he quickly pulled his burnt fingers away and stared at the soft blue light visible beneath his tunic.

The star sapphire was glowing.

Ren's mind reeled at the implications. He focused harder, releasing more of his wall and sending more of his energy into bringing his memories to life. When he concentrated on the stone his memories became more vivid. At times he thought he could reach out and touch them. Then he remembered how Galvin had told him to believe right before his eyes had flickered to the stone.

The stone would hold his memories until Markum opened his door.

A complete calm washed over him. His faith in the Maker and the Oracle flickered to new heights. He wasn't a prisoner of fate but a prisoner of doubt. If you trusted the Maker and let him steer you, even if the path looked impossible, your fate worse than death, whatever happened would be right. Trust Him to the why, Galvin had said, you just follow the how.

A door carved with ornamental runes loomed before him. As Feher opened it a soft, eerie humming drifted into the hall.

Ren shifted his gaze to where Feher pointed. A lone pedestal rested at the center of a stair-stepped platform, barely discernable among the white moonstone floors. Two steps bolstered the platform, forming an arc that swept the room. Another curved section faced the platform, but where only two steps formed the first, multiple steps marched up the second. Those steps held hundreds of white-robed Druids. When Ren stepped forward, the entire Druid clan turned his way.

Ren felt a hand on his arm and looked up into Morrus' eyes. Morrus' former mustache had been shaved, and his skin was shimmery, as if he had been in an oil bath.

"Courage to you," Morrus whispered.

Ren nodded, grateful someone in all this madness cared for him as a human being. He whispered his thanks before he walked toward the center pedestal.

The humming stopped. The only sound was the echo of his footsteps on the moonstone floor.

He wished he wore something else with color besides his brown pants and boots. The white surrounding him left him slightly off balance, like he was walking in a mystic abstraction, looking through another's eyes but feeling every emotion. The white was maddening. It went against what was about to occur and marred the color's purity.

Part of him wished the countless Druids would turn so he could see their black tufts of hair, something that would provide a concrete image.

Apparently every Druid had come for his closing. If all were needed, he was unsure. But it was no matter. He came willingly. In a few heartbeats he would release his wall completely and let them fulfill his fate.

He glanced up when he reached the pedestal. The thin pyramid ended in a pinprick of dark sky. He could see a star through the shaft and wondered if it was the synergy. He would like to think it was. The thought calmed him.

Marinus tapped his shoulder and motioned for Ren to mount the stone pedestal. Marinus sat in a moonstone chair to the pedestal's left. Feher took the seat to the pedestal's right. As soon as Ren had stepped on top of the smooth stone Feher and Marinus lifted a stone goblet to their lips and drank its contents. When Ren turned to face the assembly he saw the entire Druid clan doing the same.

Ren discerned Morrus amidst the sea of clouds, gliding past the crescent horde on his way to a small, round stone resting below the main platform. Ren followed him with his eyes, longing for an allied spirit, but when Morrus turned to face him he wore the expressionless Druid mask.

Morrus raised his hands. The stark silence in the auditorium became deafening. Not even a robe moved. One of Ren's hands clutched the star sapphire on its own volition.

Feher began to chant in the old language, and Marinus joined in. The Druids on the terraced steps started to sway, and one by one their voices merged and congealed together. The chant shook Ren's bones and rumbled deep in the hollows of his gut.

Ren concentrated on Morrus, the only Druid not singing the haunting tune. The white of his robe blended so well with the white of the floor Ren had to concentrate to find the outline of his friend's body. Then Morrus' eyes cleared and locked on Ren. It was a friend's farewell. Then the look was gone. But it was all Ren needed.

He released his hold on the wall. It faded into oblivion.

Ren forced himself to concentrate on his memories. Releasing the stone he let it fall against his chest and burn his skin. He let the memories crash over him with maddening speed.

The memories went on and on: falling, tumbling, screaming, and burning. He reveled in each wonderful heartbeat, relived each painful experience, and recalled each raging emotion. The love, the hate, and the pain flowed through him, sending fire through his blood. It caused the Quy to ignite within him.

With sudden intensity all the feelings he had ever known merged into one, shattering his vision and forcing him higher until he thought his heart and mind were going to explode with pain, hate, and love.

He screamed as his entire body was racked with the extremities of the internal elements. Then with sudden fury, they were gone.

Cold stone hit his shoulder. A sensation he knew he should recognize lingered in his arm. But, for the fates, he couldn't place the feeling.

A rill of crimson liquid seeped from beneath him and trickled across the white floor. He watched in fascination as the crimson froth soaked through the cracks and crevices in the stone, creating a web of powdery pink lace.

Color, he thought. It made him feel better, yet he couldn't remember why it should. His eyes focused on a man standing below the platform. The man had an odd look on his face.

He was tired. He closed his eyes, not wanting to think about all the new images. He knew he should know them, but he did not.

A humming echoed around him. Something tickled his mind. He batted the air with a limp hand, annoyed. All he wanted to do was sleep. The humming grew louder.

Then it seeped inside him, buzzing incessantly, rumbling his vitals. He didn't like it. He wanted it out. He managed to push a few of the whip-like currents away, but there were far too many to fight.

The whips continued to come. He could see them now. They were a dark gray, a very dark gray, so dark he could barley make them out in the darkness. There were hundreds of them. A door rose in the darkness. He lay in front of the door, facing the long, gray whips. When he managed to roll his head to the side he saw a rune on the door: an inverted triangle inside a larger triangle inside a circle.

It was the symbol of something powerful.

He turned back to the approaching gray whips. They swam through him, insistent, hungry, and then he felt them pulling something out, tearing something from him.

The last of the whips left him. He rolled over just as the door shut. He heard a sharp slap and knew the door had been locked.

His insides welled with desperation. He had to open the door. He propped himself up and pushed with all his strength. It wouldn't give way.

The air became very thin. He heaved for a breath. He shook the door.

Something wasn't right. He wasn't right. A part of him had been taken. It was a part that kept him alive.

He tried to unsheathe his sword, but it was too heavy. The raised emblems on its hilt burned his palm. He struggled to remember what they meant. He couldn't.

Losing his grip, he fell.

- - -

Morrus stumbled to Ren and gathered him in his arms, not caring if he stained his white ceremonial robe with the blood of the man who had given him the chance to live another day. He felt a tear trickle down his cheek. He hadn't cried in a long time, not even when he walked to his death that morning.

He couldn't believe what he had seen or what he had felt. When Ren had released his guard the collective force of the Druids surged forward, but instead of entering Ren's mind they had been shattered in a thousand directions.

A blinding hot light emitted from Ren's chest. It encased his entire body with a soft blue hue, forming a shield around him. But the touch of that light was like lying naked in soft grass, allowing the morning's mist to tickle your skin as the sun caressed your limbs and warmed your soul. It was exhilaration, radiance, and felicity. Morrus wasn't surprised he cried. That feeling, that faith!

But when the light had congealed back to Ren's core and Ren had fallen from the pedestal Avalon had crashed past Morrus, leading the Druids in the closing Morrus should have led.

Morrus tried to overtake the new LoDrek, but he had been whisked away by the others, wrapped up in the Druid power that had been lying dormant since the ride of the Black Knight. They had invaded Ren's mind, locked his power away and left him as quickly as they had entered. Morrus tried to stay behind and touch Ren with his own mien, but the power of the conglomerate was too strong.

Now Ren was stark white, near death.

"Does he live?"

Morrus looked up into Feher's yellow eyes. He had always despised those eyes. They had haunted his dreams since he was a boy. They were so impure their pupils were almost imperceptible. Morrus shivered, acknowledging the corruption he had denied his entire life.

The High Priest hovered over him. He licked his lips. "I asked you a question, Morrus. Does he live?"

Yellow eyes lit with salient carnality. The High Priest of Dresden, the true Druid leader, was depraved. Morrus' breath quickened. He drew Ren closer. His denial may have caused Ren's death. May the High Order save him. If, Morrus reminded himself, there was a High Order.

The rock on which he had built his foundation crumbled. All his life he had tried to obey their laws. Although they told him he would never become the High Order, if he were pure enough he may be born again to the Druid race and granted a second chance. If he were impure at death he would fall back to the lowest realm to wallow and pine until he paid for his sins and reached a new understanding. If he fell, Morrus knew, he would never become the High Order. Only a few were taken, only a few became, only a few.

"Barely," Morrus said, realizing he had done something grave and dangerous. Although Ren had agreed to go behind the door, something was wrong, and there was absolutely nothing Morrus could do about it.

Feher grinned. He actually grinned. Morrus couldn't hold his tongue any longer. "If you want to achieve the High Order you shouldn't be laughing at a man near death."

Yellow eyes darkened. "What do you know of the High Order? Contrary to what your father believed, no one can rise to Druid status again, even if he continually walks in moonstone halls. In short order you'll be sent to your rightful place. So don't speak to me, or else – "

"You'll kill me again?" Morrus was suddenly thankful his father had passed on. Now he could leave the Obelisk and discover if the High Order truly existed. "Nothing matters to me anymore, Feher. Don't think it does."

Feher's yellow eyes narrowed, but Marinus stepped between them, the ceremonial drug still laden in his eyes. "You'll have to be purified again, Morrus."

Morrus followed the Drek's gaze to his white ceremonial robe. Blood from Ren's torn shoulder saturated the front. He nodded, studying Marinus. Was the Drek corrupt as well? But no satisfaction glistened in the Drek's gaze, only a duty of station. For the first time in Morrus' life Marinus appeared old. Avalon would soon be Drek. The thought repulsed him. The New Order would once again rise above the Old. Morrus wondered if the Black Knight would appear when the destruction began again.

In a way, Morrus hoped he would.

"Morrus, you must hurry. Go to the purification chamber. We must make haste. The ship will sail as soon as you're ready," Marinus said, shattering his thoughts.

Morrus motioned to Ren. "Let me help him first."

"They'll tend to him in the purification."

Morrus blinked, confused. Why would they purify Ren? Were they sending Ren to his death as well? Marinus saw the shocked look on Morrus' face and put a hand on his shoulder. "Ren is being purified because he must travel among our kind until the One gives him to whom he should."

Morrus felt sick. Something wasn't right. The story didn't make sense. Ren was in trouble and he had helped get him there.

- - -

Neki sat on the docks, trying to decide if he was nervous, furious, or just plain bored. He had watched the Seawitch fade into the distant horizon with increasing frustration. He knew the wizard was right, but burning cinders he wanted to go.

When he could no longer see the sails he tried to decide on his next course of action. He had always loved exploring cities, the labyrinth of streets and alleys, the bustle of bars and inns, the intrigue of shops and trades, but after what he had just experienced city exploration held little appeal, and he had already scoured the countryside waiting for the blasted ship to sail. Finally, he plopped down beside the kota and started to brood.

He was good at brooding. Grauss hadn't been the finest of companions. Yes, Neki was a champion at brooding. A lot of favorable things came from it, in his opinion. If no one brooded nothing would be discovered. Grauss was also good at brooding, but he brooded with his hands. Neki brooded with his mind.

He stroked Keena's neck. She didn't purr. That bothered him. Keena always purred. Neki studied her. She had grown so fast she looked half starved, but he had nothing to worry about. He had seen her eat. Grauss had fretted over him for a time as well, but that had been unnecessary. He ate like a horse, or a kota.

Neki stretched and tried not to think about being left behind. He was beginning to feel unneeded again. He knew his feelings were irrational, but his childhood had left him with a fear of inadequacy.

Grauss was a good man, but a blasted horrible grandfather. Neki could count on two hands how many times Grauss had engaged him in games of chance or carried on a conversation without mentioning his inventions. Neki's life had consisted of running errands for Grauss, learning on his own, or brooding.

If his parents had lived he would have had a pedagogue, but Grauss had taken him into hiding and let him learn on his own. Grauss' first rule was: you don't have a last name, you're not related to me, and you don't know where you live. To a young boy it had seemed deliciously adventurous. He was a shadow with no name, a creature free to roam, a spirit without a role. But the older he grew his lack of identity and friends became tiresome.

Since he was a young boy he had dreamed of joining Ren's guard. He had managed to do so, by the Maker's fates good fortune, and had begun to make a name for himself. But now he was feeling insignificant again.

Neki heaved a sigh. Ren had given him a chance, and Neki wanted to give something back. He had been, in his mind, practically useless up to this point. He thought the Druids would give him an opportunity to fight for Ren, but that thought went up like a livery under flame. He was beginning to think his life would amount to a hill of beans.

The clouds were dissipating, granting a clear night to view the stars. Star-study was the one interest both he and Grauss had in common. Neki loved to sit with his grandfather and decipher the stars' hidden messages.

When Neki found the synergy constellation his breath faltered. The three stars around the synergy were almost in complete alignment, but the synergy, the center star had begun to move! The hazy light representing the One, though veering toward the center triangular region, was moving parallel to the center star. Hence the two would never meet. They would be two ships passing in the night.

Ren wasn't on Dresden anymore.

Zorc was going to miss him.

Neki jumped to his feet, Keena right beside him as if she had anticipated his panic.

What could he do? He was on the mainland, and he was no wizard. Although he could blow a pretty mean dust storm no one would heed him like they heeded Zorc. Besides, he couldn't waste time bargaining for a ship. He had to find one immediately.

He glanced back at the constellation. Ren was veering east, toward Zier. Maker of Fates!

Neki grabbed Markum's pallet and began dragging him toward the nearby trees. "Maker curse it, Markum! I can't take you with me. You wouldn't be good in a fight, and if I lose my skin I wouldn't want you to lose yours too."

As soon as Markum and the horses were sufficiently concealed in the thicket, Neki ran toward the dock. If he didn't steal a ship the world would suffer for it. There was no other way.

There were three ships in the harbor. Unfortunately all were large, huge even. Neki stopped beside the first only for a few heartbeats before dashing off to the next.

May the Maker be with him! Let there be a raft. Just a raft! He could handle a raft. But the others? He would either die trying to reach Dresden or arrive as gray as Grauss.

For the love of the Maker he had never so much as been on a raft before. Damn Grauss for his reclusive life! Every man should have been on a raft. Although Grauss studied ship navigation that wouldn't help Neki operate any one of the large ships, much less a raft.

Neki scurried up the third ship. It was the smallest of the three, though no less impossible, and glanced back at the stars. Thank the Maker it was going to be a clear night. He needed all the help he could get.

When he dropped to the deck his heart sank. Ropes and pulleys were everywhere, and the sail was so big it seemed to reach the stars. It would be foolish for him to try to overtake the Seawitch. He needed more men.

Neki studied the sky. The synergy star moved with slow precision. Although most would be unable to observe its slight movement, Neki had been trained by the best. It was moving. Grauss would say that if the synergy star broke through the triangle hope would be lost and the union would never be joined. Neki felt panic building inside him again.

A light shot through the darkness. Neki fell to the deck, hoping those approached wouldn't board the ship. Sailors thought of their ships as women, and if Neki had "touched" her he would have a fight on his hands.

After his heartbeat calmed, voices became clear. At first he thought he was done for. It sounded like an entire ship's crew approached, but as the fit of panic left him he heard only three distinct voices. They were just obnoxiously loud.

"Pass me whisky, Broody," the first one said

"Told ye, no more of whisky. Drank all of whisky."

The first one howled in laughter. The other two joined in. Something was struck over and over – perhaps a whisky bottle – adding to the commotion.

"Bloody need me more whisky," the third said.

"Coins? Any one ye have coins?" the first voice whispered, as if it was a felony to buy a drink.

There was immediate silence, a rustling, and a few oaths.

"A fine lot we're in!" Broody said. "No drink, no coins. A damn fine lot."

Neki slowly raised his head and peered over the edge of the railing. Three men sat in a large yet sturdy rowboat. Or was it a sailboat? Neki frowned and squinted into the dark. Four oars, two in front and two in back, were pulled in and sticking out of the boat at forty-five degree angles, making the craft look like a giant upside down bug. At the boat's middle was a sail, currently tied and bound with cords. How they had managed to float the make-do contraption up the river in one piece was beyond Neki's comprehension, but if they could do it drunk, he could do it sober.

"Maker's greetings!" Neki called.

The three men jumped like the Adderiss herself was after them. Neki watched in bemusement as the big one lost his balance and fell into the river. The other two, howling in glee, didn't lift a finger as their friend flailed in the water. When the man continued thrashing Neki realized he was truly in trouble and jumped over the side of the ship, cursing himself for not being more careful. All he needed was two drunks accusing him of drowning their friend.

When Neki reached the water's edge, the large man had managed to flail his way to the dock. Before he swallowed another mouthful of water Neki caught his burly arm and heaved him to safety.

The other two, still laughing, staggered their way, arm in arm, to the wooden planks, pointing at their companion who now appeared completely sober. Neki fell back, exhausted, wishing the man would have refused his last ten meals, but before he had time to take a breath the big man toppled his friends, accusing them of leaving him for dead. Neki, recognizing Broody's voice, scrambled up in time to catch Broody's burly arm as it reared back for vengeance. Broody turned to him, eyes red with either rage or whisky, Neki was unsure which, but he really didn't care to find out.

"Your friends didn't see the need," Neki said through clenched teeth. "They knew I'd help you. Why not forget the entire affair? I have an offer that will make all your moods better."

Broody swayed, but he finally conceded by rolling off his friends, blubber shaking when he hit the ground. "What offer?"

"Well," Neki began, scratching his head and trying to come up with an impromptu bargaining strategy, "I was just admiring your boat there. I have need of a boat like that and I heard you were wanting some more fine whiskey."

"No," the voice of the first said, rubbing his shirt where Broody had saturated it.

Neki glanced up at the stars, resolution filling him. "Not even for half a bag of gold?"

Broody's eyes widened. The one sitting next to Broody turned to the first and licked his lips. "That'll buy lots whisky, John."

John pursed his lips and shook his head. Neki knew the boat hadn't been worth a half a bag of gold when it was new. He stood for a few heartbeats, trying to decide if he should offer them the entire bag. If he did he had nothing else to bargain with. "All right. Three quarters of a bag, and that's my final offer."

John's eyes flickered to the bag of gold in Neki's hand. Neki jingled it for emphasis.

"All the bag and I keep the bloody oars."

Neki looked at John in shock. Keep the oars? The boat was half useless without the oars.

When John saw Neki's shocked expression he hung his head. "Sentimental reasons."

"All the bag and you keep one oar."

"Done." John staggered to his feet. Neki breathed a sign of relief as the other men began to laugh and dance around the dock. John snatched the gold from Neki's hand, forgetting all about the sentimental ore as soon as his hand touched the laden burlap cloth, and staggered off with his companions.

Neki wasted no time. He jumped into the rowboat and surveyed his new purchase. It was large enough to hold five men and five horses comfortably but small enough for one man to steer with only a little difficulty, or so he hoped. The more he examined it the more shocked he became. John had to have built the contraption. Although silly looking, it was bound to be useful. Surprisingly, it was very well made. He suddenly felt slightly ashamed for failing to remind John to take an oar. He could see the hard work that had gone in to shaping the wood and carving the handles with swirling designs.

John probably lived upriver and had constructed the phenomenon to make swift passage to the city: upriver use the oars, downriver use the sail. Sounded like something Grauss would invent, or at least ponder over for days.

Neki went to the mast and untied the sail. Although the night was calm, he could always hope a breeze would stir. When the sail was free he stepped to the side of the vessel and reeled in the anchor. Just as he began walking to the front there was a loud clamor and the boat rocked violently. Neki wheeled his arms, trying to regain his footing, but soon the boat's motion toppled him. Within the span of one breath he spun to a sitting position, dagger in hand, sure it was John returning to see if he carried any more gold for his life.

Instead of looking into the eyes of an inebriated man, Neki stared into the eyes of the kota. Keena blinked at him as if pouncing into a rowboat was something she did every day.

He didn't have time for this. "No," he said, striding forward, waving his hands in frustration and trying to make her jump back to the dock.

She growled.

He stopped. Had he mistaken her purr for a growl? Keena just stared at him. He walked forward again. This time she not only growled, she also bent her head and pointed her stunning horn at him.

"Whoa!" Neki said, slowly backing up. "Just trying to save you a little seasickness." With each retreating step, her stance relaxed, but only after he settled at the fore of the ship and began dipping the oars awkwardly in the water did she turn full circle and find a spot suitable to settle her large frame. There was nothing threatening about her now, only two large, soft brown eyes staring at him with complete trust.

"Ren has some good people on his side, girl. He'll be all right."

She whimpered as if she understood his words. A shiver went down Neki's spine. He shook it off, forcing himself to concentrate on oaring, or rowing, or whatever it was called, but the oars were distanced just far enough apart that he couldn't get a good grip on both at once. By the time he slid from one side to the other the boat was moving in the wrong direction. He was, at best, only compensating for his last stroke.

After a moons' click of awkward maneuvering, he was drenched in sweat and his buttocks had collected a thousand splinters. He glanced at the sky. Ren's star still continued to drift and the hazy white cloud still moved to where the star used to be. Neki rested the oars in the boat and put his head in his hands. He was going to be too late. If only there was a breeze.

Neki looked at the dormant white sail. If he could make a pebble spin in the wind, cause tree limbs to shake, and create a dust storm he could sure cause a breeze to move a boat. With budding confidence Neki concentrated on his emotions and looked at the sail. Nothing happened. He tried again. The sail only fluttered, careening to each side in a teasing manner.

Neki glanced at the synergy as a sick feeling rose inside him.

"Move!" he screamed to the night. He pulled out the sail and tried again. Tears of frustration burned his eyes. He dropped the sail

183

and sat down beside Keena. An ore pressed against his back, telling him it was his only hope.

The kota whimpered and Neki turned to her. "You think you could row?" Keena just stared at him.

Neki scratched her on the head. "Then what good are you?"

She leaned against him but didn't purr. That still bothered him. Ren was in trouble and Neki was the only one who could help. This was his chance to contribute to the cause. He looked across the black waters of the Old Sea, then back at the sail.

Neki cleared his thoughts and focused, not on his panic, but his determination. He could feel the Quy inside him, building in strength. He could sense her just beneath the surface, ready to help. Neki breathed her in. The sail filled and sprung to life. Keena's eyes opened wide when Neki slapped her on the neck and bellowed with laughter. He had never felt so good. They shot down the river like they were in the midst of a cyclone.

"Whoa!" Neki jumped to his feet. They were moving faster than dragons could fly but they were going in a straight line – the river curved.

With consternation Neki realized he didn't know how to change the wind's direction.

He dove for an oar and veered the ship back to the center of the river just before it made a disastrous course for a river tree.

Nothing was ever easy.

CHAPTER 19

They were approaching Dresden with a speed Nigel thought impossible until he realized the wizard had helped the winds a little.

During the ride Zorc had been mumbling to himself, drawing symbols on the deck with silver dust and checking the inner compartments of his robe. Nigel didn't ask. He would never understand wizardry. Although he had the power, he didn't know if he wanted to learn it. Galvin paced, shoulders and arms tensing under his dark tunic, a worried look on his face. Nigel was the only one perched on the edge of his seat with grim anticipation. The Druids were finally going to know him, this time intimately.

He watched the approaching island. Tall, spindly, white birch trees reached to the sky like pikes, warning off any trespassers. The trees had been cleared from the front of the Obelisk and cut back in a triangular shape from the entrance. The Obelisk shimmered in the rising dawn with wicked surety. The trees surrounding it matched its sinister appearance. Only the Druids could turn a sparkling white island into something that made your skin crawl.

As they moved closer even Nigel grew somber. The Obelisk's beveled peak towered over the ship and seemed to whisper a warning. Its smooth surface looked like it had been polished every day for centuries. If a window marred its great height Nigel couldn't find it. All he saw was flawless, shimmering moonstone.

The only sound heralding their arrival was the creaking wood of the ship. Nigel searched the shore for guards, expecting an alarm to sound. When none did Nigel turned to Zorc. The wizard observed the island with severe eyes. His midnight-blue robe blended into the morning's dimness but its silver swirls danced around him with a life of their own.

"Guards?" Nigel mouthed, shrugging in confusion.

Zorc's face darkened. "Every Druid will want to attend the closing."

"Then we have an edge."

"Maybe an edge to no avail."

It was the first time Nigel had heard the wizard express fear. For a few heartbeats, Nigel's confidence waned.

Before the boat had docked they all jumped into the shallow water and ran like the ten winds, each intent on the moonstone structure jutting out into the dusk like a sword's edge. The moonstone pathway led straight to the temple, but there was no door. Zorc began examining the structure, scowling and mumbling under his breath. Nigel could tell the wizard's tolerance for delay would last as long as dry grass in flame and moved back even before Zorc motioned them away.

Zorc plunged his hand into his robe, pulled out a fistful of silver dust and hurled it against the wall. Nigel dove to the ground, pulling Galvin with him as moonstone exploded in all directions. A rain of dust showered over them.

As the noise stilled, Nigel cleared the air with a wave of his hand. "What a novel idea. Alert the entire Druid cultus we're here. It has merit, wizard."

Zorc glared at him and pointed to the hollow opening.

A main passageway could be seen through the hovering dust. A young Druid cowered just beyond the wreckage. Nigel had never seen such stark terror scrawled in a face before, even when he had been on one of his execution missions. Another Druid lay dead inside the ruin, skull crushed by a large piece of moonstone.

Nigel pushed past Zorc, face hardening into an emotionless mask. "Take us to the Chosen."

The Druid cringed, eyes moving fitfully between Nigel and Zorc. Nigel leaned down and drew him up with a fistful of gray robe. "Now."

"I don't know where he is," the Druid said. "Honestly. Please. I don't know."

Zorc moved closer, eyes shining like hot coals. "Then take us to the Drek."

Nigel almost felt sorry for the youth. To be under the gaze of his people's assassin and a wizard who had just blown a hole the size of a horse in the sacred temple must approach the boy's worst nightmare.

Nodding, the boy spun and hurried down the passageway. The halls were deserted, and their footfalls echoed with ominous bearing on the moonstone floor. Nigel felt his longing to destroy the entire Druid line burgeon inside him but shoved the feeling down. His first priority was Ren. Then he would decide how many he would destroy.

Religious charlatans deserved death.

The boy turned and scampered down a narrow hallway to the right and led them to a column of winding stairs. They were moving to the heart of the Obelisk, to the temple. When they reached the landing the boy glanced back and darted away. Nigel put his hand on the hilt of his sword. He took the last few stairs and stepped into a large chamber. At least one hundred Druids were scattered over a terraced landing, chanting and swaying. One lone figure stood on the stage, long beard betraying his post.

Nigel stepped forward and strode to the Drek. His black cloak swirled about him as if a storm followed; inside, one did. Zorc and Galvin flanked him but Nigel barely noticed.

The Druids didn't hear them. Every eye was closed and raised to the hollow section of the Obelisk. Nigel recalled his pain from years ago when the three Druids had tried to claim his power. His anger boiled inside, yearning for a kill.

Nigel stopped in front of the Drek and put a hand on the wizard's arm, indicating for him to remain silent. Zorc bristled but nodded his assent.

Nigel clutched his anger to him like a blanket and pulled his sword from the scabbard. It echoed in the chamber with terminal resolution. All humming stopped. The Drek's eyes opened. His face held no emotion, but Nigel could see the recognition in his gaze. The Drek's body grew taut and a nerve began to twitch near his left eye.

Nigel smiled, free of the mask he had worn his entire life: first as a prince, second as an assassin. From that day hence he was neither price nor knight. He was who he was. And all would know.

He took a step forward. The silence was penetrating.

"My name is Nigel Augustus, heir to the throne of Oldan, known to you as the Black Knight. Years ago Druids took my sister, my love, and my life. I declared war. Today I wish to end it if and only if you honor one request."

An electric current went through the assembly as quiet words were whispered and then stilled. Nigel could smell the hate, and the fear.

"Give me the Chosen." When he was met with no reply, he lowered his voice to a harsh whisper. "I don't think you'll like the consequences if you refuse."

"The Chosen isn't for us to give," the Drek said.

Nigel could sense Zorc quaking anger and put out his hand, signaling for Zorc to remain silent. It didn't work.

Zorc pushed past him. "Where is he!"

It wasn't a question. It was a demand.

The Drek focused on Zorc for what seemed to be the first time. His brows twitched for a few breaths, but then his features smoothed into an emotionless mask.

Nigel could feel the Druids' weak attempt to gain entrance to his mind. He grinned. This would be fun. Zorc batted at the air as if a swarm of gnats were in his way. The Druids were either too few or too weak to do anything to the wizard.

The Drek glided back a step as Zorc strode forward. Nigel's eyes were drawn to the pedestal behind the Drek. Blood stained its surface. He remembered Ramie's description of the prince. Ren was a kindred spirit, a brother and a friend. Nigel took a step closer.

Zorc grabbed the Drek with both hands. The Druids rushed forward to protect their leader. Zorc was ready. He raised his hand. The Druids slammed into an invisible wall.

"You fool!" Zorc said, leaning closer to the Drek. "Did you honestly believe you had the One? Did you?"

The Drek's eyes widened.

With that look, Nigel saw the truth. The Druids had been tricked. They honestly thought they had the One. Apparently Zorc saw it too, for he released his hold, although his eyes still burned like two hot coals.

"You've sentenced the world to darkness," Zorc said. "Were you such a fool to think you were protecting the Lands? Did you honestly think closing the Chosen would force Barracus to wait for another? Now Barracus will be able to enter the Chosen with ease, for now Ren can't fight back."

Tears shimmered in the Druid's eyes. Nigel almost felt sorry for the Drek until he glanced back at the pedestal. He tightened his grip on his sword.

The invisible wall exploded with a sharp "swoosh." Zorc's scream shattered Nigel's calm. The Druids began to rush them. Nigel spun.

A Druid ran from a side door. He had the most putrid yellow eyes Nigel had ever seen, and they were focused on the wizard.

Zorc lay on the floor beside a broken bottle, dreadfully pale.

Nigel grabbed the Drek and put his sword against the hollow of the man's back. The horde of Druids stopped, unsure of what to do. The yellow-eyed Druid continued to walk forward, eyes finding Nigel.

A sharp, hard slam exploded in Nigel's mind. His internal door almost imploded. Nigel sagged backward, holding his door firm but feeling the resonant pressure of the depraved man on the other side. The yellow eyes narrowed. The pressure became stronger.

Just as Nigel felt himself weakening, his mind emptied. Nigel released a gasp just as Galvin screamed a warning.

Galvin pointed, but it was too late.

Nigel was shoved forward. His sword sliced through the Drek.

The Drek grunted as blood pounded from the wound, but instead of looking at Nigel the Drek turned to the Druid who had pushed Nigel's sword.

"My only son."

A murky-eyed Druid hid a smile as his eyes flickered to Nigel in victory. He turned to the horde of Druids and shouted, "He has killed my father. Now we must kill him!"

The Druids screamed in rage and rushed forward. Everything seemed to move in slow motion. Nigel looked into the murky eyes of the new Drek and felt his loathing grow to the very depths of his soul.

The Black Knight came to life.

He rose in a wave of black fury and grabbed the man around the neck of his white robe, raising him off the ground. Nigel brought up his bloodied sword and wiped it on the Druid's robe, signifying the betrayal.

The mass of white-robed Druids still hurled forward. Nigel felt the power inside him and remembered the feel of Zorc's fury as he unleashed it to create the invisible barricade.

He cracked his internal door and hurled his hate forward with the Quy, slamming a wall of air into the approaching Druids, hurling them back. The man in his hands squirmed and choked.

"Where is he?"

Nigel felt a hard slam in his mind. He gasped, trying to close his door, but it was too late.

The yellow-eyed one began to take his power. For the second time in his life, he felt part of his soul being torn from him.

Galvin had his sword at the hollow of the yellow-eyed Druid's neck. A small rivulet of blood oozed from the sword's tip, but Galvin had turned a ghostly white. For a heartbeat Nigel thought the Druid had somehow taken Galvin's mind, but after a slight hesitation Galvin drew back his sword and slammed it against the Druid's head, knocking him unconscious. The pressure immediately dissipated.

Nigel slammed the invisible wall back into place, but he knew he couldn't survive another attack. He turned to Galvin with unspoken haste. Galvin scooped up the wizard and ran for the door. Still clutching the Drek's son, Nigel ran after Galvin, leveling the remaining Druids with his gaze. He released the Quy and shut himself protectively behind his internal sanctuary, safe from the Druids' tentacles. A large vessel with glowing embers rested beside the door. Nigel kicked it over, spilling its contents. A white curtain shielding a side room from view ignited in flames.

The Druids screamed behind him.

He ran down the stairs, still dragging the murky-eyed Druid. Now all they could do was run, and they still didn't know where the Druids held Ren.

When he reached the main hallway he saw Galvin just ahead with Zorc slung over his shoulder like a sack of grain.

The Druids pursued them down the steps. Nigel's heart quickened. A deafening blast came from behind. Nigel dared a glance back. Fire spilled down the stairs. Whatever the Druids kept in the chamber behind the curtain didn't take kindly to heat.

The Drek's son scraped the sides of the walls, trying to slow Nigel's flight. Nigel finally turned and bashed the Druid's face. The man lost his balance and fell. Nigel hauled the Druid behind him, not caring how many bones the man broke along the way.

The hollow Zorc had blasted was just ahead. Nigel picked up the pace. Galvin did the same. When they broke into the sunlight they careened their way through the birch trees, making a straight path to the ship.

The ship was gone.

Galvin skidded to a stop, frantically searching the shoreline. Nigel turned to the Druid. There were scrapes all over him, a wicked gash on his forehead, but the fire in his eyes was still alive. Nigel put his sword against the Druid's chest. He leaned forward.

"Where's a ship?"

The man grinned. Blood oozed to the surface of his chest. "Already sailed to Agger Point, the Chosen on it." He cackled like a madman.

Nigel stiffened as a wave of Druids erupted from the Obelisk. They were going to die. It would be impossible for two men to fight so many Druids. With grim determination, Nigel tightened the grip on his sword, vowing to cut as many down as he could.

Galvin turned to Nigel and nodded. "It's been a pleasure."

"Truly said."

They clasped arms before they turned to face their deaths.

- - -

From out of nowhere Neki sprinted by them, straight for the wave of Druids, screaming like a lunatic and waving his saber in the air as if he were going to annihilate every last Druid on Dresden.

Nigel stood in stunned confusion. The Druids stumbled to a halt and began running in the opposite direction.

After the initial shock, Nigel laughed.

"Maker's fates. He has a boat!"

Nigel blinked. Galvin was right. If Neki was on the island, he had a boat.

"Run!" Neki screamed.

Nigel turned to see Neki swiveling in midair as the Druids regained their senses and resumed their charge. But it was enough. Neki had given them time.

Nigel laughed as he ran to the shore. For as long as he lived he would never forget the sight. He had never seen anything like it.

"Remind me to kiss him, will you?" Nigel shouted at Galvin.

Galvin only grinned.

After leaping into the funny looking boat, Galvin laid the wizard down and grabbed an oar, preparing to shove off as soon as Neki boarded. The kota pranced a greeting. Nigel did a double take when he saw her. Why would Neki bring the kota?

"Go, go, go!" Neki said, running toward them at full speed, saber slicing the air. Nigel took another oar and helped Galvin shove off. The kota continued to prance. Her drumming hooves reminded Nigel of a war chant.

Although the Druids weren't gaining on Neki, they could still reach the boat before it was safely away.

"Faster!"

Neki dove into the water and disappeared. Heartbeats later he was beside the boat, gasping for air. Nigel grabbed his tunic and hauled him in.

When Neki fell to the deck he wasted no time. Rolling to his feet he positioned himself behind the sail. A sudden breeze picked up and the boat lurched forward. Nigel lost his balance and fell over Zorc's sprawled body.

Nigel looked back. The Druids on the shore weren't coming after them, but they all had their hands clasped in a stance Nigel recognized.

"Neki! Get down!"

Neki didn't seem to hear. He was concentrating on the wind.

The Druids' eyes focused on Neki. Nigel didn't know how far the Druid power ranged but he intended to find out. The only thing that could save Neki was distance.

Galvin was already grunting with effort as he rowed the boat forward.

It wasn't fast enough. Neki released a scream.

"Hold on, Neki!" Nigel caught Neki as his body careened down the side of the boat. Nigel didn't hesitate. Nigel exploded out of his inner sanctuary and spun his desperation through the air. The boat lunged forward.

Neki was pale, but he twisted with effort. They hadn't closed him yet.

"More!" Galvin shouted.

Nigel didn't know how to conjure the continuous breeze Neki had, only the bursts came natural, but he released them one right after the other. The Druids' tentacles searched his mind, trying to reach his door, but with each burst the tentacles became more tenuous.

Galvin continued to row, but his face was contorted with worry. "Get him down!"

Neki moaned again. His eyes rolled back in his head. They almost had him.

Nigel covered Neki's body with his own, feeling the tentacles retreat, the wood of the boat somehow blocking the Druid power even more. After a few more bursts, Neki's eyes fluttered open. Nigel rolled away as he felt the last of the Druid tentacles fade to nothing.

Neki began the breeze again, but his face held a lingering horror of the tentacles.

"No."

Galvin's cry forced Nigel back to the task at hand. Peering over the boat, he froze.

"May the Maker's fates be with us."

Although they were well away from the island they weren't far enough away to miss the five Druids standing apart from the others: five Druids with five xectics.

A high-pitched whine screeched through the air. The kota growled in irritation.

"Burning cinders, faster," Neki whispered, more to himself than to anyone else.

The ship moved like the ten winds, but it wasn't fast enough. They were sitting targets on the Old Sea.

"Nigel," Galvin said, "how long will it take the Druidonian to find us?"

As if in reply, the water rolled with ebullient foam. The boat lurched forward, teetering dangerously to the side. Galvin dove for Zorc, catching the wizard's robe before he was flung off the side of the vessel. The kota screamed a warning. Nigel turned in time to see a silver mass begin to emerge from the turbulent waves. Silver scales glittered in the sun as mammoth shoulders crashed through the surface . . . then a head . . . then a neck. Someone gasped.

The Druidonian's neck extended skyward for almost three stories, and its head was over twice was big as their boat. Water cascaded down its silvery scales and seaweed clung to its length like leeches. Its eyes were solid silver holes, blending with the scales but glowing with an unnatural fury, even for a predator. Nigel took a step back.

The air stilled. Neither Nigel nor Neki could conjure a breeze if they tried. The waves crashed into the side of the boat, jerking them fro and back, but they couldn't take their eyes off the horror before them.

The Druidonian bellowed a warning. Teeth as long as thighbones gleamed in the morning's sun. Its head moved closer, mouth curling in a snarl.

"Holy Maker," Neki whispered as he crawled over and began shaking Zorc. Nigel remembered what the wizard had said. No magic could kill the creature, and no weapon could defeat it. He put a hand on Neki's arm, shaking his head as if to say the wizard would be of no use. Nigel didn't even know if the wizard still lived.

"Wind!" Galvin shouted as the Druidonian's head moved closer.

Both Neki and Nigel forced the sail to rise. The boat spun forward, but the creature was right behind them, tips of its wings coming out of the water like oars.

Nigel could feel the heat of its breath moving over the ship. He smelled the foul odor of the creature's latest kill. Neki stumbled backwards, but it wasn't fast enough. All Nigel could do was watch as the Druidonian opened his massive jaws to take in Neki's body.

A ray of light shot past them, hitting the creature directly in the mouth. The Druidonian froze, its teeth barely grazing Neki's flesh.

Their boat pulled ahead a safe distance. The creature didn't follow. Its eyes stared blankly ahead. Nigel could hear his own breath coming in short gasps. He looked back, expecting to see Zorc's coal-black eyes, open and fierce, but all he saw was the kota, down on her front knees, horn pointed in the direction of the Druidonian.

Neki collapsed where he stood. "And to think," he said, "I tried to force her off the boat."

CHAPTER 20

A ray of light sliced through the darkness and widened like an opening curtain. He tried to rise, but he was too tired. A heat came from his chest. His eyes flickered to it, unable to remember what it was, yet knowing it kept him alive. He tried to reach it but his hands wouldn't obey his command.

He looked at the light again and felt a soothing warmth filter through the darkness, warming his limbs. A shadow of a man stood in the light.

He tried to speak but only managed a whisper. He was dying, fading to nothing. The light could help him if only he could reach it.

Warm, strong hands looped under his shoulders, lifting him, carrying him to the light. Tingly sensations raced from his hands into his spine and then back again. The hands holding him had the power. He used to have that feeling. He wanted it back. It hurt to be separated from something so beautiful.

Light suddenly engulfed him. It was blinding in its intensity. A shadow bent over him.

He searched the face of someone he knew he should remember. His brow furrowed. The heat at his chest intensified. He tried to touch it, but his hands remained limp by his sides. The man's hazel eyes looked at him with concern and then flickered to the heat. Two other men loomed above him, one dressed in black, the other in white.

The man in the black leaned forward, took his hands and placed them over the heat.

His memories came back in a maddening rush: Zier, Aidan, the Collective, the quest, the Oracle, the Druids, and the closing.

Ren rose to his feet and stared into smiling hazel eyes. "Markum?"

Markum grinned. "I found the right door, Ren."

They stood on a walkway that wound in the darkness, dragon's tails long. The light he had seen came from a lone torch dangling in the air beside an open door.

Markum's eyes danced with the surety of a seer. Ren felt the Quy flickering inside him and turned to face the two men who had brought him to the light.

One looked at him with eyes he knew well, yet the face was older, thinner, and had been etched with anguish of unbearable proportions.

"Chris?"

As a slow grin spread across Chris' face Ren caught a glimpse of the boy he once knew, but it immediately faded. Ren drew a worried breath before he turned to the man with the golden eyes. Age-old pain still shone in those eyes, memories of what the man had once been. Ren immediately recognized the Avenger.

Ren felt the Quy bouncing from Chris and Aaron back to him. His own power was still locked behind his door. He was using Chris and Aaron's power to survive.

Ren drew a quick breath. It was the union.

He glanced through the open doorway into the darkness, his darkness. He was the Chosen. Without the power he was undefined, but he was also the synergy, or the union of the three stars surrounding his star. Grauss had said three others would help him, give him power on which to draw. Chris and Aaron must be two of those stars – two of the defenders of the Quy. He could draw from them and use their power. But he could also destroy them.

He turned back to the two men. "I'm draining you."

They both nodded.

"We're in the dream world, Ren. Your dream is in there," Markum said, waving his hand in the direction of the open door. "But what you see here," Markum turned in the darkness, bringing more torches to life, lighting up thousands upon thousands of doors with odd inscriptions and symbols, "is the land of dreams. I could choose any door to enter. Each door represents a person's dream."

"And if you had chosen the wrong door?"

"I would have been swept up in another's dream, unable to reach yours in time. You would have been lost."

Ren looked toward the open door of his dream. Somewhere inside his dream another door rose in the darkness, one with the symbol of magic etched on its surface.

Chris swayed. Ren reached out to steady his friend. When they touched he saw everything that had happened to Chris and Manda. A blinding rage churned to the surface. "Alezza will pay for this."

His friend smiled, but his smile was fleeting. "I'm sure Manda has made her pay dearly already."

Aaron stepped forward and handed him three stones. "The Quy told me to give you these." As their fingers brushed, the Avenger's memories and emotions seared inside Ren with reckless speed.

Ren looked down at the three stones in his hand. One was clear as glass, the second white as snow, and the third had a hazy gray bearing with one large blemish of devouring ebony. Ren glanced at the Avenger, asking the silent question.

"I gave all I am to make the love and pain stone. My righteous hate, along with Chris', formed the hate stone. But the hate stone isn't complete. The third member of the union needs to be found."

Ren nodded in understanding. It would take one more to make the union complete, to make the defenders of the Quy complete.

"My pain and love lasted centuries," Aaron said. "Chris' hate only lasted a brief time, and although it was intense, it wasn't enough to complete the hate stone. You must find one other who can finish the task."

Ren saw Aaron weakening and reached out to steady him. "What must I do?"

"Regain your power and release ours. Then find the other who will make the hate stone complete. Only when all the stones are complete will we be able to leave this place and help you defeat the darkness."

Ren nodded. The magic that had formed the hate stone had drawn Chris and Aaron into the dream world physically. Unlike Markum, their souls were here. They would be released only when the hate stone was complete.

Ren turned toward the open door. A torch suddenly appeared in his hand. He nodded his thanks to Markum before stepping inside his dream.

The door slammed shut behind him. The torch flickered but didn't die. The defenders' power still pounded through his temples but he felt their strength waning. He had to hurry.

Ren strode toward the door with the symbol of magic etched on its surface. It floated before him, taunting him. Ren fingered the triangle, feeling his power throb beneath the door's grain. He ached for it. The door had no handle, only a lock. He pushed on the door with all his might but it did no good.

Ren unsheathed his sword and struck the frame. Not even a divot appeared in the wood. Ren slammed into the door with all his strength. It didn't budge. He walked around it, trying to see any other way to break it down.

He circled the entire door. Where did it open? He remembered his door in the land of dreams. It didn't open where he was. It opened somewhere else. The thought didn't calm him.

He sat down, feeling himself weaken, feeling Chris and Aaron weaken.

He studied the door again. How could you open a locked door? Not only that, but how could he open a door locked by minds, not by metal?

The symbol for magic mocked him: an inverted triangle inside a larger triangle inside a circle.

What did the symbol mean?

Ren looked closer and frowned. The larger triangle was raised slightly. If the smaller triangle was inside the larger, it should be raised even higher, but it wasn't. It was on the same flat plane as the circle.

Ren traced the symbol's lines with sudden understanding. The center triangle wasn't a triangle at all: it was part of the circle. And what appeared to be a large triangle wasn't one triangle at all, but three triangles, endpoints touching.

Three triangles were floating in a circle, like the union of the three to him.

He looked down at the three stones in his hand and felt their power. He glanced at his sword. The fierce eyes of the dragons glistened in the torchlight. One set was a deep sable, one set stark white.

"Choice, Chance, and Fate," Ren whispered, reciting the words from the Oracle, "merged with pain, love and hate, can embrace the light, can embrace the dark. Heed us well, our Chosen."

Ren quickly took the ebony stone, the hate stone, and placed it inside the open mouth of the sable-eyed dragon. He then placed the white stone, the love stone, inside the open mouth of the white-eyed dragon. They clicked into place and began to glow with power. The clear pain stone he placed inside the open area of the blade, within the hollow teardrop. It lit the darkness with crystalline glory.

He clutched the hilt, focusing on the stones. Beams of light went from each stone to the others, forming a perfect triangle, the same triangle he had seen in the Oracle. It was the triangle of the synergy.

The light emitting from the hate stone wasn't as strong as the others, but it had to be enough to unlock the door. The only reason those who had been closed couldn't open their door was because they had no power to do so. He did.

Ren released the power of Chris and Aaron and called on the power of the blade. It surged inside him, singing with shrill intensity. The triangle of the sword, led by pain, pointed down through the blade. When he used the sword the power of the synergy would be sent through the sword to the target.

As he stepped forward he felt the wonder of love, the torture of love's pain, and the seduction of righteous hate. The sword glowed with a dazzling silver light. He inserted the tip in the lock and heard a "click." The door swung open.

He stepped inside.

- - -

Ren opened his eyes and winced. His head throbbed as if the Mynher himself had laid claim to it. When he touched his scalp his hand came away with blood. He must have dashed his head against the pedestal when he fell at the closing.

Druids were everywhere, scurrying across the deck of the ship like mice after a piece of cheese. Ren observed his surroundings through slit eyes. He rested on a small bunk that jutted from the ship's hull. His face was turned to the deck.

The wizard came into view, long dark hair flowing behind him. "Where?" he asked.

A Druid pointed. "It's a small craft, but it's heading this way."

The wizard shrugged. "We'll be well away before they arrive. Hurry the sacrifice. Ista is expecting us."

Ren's chest constricted. The Druids were working with Ista? Ren shuddered at his foolishness. Ista hadn't pursued him because she knew the Druids would. But if the Druids were working with her, he didn't need to go behind the door.

Ren clenched his fists. Ista would be able to control him at whim if he was closed from the power. He would be an easy target.

The wizard walked past, shouting orders to the Druids. A small hope welled within Ren. If the Druids were working with Ista, Zorc was an imposter. The One was still out there, searching for him. Ren still may have a chance to save Aidan.

His eyes drifted to his sword, resting just below his bunk. Praise the Maker the Druids didn't value weapons or it would have been left on the island. The Quy's stones were in the dragons' mouths. Their light shamed the bright of day.

A commotion came from the lower deck. Curses and a few hollow slugs drifted to him. Five gray-robbed Druids exploded from the ship's hull with a tall figure between them. Ren felt a stab of betrayal when he recognized Morrus.

Morrus' head whipped around before Ren had a chance to feign sleep. Their eyes met. Ren tensed, prepared to leap from his bunk, but Morrus turned away, a hint of a grin playing on his lips.

The Druids shoved Morrus forward. Chains bound his wrists. Why had they bound Morrus? The ship lurched to a halt and Ren tensed to keep from rolling off the narrow, wooden bunk. One Druid unleashed two hinges attaching a small section of the railing to another. He swung open the section and placed a long plank in the gap.

A large rock jutted out of the sea like the humped back of a huge sea creature. Ren had read about the small island a few times. Agger Point legally belonged to Fyl, but the Druids used it for sacred rituals. Because of that, everyone steered clear of it.

The wizard approached, scowling at the progress. The Druids picked up the pace. Morrus turned and fastened his gaze on the wizard.

"May the Maker send you to the lowest realm for what you have done and what you will do."

The wizard released a loud guffaw. "Your own kind send you to your death and you condemn me? Have no fear, I'm already among the damned, but you may want to start condemning your peers. Or do you still think them worthy of a godlike body?"

Ren's breath caught. To his death? Some of the Druids stopped and turned to the wizard with unreadable faces. The tension was high. The wizard sneered, unconcerned. Ren's brow furrowed. One wizard shouldn't debase a ship full of Druids. It was suicide.

The five Druids pushed Morrus ahead of them. The look on Morrus' face was unmistakable. Ren's jaw tightened. Morrus hadn't betrayed him. Morrus had been unaware of the Druids' intentions.

Morrus looked to the sea before he turned to Ren. His gaze settled on Ren's sword. Ren didn't miss Morrus' silent entreaty. A ship was coming. Ren needed to fight his way free. Morrus sprung out of the Druids' grip, shouting and cursing like a sailor, trying to distract them so Ren could have a chance of escape.

"Not without you, my friend."

Ren jumped from the bunk just as some of the Druids started beating Morrus with flails. The first Druid didn't see his attacker. The second didn't know much more. The third had a brief glimpse of him just as the wizard screamed a warning.

Then there was bedlam.

Morrus yelled for Ren to flee. Ren impaled another Druid and shoved another off the plank to the jagged rocks below. The two Druids on top of Morrus turned to see what had caused the wizard's alarm. It was all Morrus needed. Morrus looped his chains around both Druids and began choking the life out of them.

Ren felt a tenuous touch in his mind. They were trying to enter him again. Rage built inside him. He flung them off. Morrus grabbed his arm, and then they were running down the plank. A small ship had landed on the rocks. Neki was at the helm, waving his arms frantically.

Before Ren could take two steps down the plank, he felt the energy of the Quy being released and yelled for Morrus to drop to the ground. A bevy of swords sailed overhead, missing them both by a hair. Ren stumbled to his feet, dragging Morrus with him. A horde of Druids ran down the plank after them. With each step he felt their tentacles brushing against him.

A ripping sound assaulted the air. Ren turned to see a flail descending on Morrus' back.

A sword appeared in his periphery, blocking the flail's attack. The flail spun around it like a bobbin. Ren's eyes flickered to a face he thought he should recognize. Fear gripped him. Had they taken his memories again?

"It's a pleasure to make your acquaintance, my prince," the man said, stabbing an approaching Druid and flinging the body over the plank with effortless grace. The man turned to meet Ren's eyes and grinned. "My brother told me I would like you, but Ramie has always been perceptive. Now get to the boat." The Black Knight winked. "This won't take long."

Ren watched in stunned silence as Nigel Augustus ran off like a blur of black death. Ren screamed after him. "No! Wizard!" But the Black Knight didn't hear him. He merely struck down Druids as if they were straw and not flesh and bone.

Ren staggered to his feet, blocking the buzzing in his mind. It felt like a thousand bees were inside, not threatening, but causing a great amount of discomfort.

The wizard rose from the deck of the ship, eyes focusing on the Black Knight.

Ren pushed past Morrus and toppled Nigel before it was too late.

"Wizard," he said through clenched teeth, "won't harm me."

He was taking a chance, but if Ista had gone through this much trouble to close him she wanted him alive. He held his breath, expecting something to happen, but when he looked back up the deck was deserted.

Ren caught a movement. He turned just in time to see the Druidonian rise above the ship, silver eyes filled with rage. The Black Knight jerked beneath him, throwing him off with little difficulty.

200

A familiar cry resonated in the air. Ren turned to see the kota prancing on a ship beside Galvin and Neki.

Ren hauled Morrus to his feet. The Black Knight was quickly beside him, taking half of Morrus' weight. They hurried down the plank as the Druidonian bellowed a warning and released a blast of deadly flames.

When they reached the boat Ren dared to look back at the Druid ship. It was ablaze. The Druidonian picked entire bodies from the deck and enveloped them in its powerful jaws.

As their small craft moved away, all of them watched in stunned silence as the Druidonian took apart the Druid ship piece by piece.

CHAPTER 21

"A Druid?" Nigel asked, face twisting into something sinister.

Galvin ripped off Morrus' shirt and applied a healing salve. Morrus stirred when Galvin touched the cool substance to his skin but didn't wake. Ren was surprised Morrus had remained conscious for as long as he had. The flails hadn't been kind. There seemed to be hundreds of small, deep holes in the Druid's back

Ren turned to Nigel. The Black Knight's eyes still conveyed their disgust, but his face lost its loathing when he saw the flail marks.

"He's a friend," Ren said.

Nigel raised an eyebrow but didn't question.

Ren turned to the wizard. After a brief inspection, Ren felt foolish. Markum had described Zorc in explicit detail: the hair, the widow's peak, and the kind but determined face. If Ren had looked a little closer he would have seen the slight differences between Markum's description and the man Ista had sent to the Druids.

Nigel took off his cape and covered the wizard with his cloak. Ren leaned down beside him.

"How is he?"

"Not good, I'm afraid, although he is the first wizard I've ever examined." Nigel grinned, blue eyes dancing with resonating vigor of the morning's activities.

"Ren, I may have failed."

Ren glanced up at Galvin. The guard stood behind him holding out his sword like it was a viper. "What do you mean?"

Galvin nodded to Zorc. "He told me to kill him if the Druids appeared to be closing his door. He enchanted my sword," Galvin said, glancing down at the sword in his hand. "It was supposed to gain all of his knowledge, so as to tell you."

Nigel glanced at Galvin with concern. "The Druid with the yellow eyes?"

Galvin nodded, a wave of disgust crossing his features. "When I pricked him, I saw images, thoughts. Zorc didn't warn me the sword would take thoughts from anyone."

Nigel and Ren exchanged glances. Neither wanted to know what Galvin had learned.

Nigel heaved a sigh. "You didn't fail. It happened too fast. Even if you had reacted as soon as Zorc fell it would have been too late, but I don't think he's behind the door. No lone Druid would be powerful enough to put a century-old wizard behind the door.

"The High Priest tried to close me as well. Yes, he was powerful, but I don't think Zorc would have been taken so quickly. Something else is wrong. We need to find a healer, preferably someone who knows something about magic."

"No one knows anything about the power besides Ista," Ren said.

Nigel blue eyes regarded him for a time. Their chill intensity was vastly different from Ramie's majestic gaze. Ren could scarcely believe Nigel and Ramie were brothers.

"Presario. Since his accident he studies constantly. If any book on magic exists it would be at his home in Yor."

"Why would he speak to us? No one has seen him since the fire."

"I have," Nigel said. "When I rode as the Black Knight I was once wounded to the point of death. I went to Presario. I was sure he would never reveal my true identity, but I took a chance he might turn me away. He did not."

"And?" Galvin asked.

Nigel's eyes became distant. "I was there for a long time. He tended me, fed me, even read to me. At times the drugs he administered to lessen the pain wore off and I saw him, but he also saw me, and has never breathed a word of my identity. I won't defile his silence by revealing his mien, although it isn't as horrible as he believes. But I'm biased. I wouldn't be here today without Presario." Nigel turned to Ren and motioned to Zorc. "Presario will help, I'm sure of it. We became friends while I was there. If anyone could help, he could."

Ren bit his bottom lip. Yor was a long way from the threat he was trying to stop. "It's too far from Zier. I need to stop Ista, not run away from her."

"Presario is the only man I know who may be able to diagnose what's ailing the wizard," Nigel said.

Ren heard Neki humming behind him. "Grauss," he said.

"Grauss?" Nigel asked. "No one knows where he lives."

Ren turned to Neki. Neki was slouched against his pack, arms propped up behind him. Grauss' hideaway was a little too close to the threat for Ren's taste, but Yor was too far, and he would rather risk Grauss' closeness verses the question of whether or not Presario could or would help.

"Neki, do you think Grauss could help?" Ren shouted against the wind as he pointed to the wizard.

Neki shrugged. "I've never found anything he couldn't do. If anyone would know, he would."

"Then after we get Markum and the horses take us as close as you can to his hideaway."

Neki grinned and nodded. Ren turned back to Nigel. The Black Knight looked at him with a cocked eyebrow.

"Neki is Grauss' grandson. He led us to the sage's home once already."

Nigel shook his head, mumbling about the oddity of the crew.

Ren had to agree: two former crown princes, a grandson of the most famous sage in history, a wizard, and a Druid. But when Morrus woke Ren didn't know how cordial the group would be. Nigel was the sworn enemy of the Druid race, Galvin distrusted them, Zorc was sure to hate them, and although Neki could get along with anyone he had a way of stirring up trouble.

As Ren watched the sun send shivers of light on the water, the night on the Druid ship came back with vivid clarity. Everything seemed so obvious now. How could he have been deceived so easily? Then he remembered Fate's command: You must destroy your soul. The Druid closing was the road Fate had ordered him to follow. But why?

Ren didn't know, but he had carried out Fate's command and escaped the Druids whole. Did Choice and Chance have another purpose as well? Was Aidan still whole? Was his mother?

The more he thought, the more convinced he became. The Oracle had told him what to do, but that didn't mean what he had done had the outcome he feared. Ren thought of Aidan's words: blind faith. A small smile touched Ren's lips.

Someone sat beside him. Ren turned to look into Nigel's piercing gaze. Ren was struck again by the vast difference in Nigel and Ramie, but there was something in the shape of Nigel's face, the strong jawline and the dimpled chin, that connected the two.

"The Druids put you behind the door, but you didn't say how you opened it."

"It's difficult to explain," Ren said. "I had others helping me." As he spoke, even Ren found himself questioning his memories, but when he glanced down at the sword the stones were still there.

"How did you block the Druids when you first went to the island?"

Ren recalled his barrier of belief and tried to put it into words. "A wall," he said finally. "A barricade of my emotions, my beliefs."

Nigel nodded. "What you did was what I did when the Druids attacked me long ago. You fought them with your own strength. What I do now is different, and you need to learn what I do so you can keep your power safe from an infinite number of them. I create what the Druids do, a door, and I can leave it shut at all times. Walls can fall down, but doors have to be unlocked. Beware though, you can't use magic behind the door. All you can do is save your mind. To use magic you must crack the door open, and when you crack the door with Druids trying to enter, you could be lost."

"And the Druids can't unlock this door?"

Nigel smiled and leaned closer. "I don't lock this door with a key. I lock it with my calling power."

Ren lifted his eyebrows.

Nigel's grin widened. "The calling power isn't magical. It's an ability. Therefore you can use it behind the door. You can hold the door closed so the Druids can't reach you."

"But the Druids have the calling power as well," Ren said. "At least most of them. Why can't they use it to open the door, thus getting to you?"

"It isn't their mind. It isn't their door. Druids can't use the calling power outside their own mind. When they enter yours their only power is to lock something of yours away. Their other abilities stay with them. However, you are in you. You are you. You can hold a door of your own creation shut, and you can open it again."

"This can be done by anyone having the calling power?"

Nigel glanced over at Galvin and Neki, who were talking at the aft of the vessel. "Yes, that's why I can't teach Neki. Even though Neki has the Quy and can bring things to him as you can with the calling power, it isn't the same. He uses the Quy to do so. You, on the other hand, use your ability to sense things. You can hold the door shut with that strength. Neki would have to use the Quy, and behind your inner door you can't use the Quy."

Ren was about to reply when Morrus groaned. Ren hurried toward the Druid, Nigel following. Morrus' eyes flickered open, and like a wave of light a long smile spread across his face. "No more Druids?"

Ren grinned. "No more Druids."

Morrus struggled to rise. Ren clasped his shoulders and helped him to a sitting position. Morrus' dark eyes flickered to the Black Knight. A look between fear and respect rippled across his features before he turned back to Ren. "I'm sorry. I didn't know what they planned."

Ren nodded. "I know."

Morrus shifted his weight so his shoulder rested against the side of the boat. Ren motioned the others over. Morrus' eyes darted between Neki and Galvin with obvious apprehension.

"We all need to know what you know, Morrus. Please, you're among friends."

Morrus finally nodded and released an unsteady breath. "When the One came to us he claimed the Chosen would rebirth the power and become the most powerful man alive. When we learned it was you who had birthed the power, the threat was twofold. First, because you were a prince, if you became corrupt you could easily seize control of the Lands. Second, and most important, when magic was reborn the One claimed the spirit vacuity had been breached. When someone dies the Druids believe they go to this neutral vacuum until they are born again, either in a higher or lower realm. Because the spirit vacuity was torn the cleft acted like a slide. Powerful spirits could come through, spirits with magic."

"Through the Red Eye?"

Morrus nodded. "Only spirits with the gift of magic would be able to use the Eye, but the One said the Eye acted like a gateway to the world." Morrus paused to let the news sink in. "We couldn't allow the spirits to enter those of the lower ranks of life."

"You mean those not Druid."

Morrus' gaze settled on the Nigel. "Yes, those not Druid. When these spirits entered those of the lower ranks, the lower ranks would be unable to, shall I say, control themselves. Only those of the higher ranks would be able to contain them and use them to better the Lands."

Morrus shifted, clearly uneasy, and avoided all eyes. "The One claimed he had another guarding the gateway to stop the spirits, but he didn't know how long he could keep the spirits at bay. If a spirit came through and entered Ren . . . Well, Druids were unable to close Barracus when he was alive. They would be unable to do so to again. The Lands would be at risk.

"It was decided we would find Ren and close him. Then we would close others with magic, unless the One could find some way to block the spirits' entrance."

Ren closed his eyes. Ista would claim the needles would block the spirits' entrance. Maker of Fates, she had everything planned. He had underestimated the extent of Ista's hold. Ren glanced at Nigel. The Black Knight met his gaze. Their war with the Druids was only beginning.

"The Druids on the ship, picked by none other than Feher himself, would go to Zier and take the spirits that may escape the Eye."

Ren met Morrus' gaze. Druids had always hungered for the power. They wanted to obtain the Quy for their own. But Ista knew only those with the Quy could augment a spirit's power. She had promised the Druids something that would never come to pass.

"Marinus, the Drek, was very concerned about the threat. He's of the old line of Druids, those who keep to themselves, strive for a higher awareness, and interfere in the Lands only when they see a greater good. There's a New Order of Druids who want to obtain more power. These Druids claim it's our divine right to guide those of the lesser castes and lead them to a higher realm in their next life. The New Order believe all people have been corrupted for they worship things of the world and not things that will bring a greater good. The New Order preach drink needs to be outlawed, women need to be subdued to the old ways, and harsh restrictions need to be implemented.

"These New Order Druids want to shut everyone away from desires and vices. These are the Druids the Black Knight fought."

"It would make a boring world if everyone's vices were gone," Neki said, mumbling under his breath.

Morrus turned to Nigel. "Marinus only gained power a few years ago. He wasn't the Drek who ordered the outrage you stilled, but the former Drek, Kasim, was an avid follower of the New Order. He was very charismatic and turned many, if not most, to his views. Feher and Avalon are two of his followers."

Morrus turned back to Ren. "I thought I was seeking you to end a threat. I know you don't agree with closings, but Druids are needed. We've stifled many evil things and that's ultimately what we try to do – stifle something before it turns sour."

Galvin stiffened. "Before it has a chance to prove it may not turn sour."

"Yes," Morrus said, "before it can prove good or evil. That's something Druids seek forgiveness for after a closing. Or I should say, some of us."

Nigel exchanged glances with Galvin. Ren caught the look. They had witnessed the prayer session after his closing.

Morrus continued. "Not all Druids feel the same way. Those who don't attend the prayer session feel all closings are needed and deserved."

"Feher and Avalon," Nigel said.

"Yes, the New Order. And Feher is a powerful High Priest. He has continued to preach the teachings of Kasim. Marinus tolerates Feher because Marinus knows he's old and will soon die." Nigel glanced at Ren. Morrus saw the truth of that glance and heaved a sigh. "Kasim had no child and named Avalon as his scion, but Avalon was too young to succeed him. The responsibility fell to Marinus, Avalon's father. Marinus was a good leader. He instilled the old laws back into some of the Druids."

"So what will happen now that Avalon is in power?" Galvin asked.

"They'll try to eradicate magic after obtaining it for themselves. When they put me on the boat I overheard conversations. Feher and the One tricked Marinus. He thought Ren's closing was for the good of the Lands, not for control of the Lands."

"What do you mean by 'control of the Lands?'" Nigel asked.

Morrus shifted uncomfortably. "Druids were going to become a necessity since the spirit vacuity had been breached. They would be needed in every town, in every province, and in every kingdom. They would begin a new ruling class. They would become a residing judge of all laws passed, all commerce conducted, and all decrees given. The Druids would keep the Lands under tight control. The wizard claimed this was the future he had foreseen."

Ren leaned back on his heels, trying to piece Ista's scheme together. "Why would Ista promise the Druids power? It doesn't make any sense."

Nigel chuckled beside him. "Yes, it does. It makes perfect sense. 'Make your enemies indebted to you,' my father always said. A happy enemy is a friend. Ista wanted to use the Druids. She would make them her watchdogs. They would close any who may oppose her."

Ren turned to Morrus. "On the boat, the wizard didn't fear the Druids. Why?"

"He was blocked."

Ren sank back against the mast. "You're right, Nigel. She already knows how to keep the Druids from closing her followers. Somehow, the needles block them. Those who oppose her, those without the needles, would be closed by the Druid overlords."

"Morrus," Galvin said, "you said Feher was the one who wanted this to come about. Why wasn't he on the Druid ship bound for Zier?"

Morrus' lips twisted in a sneer. "Feher will, no doubt, arrive sooner than we do. Feher and a few attendants planned to depart on a much smaller vessel this morning. The High Priest of the Druid cultus is revered. He isn't allowed to leave the island, but this time Feher made an exception. Feher sent the sacrifice to the Druidonian so he could sail safely in the opposite direction to the mainland."

"And Druids sacrifice Druid women to the Druidonian to appease it?" Nigel asked.

"Yes."

"There were no women on the ship, Morrus," Ren said.

Morrus paled and he chafed his hands before him. "The few Druid women remaining cannot be sacrificed."

Ren waited in silence. Morrus was about to reveal something sacred. The look in his eyes was that of a frightened animal, an animal that had been rescued from wolves but was now in a foreign land, being questioned to betray his history. Although Ren knew Morrus was relieved the choice was finally before him, the Druid's eyes still held the fear of the wolves.

When Morrus spoke, his voice was soft. "I've never even seen one. Feher is in charge of them. Rumor holds only a dozen or so remain. They are bred, nothing more."

Nigel cleared his throat. "How was the sacrifice of women justified?"

"Blemishes. Ugliness. Our teachings say the women who remain are only with us to bring across the worthy, and all worthy will be born in the Druid way."

The wind picked up. It made a hollow lapping sound as it lashed the sail. The crinkle of Nigel's leather sent shivers down Ren's spine. He didn't know if he wanted to hear any more.

Nigel leaned closer. "Druid way?"

"I don't know how they do it." Morrus' said with a sigh. "But the women birth Druids who are dual-sexed. Druids believe their dual nature is godlike. It's a sign they'll congeal to form a god at death."

"Then why do they need the women?"

"Dual-sexed Druids can only impregnate. They cannot bear children. At times, Druids are born with one sex. If they are born women and found good enough, they are bred. If they are born women and are marred in some way, they are sacrificed. If they are born male they are killed immediately. There's no use for male Druids. They are unable to bear children, and they will be unable to reach the higher realm."

"You?" Ren asked.

Morrus hung his head. "Yes. My father hid me from them. He was the Drek before Kasim took power. At that time the women were under the Drek's charge. He fell in love with my mother. I lived until my teens unnoticed by others. I was to rise to Drek status. I studied everything I could, learned everything I could so I could do what my father wouldn't and change the Druid ways. But one day I was stripped before the council. I had begun to broaden, my voice deepen. I tried to conceal it for as long as I could but there was only so much I could do.

"Kasim killed my father for his lie. My sentence was to live among them, as LoDrek. There were many times I wished they would just kill me. I was shunned and scorned by everyone. My words weren't listened to so I learned not to speak. Then I came for you. It was the first time I had ever been in command."

"They sent you because you were expendable," Galvin said.

"Correct."

Neki's brow furrowed. "Then why Avalon?"

"Avalon needed to do something for the Druid good before he could rise to LoDrek status," Morrus said, picking at a loose thread on his tunic.

Galvin put a hand on Morrus' shoulder, his deep voice soft and comforting. "You aren't a Druid. You've broken from their ways since birth. That's why you felt the way you did about Ren. The New Order would have killed him. The Old Order would have questioned Feher's intent, but they too would have followed the High Priest. You broke, and you broke at the first opportunity the Maker provided."

Morrus smiled at Galvin. "I would like to think that, I truly would, but I'm a Druid. I didn't begin questioning Druids because I disbelieved their teachings, but because I feared death without higher attainment. Do I break from the Druids because it's right? Or do I break from the Druids to cling to a hope that's futile?"

"Look inside you," Nigel said gently. "The answer lies within. No one can tell you who you are. You know who you are. You know right from wrong. You just have to be strong enough to grasp it."

Morrus nodded, a small smile spreading across his face. "Thank you."

Nigel cleared his throat. His soothing tone vanished like a fleeting wind. "Feher did something to the true wizard. Do you know what it might be?"

Morrus frowned. "Let me see him."

Ren helped Morrus rise to his feet and walk to the wizard. Morrus felt the wizard's forehead and checked for a pulse. After a time he turned to Ren, clearly confused.

"I've never seen anything like it, but I don't think Feher could have caused this. If I've your permission, I'll enter his mind and see what I can."

Nigel tensed, but Ren nodded for Morrus to continue. Morrus turned to the wizard and closed his eyes. After a short time he opened them, bewilderment scrawled in every feature.

"His power is there, everything is there that I can see. Wait. Did Feher use a bottle?"

Galvin and Nigel exchanged glances. Nigel nodded.

Morrus turned grave. "The wizard used magic trapped in bottles. That was how he gave our horses their speed. He broke bottles beneath them. Feher had some bottles as well."

Ren turned away. "Wizards don't need magic trapped in bottles. It wasn't the power of the Druids that did this to him. It was Ista."

CHAPTER 22

After they landed on shore and made Zorc a stretcher, it was getting dark. The work was cumbersome, but soon they were on their way to Grauss' hideaway, Ren carrying sinking hopes.

Zorc was dangerously thin, and his pulse was weak. Ren was uncertain the wizard would last the short distance they had to travel.

The road they were on would lead them to the Sierras near Grauss' home. The farther they went the denser the trees became, but for the first time the forest didn't bring Ren comfort. Instead the trees looked like demons sent to ensnare his hopes.

A light rain began to fall, but they continued on, each intent on traveling until well in the night. The air was cooling. Soon the nights would begin to drop to near freezing, especially in the high country, and they would have to purchase additional clothing to keep warm.

A horse cantered up beside him. Ren turned to see Neki pointing to the stars.

The night was clear, the moons full, and Ren found his constellation easily. A white mist now surrounded his star, as it should be, but two of the outlying stars were disappearing.

The cold seemed to deepen around him.

Chris and Aaron were dying.

Ren jumped off his horse. He had to find "Hate" or the union would not be formed.

He unsheathed his sword and looked at the incomplete hate stone. His heart pounded so hard he didn't hear the voice beside him. Only when he felt a hand on his shoulder did he turn and look into the Black Knight's eyes.

Nigel's brow creased in concern. He took off one black glove and raised his hand to feel Ren's forehead.

The symbol of hate was burned in Nigel's palm.

Ren caught his wrist. "You must give me your hate."

Nigel stared at Ren with questioning eyes.

"I've no time to explain. You're the third. You'll make it complete."

"The synergy, Nigel," Neki said, stepping forward and pointing to the stars. "If you don't the darkness will take over the Lands. Without you Ren can't do what he must."

Nigel's blue eyes flickered in the dim light. "No, Ren is in control of the darkness, not I."

"I need three to help me," Ren said. "Without you, I'll fail."

"I can't. Hate's the only thing that keeps them alive."

"Who?"

Nigel closed his eyes. "Sherri and Megglan. I can't see them otherwise. I forget their features. Only when I become enraged with their deaths do I see them."

Ren tightened his grip on Nigel's wrist. "Nigel, you must, or the world is lost."

Nigel shook his head. Ren glanced back at the stars. The two points had almost faded from vision. Chris and Aaron had been in the dream world for some time. Unlike Markum, they couldn't live there indefinitely.

He turned to Nigel once more, not wanting to do what he was about to do but knowing he must.

"So you condemn your brother to die."

Nigel clenched his fists. "No."

"His children."

"No."

"That's what you do if you refuse to give me your hate."

Ren hoped he hadn't made a fatal error, but he didn't know what else to do. They had no time. Chris and Aaron had no time.

Nigel gazed at him like a man sick with a fever. "How do I give it?"

"I don't know," Ren said. "But we have to try."

Ren stepped back and impaled the ground with his sword. The love and pain stones glimmered in the darkness. The sable stone was dull, placid. Nigel reached out with his gloved hand. Ren stopped him. "No, your left, the one with the brand."

Nigel nodded and clamped his bare hand over the hilt of the sword. The hate stone began to glow. Nigel's face contorted. He fell to his knees. The scream he emitted came from the depths of the earth. It sounded as if he were being torn in two.

Ren tried to reach him, but the force of Nigel's emotions threw him back. The sword glowed with an intense silver light, but the hate stone pulsed with black heat, marring the silver brilliance. The black heat began to grow more intense, eating away at the silver light until Nigel's form was completely concealed behind a wall of sable.

Then, as quickly as Nigel's screams had come, the night was immersed in silence. The black light blinked out. In its place, white, clear and black lines merged to one, forming a solid silver triangle. The sword faded into the darkness, but the light of the triangle remained.

Nigel collapsed on the ground. His lips were chalk-white and his skin shimmered with sweat. Ren wrenched the sword from his grasp and stumbled backwards as the power of the blade roared through him: rage so hot it burned his soul, pain so intense it ripped his heart, love so deep it shattered his resolve. They became richer, fuller, brighter, and darker. He strained with effort, feeling his insides smoldering with the severity of the internal elements.

He ached everywhere. The love was so powerful it hurt, it seared, and it burned. The pain was so intense it gouged, it tore, and it ached. He saw Kyra being skinned alive, Manda raped, Sherri and Megglan stabbed, Aidan falling . . .

Hate filled him. It was a hate so intense he panted with its power. And in the hate there was no more pain. He felt himself begin to lose control. The hate was seduction. It was strength. It was domination. He screamed with effort, knowing he had to release the sword, but almost yearning to use the hate Nigel had just released into the blade.

The horror of it was that he hungered to wield the blade for hate itself. The warnings of the Oracle stole over him like a shadow.

Hate was easier to feel. It sheltered you from pain.

Ren fell to his knees and sheathed the blade. The emptiness he felt without the emotions left him slightly off balance, and then his own pain welled within the pit of his gut. After the hate, it was all the more painful.

He looked at the others.

All eyes were on him, but no one moved. Fear was etched in every face. Ren turned from his friends' terrified faces when he remembered his sinister eyes in the Oracle.

The three stars were now in perfect alignment. The middle one glowed with a brilliant intensity. Ren wondered where the others were. When he closed his eyes he only felt Nigel's mien, but then Nigel was beside him. He walked a short distance away and focused on Chris and Aaron. Their connection wasn't as strong, but he could sense them somewhere in Crape. Instinctively, he knew they felt him too. Turning, Nigel nodded. Nigel was aware of the others as well.

The synergy was complete.

On instinct, Ren looked toward the Raven. It had grown bigger, but they still had time before it would overcome the synergy. Neki followed his gaze and turned to him with a poignant stare.

"Its growth has happened in the past day. If it continues at that rate it will engulf your constellation within one week."

Ren's hopes withered. That quickly? He looked back at the unconscious wizard and fingered the hilt of his sword, remembering the hate. He needed to learn how to use the elements and only Zorc could teach him. They all were thinking the same thing as they climbed back on their horses: if they only had a little more time.

- - -

In one heartbeat the air was being sucked from his lungs. In the next it came back in a maddening rush. Chris opened his eyes. Aaron stood above him, sword in hand. They had returned to the Crape castle. Ren had found the third defender and formed the stone.

When the realization flooded into Aaron's eyes, he lowered his blade. Chris rose from the bed and looked around him. They were in the marriage suite. He had little recollection of what occurred here, but he did recall the emotions: the pleasure, the pain, and the rage. He especially recalled the rage.

He almost yearned for those emotions to rekindle: the biting flame of pleasure, the cutting blade of pain, and the searing scream of rage. But they only smoldered deep below the surface. Now all he had was the memory, the resonance. It was nothing compared to the emotions he had felt before. No pain could ever match the agony he had lived. No pleasure could ever compare to the ecstasy he had suffered.

From now on any emotion that claimed him would be drowned in the memories and washed away. He would be surprised if he ever felt anything again. He was a shell, nothing more.

Aaron hadn't spoken, but they needed no words. Both knew they had to reach Ren. Chris could feel Ren's mien. It was a beacon in his mind, calling him to hurry. That beacon was moving toward Zier.

When Chris looked at Aaron, Aaron made no move to leave. Golden eyes held his own with an understanding so rich, so deep, Chris could only nod. Aaron knew Chris couldn't leave the castle until he had found Alezza and destroyed her.

Chris opened the door to the suite and gazed down the stairs to the halls he had once called home. Everything had changed. The preposterous array of colors Valor had lavishly thrown in every haven was gone. Instead, rich reds and verdant greens, the colors of Quar and Crape, carpeted the castle's interior. Splashed amidst the new textures were ornaments displaying Zier's colors of black and gold. The entire castle was a celebration of Alezza's triumph.

Chris' eyes shifted to the wall directly opposite him where a large, detailed painting of Alezza now hung. Her eyes sought the painter with a flirtatious glint. Her lips opened in a slight smile. Her hair twisted sensually down her back. The painting was a masterpiece, but the beauty that radiated from its strokes faded under Chris' glare.

Beneath the surface, Chris felt his hatred boiling, but that hate was only a distant cry. His eyes swept the room, surprised to find none of Alezza's guard in sight. Only green uniforms ambled below. The gold-braided uniform marking Harman's high rank glittered in the torchlight.

A servant girl glanced up at Chris and gasped. When Harmon turned to see what had caused the girl's outburst, shock riveted across his face.

Chris started down the steps, Aaron close behind. The hall filled with a tense silence as servants stopped and watched their descent.

When Chris reached Harmon he spoke only one word, but that word was so biting it seemed to pierce the air like an arrow. "Alezza."

His voice was odd to hear now that he knew his identity, for it had changed. Where before his voice held slight buoyancy, now it was as flat as a blade was straight. It was a voice of a shell of a man. That fact brought neither sorrow nor pain. It brought nothing.

Harmon cleared his throat, eyes still shimmering with surprise, but beneath the surprise joy bubbled to the surface. "Gone, my lord. After Manda told me what she did I thought it in everyone's best interest she leave until the mystery was solved."

Chris nodded. The fact brought him neither disappointment nor joy. "Harmon, I leave you in charge of the castle."

Harmon's brow furrowed in confusion. "My lord, where are you going? We need you here. You're the new leader of Newlan."

"No, Ren is still the leader of Newlan. Soon he'll return, and when he does I'll return Zier to him. I'm riding to Zier, Harmon, to war."

Harmon studied Chris in the soft light before he nodded, as if what he had seen had answered all his questions, but when Chris turned to leave Harmon spoke again.

"My lord? What of Alezza? Do you want me to send word for her return?"

Chris' eyes flickered to Alezza's portrait. As soon as his eyes grazed it, it exploded. Everyone but Aaron and Chris cowered on the floor and covered their heads as shards of wood rained down upon them.

In the lingering silence, Aaron and Chris walked from the castle. In the far corners of his mind Chris heard Harmon shouting orders for the troops to prepare.

They were riding to war.

CHAPTER 23

They rode hard through the night, the next day and the next night. They were exhausted, but they could afford no sleep. The darkness was growing in the sky. Each time Ren looked at it his skin prickled.

Ren spurred his horse into a gallop and careened down the steep cliffs toward the entrance to Grauss' hideaway. Neki overtook him and led them down, finding footfalls and avoiding crevices that couldn't be seen by the naked eye. A few times Ren heard a horse stumble behind him, but no one cried out, and before long they were standing in front of Grauss' hideaway.

"We all go in this time," Ren said.

Neki didn't argue as he took Markum and placed him behind a large bolder. Ren tethered the horses out of sight. Morrus untied Zorc and motioned to the others. "I'll carry the wizard. His weight won't bother me."

Ren nodded and within heartbeats the five of them slipped quietly through the crack in the mountain.

The only sound was the running water far below, now a steady drumming instead of the soft trickle it had been before. The fall rains had come early. Soon the rift would be filled with winter runoff.

The nightmoss shimmered brilliantly, so much so their torches weren't needed. They walked in silence, each knowing how much depended on Grauss' wisdom. Just before they reached the sage's cavern, they heard Grauss' scream.

Neki ran down the remaining path at full speed, calling his grandfather's name. Ren and the others followed as fast as they could. When they finally stood in the cavern, Ren found Grauss swinging from one of his dangling chairs. By its movement, Grauss was frantic.

"Grauss?" Neki said again, a slight nervousness to his voice.

Grauss turned and surveyed them with a blank stare. His skin matched his white hair. He blinked a few times before recognition came to his face.

"Choice!" he shouted with glee as he reached above him and pulled the lever. The chair moved down the rope with incredible speed. Before it could land, Grauss jumped to the floor and ran to Nigel.

"Choice!" he said again as he clasped Nigel's face with two bony hands.

The Black Knight looked surprised before he grinned. "Grauss the Sage. Now I know you're more mad than I even dared dream."

Grauss chuckled before turning to Ren, face suddenly serious. "I don't see Chance or Fate."

"They're coming."

"Coming? Have you seen the Raven? My boy, there isn't much time!"

Ren looked down at Zorc's limp body. "I know. That's why we're here. We need to wake the wizard."

Grauss peered at Zorc as if he were death come to life.

"We don't know what happened to him," Neki began, relaying the story of Dresden. With each sentence, Grauss turned more serious. Soon a frown consumed his entire face.

Grauss ushered them inside and pointed to a nearby table. Morrus gently laid Zorc down as Grauss ran to a large crate. After throwing out the top layer of gizmos the sage buried his entire torso in the crate and selectively tossed more things over the side.

Ren stooped over him. "Can I help you find something?"

Grauss jumped, hitting his head on a large round metal device. After some exclamations and curses Grauss' head reappeared. "My dear boy, don't speak while I'm in the midst of something. I forget people are here. Silver dust is what I need. I know I have it in here somewhere."

Ren reached into his pocket and withdrew the small bag of silver dust he had carried since Michel and Galvin had recovered the bags from Ista's camp. "I have some."

Grauss pushed himself up and peered at Ren as if he had gone mad. "Well, why didn't you say so, my boy?" he asked, snatching the bag out of Ren's hand and scampering back to the wizard.

"What's wrong with him, Gramps?" Neki asked.

Grauss plopped the bag of silver dust on Zorc's chest. "Nothing's wrong with him. He just used a simple trick called the 'wizard's defense' to avoid whatever magic was in that bottle."

Nigel moved out of Grauss' way. "And that is?"

"Sleep."

"Sleep?" Neki and Ren asked in unison.

"Yes, sleep," Grauss said, peeling the wizard's eyelids back. "Some magic is so powerful it can only lock onto something or someone with a great deal of strength or learning. From what you tell me, the bottle the High Priest broke was made specifically for Zorc. It

218

would have been extremely powerful. In order to divert it the wizard went to sleep, for that is when they are at their weakest, hoping the magic wouldn't catch hold. And the magic, without its true maker present, didn't know where to go, so it died out."

"But he's been asleep for days," Nigel said in frustration.

"Yes, dear boy," Grauss said. "Wizards fall into the wizard defense only in desperation for they never know if they're going to wake up in greater danger than they were in before. Most wake within a sun's click, but this wizard is different. This wizard is – "

"Four centuries old," Ren finished.

Grauss smiled, pleased the synergy had found the answer before it had been revealed. "Yes. He hasn't slept in almost four hundred years. He can't wake up. He's making up for lost time."

They all stared down at Zorc.

Nigel frowned. "Why hasn't he slept in all those years?"

"No need. If he's survived since the Wizard War a time weave was placed on him, and there's no need of sleep during the duration of the weave. Now that time has once again started turning for him, his body is slowly starting to need more things, like food and sleep." Grauss looked at his grandson. "Has he slept before this?"

Neki shook his head. "No time."

Grauss grunted his confirmation.

"So that's why he refused all food. His body was adjusting?"

Grauss nodded.

"No wonder he's lost so much weight," Neki said.

"The wizard's defense is the most powerful sleep there is. Because he hasn't slept in four centuries it will be nearly impossible to wake him until he's slept his fill." Grauss peered at the wizard. "He's in dire need of food. He'll starve if we don't wake him soon."

Ren heaved a sigh. "What can you do for him Grauss?"

Grauss blinked up at him. "I can't do anything. One of you has to wake him. Mere noise or slight physical disruption won't even cause him to stir. Magic needs to be used, hence the silver dust." Grauss held up the small bag before plopping it back down on Zorc's chest. "It'll help intensify whatever you decide to do."

Neki stared at him. "But what are we supposed to do?"

"Wake him. Do something to wake him."

"How do we know what will wake him?"

Nigel placed a hand on Neki's shoulder. "Think about it. What wakes you? Something tickling you perhaps? Being too hot? Too cold? We've kept the wizard well covered and relatively comfortable. Maybe that's part of the problem."

Neki released a guffaw. "Galvin drug him out of the Obelisk, the Druidonian almost ate him, and he was dragged across half of the Maker's forsaken country. " Neki waved his hands in the air. "What do you mean he's been comfortable?"

Nigel grinned. "Relatively. I said relatively."

Ren felt helpless. "You two need to wake him. I can't do anything that simple."

Grauss peered at Ren for a brief time before he nodded. "Yes, that makes sense. The synergy is so strong the simple things evade him. That's what keeps him strong, and that's why he needs the three defenders. Yes, that makes sense, but why didn't I see it before?"

Grauss wandered off, intent on the new information.

Neki picked up the bag of silver dust and heaved a tremendous sigh. "Wake a man who hasn't slept in almost four centuries, Neki. It won't be hard, Neki. Burning cinders on dragon's tails." Neki paused to run a wary hand through his thick black hair. "The Adderiss may be more pleasant than this."

- - -

Neki peered down at Zorc. "I think I burnt him."

They had tried everything they could think of but the wizard hadn't even stirred.

Ren stepped closer. Sure enough, red welts were beginning to appear on the wizard's exposed skin.

"Well eternal damnation!" Neki stepped back and crossed his arms. "What's going to wake him if that didn't?"

"I don't know, but we have to keep trying."

Neki sighed and nodded. He stepped back to the table and touched one of the red sores on Zorc's neck. "I don't think Zorc will be too pleased with me when he wakes."

Although Neki grinned, Ren could sense his exhaustion.

"Why don't we take a break and get something to eat?" Ren suggested. As soon as food was mentioned, his stomach growled. They hadn't taken the time to eat a full meal in almost two days.

Neki nodded, visibly relieved, and walked over to the small smokeless fire Grauss had lit. After heating some water he tossed in some herbs and dried chicken. Soon a savory scent of basil and dill wafted through the air.

Zorc moaned.

Neki dropped his spoon. Nigel and Ren glanced at each other as wide grins stole across their faces.

"Hunger," they said in unison.

Neki picked up the kettle and hurried over to Zorc. "Well, we don't need magic to help that along."

Neki dribbled some of the broth into the wizard's mouth. Zorc's stomach made a horrible grinding sound. Before Neki could dip the spoon back into the kettle, Zorc's eyes flew open.

Neki grinned down at him. "You're one tough wizard to wake. I nearly turned your robe into cinders."

Zorc pushed himself up. "The Chosen?"

Neki pointed to Ren. Zorc turned.

The wizard's eyes were just as Markum described: timeless, and filled with ageless understanding and depth. Ren felt like one of Grauss' experiments under the watchful gaze of a master.

Then Zorc did something unexpected – he grinned. Zorc grinned to such an extent it was comical. Ren smiled back, too relieved to move.

"You're whole?"

"Yes, I'm whole."

Zorc drew in a deep breath. "I'll be staggered. Tell me how. The Druids seemed to have closed you already. How did you escape?

"No, no," Zorc said, shaking his head as an afterthought. "Start from the beginning. I haven't heard everything."

Neki forced a bowl of the chicken stew in front of Zorc. Zorc grabbed it and without bothering to cool its contents shoved a spoonful into his mouth. His pointy eyebrows rose to meet his widow's peak as he swallowed and sat where he stood. "All these years I thought I'd imagined food tasting this good. But I was right," he said, raising his spoon in the air for emphasis.

He motioned for Ren to begin as he held his empty bowl out to Neki. During Ren's recount, Zorc mumbled curses directed at Ista under his breath, but didn't interrupt. He only nodded on occasions when he agreed with Ren's chosen course. Zorc hesitated when Ren had said he had met the Quy, raising his eyebrows even higher, in respect if nothing else.

When Ren mentioned the Oracle, Zorc leaned over and grabbed his hands. Pulling him forward, Zorc searched his eyes. A current of energy passed through Ren. Zorc's eyes shone with intense power, but when the wizard released him they softened.

"I'm truly sorry you had to learn what you did, Ren. It would have been better if you hadn't known what needed to occur before it did, but it seems what you did was necessary. Although I don't know why, you're whole, and now you know how to unlock the door. This will help you defeat the darkness."

"You read my mind?"

"Not exactly, but close." Zorc's voice sounded almost as ageless as his eyes appeared. It was hollow and slightly deep, but soothing. The knowledge it conveyed contrasted greatly with Zorc's young appearance, although some streaks of gray did frame his face and run the length of his hair.

"I read your emotions and those emotions brought me images. I may not know exactly what the Oracle told you, but I have an idea. Emotions tell us more about a person than the person's own thoughts. Emotions are stronger than thoughts. They bring pictures of feelings instead of just words. Although pictures, like words, can be interpreted many different ways, if you know the emotions of the person, images take on a life of their own. For instance, because you know Markum's personality, his emotions, you are able to interpret his dreams easier than you would written prophecy. Written prophecy is without images and can be interpreted a billion different ways. The written word's interpretation is based on the decoder and the decoder's opinion of what the words bring to mind, which won't be the same as the emotions of the seer.

"The internal elements are the driving force of the Quy, and learning to use them will be your first lesson. The love inside you was strong already, now the pain inside you is intense, and the anger is waiting to be released. The path you have walked may have been a tool to show you how to elicit these emotions. You need all emotions to be in balance, to be strong. It's my job to show you how to use emotion wisely."

Ren frowned at the thought that everything he, his friends, and the Lands had suffered had only occurred to teach him emotion.

"Will we be able read someone's emotions?" Nigel asked, interrupting Ren's thoughts.

"Maybe, depending on your strength and your talents." Zorc turned back to Ren. "Continue."

When Ren had finished, Zorc stood, pulled something from his robe, and tossed it on the floor. There was a silent impact to the air as three shining silver dragons rose from the ground in a circular configuration, necks stretching in a roar, wings billowing up and out, and blue sapphire eyes shining with brilliance. The pewter creatures stood as tall as Zorc's waist. Ren half expected the dragons to come to life, but they remained still, watchful. Zorc placed a small round globe in the midst of the stand. It immediately exploded to full size, cradled among the dragon's wings.

It was the Silver Eye.

Grauss hastily began scrawling notes on a parchment. Morrus, clearly uncomfortable, took a step back.

Zorc cleared his throat and looked at each in turn. "The Eyes contain the extremes of the Quy, one holding good, the other holding evil. Long ago they resided in the Oracle, kept by Choice, Chance, and Fate. The Oracle guarded the Eyes from all who would covet them. As you know, the Oracle appears to who it will, but it wasn't always so. The Oracle used to be a temple where everyone could go for answers. If questions were asked without malice or greed the guardians of the Oracle gave direction to those who entered. At one point they were deceived and the Eyes were taken. It was then the Oracle disappeared and was only accessible as you know it today, guarding its knowledge and its power to all but a chosen few.

"When the Eyes were taken a mage named Magnus went after the one who had betrayed the Oracle. The Silver Eye was recovered and given to the wizard leader for safekeeping. The Red Eye was hidden until the time of the Wizard War, when the Red Eye was given to the Maritium for protection."

Zorc's words were hypnotizing. Even Grauss remained silent. It felt as if Choice, Chance, and Fate were watching them, ensuring the story was told true.

"Ista was an avid follower of Barracus. She knows about the power of the Eyes and has probably been searching for the Red Eye since the Wizard War."

The wizard creased his brow and gazed into the crystal. There was a sizzle as the ball began to glow with a brilliant light.

"Yes, Zorc," came a monotone voice.

Ren blinked in shock. Grauss wrote a hurried note on his parchment, mumbling to himself. The crystal sent a sheen of milky light over Zorc, but as Ren gazed into the crystal he didn't see an image as he expected. All he saw was swirling mercury, billowing as if a mass of clouds were trapped beneath the surface.

"Krov, you're in the Silver Eye. Can you detail its function?"

"It's called the Dragon's Eye and was forged in ancient times. It can be used to create life."

Zorc mumbled something under his breath. "Can you use it for anything else, Krov?"

"Yes. Whoever controls the Eye can call good spirits into the Eye and speak to them, but the Maker forbids this. It can also seep goodness into the Lands. It can do so in a slight way or in a great way. If used incorrectly or by someone weak or untrained in magic the crystal could drown the world with moral righteousness. It's so powerful it would change everyone in the Lands. Evil would be defeated forever."

"That doesn't sound too bad to me," Neki said.

It didn't sound bad to Ren either, but as he looked at Zorc he knew the wizard wasn't satisfied.

"Krov, how would the crystal drown the world? Describe in detail please."

"Those inherently good would become better, those bad would become good," Krov replied. "All would agree. No pain would ever be felt."

Neki raised an eyebrow and looked at Ren. "Looks like we've found a solution."

Zorc stepped closer to the Eye. "Do you mean there would be no killings, no picking of crops, no work, no lust, no sin, and no leadership?"

"That's correct."

"So, no one would eat, no one would be born, and in time all would die?"

"Correct."

Nigel's smile withered. Ren felt the hairs of his neck stand on end. Neki gave a low whistle and mumbled that it wasn't the solution after all.

Zorc raised a bony finger. "But you said *if* it's used incorrectly. If someone is powerful enough he can control the Eye and not release this destruction. That is, if someone is powerful enough he could use the Silver Eye to create life or release what goodness they desire?"

"Yes."

"So the Silver Eye could release destruction, but it doesn't have to be so?"

"Correct."

Zorc began to pace. He turned back to the Eye after a brief span of thought. "Are you guessing this time, Krov?"

"No."

Ren glanced at Nigel and Neki, unsure of what had just passed between the crystal and Zorc. Neki shrugged and turned back to the wizard, undisturbed. Ren felt a little uncomfortable. Guessing?

"Tell me about the Silver Eye's twin, Krov. What can the Red Eye do?"

The crystal grew a shade brighter as Krov began to speak. "For the Silver Eye to be formed, the Red Eye had to be made. The Red Eye is the Dragon's Fire."

Ren glanced at Zorc. The Adderiss had wanted his fire. Could she have meant the Red Eye? Zorc held his gaze for a few heartbeats before turning back to the Silver Eye, but Ren didn't miss the worried glint in his eyes. Although they didn't have the Red Eye now, they would.

"What can the Red Eye do?"

"The Red Eye holds the power over death. It can call forth evil spirits. Again, this is forbidden by the Maker, but many who use the Red Eye will care little for the Maker's commands."

Ren knew that to be true. Ista's entire plan hinged on calling to evil spirits. He shivered. It amazed him how much one person could affect an entire race, but Ista's disobedience could be the Land's undoing.

"Unlike good spirits," Krov continued, "evil spirits want back into this world. The Red Eye can release them into a vessel. Hence it can create death."

"If all the Red Eye's power was released what would happen?" Zorc asked. Ren didn't want to hear the response. If the Silver Eye could destroy the Lands the Red Eye should be able to do so as well, and its destruction wouldn't be as kind.

"As the Silver Eye is good to the extreme, the Red Eye is evil to the extreme. If used improperly, the Red Eye could wreak havoc on the Lands. It calls to evil and can twist righteous minds to be suspicious and jealous of others, causing brother to rise against brother. Evil would prevail. There's no love in a world controlled by the Red Eye, only lust and desire for more. Soon all would be destroyed by their own destruction."

"But this Eye is also like the Silver, is it not? If someone is powerful enough it can be used for its true purpose. In other words, the Red Eye's power can be controlled?"

"Yes."

"If someone were to release either crystal's power to the extreme," Zorc said, phrasing his words carefully, "is there any way to stop the destruction?"

"There's no controlling what happens if an Eye's complete power is unleashed. There's only chaos."

Zorc began to pace again. Ren knew what he was thinking. If Ista used the Red Eye would she be powerful enough to control it?

Grauss stepped forward and cleared his throat. "If I may," he said to the wizard. Zorc waved his hand in frustration, indicating for Grauss to ask what he would. The sage stepped forward and bowed to the crystal.

"Grauss the Sage at your service, Krov the Silver Eye."

The crystal didn't respond.

Grauss smiled, unaffected by the crystal's silence. "If someone unleashed the chaos you described, could the other Eye be used to counterbalance the destruction?"

"Yes."

Zorc glared at the crystal. "Krov, why didn't you say this before?"

"It's impossible."

Zorc's eyebrows furrowed as he stepped closer. "Why?"

Grauss' blue eyes sparkled with his newfound discovery as he answered for the crystal. "When one Eye's power is released the world is all good or all bad. Therefore, all would be good or all would be bad and no one would be whole enough to release the other crystal's power. No one would want to."

Zorc nodded in respect to Grauss. "Is this correct, Krov?"

"Yes."

"If, for the sake of argument," Grauss began again, "two were at play together, would the threat neutralize completely or would there be repercussions?"

"It depends on who is in control of the two crystals," Krov said.

"Describe," Zorc said, still visibly irritated.

"Once together the twin magic will work automatically. The good and evil of the two Eyes will balance each other, neutralize each other. But they can't go on forever. Soon the Eyes will begin battling for power. If the person controlling them is strong enough he can shut off their power. If the person can't control them anything can happen. One or the other or both Eyes' power could be released.

"The person in control of the Eyes is who you need to fear, not the Eyes. Together the Eyes can capture or release whatever you wish if used by someone powerful enough, but before you use them you must think through your wish carefully. Things wished for may not be as they appear."

Galvin let out a low whistle as Grauss muttered something under his breath. Ren just stared at the crystal, unsure of how interpret the response. How could they prepare to fight something they didn't fully understand?

Zorc continued. "If a spirit passes through the Red Eye, does it have its own strength, or does the Eye magnify it in some way?"

"On the first passing the Eye makes the spirit stronger."

Zorc closed his eyes. "May the Maker have mercy on our souls."

The cave filled with a tense silence. Although Barracus' name had yet to be spoken it seemed the very walls of the cave whispered it.

Zorc tapped the bridge of his nose. "What do you do to defeat a spirit who tries to merge with you?"

"Banish it."

Zorc's eyes narrowed in concentration. "Describe this banishment."

"Once a spirit is called to the Eye it must merge with life or it can't exist. If the vessel fights the spirit, weakens it and refuses the spirit, the spirit can be banished back into the Eye. Depending on how much strength it has left it may or may not be able to leave the Eye again. If it can't leave the Eye, it will become part of the Eye."

"So the spirit can't be destroyed once it's in the world but if it's weakened and banished back into the Eye, the Eye could claim it?" Zorc asked. Ren stepped forward with growing hopes.

"Yes."

"So if someone were to banish the spirit back into the Eye, the spirit may forever remain inside the Eye to never threaten the world again?"

"Yes."

"For all time?" Zorc asked.

"For all time."

Ren recalled the painting in the Oracle. Now he knew what the Oracle meant. If he wanted to defeat Barracus he would have to become Barracus. It was the only chance to destroy the mage. He had to let Barracus inside, drain his strength, and put him back into the Eye. The Oracles words burned in his mind. *Take heed our warnings. Both you will be. One you will become. Which on depends on thee.*

The Oracle's warning about hate was real. He would have to battle a spirit carrying profound hate. The Oracle had warned him pain couldn't be felt in complete hate. When Barracus' spirit entered him he would be seduced by hate, beseeched to give away his pain.

"Krov," Zorc said, "how can you awaken an Eye's power? I've been using the Silver Eye to speak to you for centuries and I've never touched its true power."

"The Eyes contain powerful properties. They were formed by the most powerful elements. Only the most powerful can awaken them or

227

close them. Only those with the Eyes' dominant element can awaken them. Only those with the counter element can close them."

Zorc tapped his chin. "You mean a mage. And that mage has to have love to open the Silver Eye and hate to close it, hate to open the Red Eye and love to close it?"

"Correct."

Zorc's face twisted in confusion. Ren understood. Ista was a sorceress. It was impossible for her to have a mage's power. Zorc waved his hand in frustration.

"Once the crystal's destructive power is released, how fast does the second crystal have to be put into play?"

"Quickly."

"Quickly, as in heartbeats or days?"

"Quickly."

Zorc rocked forward to his toes. "If one Eye is put into action first, will it affect the equalization of the two?"

"No, but things can escape permanently from the first Eye played before the other is there to neutralize the threat."

"There?" Zorc asked, furrowing his brow. "Do the crystals have to be together, or can they be separated by distance?"

"They have to be side by side."

Ren sighed. Even if they were in the city of Zier itself there may not be enough time to reach the Red Eye if Ista tapped into its power. He looked at the crystal with sinking hopes. "Is there a way to tell if the Red Eye's power is released?"

The crystal pulsated with bright force and then settled back into its wintry glow.

"The sky will turn to blood."

Ren hung his head as the main prophecy came back to him: *The world will drown in blood.*

- - -

Ramie walked from camp and gazed toward Zier. He had been on edge for far too long. He needed to relax. Ista wasn't coming, just as Lazo said. She thought his army a mere irritation.

Bostic had joined them last night at the base of the Sierra Mountains. Ramie hadn't allowed Bostic's army to mingle with his until they had searched Bostic's soldiers. They had found two more crystals. Presario had begun intense training of the newcomers as soon as the search was over, while Lazo continued with the old.

Lazo and Presario had become fast friends and Lazo had begun to learn the patoi of magic as soon as Presario had shown it to him. With the intelligence of a triplet, Lazo's learning had shocked even Presario. Although Lazo's abilities had diminished because of the twins' deaths, he was in no way less intelligent, and his power far surpassed most in the army.

Even if their magic didn't stand a chance against Ista's, Ramie was glad Presario had come. His skill and training had given everyone confidence, and confidence was something they desperately needed. The men were now eager to march and use what they had learned.

Those with the Quy would be the first to approach Stardom. Those without would remain behind until the first division had cleared a path with magic. If Renee had touched any hearts many of the Collective would be dead when they arrived. Some citizens may even help them open the gates. Ramie smiled as he pictured the queen's defiant gaze. Ren had some very good people on his side.

Although Lazo said the Collective were grains of sand on the shore they couldn't be as many grains as the armies of three nations. The armies had to outnumber them at least three to one. Even though someone with magic could do a great deal of harm, someone untrained with magic couldn't fight off three trained soldiers with a sword all at once. Sooner or later the sword would win. At least that's what Ramie was telling himself.

Ramie turned and looked in the direction of Fraul's tent. Sure enough, Fraul was deep in a lesson with Manda. Ramie had to close his eyes when his gaze brushed Manda's form. He had never seen someone with so much determination, so much energy and life, but also with so much brash disregard for customs and traditions. Even Nigel was more covert with his feelings. But Manda? Manda was a bonfire.

She laughed when he demanded silence. She teased when he had no humor in him. She screamed when he tried to tell her he wouldn't allow her to ride to war.

And he wouldn't. The battlefield was no place for a woman. Even Marva and Renee seemed to realize that. They weren't planning to fight with a sword, they were planning on entering the city through the passageways, and if the army needed help on the inside they would be prepared.

But Manda glared at him when he made any mention of her remaining behind, and Fraul wouldn't help him. His captain only laughed, insisting Manda was a better fighter than his own king.

That comment always made Ramie's anger rise to new heights. A few days prior, he had flown into a rage, grabbing Manda by the arm and shaking her almost senseless.

She had slapped him. The shock of that slap had knocked him out of his fury, and when he found himself looking into her fiery green eyes he realized why he was so infuriated with her.

He was in love with her.

She was not only defiant, she was beautiful, and it drove him mad.

Ramie wiped his brow. He couldn't stop thinking about her, and that really infuriated him. He was married for the love of the Maker! He had never so much as looked at another woman! But his eyes sought Manda more than he would care to admit. He was petrified she would come to harm.

Ramie forced his eyes from Manda and as his eyes caught a movement in the distance.

A brigade of soldiers marched toward them from the west. Shouts of alarm sounded in the camp, but almost as soon as the cries went up they turned to cheers. At first Ramie didn't understand, but when he heard Manda's burst of unrestrained laughter and saw Crape's colors of green and gray, he smiled.

Leading the army was none other than Chris Kahn himself, and next to him, dressed in black and donning an ornate sword, was the Avenger.

When Fraul had relayed what had happened to the Kahns, Ramie had been furious. If he still had breath after the battle in Zier he planned on marching to Crape and relieving Alezza of the throne himself. Now it seemed he wouldn't have to do that unpalatable task. Ramie couldn't quite understand how Chris had returned, but he wouldn't question the Maker's fates.

Now they had four armies.

Ramie chuckled under his breath.

In his peripheral vision, he saw Manda mount her black stallion and gallop to meet her brother. Ramie watched with a mixture of joy and jealousy as she embraced both Chris and Aaron. Even from his distance he saw the love Aaron held in his eyes as he looked at Manda, but Ramie couldn't tell if that love was something with which he should concern himself.

Ramie guffawed. Concern himself! He was married, for the love of the Maker!

Cursing, he turned and walked back toward camp as Chris, Manda, and Aaron rode to meet him.

When Chris stopped before him, Ramie had to consciously keep from flinching. Chris' gaze was apathetic and cold.

Ramie inclined his head. "Welcome to the resistance."

Chris' lips twitched into a slight grin. Scant humor lit his eyes. "It's a pleasure."

"We march tomorrow at dawn. Will that give you enough time to prepare?"

Instead of answering, Chris looked to the sky. Ramie followed his gaze to the triangular-shaped constellation he had read about multiple times before. A large dark spot in the sky was almost touching one of the points of the triangle.

Chris turned back to Ramie, green eyes holding an intensity Ramie could only wonder at. "Tomorrow won't be soon enough."

Aaron nodded beside him. "If we march now we could reach Zier by dawn."

Chris' eyes bore into Ramie. "We leave now. Prepare your men and follow as soon as you can."

Without another word, Chris and Aaron passed him. Manda glanced at him only briefly, as if daring him to order her to stay, before bolting after Chris.

Ramie gritted his teeth. How dare Chris Kahn tell him what to do! He was the one who had organized this revolt! And Manda! Ramie released a heavy grunt and watched Manda ride farther away from him. Clinching his fists, he felt the sudden need to throw something – anything!

He looked back at the sky. Was the black spot closer? A sudden chill, colder than the Mynher himself, shivered through him. Without further ado he spun and marched toward camp, mumbling that this wasn't the time to let his anger get the better of him.

He shouted for Fraul. If the troops weren't ready in a moons' click he would leave without them.

- - -

Quinton tried to regain his balance, but it was futile. He fell. Cursing the night, Quinton watched as the Crape army surged passed him. How he wanted to join them. How he wanted to destroy Ista. If only he had a horse!

If only the wolven hadn't come.

Collapsing back into the grass Quinton screamed in frustration. It was dark. No one in Crape's army had seen him emerging from the nearby trees, and the pounding hooves would drown his scream.

Ramie's army had yet to leave but Quinton knew he would be unable to reach them in time. They were already abandoning camp and mounting their horses.

With a heavy grunt, Quinton pushed himself up and looked at the bloody stump that had once been his left leg. He would never be able to run again. But with the Maker's help, he would learn to walk. Taking the two long, thick branches he had whittled to staffs, Quinton pulled himself up and managed to stand. His right leg shook with effort.

When he fell for the second time Quinton bowed his head and heaved a sigh. He was too tired, far too tired.

For days he had lived with the pain. For days he had risen only to fall. For days he had lived with the horror of the memories: Michel's eyes, shifting between sanity and insanity; Michel's terror of what he had become, of what he didn't want Ren to see.

Quinton pinched the bridge of his nose, trying to banish the images. When Michel had finally pinned him, he thought he would never again see the light of day. He knew if Michel didn't kill him the wolven would.

As the wolven bounded toward them, eyes fixed on the kill, saliva running down their gaping jaws, Michel had released him. The wolven, smelling the fresh blood from the knife wound in his thigh, had attacked, taking his leg with only a few bites of their powerful jaws.

But instead of Michel leaving him for dead, he had once again transformed into the man Quinton knew well. With a strength Quinton could barely fathom, Michel had taken him and lifted him into a nearby tree. He had barely been able to grab hold and swing his body over the branch. He had screamed for Michel to follow, but it was too late.

The wolven were all over him.

Michel had saved him. In the end, Michel had defied the animal Ista had created.

Quinton looked up into the night and studied Ren's constellation. The Raven had almost reached the first point of the triangle. He had to hurry, but his leg still throbbed from where he had cauterized the wound, and in the distance he heard Ramie's troops begin to march. With rising conviction Quinton pushed himself up and shouted for help, but the soldiers were too far away to hear a lone scream, too preoccupied with their purpose to give notice to a small movement in the trees.

- - -

"We must leave," Zorc said, tucking the shrunken crystal back into the folds of his robe.

The group fell to silence as they ambled to the cavern's entrance. Grauss put a hand on Neki's arm, motioning for him to remain behind. Neki was about to question when Grauss' piercing gaze stopped him.

Over the years he had learned not to question his grandfather. If Grauss wanted to have a word with him without the others, he had good reason. It may be a reason Neki would never know, but a reason nonetheless.

When the others had disappeared from sight, Grauss tapped the side of Neki's face. "You must watch the stars, my boy. Something is wrong." Grauss turned toward the window. His eyes darted nervously to the side. Neki almost drew back. Grauss was shaking.

"I said nothing to your prince because I don't yet know the implications."

"What is it? What did you see?"

When Grauss turned back to him, his eyes were crazed. "The twin moons, Neki. Look at them. Really look at them when you leave here. You'll see what I mean."

Neki was about to ask another question when Grauss flung his arms around him. "I'm proud of you, my boy. Be safe. And watch the stars."

Before Neki had a chance to reply, Grauss broke from him and scampered to the nearest dangling chair. After hoisting himself up to the window, Grauss began writing frantically. Neki watched Grauss for a few heartbeats before turning to leave.

He walked slowly at first, needing to be alone with his thoughts. The twin moons? What did Grauss mean? He had seen the twin moons every night and he hadn't noticed anything unusual. Neki heaved a sigh and picked up the pace, watching for any sign of the others. He should have seen their torches by now, but the trail was dark. He ran on instinct.

The green glow of nightmoss began flickering around him.

Neki stopped. It was the end of summer. Nightmoss was only green in the spring. Neki drew his saber. The emerald glowed with a brilliant intensity. It was almost blinding.

The emerald wards off evildoings.

His shadow hit the rock wall beside him, making his countenance appear as vast as the Druidonian. Neki only hoped the enemy would think so as well.

Neki sensed them before he felt the air stir behind him. Spinning in defensive posture, he faced Feher and Welch. Feher's putrid yellow eyes glowed with a deep-seated hatred. Welch appeared smug. It was that smugness that gave away the third Druid creeping up from behind. When Neki spun, his saber sliced through the approaching Druid, spilling his insides across the cold, gray stone.

Neki whirled back to face the other two. Feher only chuckled. Neki remembered the feeling when the Druids tried to close him and slunk back, trying to find the others in the dimly lit passage. He spotted the silver dust on Zorc's robe first, about ten paces down the ledge. Galvin, Nigel, and Ren lay with him. Morrus wasn't there.

Morrus had betrayed them.

Neki's body slammed into the mountain's face as a mighty force entered his mind. He felt strong tentacles searching for his power. They grabbed it, encircled it, and began to pull, but as quickly as the feeling came it went. Neki careened down the wall, exhausted, and watched in shock as Morrus hit Feher. Welch lay dead, a knife in his chest.

The High Priest faced Morrus with a long dagger. Morrus looked into Feher's eyes without fear, but he had no weapon. Feher grinned.

In that grin was victory.

With rising dread Neki saw what Morrus was about to do. Morrus was next to the mountain's face, Feher next to the edge. Morrus was going push Feher over the edge, but in doing so he was prepared to sacrifice himself. If Feher grabbed Morrus, Morrus would be unable to stop his own fall. His bulk wouldn't allow it.

Neki pushed himself off the rocks just as Morrus broke into a run. Worry stole over Feher's countenance. Neki jumped, knowing full well it may be the last jump he ever made, but he knew it would be next to impossible for him to pull Morrus back from Feher's grip without toppling into the fissure himself. He had to trust Morrus to save him if Feher grabbed him before plummeting into the crevice below.

He hit. Feher screeched in rage as he groped for Neki's tunic. Feher stumbled backwards, clutching Neki to him, and fell. Neki held his breath. The darkness bellow came closer as his feet lost contact with the ground.

Then strong hands encircled his waist, jerking him from Feher's grasp.

Neki fell to solid ground as Feher's shrieks became distant echoes and were finally silenced.

Neki's head sunk down in relief. "Thank you."

Morrus chuckled. "I should be thanking you."

Neki felt a stab of regret for doubting Morrus' loyalty, even for a heartbeat. He rolled to his side and looked at the Druid who had hereto been an enigma to him.

"Forgive me."

Morrus looked surprised. "For?"

"When I didn't see you with the others I thought the worst."

Morrus nodded, but no emotion touched his features. "There's nothing to forgive. I'm a Druid. I can understand your doubt."

"Do you have go through some ritual to become a Druid?"

Morrus frowned. "Well, there's a coronation at birth. But no, not really."

"Can you be de-coronated?"

"De-coronated?

"Yes, de-coronated." Neki stood and slapped the dust off his pants before he offered Morrus his hand. Morrus helped himself up and they both walked to the others. "What do they do at this coronation?"

"The father immerses his new born in water and holds him up to the heavens, asking for his child to be worthy of the omniscient state."

Neki cocked his head to the side. "That's it?"

Morrus nodded. "That's it."

Neki recorded that piece of information for future reference as he bent to examine Ren. "That doesn't sound too difficult. We just have to have you de-coronated."

Morrus frowned, but before he had a chance to speak Neki pointed to Ren and the others. "What happened?"

Morrus lowered his voice and took Ren's hand in his own. "Feher surprised us. I managed to hide before he realized I was with the group. Feher sprayed Ren and the others with a mist. They immediately lost consciousness."

"From the numberry bush," Neki concluded. One dose of the potent plant could put an angry dragon to sleep. The plant was rare, and although the plant's effects didn't last long it was enough to down an enemy.

Morrus heaved a sigh. "They were planning on taking them to Ista."

Neki nodded, knowing full well what the Druids intended.

"I was trying to find a way to free the others when you came down the passage," Morrus said. "You gave me the diversion I needed."

"Well, at least that does away with them."

Morrus glanced at the ledge. "Feher is still alive. I'm afraid we haven't seen the last of him."

"How could he have survived?" Neki's voice sounded frantic.

Morrus' eyes were hard when he turned back to face him. "High Priests are stronger than other Druids. Druids can use the calling power, but High Priests can use an opposite phenomenon. Instead of bringing an object to them, High Priests have learned how to send their body to an object. Feher found a way to land without harm. Rest assured, we'll see him again."

Neki was about to ask more when he decided against it. He didn't want to know any more about the Druid cultus.

Nigel moaned and reached up to rub a nasty knot on his head. In the next heartbeat Nigel's eyes opened and he sprang to his feet, drawing his sword.

"Easy Blackie," Neki said. "The threat has been deterred."

Nigel looked down the passageway at the two dead Druids. "All of them?"

"Not all," Morrus said. "Feher went over the edge."

Nigel stiffened, face grave. It took a little longer for Galvin, Ren, and Zorc to wake, but when they did Zorc was furious. He mumbled under his breath and peered over the edge like he was about to jump after the High Priest.

When they finally made it out of the mountain it was far into the next day and they were surprised to find Markum sitting on a rock. He looked tired, but a large smile lit his face when he saw Ren.

After a heartfelt reunion Zorc led the way down the mountain, taking them on a course that led straight to Zier. Neki wondered what Zorc was doing but didn't question the wizard. It wasn't his place. Soon darkness surrounded them, but they continued on. Zorc insisted that after this push they would settle in until they went to take the Red Eye from Ista. The mood of the group was dismal and no one spoke after Zorc had reiterated everything about the twin Eyes. Neki tried to tune out the wizard's words but he couldn't. He finally busied himself by studying the twin moons. They were bright that night, and for a time Neki found nothing unusual about them. Then he saw it.

One of the moons was larger on one side. The more he studied it, the more concerned he became. It wasn't larger at all. Another moon was emerging from behind it. Three moons?

Neki began to wonder how any of them were going to make it out of this alive.

CHAPTER 24

Ren turned his head and glared at Zorc. "I feel ridiculous."

Galvin grunted his agreement from where he played a game of Chance with Markum and Morrus.

Zorc had taken them as close as he dared to Zier. They had found a small rise in the foothills of the Sierra Mountains that overlooked the city. Thick foliage surrounded them on three sides, protecting them from a surprise attack.

Ren, Nigel, and Neki had perched on boulders near the embankment's edge at Zorc's command. All were leaning forward with their backs parallel with the ground and one leg in the air in line with their spine. Their arms were spread to each side, as if they were preparing for flight.

Zorc raised his pointy eyebrows and lifted a finger. "Ridiculous but effective. Here, let me show you." Zorc jumped on Ren's boulder and shooed him off. He bent into the pose, dark hair falling to brush the ground. Zorc closed his eyes and raised his head to face forward.

"The elements are powerful things. If you don't feel them and know where they reside inside you, you'll fail in your task. I'm showing you 'love' in the best way I know how. You must believe it, feel it, live it, be it. Relax your body, feel your heart, feel the wind and the freedom of love's choice. It's there, inside all of us, and only we can choose to feel it. When we do we can fly!"

Zorc slowly lifted the only leg he stood on and hovered in the air, all muscles relaxed. The wind hit his face and caused his blue robe to ripple like an expanse of ocean. He grinned at their astonished expressions before languidly lowering both legs to the rock.

"Come," he said, waving them over. "First I should explain how the Quy works." All three of them approached, humbled by the wizard's display of power. Zorc grabbed a stick and drew an equilateral triangle in the dirt, placing a small stone at each point.

"Ren, this is what you saw in the Oracle, the internal elements of love, hate, and pain. The Quy uses these elements to create magic. Magic can be woven from any of these elements and any combination of them," Zorc said, tracing the lines of the triangle.

"But," he said, "the Quy is strongest when it's here." Zorc placed a stone in the air above the center of the triangle. It hovered above the ground, creating a pyramid effect.

"It's the synergy," Neki said. Zorc smiled and nodded.

Ren studied the hovering stone. "What does it represent?"

"That is the pinnacle or, as Grauss calls it, the union, or the synergy. The synergy, or pinnacle, draws on all three of the elements. None are stronger than the other in the pinnacle. The pinnacle is the calm."

Ren glanced up. "I didn't think you were supposed to use hate."

Zorc smiled. "No, you shouldn't use hate in the sense of the word 'hate.' For instance: If I hate you because you have more power than I do, that's hate, and that hate is evil. Let's say you hated this way, your hate is birthed by no other emotion than hate itself. Watch what happens to the pinnacle."

The hate stone on the ground grew, causing the triangle to become unbalanced. The hovering pinnacle rock began to sink, slowly at first, and then it plunged down to crash into the hate stone. This caused the large mass of hate to sink into the opposite leg of the triangle, which in turn caused the love and pain stones to collapse into it as it hit their center, leaving only one large rock mass.

Zorc peered at each in turn. "If you begin to hate for hate itself, for evil, such as greed or jealousy, without love or pain originating the hate, you'll become hate. Hate will envelop you and take over your soul. Barracus proved that. He allowed hate, in the form of greed, to consume him.

"Barracus was a mage, and very strong, but he was like this." Zorc swept his hand over the one large stone. "But beware, this configuration of one emotion to the extreme is powerful. It can overtake someone who uses the pinnacle as if the pinnacle is nothing more than a piece of glass. However, the pinnacle, the synergy, is ultimately stronger than the intensity of the one emotion. If the pinnacle can withstand the intense emotion's first attack it has a chance. If you are strong enough to hold the pinnacle, the attacker with the one dominant emotion will weaken. The pinnacle won't. That's why I'm teaching you to find the calm, the pinnacle. Barracus has intense hatred inside him. If you're forced to face him you'll have to overcome that intensity and push off his hatred."

Zorc leaned closer, eyes piercing. "Ren, you'll have your own hatred inside the pinnacle. It will be the righteous hate, the good hate, but you'll have it all the same. Your hate will be attracted to Barracus' hate and together it may cause what I've just described – the collapse of the union. Only if you're strong enough will you be able to resist and hang onto the pinnacle, thus pushing Barracus out."

The day seemed to darken with the wizard's words. Ren released a breath as Zorc turned his concentration back to the stones.

Suddenly, the large rock mass broke apart and the stones soared back into their earlier positions.

"The reason the mass of hate is ultimately weaker than the pinnacle is because of love and pain," Zorc continued. "They're both stronger than hate. Hate, though, doesn't have to be pure hate as in hating for hate's sake. Hate can be stemmed from goodness. Although you hate, your actions are truly originated from love or pain. For instance, hate could stem from a man's daughter being raped. The man loves his daughter. He hates what happened to her. He hates that he couldn't prevent it, but he doesn't hate for hate's sake, he hates because of love. A better term to describe this righteous hate is anger or rage."

Zorc tapped the Black Knight's chest with a long, bony finger. "You've lived long with this righteous hate. I commend you for not giving in to true hate long ago. Many who carry that much righteous rage can't withstand the pain. Take the man and the rapist for instance. The man's righteous rage transforms into hate for the perpetrator. He kills the perpetrator. He feels power by doing so. He forgets the pain of his daughter because he can't bear to carry it with him. He begins to scheme of ways to hunt down more rapists, not because of love now, but out of lust. So beware, righteous hate can grow into evil hate within the blink of an eye.

"But if you hold on to this righteous hate, this righteous anger, and remember the love and the pain it stemmed from, the hate will be the good hate. This type of hate drives you to correct those who use hate in other ways. If you have this righteous hate it's powerful, and it's needed to create the calm.

"You're a mage, Ren. And you're the Chosen. The two together are powerful. The evil of this world will try to make you one of them. When people die and destruction happens hate is an easy thing to feel for it doesn't come with pain. If you remain in the calm you'll feel pain. Pain is pain and love is painful. Hate doesn't deal with any pain. You must make sure your hate won't grow into evil. You must make sure love and pain balance it and bring it."

Zorc paused, making sure his words were being understood. "Only a mage can control the pinnacle. Others of us never reach it or only reach it a few times in our lives. And only a mage can destroy another mage. The first mage was Magnus, a wizard who lived before the Dark Ages. Magnus found the calm and used the pinnacle. Years later Barracus found the calm, but his hate collapsed the pinnacle. If the two were in battle for power, I'm unsure who would survive. Magnus, though stronger in the calm, would be aware of the consequences of his actions. Barracus, in his hate, wouldn't care whom he hurt and would hurt many to wear Magnus down.

Zorc focused on Ren. "If Barracus enters someone other than you, you'll have to battle him outright, not internally. You'll be concerned about your actions – he won't. Even if you find the pinnacle you could lose. But," Zorc said, raising his finger in the air, "if the mage enters you, you're on your terms, your actions affecting only you. If you reach the pinnacle you have a chance of ending the threat forever by banishing the mage back into the Red Eye." Zorc nodded to the boulder Ren had been on earlier. "You must learn to find the calm so you'll be at your strongest. That's why I show you the exercises I do.

"You have to learn fast. In my day it took years to find the elements within. Over the centuries I've searched for a quick way to teach you, fearing we wouldn't have much time. The exercises I show you are what I discovered to work best for me and I think will work best for you. Ren, you're strong, and the Quy has gained in strength since the Wizard War. You'll be able to do things in a day that took me years of training, but I don't know how much time we have."

Ren nodded. "I'll do whatever you ask," he said, meaning it more than he had ever meant anything in his life.

Zorc smiled. "Then find love."

- - -

Sim shivered by the brook. He couldn't move. Fire spread through his right thigh, his underbelly, and his flank. He released a pent-up roar. Men began to emerge from the woods. A black citadel glittered on their tunics. All their heads were shaved.

He had been running for days, fleeing their poisoned arrows. But he had to rest, he had to eat, and when he had landed for a drink they were there. Magic had made them swift. His skin may repel magic but he couldn't outrun it. He released another bellow.

The men stepped closer. Some held flails, others held whips, and others drug a long wooden plank behind them.

Sim couldn't resist on any longer. His head hit the ground, causing one of the arrows to embed further in his flesh.

CHAPTER 25

Ramie gazed at the scene before him. The Collective stood on top of the outer wall of Ziera, watching their every move. It made Ramie's skin crawl.

Every ten or so cubits large bundles of supplies marred the perfect circle. Supplies for what, Ramie was unsure. He really didn't care to find out.

The still air hovered around them like a thick fog. The Collective hadn't stirred, but the clouded look in their eyes wasn't quite right. Ramie scanned the wall again as his hackles stood on end.

The Collective were united as one mind.

Lazo was right. The Collective were grains of sand on the shore, but now they were grains united as one mind. Only time would tell if his army would be able to counter the Collective's magic.

Beside him, Lorlier and Bostic paled, but Chris and Aaron seemed undaunted by the horde before them. The two were as opposite as day and night: Chris, dressed in all white, with tan skin and blond hair; Aaron, dressed in all black, with pale skin and hair as black as midnight. Each held an intensity Ramie had never seen before. When you looked into their eyes you drowned in emotions that could only be felt through hundreds of lifetimes. When Ramie looked at them he felt like a paltry babe. He didn't like the feeling.

He turned and motioned for Presario and Lazo. Presario still wore his cowl, but it was pushed back so that much of his face showed. Ramie had grown accustomed to the molten flesh, as had all his soldiers. Now, instead of appearing horrific, Presario's features held a profound beauty.

Lazo's contrasting eyes studied him briefly before turning back to the walls. "Don't fear, my king. We may only be a pebble, but we're prepared to become much more on your command."

Ramie nodded. "You know what to do. On my command."

Lazo and Presario rode forward, those with the Quy following. Soon the first division stood hundreds wide and four thick. Ramie's eyes darted to each side, looking for any sign of movement on the wall before turning to Fraul. His captain would lead the attack without magic, but it would have to be timed with precision. "Fraul, prepare to attack on my command. But don't be a hero. Wait for my command."

Fraul's gray eyes danced with delight, as if preparing for a ball and not a siege. He turned to his men. "On guard!"

The drawing of swords and the clinking of lances echoed in the dawn.

Ramie raised his hand in the air, but before he could give the signal someone caught his wrist. He spun only to be greeted by the commanding eyes of the queen. Just as Ramie's anger was about to ignite, it dissipated as Renee offered him a jester's grin.

She nodded to the walls. "It would be wise to hold your position, my king. It seems my speech struck a cord."

Ramie followed Renee's gaze to a large tree beside the walls. Upon closer examination Ramie espied a small, dirty face peering from the branches. The small boy jumped from the tree, light blond hair shimmering like spun gold, and waved. The boy turned to the walls, placed a wooden horn to his lips, and blew.

A loud hum inundated the still air and suddenly the bundles dispersed throughout the Collective came to life. Men from the city, with black sashes tied to their arms, leapt from the mounds. Each man flung two, if not three, of the Collective to their deaths before the Collective had a chance to retaliate.

Before Ramie could whoop in delight the rebels dropped to their knees and screamed a gut-wrenching cry. Although the Collective's magic couldn't be seen, the men's screams heralded the terror the armies in the field were about to face.

"Presario!" Ramie yelled as he brought up his hand and signaled. "Now!" Although the Collective still outnumbered the rebels on the wall by five to one, the rebels had given his army the diversion they needed.

Presario shouted a command. The first division brought up bows, aimed, and let their arrows fly. They didn't fly like normal arrows. They flew with magic. Ramie watched as a few caught their targets. The remaining Collective stopped their assault on the rebels and refocused on the army.

"Go, Fraul! Go, go!"

The secondary division speed past, bellowing a battle cry. The air was immediately replete with screams of the dying and the roar of soldiers.

A torrent of wind hurled from the Collective. The arrows of the first division halted in midair as the magic in them strained to penetrate the wind of the Collective. Ramie shouted for Fraul to hold, but his command was whisked away by the wind.

Ramie tried to spur Mortar forward, but the air was like a brick wall. He couldn't move. With rising dread he watched Fraul and his army plunge forward, intent on breaching the gate. The Collective were letting them come, leading them to their deaths.

"No!" Ramie shouted, but again his voice was whisked away.

Ramie turned back to the arrows. A few of them broke through the wind to successfully pierce their targets, but most of them fell to the ground as the power of the wind forced all magic from them.

- - -

Presario lifted his arms. "Prepare to form a gale on my command!" It was the only counter measure he knew against gusts of air that powerful. They had to form a windstorm that would hurl the air back at the Collective. Just as he was about to command his men to form the magic, the wind stopped.

Presario hesitated, unsure of his next move. Then the power of the Collective's new magic surged toward them.

It wasn't the strong gust of air as before, it was a scant breeze, but it was hotter than flames. It stole over them like a shadow, coating them with fire. Presario screamed as the flames engulfed him, burning him as they had years before. Some of his men dropped from their horses, no scar or blister on them, but their faces were clenched in the terror Presario had once lived.

Suddenly Lazo was beside him, keeping him upright. The flames quickly dissipated. Lazo spun to the men. "Shields! Everyone, individual shields!"

Presario nodded his thanks. His entire body still held the resonance of the flames, but he would survive. Presario embedded his emotional shield into place. Shields would deflect most magic, but you couldn't use any magic behind them, and they were so difficult to conjure without silver dust most would be unable to summon them more than once in a day. Shields wouldn't save them again.

When Presario rose to his feet he saw Fraul leading the second division to the outer gate. His eyes scanned the wall. The Collective were slowly beginning to turn, eyes reaching for Fraul and his army. In heartbeats the army would feel the heat of the flames and they would be unable to counter the threat. They were riding into a trap.

Frantic shouts caused Presario to turn. Chris and Aaron rode toward Fraul's division in a blur of white and black. Presario blinked in shock. What were they planning to do? Even if they were strong enough to conjure their shields again those shields wouldn't be enough to save the entire division, and when they weakened Aaron and Chris would be sitting targets.

As the Collectives flames reached the soldiers, horses reared and men began to topple. Presario watched helplessly as many soldiers weren't killed from the inner flames but from their own horses as they were trampled underfoot.

Fraul turned in confusion as the screams of the dying reached his ears. Then the flames engulfed him. Fraul's eyes widened as his body took in the heat. Heartbeats later the wave of fire swept though the entire army and harrowing screams saturated the air.

When Aaron and Chris reached the troop of soldiers they turned as one body. Presario could see the power lighting their eyes even from his distance. Presario watched in awe as the air before Chris and Aaron twirled in a circular pattern, forming a lip as wide as the wall itself. The cyclone roared in the dawn, masking the screams of the dying, and moved forward. Just as Presario thought it would move over the Collective on the wall it stopped. A thundering implosion echoed over the horizon as the cyclone collapsed inward, forming a funnel that led to the two defenders. Presario could almost see the power of the Collective being drawn into the funnel. He could almost hear the heat sizzling down the tube.

"May the Maker's fates be with them," Presario whispered.

- - -

Chris collapsed on the back of his mount as the first wave of heat tore through him, transforming his body into an inferno. Beside him, Aaron screamed, but Chris knew it wasn't a scream of a dying man. It was a scream of determination. Even as the flames engulfed his body Chris forced himself to straighten and look through the funnel. Their conjuring was so strong, the collective force behind it was wrapped up in its strength. As long as they held the funnel the Collective would be unable to turn from their magic. They were trapped.

Chris found Presario through the torrent of wind. Presario's eyes were wide. In those eyes Chris saw the pain of the flames and the pain of realizing Chris and Aaron would be unable to survive the intensity of the conglomerate fire.

Little did Presario know Chris and Aaron had survived much worse than the flames. They wouldn't only survive, they would also give Presario the time he desperately needed.

Chris nodded to Presario. "Now."

- - -

Ramie watched as the messenger spurred away before turning his attention back to the battle. Both the first and the second division were trying to recover from whatever horrors the Collective had used against them as Chris and Aaron took the brunt of the attack.

Ramie hungered to join the fight. Even Mortar pranced impatiently, ready for action. It was both the curse and the blessing of a king. He needed to oversee the battle, ensure the full picture was being realized. He needed to give commands others would follow blindly, even if those commands went contrary to their views. For in the midst of battle you missed other options, other threats that could emerge. Messengers took his commands to the front lines. Ramie turned and caught Tec's eye. The boy sat forward in his saddle, eyes wide with eager bravado and mistaken immortality. If Ramie needed a messenger he wouldn't send Tec. He wanted the boy to live.

Presario shouted a command. The men of the first division rushed forward. Many of the Collective fell from the wall as magic Ramie couldn't see spewed from the first division. His hopes rose. Somehow, Chris and Aaron had trapped the Collective. Now Presario had the Collective in the palm of his hand.

A mass of red hair shot past. Ramie cursed. When he hadn't seen Manda with Fraul's army he thought she may have come to her senses and left with Renee and Marva, who had entered the tunnels in case the attack went sour. Renee thought she could rally more people to fight the Collective internally. One of the tunnels led directly to the Dragon's Bane, where they had spoken to the people before.

Manda hadn't gone with Renee. She now galloped from him faster than a dragon could fly. She was riding to the gate, skirting around the stunned army.

What Manda didn't realize was what Ramie had already seen. Behind the gate more of the Collective waited, more who weren't wrapped up in the defender's magic. He had just sent a messenger to inform Fraul to retreat immediately.

"Manda!" But Ramie knew even if Manda heard she would ignore his plea. "Maker curse it," he mumbled before spurring Mortar into a gallop. Behind him, his personal guards jumped on their horses to follow. He had no time to order them to remain behind. His only intent was to follow the blur of red hair. Although Manda's stallion was fast, Mortar was faster. He was gaining ground with each stride.

The Collective behind the gate were beginning to move. Ramie watched helplessly as Fraul's army was assaulted from behind. Ramie didn't know what magic the Collective was using, but it was worse than the first. Men fell from the saddle, screaming a horrific cry. A few quickly died as blood seeped from their eyes.

Manda didn't slow. In precious heartbeats she would be caught up in the Collective's magic. She wouldn't stand a chance.

Ramie shouted Manda's name once more, but it was met with deaf ears.

- - -

Manda stood apart from the others, almost dizzy from the feelings churning within her. During their ride to Zier she felt the avenging power building inside her. She cultivated it, encouraged it, yet she still didn't know what it would help her do. She had planned on marching with Fraul's army, but had retreated just before Ramie's command, the feelings moving inside her too fervent to ignore.

The power surged through her with the strength of the ten winds, boiling her blood and sending her into a spiral of intent. As she watched the battle before her, everything else around her went black. In her mind there was no sound. All was silenced, and in that silence she listened to the power becoming something she couldn't define.

The love came first. It welled in her soul: the love she carried for Chris and Ren and all others who had been touched by Ista's vile hand. When it reached a zenith the pain rose inside her: the pain of the death and destruction happening before her eyes. Once the pain overwhelmed the rage burned hot within her: rage at the woman who had stolen her father and who had stolen Zier. Her emotions screamed for her to fight for justice. It was almost blinding.

And so it continued: the love, the pain, the rage, and the scream for justice. She was like a rod electrified with the three internal elements.

As Manda watched the destruction before her, she saw more of the loathsome Collective gathering at the gate. Her blood boiled hotter. And then the spiral went again: the love, the pain, and the rage.

Glancing down at her fingertips she saw sparks of power seeping from her skin.

She blinked, stunned her inner feelings could create such intensity. She thought about the Avenger's power. She had taken a piece of that power, that scream for justice, that righteous judgment, that rage. The Avenger's power helped protect him from those who would stop him. One spark of it would ensure complete destruction.

Would her power, as Aaron's power, protect her from those who would try to stop her? Would her power, as Aaron's power, protect her from those who would try to stop her with magic?

Manda's eyes flickered to the gates. The Collective were merging. Fraul's army was still recovering from the magic Chris and Aaron had taken. Chris and Aaron were intent on delaying the Collective's attack. Presario aim was the Collective's destruction. None would see the lone few gathering at the gate.

Manda snapped her reins. She heard Ramie call her name but ignored him. She didn't care at all about the king's commands. Her only goal was saving Fraul's army from whatever those vile creatures were about to do.

She heated her intent still higher. The internal elements tore through her with the force of a catapult.

As she paralleled the army she saw the Collective at the gate begin their chant. She wheeled her horse in front of Fraul just as the incantation was hurled through the air. Her skin was light, her eyes were flame, and when the magic washed over her she felt it, yet she felt no pain. She felt their power, yet she had more than enough to counter it. She also felt the Collective's screams, their dying breaths as the intensity of her emotions bounded to them, sending their bodies into convulsions. She watched with only mild interest as the Collective before her shriveled to the ground as the avenging power seared their bodies from the inside.

- - -

When he heard Manda's name being yelled in terror, Aaron faltered. Chris did as well, but now the Collective on the walls were few and far between. The first division could take them easily. As one mind, Aaron and Chris released the funnel of air and spun, barely aware the remaining Collective collapsed as they were released from the strain of the funnel's hold. Aaron had to blink in shock at the woman standing before the army. She seemed to glow with light, just like his Kyra, and as the sun's rays caressed her long hair at first he thought it was Kyra. But when she moved and the red locks caught the light he smiled with doleful rapture. It was his Manda, learning the power he had bestowed upon her.

He hadn't known the extent of his transfer, but when he had held her after he had killed Valor he had allowed his remaining sparks to disseminate inside her. Only an avenged could take his sparks, and only an avenged strong enough could cultivate those sparks to their own purpose.

Now he saw that purpose. His sparks had been too painful for anyone to withstand, even someone who touched him with magic. Manda had taken those sparks and formed them to her own emotions. Now, when Manda looked on depravity she would become the hand of justice, and her power would ignite not pain, but rage, righteous rage.

And if any touched her, they would die.

Beside him, Chris grinned, transforming his melancholy countenance into whimsical charm. Chris spurred his mount forward.

Aaron followed, passing a wide-eyed Fraul. Looking down at his friend, Aaron winked.

Renee and Marva had already reached the gate and had opened it for Manda. The remaining Collective could be seen weaving their way through the streets toward the castle. Some brave rebels ran after them.

When Chris and Aaron finally flanked Ramie, Manda was already halfway down the main street. Behind them, Fraul and Presario's army could be heard barreling though the gate.

They had won their first attack.

Manda spurred her mount to a stop and wheeled around in the circle. She still shone like the stars, and as she spoke the power of her words echoed down the streets.

"Citizens of Zier!" she shouted. "I implore you to take up arms and fight for justice! If you want to be free men, if you want to live in peace, you need to fight for the true king of this Land! Our army has defeated Ista's first attack. Now we march to Stardom to defeat Ista's forces there. If you want to defend your home, your king, and your honor, I implore you. Follow me!"

Aaron shivered at the power of Manda's words. Behind him a roar went up from the army as people came out of houses, tying pieces of black cloth around their arms – Razon black.

Manda surged forward, red hair flying behind her like a war banner.

Ramie scowled as he stepped beside Aaron, but Aaron could see the sparkle in the king's eyes as he gazed at Manda. There was also a profound relief in his stance, and perhaps even adoration.

Hearing a chuckle, Aaron turned to Chris.

"Sis never cared for war, Aaron. It seems you've given her a taste for battle."

Aaron lifted a sarcastic eyebrow. "I don't know if I've given her a taste for battle, but I've given battle a taste of her."

CHAPTER 26

Ren hovered in the air, feeling the love flowing through him. He reached for it, yearned for it. He was buoyant. He was light. He was love.

"Now try pain."

Zorc's words came from far away. Ren opened his eyes and released love, letting his legs sink to the ground. Ren was unsure why Zorc wanted him to find pain. He had mastered pain days ago, but he didn't question the wizard. Ren rested on his knees and leaned forward, forming a ball, focusing on the ache inside him. Pain was an inward emotion, not open like love. Pain was in the upper chest. Love was deeper and lower, almost where the soul should be. The pain tore through him, searing his mind.

"Look now. Hold it and look."

Ren lifted his head and stared in stark amazement. Standing, he turned full circle, holding his pain, breathing it. Everything around him bent in his direction: the trees, the grass, and the air. Even his friends had their heels implanted in the soil, muscles straining as they resisted being pulled toward him. Only Zorc sat untouched, somehow blocking his pull.

"Hate," the wizard demanded.

Ren was already in hate's stance, standing straight. All he had to do was bow his head and clench his fists. He found hate immediately, on the surface of the chest. He felt himself rising from the ground, hovering above it, his hate forcing itself out of his hands, lifting him.

"Look."

Ren raised his head. Now everything blew away from him. He suddenly understood why the three worked together. Hate blew out, pain blew in, and love was the balance.

He pulled on each with quick surety, forming all inside him at once. He let each emotion roar through him, tumbling over the others, caressing the others, learning the others, until they churned to a stop and formed an impenetrable whole.

He was above the elements, looking down on them but together with them. He felt each one, but he felt them like a whisper. He could see their intensity, but he kept their fervor from him. He found the calm. He was the calm. He was the synergy, the union, the pinnacle.

All was back to normal. The grass didn't bend, the trees didn't shake, and the air was tranquil, but he was far from normal. He looked through wizard's eyes.

He saw the Quy everywhere. Images blurred and edges glowed with strength. Nigel was replete with black sable. It shimmered around him in a haze of power. At his core was love's white diamond trimmed with a crystal of pain, but his righteous rage radiated from him so much it darkened the day. Neki glowed with all three elements. They spun from his center like a whirlwind: black rage, white-hot love, and crying pain. The tones, however, were subdued, not vivid, but with the way they churned, Ren could sense Neki's power. Markum was a haze of murky white, but his eyes were lit with a deep sapphire blue, a symbol of his seer status. And Galvin, although he didn't have the Quy, had poignant steel gray effulgence emanating from his chest.

Ren turned to Zorc. The wizard was surrounded with every hue imaginable. Not only did blacks and silvers careen from his persona but emeralds, sapphires, rubies, ambers, and amethysts. Ren looked down at his own body, seeing for the first time what Zorc saw when he looked through wizard eyes.

Black was at his core but white surrounded it, so much so the black seemed to be a moon drifting over the sun, shielding its rays only briefly. The white core at his chest radiated a light so intense even the black moon radiated the light, causing black to surround him as well as the white. Then, at his edges and seeping a glow, was his pain, emitting a crystalline brilliance, and causing the lights to merge together and become one large shield of silver platinum.

Ren let the calm flow through his entire being. He pulled from each emotion, was one with each emotion. Zorc grabbed Neki's saber. His eyes glimmered with an inner fire.

Zorc raised the sword in an attack position. The silver blade flashed wickedly in the sun. The emerald, ruby, and sardonyx were dull without Neki's hand, but they appeared to be watching, boring into Ren's soul.

"Love, hate, pain!" Zorc said, moving the sword faster than possible without magic.

As Zorc screamed the internal element's cognomen Ren instinctively pulled from each emotion, blocking the blow of the blade. He held the pinnacle inside him, lifting each leg of the triangle to his wishes: love, then hate, and then pain. Each time he lifted the triangle he felt the intensity of the emotion he used, but although he could feel the intensity, it was a distant memory, a storm behind a windowpane.

None of the emotions took him off balance. None seared his heart. In the calm the emotions couldn't claim him. They couldn't hurt or overwhelm him. As the sword continued to pound the air he learned how each emotion worked and how much to drain from his wealth of feelings to keep himself from harm.

Zorc stepped back, panting with effort, and smiled. He sheathed the saber and tossed it to Neki. "Good work, Ren. The more you use the pinnacle the longer you'll be able to hold each emotion and the more you'll be able to draw on all equally. Magic always needs certain degrees of each one, and the more in balance you are the more you'll be able to detect how much of each emotion you'll need. You've now mastered something that's taken me over a century."

Ren started, surprised by Zorc's statement, and released the calm. His emotions washed over him in full force. They were random and uncontrollable. In the calm they had been controlled and predictable, almost purposeful. He suddenly felt alone and weak, unable to control his thoughts to one purpose. He began to reach for the calm when Zorc stopped him.

"Don't go to the calm for the calm's sake. It's peaceful and powerful, but it will destroy you." Zorc's voice was low and grave. It shivered down Ren's spine like a cold rain. Somehow Zorc had twisted his words with magic, breaking him from his desire to reenter the calm.

"How?" Ren asked.

"If you go to the calm for the calm's sake you'll eventually not see, or hear, or smell, or feel anything. You'll just sit and feel nothing, sit and slowly die." Zorc paused to make sure Ren understood. When Zorc found what he wanted in Ren's eyes, his voice softened.

"I know how it feels. Not many wizards are able to feel the calm. Only a handful of us have ever reached it. We just aren't powerful enough. When I did reach it I almost gave in and let my mind become washed away. Feeling no loneliness or pain or hurt is a wonderful thing, but I've seen what the calm can do. There's a wizard in the fields of the Alcazar, body alive, mind dead. He's called the Residuum Man. He isn't human, animal, or plant. He rests cross-legged, moss and fern coating his body, limbs rooted to the earth, eyes staring blankly ahead, breath and pulse nonexistent. When he reached the calm nothing else mattered. He gave in to that peace, and that peace destroyed him."

Zorc's dark eyes studied him, waiting for the shock to spread over his face. Ren drew in a breath, still yearning for the calm, but now revolted by the seduction of its peace.

Zorc started toward the camp. Ren was surprised. It was only midmorning and there was still much he needed to learn.

"Wait, I'm not tired. Now that I can reach the calm you can teach me how to use it."

Zorc grinned. "You have the calm, Ren."

"Yes."

"You know the pinnacle. You are the pinnacle. That's all I can teach you." Zorc turned away, muttering that he was half starved.

Ren watched Zorc walk away, unable to find the words. When they finally came, they exploded from him. "I don't know anything about the Quy. What do you mean that's all you can teach me?"

Zorc turned back to him, holding up a finger with a winsome expression on his face. "You're a mage. I'm a wizard. Wizards can't teach magi. Magi teach wizards."

The others turned to listen, interested in the sudden change of conversation. Ren felt his frustration building. Zorc saw it as well. He crossed his arms, grin spreading.

"What do you want to know?" Zorc asked. "Do you want to know how to meet the Quy?"

Ren frowned. "No."

"Do you want to know how to merge a body with a spirit? No, that can't be," Zorc said, crinkling up his face, "you already know how to do that. I know! You want to know how to light a wolf on fire, or cause a castle wall to crumble. No," he said again, scratching his head in mock confusion, "you already did those things now, didn't you?"

Ren was beginning to feel foolish, but he was unsure why. "But what about all the instructions in the books we found about how to use the Quy?"

"Instructions for wizards, Ren. Merely words that help wizards harness their emotions so they can create magic. Those words are a guide, a blueprint for those who do not have the calm." Zorc held up a finger. "You do. What I could teach you about using the external elements, what I could teach you about using the internal elements of the Quy, what I could teach you about rules and guides would serve you no purpose. In fact it would clutter your mind and serve to bring you doubt when you're instinctively reaching inside yourself to do what you must.

"The more recipes you have for magic the more those rules will clutter your mind when your instincts are needed. You've learned the first truth. Yes?"

The question took Ren off guard. He thought about the Druids and the closing. He thought about his faith in the Maker and his faith in himself to listen and give in to that power. Belief was a powerful thing. It could damn you or it could raise you. With belief anything was possible. He could only nod.

"Then you know how much danger and destruction doubt can cause. Doubt can destroy your conviction and clutter up your thoughts until you begin to believe what you need to accomplish is too unreachable to try. The small doubt will snowball and you'll think of it over and over. You'll fear it. You'll run from it. One doubt can ruin every chance of happiness, can damn your hopes, can mar your dreams, can change your destiny, and can destroy your soul.

"But if I leave you to your inner strength, as all teachers should do with magi, you can build on your strength, intensify it, and become something far more than you can imagine. The first truth is the most powerful truth there is, others follow. But this truth and this truth alone can help you defeat the darkness, can lead you to the second truth.

"So don't doubt yourself. I'll be your guide. I'll answer any questions you have. I'll teach you the Code of the Alcazar. I'll guide your through the Code of the Quy. I'll encourage you to seek the Truths, for only with them can we grow stronger. But I won't teach you how to use the Quy. It's in here," Zorc said, tapping Ren's chest, "and that's where it belongs."

Zorc smiled at Ren's frown. "Do you know why you're the Chosen?"

Ren remembered the day he had asked Zorc's impostor the same question. "Grauss said I was born on the equinox, under all three internal and external elements. The Quy said I only use her in love."

Zorc's grin broadened. "They are both correct and incorrect. Yes, you are the Chosen, and yes you were born on the equinox. Yes, you only use the Quy in love. But the synergy constellation was only a sign in the stars, it doesn't make you the Chosen, and your use of the Quy is how all righteous people strive to use the Quy. The stars symbolize what you are. The way you use the Quy represents the side you're on. But that isn't why you're the Chosen."

Ren was unsure if he really wanted to hear what Zorc was about to reveal. Grauss' explanation had been external forces forming who he was, and the way he used the Quy was a conscious decision, alive heartbeat by heartbeat and not inherently inside him. By the way Zorc spoke he was the Chosen because of something internal. Ren didn't know if he wanted to believe that his naming was internal. The external explanation gave him a humble justification as to why he was the Chosen. Internal forces were something altogether different. They marked him as strong, as someone who formed himself into the mold of Chosen.

"You're the Chosen because of one simple thing."

Zorc paused. Ren would have given anything to halt Zorc's words, but he couldn't force his mouth to open or his arm to move to stop the wizard.

Zorc leaned forward. "I don't know."

Ren was too stunned to speak.

"Only you know," Zorc said. "You tell me."

Ren remained silent for a time. "But, I don't know."

"Yes, you do. Yes, you do. It's in your soul, Ren. It's the one thing that sets you apart from everyone else. It's the one thing that makes you who you are. It's something that cries to you every day. Take it and use it. Use it with all that you have. It has made you strong. It will make you stronger still. Barracus will try to take it from you. Don't let him. If he takes it you'll fail. No pinnacle will save you because you will have lost the essence of yourself, the one thing that makes you the Chosen."

CHAPTER 27

Marva studied a man beyond the glowing orange light as the others talked in angry voices. His pale eyes stared blankly ahead, his lips were open as if he had just taken a shallow breath, but he neither breathed nor moved. It was as if he had turned to stone.

When they had reached the castle the Collective hadn't been standing on the interior wall as they had the outer. Instead they had found the Collective outside the wall, skirting its entire length as if guarding it from entry. They stood at attention, arms stretched to each side, linking hands.

They were linked so well their hands had melted together, forming an impenetrable circle, a circle not of hundreds but of one: one mind, and now one body. Marva shivered.

The magic they had conjured cast them in a pale orange glow that hovered a hand's width from them and then abruptly stopped. Nothing Presario had tried could penetrate it. Instead of attacking, Ista had chosen a shield of protection.

Marva turned her attention to the conversation behind her.

"There has to be something we can do! Nothing is impenetrable," Ramie said, trying to shroud his panic. "We haven't thought through every contingency. A weakness has to exist!"

"There's a weakness," Presario said, "but we can't reach it."

Marva stepped forward, curious. Beside her, Renee lifted her head and looked at Presario with a twinge of hope.

"What do you mean?"

Presario nodded toward the circle of men. "Ista has formed a conglomerate weave. One of the men you see originated it. He is the weak link, the vulnerable link, but there are hundreds of the Collective forming this weave. We cannot with any certainty distinguish the weak link from any other. Hence we cannot focus our attack, and if we can't focus our attack, we'll be unable to penetrate the circle."

Ramie turned to the circle, eyes conveying his panic. "So we just try each one until we find the link."

Presario heaved a sigh and shook his head. The light of the fire played on his face, making his flesh appear to be melting once again. Marva barely took notice of Presario's wounds. To her they were strangely beautiful.

"That would take years, centuries even. A conglomerate weave is acutely unique magic. Once you discover the link you have to discover its vulnerability. By this I mean there will be a slight marring, a slight characteristic of the link that's contradictory.

"Take that one there." Presario pointed to the man Marva had been studying. "He appears whole but there's something peculiar about him. I've been examining him for a sun's click and have just now identified his idiosyncrasy."

Marva nodded. She had noticed an oddity as well. "One pupil is larger than the other."

"Yes. That's his weakness. If he was the link no magic directed at him would destroy him, no sword could penetrate the shield surrounding him, unless that sword hit the exact air pocket that led to his eye, his one vulnerability. All other areas of his body are now the conglomerate and unbreakable.

"That's the power of a conglomerate weave. You have to ferret the link, espy the flaw, and hit the exact air pocket leading to that flaw. Even if you did the first two, the third would be virtually impossible. The weaver can link random air pockets to the flaw. The air pocket that finally touches the flaw in the eye need not necessarily be directly facing the eye. It could be anywhere near the body.

"And the weaver doesn't just give a flaw to the link but to every person in the weave so the enemy will have to search each man to find his vulnerability and try to destroy him before approaching the next man. But to find the link, the vulnerability, and the air pocket . . ." Presario's voice dwindled in the twilight. The crackling fire seemed too lively in the following silence.

Marva turned back to the glowing circle and stepped up to the next man, determined to find his vulnerability. The fury she carried boiled just beneath the surface. Behind her, she heard Ramie's muffled cursing but ignored him. She had grown used to Ramie's outbursts and paid about as much attention to them as a fly on the wall.

"You mentioned the weaver. Is the weaver the same as the link?"

Marva turned to Renee. She hadn't given the weaver Presario mentioned a second thought. The queen may have discovered something. All eyes turned to Presario, eagerly awaiting his reply.

Presario shook his head. "No. Although there's someone in the conglomerate who originates the weave, another, free of the conglomerate, must weave the magic."

"Ista." Ramie almost spat the word.

"I don't think so," Lazo said. The triplet stood a short distance from the fire, hands clasped behind his back. He had traded his black advisor's robe for a rust-colored tunic and cream trousers. The clothes still looked out of place on the man, but the look in Lazo's eyes left no doubt that his attire was the only feature he had sacrificed to the Mar.

"Ista wants to tap into the power of the Red Eye. She wouldn't deplete her strength to form the conglomerate. She would use one of the Collective as the weaver. Besides, Ista is a sorceress, let us not forget. Though powerful, she would be unable to control the conglomerate at whim. She must plan for things well in advance. This was something she didn't foresee. As I said, she ignored us until she saw we could use magic. She couldn't have woven her emotions so quickly. A man, a strong one, is assisting her."

Aaron's brow furrowed. "But magic like this must take years of training. Could one of the Collective actually weave this? So soon?"

Lazo's contrasting eyes flickered to Aaron. "No, but someone from her camp could, someone who has had years of training."

"And if we could kill this weaver, would the conglomerate weave be broken?" The hope had returned to Ramie's voice.

"Yes."

Ramie grinned. "The tunnels."

Lazo nodded again.

"I'll summon some men." Just as Ramie turned to shout orders, Lazo put a hand on his arm.

"My lord, we must send the women."

Ramie's eyes darted to Manda, who had remained silent throughout the exchange. Manda's green eyes ignored the king and flickered to Marva and Renee. If Marva wasn't mistaken, she saw a slight smile on Manda's lips. She felt her own begin as well.

Heat rose to Ramie's face. "I'll hear of no such thing!"

"The Collective on the wall, my king, and the Collective surrounding the keep are all male. Ista doesn't use women, and she pays little attention to them. Only a woman will be able to pass through the castle without notice. The women are the only chance we have."

- - -

Manda touched the snood encircling her head. Lazo had seen some women wearing the coverings to hide their baldness before he left the castle. It was the perfect disguise.

In front of her, the queen took a passage to her right. Manda brushed her hand against the cold stone of the tunnels. They had finally reached the walls of the castle. Every so often hollow laughter or soft voices wafted to them. But the sounds were sparse. Ista seemed to be using every able body in the keep to work her magic.

They had agreed to use the entrance in Ren's closet because Manda had used it once before. It was also near the servant's staircase, allowing them quick access to the other floors.

For the thousandth time, Manda recalled Presario's words. The weaver would be a man, in a state of confusion, almost unconscious from the strain, but conscious enough to speak. His eyes may be clouded, and his hands may be hot. Look for one who appears near death, Presario had said, and kill him.

They would separate and search the castle: Manda the lower reaches, Renee the middle, and Marva the upper. After each had swept her floor, they were to regroup, and if nothing had been found try again.

Renee stopped. Manda bumped into her and mumbled a quick apology. She could hear Marva's quick breaths right behind her. Manda worried Marva would give them away. Marva had the temper of a wet cat in heat, and if something went awry, Manda was sure Marva would kill first and ask questions later.

Ramie had warned Marva to keep calm, but Manda knew Marva listened to the king of Yor about as much as she did. Ramie was the epitome of a king: pompous, arrogant, and demanding. Manda deemed him completely unsalvageable.

Renee pointed to the wall beside her and lifted her eyebrows. Manda looked down the passage to get her bearings. Looking back into the queen's eyes, Manda nodded.

Renee put her hand in a small indention that formed a handle and placed her cheek against the wood. After a brief pause, Renee shook her head.

"Nothing," she whispered. "I hear nothing."

A sudden snore ripped through the air. They each exchanged glances. A soft 'click' echoed in the corridor as Renee snapped the passage door open and stepped into the narrow closet.

Another snore echoed around them. Beside her, Marva mumbled something about Quinton. Manda motioned for her to keep silent.

Renee moved to the cracked closet door. Manda held her breath as Renee pushed the door open and ducked inside.

The room was a mess. Dirty dishes were scattered on the floor, curtains were stained and ripped from greedy hands, and the large red couch standing in the far corner was covered with dirt and grime.

The rotund man reclining on the couch was naked and uncovered. His mop of dark hair marked him as a mere servant and not one of the

Collective. When they saw the empty whiskey bottle at his feet none of them gave the man a second glance. He would be unconscious for a long time. They passed him quickly, stepping over that night's dinner, and paused at the door. After listening for voices, they stepped into the hall.

Renee's eyes flashed between them. It was a queen's order to hurry. Manda and Marva nodded, well aware time was of the essence. Renee pointed them down the hall to the servant's staircase before trotting in the opposite direction. Manda and Marva hurried down the hall, eager to reach the stairs that would lead them to the upper and lower reaches of the keep. Before they made it to the stairs, two guards rounded the corner.

They were in a hurry, sure to be on a mission for Ista. When the men saw them they paused and glanced at each other. A silent exchange passed between them. Manda could sense Marva tense beside her. She mumbled for Marva to remain calm.

The men stopped, waiting for them to approach. The dark one put his hands on his hips and narrowed his eyes in suspicion. "Haven't you heard Ista's orders," he said. "All Collective women are to meet her by the New Alcazar. Why are you still here?"

"We're going to meet her now," Marva said. "But it's hard when two oafs are blocking your passage."

Manda silently praised Marva's quick mind. She would have only managed a choppy apology.

The dark one grinned. His teeth were crooked, a few of them rotten. "Well, if that's true you're walking in the wrong direction." His grin faltered. "Don't I know you?"

Marva stiffened, but her voice didn't betray her unease. "I don't think you've had the pleasure of my acquaintance."

The guard perused Marva's build. When his eyes flickered back to her face, they were glittering dangerously. "Yes I do," he said, reaching out and grabbing Marva's arm. "You're the woman from the cell block, the one who escaped with the crown prince."

Before Manda could reach for her concealed sword the other guard had pinned her against the wall. The guard with the rotten teeth laughed. Manda panicked. It couldn't be over so soon. She tried to reach for her power, but her panic had drowned her rage. She was at their mercy.

The guard rubbed places that brought back memories of Bort. A low moan escaped her lips as the terror of the hands came back in a maddening rush. The man forced her to her knees as his snickers escalated. When he leaned into her, she tried to fight, but with the way he had her pinned she only succeeded in hurting herself.

Just as she thought the terror of her memories might overwhelm her, the guard heaved a grunt and collapsed on the ground. The snickers were suddenly silenced.

When Manda turned, Marva stood above her, long dagger in hand, blue eyes glowing with molten fury. Both guards lay on the floor, blood pooling by their sides. Manda stood and nodded her thanks. But now they had to hurry. The men's bodies would be discovered soon enough. The woman exchanged glances before they turned and went their separate ways.

When Manda reached the halls of the lower reaches she had to blink in shock. The once glistening Razon castle had been plundered. Dirt and grime coated the black floor. Golden statures and ornaments were few and far between, and when they did appear they were tarnished and broken. Clothes and packs lined the halls. A few children wandered aimlessly around their possessions, but no one else could be seen.

Manda quickly made her way down the hall. The children eyed her with wide-eyed stares. Their bald heads froze her blood. She almost felt Ista peering through the children's eyes, watching her progress down the desecrated hall.

Shaking that thought off she concentrated on the task at hand. But everywhere she walked she saw no sign of life. All the men were in the conglomerate. All the women were meeting with Ista. The castle was deserted.

After skirting the main portion of the floor, Manda turned down a side corridor. A large iron door appeared a few cubits down the hall. Manda froze. They had forgotten about the dungeon when they had assigned floors. Manda paused. Surely Ista wouldn't use anyone in the dungeon as the weaver. Then again, if Ista wanted to hide someone what better way to keep him out of harm's way than by placing him in the dungeon? Manda pried open the heavy door and made her way down the stairs.

Torches lined the stairwell every ten paces. Because of their distance there were times Manda couldn't see the stairs beneath her. Keeping her hands on the damp wall, she descended slowly, listening for any sound. She heard nothing, and the deeper she went the more foolish her idea seemed to become.

When the stairs ended the empty cells to her right whispered of her folly, and the stench warned her that if she did find someone it would only be a dead man. She jumped back as a large rat scampered past, unafraid of her approach. A few soft scrapings told her more awaited her in the distance.

Sure the only things living in the dungeon were creatures of the four-legged kind, Manda quickly walked by empty cell after empty cell, but as she approached the last cellblock a shimmer of gold caught her eye. She stepped back into the shadows, but there was no need. The man who lay near the bars of the last cell was as still as death. His golden hair shimmered in the torchlight as if a halo were stationed above him. It appeared as if he had been sent from the Elysium only to land in the gates of the Abyss.

A few rats sat by his feet, feasting on the tender flesh at his ankles. Manda clenched her jaw. The man before her was an enemy of Ista. That made him her friend.

"Shoo!" she said, clapping her hands. The two rats glanced up but quickly went back to their task. She stepped forward. "Shoo!" This time the rats scampered a few paces from the man. Manda's determination deepened and she strode forward. The rates scurried away, but she could see their eyes shinning in the dim torchlight patiently waiting her departure.

The man hadn't stirred. Manda crouched before him and reached through the bars to feel for a pulse.

It was racing. And his skin was hot to the touch.

Manda drew a deep breath as Presario's words came back to her. The weaver would appear near death, in a state of confusion. His eyes may be clouded and his skin may be hot as his mind burned under the strain of the conglomerate weaving.

Manda recoiled. The heat the man radiated repulsed her. She shifted so the torchlight could play on the man's features. She had to see his eyes. She had to be sure. When the light hit his face, Manda froze.

His eyes were a deep, midnight blue. And although they were unfocused, clouded, clearly the eyes of the weaver, the emotions they held took every breath from her lungs. They were filled with repulsion and horror. This man hated what he now did. And he hated himself.

But Manda did not. Manda knew him and loved him.

Manda released a soft cry, remembering the weaver's eyes at another time, boring into her, imploring her to fight, entreating her for forgiveness for only being able to do so much.

It was Korin. The man had been her salvation when her father had betrayed her. He had given her the dagger that ultimately set her free. With the dagger, Manda had broken free just in time to save her brother. With the dagger, she had taken Yov's life.

Somehow Korin had denied Ista, but he had been discovered, locked in the dungeon, and forced to weave the magic Ista now used to keep the armies at bay.

Manda couldn't kill him. There had to be another way. Manda's resolve deepened as she reached in and grabbed his hand. This time she didn't recoil.

"Please, I want to help you," she said. "Speak to me."

Korin's eyes wavered. They were filled with a pain Manda knew well: the pain of rape, to be stripped of pride and forced to do something against your will. He had been raped his entire life, and his eyes held the horror . . . and the guilt.

"No." Manda placed a hand on his feverish cheek. "You're not to blame."

Korin forced a small smile. "You're safe, my lady. I hoped it would be so."

His voice was soft, but filled with so much caring it echoed in her heart like a chiming bell. He closed his eyes and tightened his grip on her hand. His pulse raced faster. He couldn't hold his concentration much longer.

"Tell me how to break the conglomerate."

"My lady, to break the conglomerate you must kill me."

Manda shook her head. "No. Tell me who the link is. Quickly."

"No time," he said softly. "You have to kill me. It's the only way."

Manda lowered her voice, taking a chance. "Then Ista has won, because I refuse to kill you."

Korin closed his eyes. A small bead of sweat trickled down his cheek. "Please, my lady."

"It's my turn to help you, as you helped me. Tell me who the link is. Quickly."

A small hope flickered in Korin's eyes, but it quickly blinked out as the magnitude of her request settled over him. "The link stands near the gate, the fourth from the entrance. He's taller than the others, with dark eyes and a red beard." Korin paused and forced another small grin. "Ista controlled the magic through me, but she couldn't control whom I chose as the link. I chose someone close to the gate so your armies would have a chance." He closed his eyes again, muscles straining.

"And his weakness?"

Manda thought Korin would be unable to answer. His face contorted as the magic once again took control. "The little finger on his left hand is slightly twisted. The air pocket is a pinprick up and to the right of the flaw."

CHAPTER 28

They sat around the camp, each asking Zorc questions. The wizard didn't seem to mind. Now that Ren had mastered the Quy's emotions, the lines in Zorc's brow had smoothed from their constant concentration, and he chuckled more often even though Ren could still sense worry underneath his exterior façade.

When no one was watching, Zorc turned toward Zier, as did they all. Though the conversation was light, there was an undercurrent of tension, and all eyes held a hint of fear.

Ren expected Zorc to insist on leaving for Zier immediately, but instead Zorc had settled down for the night. Rest, Ren suspected, was what the wizard thought they all needed. They would leave the following morning, though none spoke of it, not even Zorc.

"Silver dust is a conduit, correct?" Neki asked. "But what about the other sands?"

Zorc plopped another piece of roasted deer into his mouth before he replied. "Everyone besides a mage should use silver dust when using their emotions to create magic. Although some magic can be evoked by habit and training, and some magic is simple enough for a lowly apprentice to weave on his own, silver dust not only conducts the wizard's emotions, it intensifies them, thus allowing you to save your strength."

"Why not a mage?" Ren asked.

"A mage?" Zorc said, pausing to tap his chin and focus his keening gaze on Ren. "Well, let's just say you never should."

Ren frowned.

"Too powerful," Neki said. "Imagine if you had used the dust when you imploded the castle wall. You would have hemorrhaged the entire castle."

The group chuckled, but Ren did not. His eyes were fixed on Zorc. The wizard was peering at Neki in a strange fashion. Ren realized Zorc was using wizard's eyes. "Neki, don't use any more of the dust. It's too early to tell, but you may be another mage."

Neki's face flushed as the entire camp quieted, but before the silence could linger Zorc continued.

"The white sand is called enchanter's sand. It's much stronger than silver dust, just as the black sand, scoria, is much stronger than enchanter's sand. Enchanter's sand is made from wizard's bones and is used when emotions are needed to heal and protect. If mingled with silver dust it strengthens the emotion's magic.

"Scoria is gathered from wizards who have given their life with the Quy." Zorc paused to touch a place in his robe with tender affection. "Scoria won't only conduct and intensify magic, it will also amplify it one thousand times over. Use scoria only when you want to conserve all your strength, or only in dire need. One grain of it is deadly. In the right hands it could obliterate kingdoms.

"All of the dusts have their uses, and if used wisely can save lives. For instance, fire is the one physical element wizards have hitherto been unable to utilize." Everyone glanced at Ren before turning back to Zorc.

"With the dusts any wizard can amplify fire, though not from his own emotions. Silver dust can cause a fire to burn hotter, but because it intensifies the heat it makes the logs burn more quickly. The other two dusts can act as a counterbalance to the silver dust. Enchanter's sand can make the logs stronger, and scoria can explode the flame without utilizing the log, hence making the fire burn for a longer time."

Zorc leaned back and looked at each one in turn. "In the future, those with magic may be able to conjure fire. Though magic is being reborn, it's also starting over. No wizard in history has been able to invoke fire, with or without the dust, but the Quy is stronger than ever and the rules have changed. All of you are far more advanced than you should be. In my day it took years to move past an apprenticeship. Even Barracus required years of training, and he was a mage."

Ren leaned forward. "But you said magi couldn't be trained."

"They can't, pardon the expression. Barracus required years of study, of growing, of learning, until he could find, through guidance," Zorc said, raising a finger, "what he was capable of doing."

"There's something I don't understand," Markum said. "How did I end up with the prophecy book?"

Zorc smiled. The fire reflecting in his eyes caused them to blaze with a reddish hue. "You're a direct descendant of Galor, Markum."

Markum lifted his eyebrows in surprise. "The seer who was with you in the Alcazar?"

Zorc nodded. "Yes. Galor didn't have the Quy, just the sight, and was my only companion when I fled the Alcazar. He stayed with me until he was told by the Maker in a dream to leave and begin a new life. I formed the prophecy book to hide its words until the time was right. I gave it to Galor, knowing the Maker would lead him to the right location so that the Chosen would find it. I never heard from Galor again."

"I'm sorry you had to live alone for so long," Ren said.

All former sadness dissipated with Zorc's grin. "I'm the lucky one, Ren. I'm alive, and I have the great honor of knowing you, the one we put our hopes on. To be able to smell the air, see the stars, and feel the grass beneath my feet is an extra bonus. I vow to extract all I can out of the rest of my life. I'm lucky I have any time at all."

Ren tensed, once again noticing the streaks of gray in Zorc's hair. They had become more profound over the past few days. "What do you mean? I thought you would just now begin to age. You were only forty-one when you received the time weave. You should live a good while yet."

Zorc's eyes softened. "Before me, magic had only been used on a few occasions to extend a human life, and only for a span of a few years. Time stopped for me for almost four centuries. No one knew how the magic would affect me. I won't die tomorrow, but I'm aging faster than I would like."

"How long?"

"A year, possibly a little longer. I've probably aged one year in the past week. If I live to a ripe old age of ninety that would give me forty-eight more weeks."

Ren didn't know what to say. In the short time he had known Zorc a strong bond had formed between them. Ren knew that bond would strengthen with each day and each lesson taught. He thought Zorc would be there to guide him for years to come.

Zorc patted Ren's arm. "I've become fond of you too."

Just as Ren was about to speak, Markum gasped.

He was having another vision. By the look in his eyes it was the worst yet.

"It's coming." Markum's voice was soft, but the way he spoke chilled Ren to the bone.

Ren knelt beside him. "What's coming?"

Then Ren felt it. It came from all directions. He scanned the woods.

Galvin drew his sword as Markum moaned.

"Burning cinders, do you feel that?" Neki said, eyes darting everywhere at once.

Nigel rubbed his arms. "Crawling. My skin is crawling."

Blood pounded in Ren's temples. The sword quivered in its scabbard. Ren remembered what had happened the last time he had held the sword, after Nigel had completed the stones. He didn't know if he could control the sword if he drew it again.

Leaves began to rustle. Twigs snapped.

Ren didn't hesitate a second time. He drew his sword and reached for the calm, hoping he would be able to overcome the intensity of the stones. The hate hit him first, righteous rage; then love washed over the hate, purifying it; then came a keening pain.

As quickly as the emotions came they mingled into one. Ren became the calm, rising above the emotions, looking down upon their intensity. He felt the sword screaming for him to draw upon the power of the stones.

The sword became an extension of him, a weapon of emotions, a herald of light. The triangle of stones glowed with a silver brilliance.

"It's coming," Markum whispered.

The pages of the prophecy book flipped wildly, but there was no wind. Markum moaned again. Ren clutched the sword's hilt, letting the power of the blade oscillate through him. The internal elements pulsated with strength. He reached higher and soared above the pinnacle. Inside him, the feet of the triangle came together and merged until only a straight line remained.

The power was no longer a pyramid but a needle-sharp shaft. The sword he held was an extension of that shaft. It was the true synergy, the true union. It was the syzygy of three to one. He was the sword. He was the elements. He was the Quy's deadly weapon.

Trees began to break as if they were mere twigs. The night air became stagnant, like a blanket of frost. Corruption seemed to surround them.

Ren gripped the sword tighter. The sky flickered with light, and clouds started gathering, swirling as if a giant force stirred the heavens.

"Ren, look," Morris said.

"I see it," Ren said through clenched teeth. Shadows stirred in the forest. They were moving closer.

"It's coming," Markum whispered again.

"No, Ren, over there."

Ren broke his gaze from the forest and turned to where Morris pointed. A blood-red beam of light exploded over Zier, reaching toward the heavens like a blade of death. Clouds rolled and twirled by the light until they too were washed in blood, spinning, churning, whirling out from the light, infecting the clouds beside them until the sky exploded in crimson, rolling toward them and past them, outward over all of the Lands. As soon as the red clouds roared by them the air changed. It became thick, hard to breathe, almost as if you were breathing cinders. The evening dusk was gone. All that was left was a sickening red glow.

The world had drowned in blood.

The Red Eye's power had been released.

The forest moved again.

"It's coming."

- - -

Chris watched the sky turn to blood. He barely heard the commotion behind him as horses reared and men screamed in terror. He paid no heed to the change in the air or his deepening breaths. He didn't listen to the king of Yor shouting for men to enter the tunnels and search for the women. His mind was focused on one thing and one thing only – hate.

It sifted through the air like smoke. It wasn't powerful enough to be detected by the normal man, but he wasn't a normal man. He was a man touched by profound emotion. He was a shell, but he was also a man who could sense the undercurrent of exceptional emotion. The hate the red glow emitted was an emotion that was now a shadow, but would soon become a disease. It was an emotion that could destroy everything it touched. It could destroy their world.

Aaron silently stood beside him, but Chris felt the Avenger's fear. It wasn't a fear of death, but a fear of the unknown.

The conglomerate circle remained unbroken, and Ista had tapped into the Red Eye's power. If the women didn't find the weaver soon all was lost.

Chris wasn't worried about Manda. Each time he looked at Aaron he knew his sister was safe. Although Aaron couldn't discern Manda's location he would know if she came to harm. Their connection was still strong.

Chris turned his attention back to the sky. "Hurry, sis," he whispered. "There's no more time."

- - -

Galvin shouted, but it was too late. Before Ren knew it, something knocked him down. A biting cold tore through his shoulder as if part of him had died with the touch. He rolled to his feet as Galvin screamed another warning. A black fog sailed toward him, whistling with speed. Ren brought up his sword, called on its power and watched the silver triangle pulse with life.

The black fog soared right through the blade. Ren felt a frost shiver down the metal. The kota wailed and bowed, sending her stunning ray into the fog. The ray did nothing to it. The fog turned for another attack.

Neki nocked and arrow and let it fly. The arrow was true. It hit the black fog directly at its center.

The fog evaporated before their eyes.

"Ista calls to the dead."

Ren spun, not daring to believe what Zorc meant.

"What are they?" Neki said.

"The shadows of the Mynher," Zorc said, backing up to the fire. "If a shadow passes through you it will strip your soul, force the life from you. The Mynher hungers to live, to feel life. The only way he can feel life is to pass through you. If he does he will absorb all life from you. No one knows how the Desolation Plains were created. The Mynher shouldn't be able to stay in the void between this world and the Abyss, but he does. To do so he has to claim live souls and slowly drain their life force from them.

"The Red Eye is somehow breaching the Plains, allowing his shadows into our world. The more souls he claims the more powerful he'll be."

Ren sucked in a breath. He felt his shoulder. It felt as if all the heat had been drained from it. The moaning grew loader. Galvin and Morris dropped to their knees, shielding their ears from the pleas of the voices. Those with magic held their ground, but both Nigel and Neki had a haunted look in their eyes.

"How do we stop them?"

"You can't."

Shrill wails of anguish rose from the surrounding woods, prickling Ren's skin. Although it sounded like one wail, it wasn't one voice. It was thousands of voices together. They moaned for assistance, for hope, for life. They cried for him, for all of them, promising them things, promising him Aidan. They had her, they cried. If only he would let them have him. But Ren was in the calm, and in the calm there was truth. In the voices there was deceit.

Cadaverous specters come out of the woods, all with hideous wounds marring their visages. Hands of murky white flailed in front of them as they reached for life. Their lips were opened in a unified scream.

Neki paled. "What about them?"

"The undead," Zorc whispered. "The Mynher's army. They can only appear where they died before the Mynher denied them eternal damnation."

"Do I want to know what they can do?" Nigel asked.

"With a touch they strip your flesh to feel your life."

"May the Maker be with us," Neki mumbled.

Galvin inched toward the horses. "In the first war there was a battle on this hill."

Nigel's eyes darted everywhere at once. "We're in the middle of a graveyard."

A deep laugh echoed around them.

Ren turned and looked over the distant treetops. The trees bent as if under a massive weight. Protruding from the trees were two jaundice eyes. They were looking directly at him.

It was the full shadow of the Mynher.

Although its body was cast in shadow, what Ren saw was enough to cause nightmares for the remainder of his days. The face was that of a man, but the skin was chalky white, with pulsating festers. Three horns crowned the Mynher's otherwise bald head, two on each side and one in the middle, all curving back and in. The Mynher's form was made from bodies, writhing just beneath the surface, trying to tear themselves free from the thin membrane of the Mynher's flesh, mouths open in silent terror.

"You can't fight them," Zorc said, shouting over the plaintive cries. "You can only slow them. If your aim is true the black shadows will evaporate and return to the Mynher to gather again. The undead also reform, but they will do so more quickly. We have to run. We have to run now."

"Ren, look out!" Nigel screamed. A black fog formed in front of him. The kota wailed. Ren rolled from it. He felt its frigid, tenuous mass suck in the heat of the air around him. Neki lunged for it and the shadow shot in the other direction. Ren stared at the saber in Neki's hand. The red lines of the sardonyx were glowing in the darkness.

"Neki, Grauss said your sword could ward off the dead. Get between us and watch for more shadows. Everyone move!"

Neki positioned himself at the center the camp and twirled his saber above them. "Hurry, they're moving closer."

Ren risked a glance back as he strapped the dazed seer to the nearest horse. Neki was right. The undead were slow, but they were coming. Some were only cubits from them. But the specters didn't frighten Ren, the Mynher did. The master of the Desolation Plain was moving closer. Ren could almost make out faces under its translucent skin.

Heartbeats later they were on their horses and galloping over the steep embankment that led to Zier.

Neki took the lead, waving his sword above him, warding off the dead. Specters came from all directions, wailing in sorrow. Black shapes flew overhead, but all strayed from Neki's sword as if the sardonyx's path left them blind.

A black fog rose from the forest, far larger than any Ren had seen, and bolted through the reddish air. Ren realized the Mynher strove to stop him from neutralizing the Red Eye. The keeper of the undead would do anything to trap him.

The shadow swooped closer, whistling with speed.

Ren did the only thing he could: he dove off his mount. Oblivious, the others rode on. The undead moved closer.

His horse screamed as the black shadow pounded into her flesh. Ren watched in horror as the mare shriveled before his eyes, then collapsed in a heap of bones.

He felt a chill behind him and spun. Bloodless, pallid eyes looked at him. The specter reached out to touch him. Ren plunged his blade into the apparition and watched it dissolve. Its screams rose above the plaintive howls of the others, but as quickly as he could draw a breath the same specter reformed. Ren took a step back, but more of the undead came, and even more were forming.

The others were already halfway down the embankment. Galvin turned and called his name, but Ren knew his friends would be unable to reach him. He spun, impaling a few more specters, but they only reformed heartbeats later.

One specter came from the left, another from the right. Before him were two more. When he backed up he saw others. If he ran between them one could easily touch him.

The hooves of Galvin's mount pounded up the hillside. Ren swung his weapon, impaling the one to his left, but it only reformed closer. He was surrounded.

A keening wail caused him to turn. Keena rose against the blood-red sky, hooves pawing the air, and impaled two of the specters. Without thought, Ren jumped on her back. She reared, scattering more specters with her ivory hooves and sprang forward. As Ren released the calm, emotions pounded inside him. He clutched the kota's neck and whispered his thanks. When he looked back at the distant camp the entire hillside was flooded with specters.

They would have never been able to fight so many.

The Mynher watched him, jaundiced eyes filled with rage. The black fog remained behind. It needed to stay close to its master.

He spurred Keena faster. Specters came from everywhere, but they were sparse, not concentrated. It was easy to evade them.

Ren looked up at the sky. He could almost feel the hate churning to be released. How much time did they have?

As if reading his thoughts, Zorc rode to flank him. "Ista wants us to come."

Ren turned toward him, the silent question in his eyes.

Zorc's eyes blazed. "She knows I'll come to stop her with the Silver Eye. She knows you'll be with me. Let's pray she's able to control the hate until we get there. We have no defense if the full power of the Red Eye is released."

Ren turned to the rolling hills of his home, now bathed in a revolting red luster. It seemed like his old life was only a brief dream. In a way, he supposed it was. He would never go back to that life or be that man.

His spiral had started.

The blood-red sky mocked him. Clouds churned violently as dawn finally broke.

Over the next rise was the city of Zier.

CHAPTER 29

The closer they moved toward Zier the more worried Ren became. They had passed hundreds, if not thousands of specters since leaving the hideaway. The Desolation Plain's dead came from all directions, as far as the eye could see, slowly creeping closer to Zier. None of them paid Ren and his companions any heed. They just ambled on as if pulled by invisible threads.

Ista was calling them, but why?

Zorc's somber gaze only emphasized Ren's worry. Zorc didn't know either, and the ramifications were too fearful to imagine.

Ista's reasoning became clear when they reached the outer wall. Bodies littered the countryside. Although most were from the Collective, others were soldiers from Yor, Crape, Ketes, and Fest. Ramie had mounted an offensive. The outer gate hung open. There had been a fight here, and Ista had lost. Ramie had marched to the inner wall.

Specters slowly inched toward the open gate, arms outstretched in answer to Ista's silent demand. Many had already migrated through. Ren could see them in the distance, slowly making their way down the main street of town.

"She's trapping them," Nigel said. "The armies won't be able to retreat. We have to warn them."

Nigel spurred Rage forward before Ren had a chance to reply. Ren rode to flank him. "Follow me. I know a back way."

Nigel fell in behind Ren as the others followed. They dodged thickening specters as they entered the open gate. Ren took a sharp left, veering through back streets that wove their way down the poorer sections of Ziera.

The streets were deserted. The clipping of their horses' hooves ricocheted off buildings, making their small group sound like a passing brigade. Doors stood open and smoke from deserted fires billowed in the cool air. A few discarded black garments littered the ground. Stray dogs roamed in and out of houses to claim whatever morsels had been left in the open.

The dark structure of the New Alcazar loomed in the distance, dwarfing the Stardom castle. Its black surface devoured the early dawn light. From the base of the Alcazar the red light emanated its fury. Death and destruction seemed to lurk around every corner. The red sky did nothing to soothe Ren's nerves.

Ren glanced down a side alley. Although he didn't see any specters, he knew they weren't far behind.

He urged Keena faster and soon they had broken into the fields. Yor's colors of navy and white, Fest's colors of maroon and silver, Crape's colors of gray and green, and Ketes's colors of rust and gold were commingled as one.

But the armies weren't what brought tears to Ren's eyes. Hundreds upon hundreds of commoners from Zier had black sashes tied to their arms. They surrounded the army, many holding up flags of the Razon dragon. Little did they know within a few short breaths they would be fighting the unthinkable. The specters were heartbeats away.

Ren felt something in his palm and turned to see Zorc wrapping his hand around the shrunken Silver Eye. "The specters will be banished once you neutralize the Red Eye."

Ren took the small crystal, overwhelmed. Although he knew how to reach the calm, was that enough? Would he be able to awaken the power within the hazy glass?

When Ren turned to dismount, Zorc stopped him. "Not here. If you open the Silver Eye now its complete effect will be lost. It has to be beside the Red Eye to exert its full influence."

Ren turned his gaze to the army. A lone sentry released a shout and pointed down the main street. The masses at the edge of the army turned as one. Ren watched helplessly as many ran toward the new threat without knowing the futility of their bravado. Others fell back, causing mass panic. He would never be able to pass through the horde.

"The Dragon's Bane," Ren said. "There's a passage there."

- - -

Chris barely took notice as Presario swung his sword at the haze of orange light where Manda indicated the flaw resided. He didn't step back as the Collective circle shuddered under the blow. He didn't realize until too late how their attack would force Ista's hand.

As the circle fell in one horrendous shriek, Chris' eyes were on the red light. They should have thought it through. Ista only had one counter defense.

Chris watched as the red light slowly turned dark. Presario yelled for everyone to move toward the gate, but now the light was almost black at its core.

And then he felt it, sluicing its way under his skin, claiming his soul – hate.

- - -

Ren clutched his head as the dark tendrils of evil seeped inside him. He gritted his teeth as a dark anger boiled to the surface. Then the hate came. It was a hate so intense he could scarcely breathe.

He fell to his knees, clawing at his chest, trying to banish the hate. It only intensified. He felt himself start panting with the need to kill.

No!

Opening his internal door, Ren slammed all of himself behind it, like Nigel had taught him. He held the door firm with his calling power. He stood back inside his mind, searching for the evil he had felt only a breath ago. It was gone.

The hate was gone.

His mind cleared.

Ren opened his eyes and looked at the men around him holding their heads, faces twisting into heinous paradigms of who they truly were.

Because the Black Knight was used to the brush of hate, he fought better than the others, but even Nigel screamed in effort as the hate began to take control. Ren grabbed Nigel and forced the Black Knight to look at him. "Go behind your door, Nigel!"

Nigel squeezed his eyes shut. When he opened them again, he nodded. "I'm there."

Ren watched in complete horror as his friends began to fight, the hate of the Red Eye overcoming their reason. In the distance he heard screams of bloodlust. The army was falling by the hundreds, not battling the specters, but their own kind. Voices mad with hate echoed through the murky light. Ren felt as though he looked in on a nightmare, observing, as Markum did, another's dream.

Nigel clasped his arm. "There's nothing you can do, Ren. Many will die this day, but many more will die if you don't leave them. You have to do what you came to do, even though they're your friends."

Ren knew Nigel was right, but that certainty made it no easier. He remembered the first truth. If a doubt enters your soul you will give it fire, and if the fire glows hotter it will cause you to fail. He couldn't let any doubts cloud his judgment or impair the true mission. With the Maker's help, he had to stop this destruction.

"We must hurry," the Black Knight said, "the more we wait the more our friends will tear each other apart."

Ren didn't hesitate a second time.

He drew his sword and urged Keena into a gallop, back the way they had come, toward the Dragon's Bane. The three elements inside him quivered in response to the stones. Then a thought struck him. He couldn't use magic behind the door. He couldn't open the Silver Eye without magic.

Panic gripped him, but then he sensed Nigel's presence beside him. Ren turned to the third defender with sudden understanding. Although he couldn't use magic behind his door he could use the calling power. And with it he could draw upon the defender's power.

Ren reached out for the defenders with the Druid ability. He tugged their miens to him, calling them to him.

The sword's triangle roared to life.

Ren turned to Nigel. His friend smiled and nodded, indicating he felt Ren's drain. Ren took more, testing the limits. He brought all three powers together, each with its own distinct colors and emotions. He merged them to one and rushed upward to claim the calm. Before he could reach it, he stopped with a sudden impact, unable to rise higher, unable to find the pinnacle and make the feet of the triangle collapse into the sharp sword of the Quy. That was his power, the synergy's power. Only the union could make the straight-line syzygy; the defenders could only strengthen it.

He felt Chris, Aaron, and Nigel's strength individually and collectively. He could pull from each of their emotions at whim, and although each contributed to the legs of the whole, each had his own hate, his own love, and his own pain. Some were more or less excessive, but together they made a virtually unbreakable force.

Around the next corner was the Dragon's Bane.

- - -

Ren chose a small entryway under the castle's main stairwell to emerge. He didn't have to hide his sudden appearance. The halls were deserted. Ista had used everyone, down to the last man.

The castle was filthy. Bedrolls and garbage littered the grimy black floor, curtains hung in shreds, and the carpets' golden threads had turned a somber gray.

Ren led Nigel through the desecrated hallway onto the main landing. The Alcazar towered over Stardom. The symbol for magic was spaced intermittently on its surface, and as they approached Ren saw heat waves seeping from the runes to shroud the temple in a slight fog.

Ista stood in the fog beside the Red Eye. Collective women's lifeless bodies were heaped in one corner. Ista had somehow drained their power in order to control the Red Eye.

The strain of keeping hold of the Red Eye without the calm had weakened her, but it by no means drained her. She had released the wrath of the Red Eye by choice, not by necessity. But she couldn't reclaim it. Although you could contain a power stronger than yourself, you couldn't overcome it. Now that the Red Eye's power was released only the Silver Eye could subdue it.

The silver dragon stood behind Ista, glistening amidst the dark walls of the Alcazar. It was chained, just as the painting in the Oracle portrayed, and there were lacerations marring its beauty. Its violet eyes sent a splinter into Ren's heart. Aidan had merged with the dragon. That realization startled him and saddened him at the same time. Aidan would never know his feelings. He would never know if she reciprocated those feelings.

When Ista saw Ren the avarice in her gaze deepened, but so did the hunger. She wanted him for his power, and she would do anything to claim him. He stepped in front of Nigel, suddenly fearful Ista would use his friend to force his hand, but Ista only smiled and motioned him forward, inviting him to do what he came to do.

A shiver of warning overcame him, but he quickly shook it aside. No matter Ista's reasons for letting him neutralize the threat, it still had to be done.

Ren dropped the Silver Eye on the ground. Three roaring dragons, blue eyes glimmering in the darkness, exploded to life and cradled the Silver Eye in their wings. The Red Eye's stand mirrored the Silver's, but its dragons' eyes were blood, and the dragons held the Eye in the hollows of their backs.

Just as he was about to call upon the defenders' power to awaken the Silver Eye, he realized the full implications of the Red Eye's hate. Without the synergy's power the calm was unreachable. He couldn't awaken the Silver Eye.

Then he knew what he had to do. He understood the prophecy. He understood the legend. He understood the Oracle.

His eyes flickered to the dragon.

Although the Silver Eye was cast out of the essence of the silver dragon, the silver dragon couldn't awaken the Silver Eye because dragons were incapable of love.

Until now.

When he had denounced Aidan he had started her merging. The roar of the dragon wasn't one of rage, but one of pain – love's pain. This dragon knew how to love. Aidan had taught it.

Although a vast sorrow engulfed him, acceptance did as well. Aidan would save the lands with her love. She would have chosen this course if she had known the outcome. He could only pray she had found some form of contentment. She deserved that, and more.

Ren stepped back from the Silver Eye and turned to the dragon.

The screams of the dying drifted on the wind like tolling bells. Some, Ren knew, belonged to friends. Ren felt a dragon's breath of uncertainty, a doubt that his intuition was wrong. Then the dragon drew a deep breath and sent a blast of fire over the Silver Eye.

A white ray exploded from the top of the Silver Eye, mirroring the black now coming from the Dragon's Fire. Ren felt the intensity of its love even from behind his door. Shouts echoed in the distance as people woke from their hatred and realized they had killed those they knew and loved. Wails of the undead thundered on the winds as the effects of the Silver Eye sunk them, once again, into eternal nothingness.

The white and black light from the crystals slowly moved toward each other, each drawn to the opposing power. With each tiny movement love and hate became more in balance.

A sudden flicker caught Ren's attention. At the Red Eye's core were two dark incessant red eyes, and they were looking at him.

Before Ren had a chance to prepare, something crashed into his mind. Ren fell to his knees, feeling the dark clutches of Barracus' spirit claiming his body and demanding entrance to his mind.

Even though his essence was safe behind his door, Ren could feel the evil on the other side. His breath quickened as he realized what he had to do.

The defender's power would be inadequate to banish the mage, but if he reclaimed his own power Barracus could use it against him. He couldn't allow that to happen. First, he had to weaken the mage with the defender's power. Then, and only then, could he reclaim his own.

Without warning his door crashed open. Ren found himself looking into the red eyes of a madman. The mage's essence began searching for his power, reaching for his thread in order to claim the Quy once more.

Ren gathered all his strength and flung the force away, but not far enough. It immediately came back. Ren then did the only thing he knew to do.

Stumbling backwards he reached for the open door behind him, the one etched with three triangles in a circle. It was his only defense. Taking his power, he flung it through the door and quickly slammed it shut. The Druids had taught him a valuable lesson.

A deep growl of rage came from behind. Ren turned to face Barracus. He reached for the defenders, but before he could lock hold of them Barracus surged forward.

As the demon entered him, his memories were crushed beneath Barracus' extensive diablerie. He felt his entire essence being used, down to the very hairs on his head.

Hate bubbled inside him. He felt his blood almost boiling as the hate took over, wrapping around every pore, taking control. He gritted his teeth as he felt the power of hate, the ecstasy of feeling no pain, start to seduce him by its allure.

As the hate tore through him something else did as well, and it was something that rose from the depths of his soul. It was a call he had felt his entire life, a whisper he had always respected yet never completely understood. And there it was, pulsing at his core, entreating him to deny the hate and fight for the light. As he had done so many times before, he obeyed the call.

Tightening the grip on his sword, a residue of emotion tingled through his hand. That emotion clashed with the hate he now carried.

Suddenly the hate repulsed him.

He looked down at his sword. The white stone seemed to call to him. He beckoned to it.

Love swelled inside him, washing through him, drowning the hate in its complete purity.

But the hate seeped inside him again, slowly eating away the love. He didn't want the love to leave. He pulled for more love, but found the end of it. He hesitated. He didn't want to take it all. He was afraid it would vanish forever if he did. Nothing should ever destroy something so beautiful. He needed something stronger than love, something strong enough to quench the darkness.

He looked down at the sword again. A second stone shivered with an emotion far different from hate. He called to it.

He felt a flicker of pain, an intense pain, and released his hold.

After the love, the pain was soul crushing, but the darkness was even more repulsive. He called to pain. It seared him, taking more of the hate away but filling his soul with anguish. It was hope crushed, betrayal, love lost, friendships broken, love denied, torture and death.

When he thought he couldn't take any more he released the pain and looked inside to see the hate still there. It had weakened, but it wasn't gone. If he refused to draw more pain the hate would begin to grow again. Taking a deep breath he summoned more pain. It enveloped him. Leaning his head back he screamed at the intensity of all who had been betrayed by the ones they loved. But the hate was still there, pulsing at his core.

He reached for the door standing in his mind's eye. It was the door with the symbol of something powerful etched on its surface. Whatever lay beyond that door could help him. He put the tip of his sword in the lock and the door clinked open. He stepped inside.

His own memories and emotions hurtled over him, bringing the triangle together. He rose higher, reaching the calm, forming the straight-line syzygy of the Quy. He drew on the pain and love of the union, commingled the two emotions to one, creating the strongest emotion of all – love's pain. It was the emotion that could banish the darkness. But as he stood, becoming the pain of love, he suddenly knew –

It was not enough.

CHAPTER 30

The air began to quiver as the two extremes of the crystals battled for control. Soon their powers wouldn't be in balance and each would fling off things no one wanted to escape.

Aidan looked through Sim's eyes, sending a silent prayer to the Maker to help Ren prevail, but as she watched, Ren's eyes, tinted a slight shade of red, grazed over Sim without any recognition.

"No," she whispered.

"There's nothing we can do, dear heart. We've done our duty. We've awoken the Silver Eye. Now only your Ren can end this. There's hope yet. Have faith."

"Sim?"

"Hmm?"

"I want you to stop him if he's the other."

"Yes, dear heart, but you have the power as well."

Aidan knew she did. She could feel it inside her, but she couldn't do it, not to Ren. "I can't, Sim. I'm not that strong."

"Yes, dear heart. I'll do so if it comes to that."

The wizard rounded the corner and skidded to a halt. When his eyes locked on Ista, his face became stone. Before Aidan could blink, Ista was lifted by invisible threads and hurled into the wall of the castle.

The wizard's eyes were disks of hate, but Ista smiled in victory. Her eyes flickered to Ren. Ren immediately crumbled to the floor, clutching his head as if he wanted to tear it off. Aidan's heart skipped a beat, hoping against hope Ren was fighting back.

Ista gave a wheezy laugh. "Don't you see, Zorc? I'm in control of you, of Ren, and of the Lands. I had the Druids implant the needles in Ren's mind after his closing. I control him whether or not Barracus has successfully claimed his body."

Zorc stepped closer, undeterred.

"And if you kill me I'll just pass through the Eye. I've already locked my calling and targeted my host." Ista chuckled. "You're my host, Zorc. I control you alive or dead."

Zorc raised his eyebrows. "I'm stronger, Ista. You will be unable to claim me."

"You seemed to have forgotten the redhead beauty of the Alcazar."

Zorc paused.

Ista heaved a hearty laugh. "Have you failed to think through the full implications for Christa's spirit?" Ista waited until the horror flashed across Zorc's face. "She'll be lost for eternity if she doesn't join with her other half inside you. The only way she'll be able to join with you is if I join with you. What will it be, Zorc? Do you choose to have my spirit residing inside you and Christa free from eternal loneliness, or my control of you? It matters not which."

Zorc's face softened into an emotionless mask. The Eyes still battled behind him, their light becoming more violent with each breath. Zorc bent to grab a smoldering stick that had received some of the dragon's fire.

"Give her to me."

Ista laughed, eyes alight with the pain of thousands. "Never."

Zorc pulled a red velvet bag from his robe. "Never? Never is a word that should be wiped from the lexicon."

Ista's eyes narrowed in suspicion. "The Eyes are about to break free, Zorc. Free me or kill me. It's your choice."

Zorc stepped forward, torch in hand. For the first time, Ista's eyes flickered with fear.

"I'm not going to do either," Zorc said, moving closer. "But you'll choose death won't you, Ista? Or do you want to feel the flames again, feel your skin melting as the fire churns around you?"

"No."

"Oh, yes." Zorc said, pushing the torch closer. Ista's chest heaved as the panic overtook her. Her claw-like hand clutched Zorc's arm.

Zorc smiled. "The only way to escape the flames is to give yourself to the sorceress's death, and you need every ounce of energy to do so. You'll have to release your bond to the Eye. You'll have to release Christa."

Zorc's smile broadened. He moved the torch closer. Ista shuddered beneath his grip. The Eyes were flickering back and forth. The day was dark and then it was light. Soon the Lands would be flooded with love or hate, or both. Zorc ignited Ista's hair. Zorc stepped back and rocked forward to his toes as he untied the string that kept the red pouch closed.

There was a loud implosion as Ista gave her life to the sorceress's death, the only magic sorceresses could evoke at whim. Zorc whispered words, waving his hands over the small bag as ash rained down over Ista's burning, empty robe. A thin stream of dust careened toward Zorc and wafted into the open velvet bag. When the last of the dust had entered, Zorc tied the bag closed and placed it back inside his robe.

- - -

Ren stumbled to his feet as the pain in his head dissipated only to find the presence inside had grown. He had thought love's pain was the strongest emotion of all, but it couldn't be, not if it wasn't banishing the darkness.

The darkness inside him continued to grow. Ren tried to hold it, calling on the sword, the defenders, and his own emotions in the calm. Soon he had created a shaft of white-hot power inside him, but slowly, piece by piece, Barracus was eating through the light of the internal elements.

Zorc had told him the first truth could help him defeat the darkness, could lead him to the second truth.

Ren searched his heart, trying to find the answer. There had to be more he could draw on. He murmured prayers to the Maker as he thought of the first truth. His faith could damn him or raise him. He clutched his faith to him like a blanket, letting his heart fill to overflowing.

Love was stronger than hate. The pain love brought was stronger than love. But what was stronger than the pain of love?

Ren rose above the hate, the love, and the pain. The shaft of light glowed below him, but still the darkness continued to rise.

And it was complete. He could almost feel the terror of the lower Plains in the growing hate. It was saturated with corruption. He pulled on more love, calling it forth from the blade of light, but the love only caused the hate to pause. It by no means ate the darkness.

He studied the love. He could feel its brilliance, its intensity, but he also sensed a slight marring of its pureness. Ren realized the love of man wasn't the opposite of the hate Barracus carried.

The love of man could stem from lust, from betrayal, from pain itself. Love, like the Silver Eye, could be used for evil.

Slowly, Ren felt the answer surfacing. There was only one way to banish Barracus. He had to rise above all the internal elements to find the only true, pure emotion.

He had to confront Barracus without hate of fear, but compassion. Barracus was the Maker's creation. The Maker loved Barracus just as much as He loved a child of light. Barracus had strayed, he had turned to evil, but Ren couldn't succumb to the same hate that drove Barracus to the darkness. He remembered the Quy's words: *Before you strike make sure you do so out of love. If you begin to use other emotions like hate, lust, envy, or desire you'll fail. Sometimes you'll strike in anger, or shun the one you strike at, but if you remember the love inside, if the love inside is what drives you, all will be well.*

"Only use me in love," she had said. But not just love – the emotion that mingled with pain and hate, but the Maker's love. It was a love that was unbounded, a love that loved despite pain and corruption.

Ren cast one final glance at the darkness before turning his head to the sky. The shaft of light brightened as he reached for a love no evil could touch.

- - -

Zorc watched Ren stumble forward to place one hand over each Eye. The twin lights cut through his hands like a saber. Within heartbeats, the Eye's flickering slowed. A glow came from within Ren and a silver shaft of light appeared, cutting through him and slicing through the lights of the Eyes.

Zorc turned away, shielding his face from the light. When he looked back the twin lights had separated and were slowly moving back to their individual crystals. Ren stood between them, a saber of light shooting through him. He drew breaths so deep Zorc thought he would collapse from the strain, but the lights quickly dissipated and the humming of the crystals soon silenced.

Ren dropped to his knees and held his sword above his head, muscles tensing. The stones in the sword shone with an ardent intensity, forming a triangular glow. The beam of light that had cut Ren before appeared again, this time slicing though the sword as well. The sword slowly turned black. Before Zorc could blink, the darkness shot from the sword and plummeted back into the Red Eye.

CHAPTER 31

Morrus' laughter boomed over the courtyard as Neki and Galvin plunged the Druid into the garden's pond for the second time. Morrus, naked as a newborn babe, emerged grinning like a dragon.

Neki nodded his approval. "Morrus, you're now officially de-coronated."

Ren smiled and turned away, noticing even Nigel had a grin on his face. But Ren's thoughts were elsewhere. His focus shifted to the silver dragon. The dragon hadn't stopped watching him since the Eyes' power had been stilled. It was waiting for something, but Ren was unsure what.

The dragon's focus shifted. It's eyes appeared clouded, as if the dragon itself were a twin, listening to its other half. Ren's brow furrowed. The dragon had the same clouded look just before Aidan had merged with it. It was as if the dragon had a human understanding.

Then something strange happened. The dragon's eyes faded to their true silver sheen. It refocused it gaze. Ren could almost hear the dragon's unspoken plea.

Ren rose to his feet as a desperate hope rose within him. Was Aidan whole? Did Aidan have to merge to teach the dragon how to love? The dragon watched him with neither blue nor violet eyes, but silver.

An understanding began to take shape. Aidan was whole. She was waiting for him to help her re-form, but the dragon had an even greater purpose than Ren had first thought. Not only was the dragon a sign of magic's return, it was carrying another. Like Aidan, someone else lived inside the dragon, someone who had brought it into the future, someone with blue eyes.

Ren looked down at the Silver Eye. Krov said it could create life. If it could create life, it could also rejoin life.

Ren brought to mind the day he merged Aidan's body with her spirit. He relived each heartbeat, remembering her essence and her shape. When he was sure he had recalled every nuance, he glanced at Zorc. He couldn't tell the wizard what he planned. Zorc may try to stop him.

Zorc and the others weren't paying him any heed. They were chuckling at Morrus who was walking out of the water, almond skin glistening in the sun's rays.

Ren put his hands on the Silver Eye. The dragon lowered its head as if to say it was ready. Ren rose above the internal elements until he reached the calm. He called upon the Silver Eye's power. White light exploded from the crystal. Ren heard Zorc's intake of breath but didn't turn.

He felt the man first. His mien was powerful, so powerful Ren knew he was a wizard. Ren didn't have to do more than call. The wizard's essence seeped though the dragon's skin like a mist and funneled through the Silver Eye. The mist careened out of the Eye and began to take shape.

The man's curly brown hair stirred in the slight breeze. His eyes were as blue as the sky. He wore a long blue robe, belted at the waist with a silver cord. He nodded to Ren, but almost immediately his appearance began to change. His hair began to gray and his skin began to wrinkle. His eyes sent Ren a silent plea.

Hurry.

Ren turned back to the dragon and called Aidan. The dragon slouched forward as Aidan's essence seeped from its skin. Because she possessed no magic both her spirit and body tried to dissipate with the wind, but Ren caught her before she was whisked away. Then slowly, carefully, he siphoned her essence through the Eye. When the mist reemerged on the other side, she began to take shape.

Within heartbeats Aidan stood before him, a faint silver gleam to her skin and hair.

Ren released his hold on the Eye and let go of the calm. As his emotions washed through him, instead of overwhelming him they were a mere trickle as Aidan stepped forward and took his hand.

"I didn't know if you would remember my promise," he said.

Aidan smiled. The slight silver tint to her skin made her appear as if she were riding the moonlight. "Faith is a powerful thing," she said. "Your words were such a shock I immediately began to give myself away, but then I realized a profound truth."

"If a doubt mars your soul," Ren said, "you'll give it fire."

Aidan gave Ren a smile that took his breath away. "Faith is a powerful thing. It can damn you or it can raise you."

"Ren."

At the sound of his name, he felt his friends form a tight circle around him. Ren turned to the newcomer.

Although the man gazed at him with conviction, his skin pulsed with constant aging.

"I don't have much time. You must hear what I have to say before I cannot say it."

Aidan tightened her grip on Ren's hand. The defenders closed the gap between them. Even Zorc stepped forward, as if protecting him from the newcomer's words.

"The Eye of the Dragon is a gateway of sorts. I came through the Eye inside Similian to bring you a message. Now I need to tell you much more than I thought."

Aidan stiffened at his side. "It's over, Magnus, isn't it?"

Magnus, the name sounded familiar. When Zorc drew in a sharp breath, Ren remembered where he had heard the name before. Magnus had been the first mage, the same mage who had sought the Red Eye when it had been stolen from the Oracle. He had lived before the Dark Ages.

Magnus's uncanny blue eyes flickered to Aidan. "Oh no, my child. It has only just begun."

THE END

*Ren's adventure continues in Book Three of the Oracle Series.
More information at www.colepain.com*